The
High Priest of Prickly Bog

Hiram Blunt

BVP

BONGOVISTAPUBLISHING
Hackensack, NJ

BONGOVISTA PUBLISHING is a division of
MOTIFF PRODUCTIONS LLC
The High Priest of Prickly Bog: First Edition. 2007
ISBN 978-0-6151-7068-8

How The Great God Bongo
Created The World

I

One day, before the beginning of time, the Great God Bongo was surveying her dominion, which was the void, when the thought occurred to her that she held dominion over nothing, because in the void nothing had ever existed. She had no place to go because there was no place in the void. There was in fact, no other place either. And for One such as she, who craved the experiences and actions and adventures of all things material and immaterial, the situation in which she presently found herself did leave much to be desired.

II

All was not lost however. Surely— he thought to himself— something could be brought into existence. He was, after all, The Great God Bongo. And the matter of creation should be a simple thing. A natural ability for the Divine; flowing easily outward from his infinite fingers... and yet— he wondered— from where could this creation be summoned?

From nowhere. For there was nowhere... and there was nowhere else either.

III

She knew that she must therefore create it out of the very fabric of that which already existed, which was... the void. And although her expectations were not encouraged by this assessment, neither was her resolve undone. This is what she did.

He stroked the fabric of the void ever in the same direction as if he were rubbing his hands across the surface of a Persian rug, until slowly the fibers, electrified by his touch, rebelled against the perfect order and rose into a blister.

Immediately she realized that she had done exactly what she had wanted. She had conjured a grotesque ripple upon the waters of the sublime; disturbing the button-down perfection of nothingness until deformity had become its own reward. It was the first "Thing." A lump... a bubble... a stroke... a pulse... a rumple... a beat. It was the first thing that had ever existed, and she was so very proud of her creation. And one must concede that it could not be compared with the wonders of modern technology, or the subtleties of fine art, but yet it was a beginning. Some "thing" as opposed to nothing at all. And, as with most new inventions, there were minor imperfections to be ironed out. But that, in an odd way, was the very problem with this case. For this invention, unlike the multitude which were to follow, was by its very nature... an imperfection. And the damned thing was ironing itself out. The rug was falling flat, as it were. No sooner had it begun to exist... than it ceased to exist. It was a momentary existence at best. In fact, its entire existence actually spanned no time at all, but merely marked a point.

Now this consequence, of course, might not have been entirely unforeseen by a god who was paying attention. For, as we all know, the fabric of the void contains no time. Nonetheless, The Great God Bongo tried... and tried again. And each time he did, the result was no less predictable. The thing would exist momentarily, and then, just as quickly, it would disappear. And although he did feel some slight success, inasmuch as he had created several "things," he did also feel somewhat frustrated at his own inability to maintain their existence. Like a mother who has lost his children.

VII

Being, however, the type of great god that she was, Bongo would not be defeated. And she persevered for the remainder of that day, and in fact, well into the night. Eventually though, she grew weary of pursuing this unresponsive course, and she gave in to her need for rest; conceding (privately) that perhaps her reality was not availed of that particular temperament which might support permanence. She admitted, in short, that perhaps nothing lasts for long.

VIII

The next morning, however, the divine Bongo awoke to a fresh perspective on the situation. It may be— he thought— that true permanence is unachievable. But that doesn't mean that the illusion of a sort of temporary permanence could not be achieved. And so, by stringing together, at regular intervals, like beads on twine, an array of these short lived pulses, The Great God Bongo was able to create a linear structure which boasted the attribute of consistency, which is – if not the same as, then at least – the next best thing to… permanence.

IX

This new activity kept the great god quite busy. It entertained her considerably so that she didn't notice the hours slipping away. It was as if this consistent rhythmic pulse she was drumming out was mesmerizing her in some way. Pulling her into it. Making her conscious of only the illusion which she herself was spinning. It was the illusion of repetition in a timeless dimension. It was the illusion of consistency where consistency could not exist.

This then… was how time began. And, at the end of the day, when it was time for her to rest, she found herself unable to stop. She was not tired. This new pastime had rendered her great energy. This rhythm had revitalized her. It had given her great power to continue. It had made her into that which she had always been. It had made her into:

"The Great God Bongo."

For without the power of creation... what is a god?

X

Finally he knew that he was The Great God Bongo, Master of Time. And he reveled in his own glory. And he gave honor unto himself. And he was raised upon high within the sepulchre of his own mind.

She was truly now The Creator, and her creations inspired her to create again. And so she did. But even as she created more and more, the future spread itself infinitely ahead and she came to realize that there was still a long... long way to go.

XI

For example, the intervals that he was maintaining could be changed and added to in a myriad of ways. He could create many different rhythmic patterns... and also colors, of an infinite variety and hue. And all of these colors and textures could eventually be woven into an equally infinite variety of illusions. And slowly... slowly, as the eons passed, The Great God Bongo created all of the illusions of the world. And she immersed herself within them so that she could experience them all. And she split herself into two, at first, so that now he was no longer she, but she and he, and then they split themselves into many, and the many into millions and then trillions, and eventually into an infinite number.

XII

And they all... who were The Great God Bongo, drummed out their rhythms of creation, creating illusions everywhere they went. And they experienced all those illusions separately, pretending to themselves that he or she were not experiencing them altogether.

One way or the other, they experienced all the illusions of the world. The earth and the water and the trees and the fields... and the goats and the chickens and the pigs and the gooses and the big clouds and the blue skies and the ducks that fly-aye-aye. And the Africans and the Indians and the Europeans and the Chinese and the Serbo-Croatians. And the Stone-Age and the Bronze-Age and the Ice-Age and the Golden-Age and youth and old age. And the Egyptians and the Greeks and the Romans and the Sophists and the Gnostics and the Existentialists and the Antidisestablishmentarianists. And Proust and Goethe and Chekov and Ibsen, and Wally Shawn and Jack Kerouak and Jack Nicholson and Jack Cheese and Jumping Jack Flash. And Muhammed Ali and Marcus Garvey and Mickey Mouse and Mitsubishi... and Delius and Gustav Mahler and Gustav Holst and everyone else named Gustav... and Stravinsky and Stalin and Lenin and McCartney. And... Frank Lloyd Wright and falling skyscrapers and skyhooks and cons and con-men and rip-off artists and strippers and painters and exhibitionists and flashers and rapists and terrorists and bombers and cops shooting black kids in the back... and abortion and the death penalty and heroes and villains and social workers and Idi Amin and crackpots and cracking jokes and crack pipes and needles and hookahs and hookers and hippies and hetros and homos and AIDS and the big lie and "freedom and justice for all" and justice and injustice and happiness and unhappiness and...

Conclusion

But you know... if you look closely at all these things which really do seem to exist, you'll start to see that they're not at all what they appear to be. In fact, if you get up really, really close you'll start to notice that they're made up of nothing more than rapidly disappearing pulses of nothingness, which just hover momentarily in space-time for less than even a micro-millisecond, and then... are gone, only to be replaced by another rapidly disappearing pulse which is replaced by another and then another and on and on in a complex and unfathomable rhythm.

Well... since then, since the beginning of time that is, The Great God Bongo's drumming has improved considerably, and has in fact developed quite a repertoire up to this point. But you know something else? Bongo isn't tired at all and loves to keep on reminding us that we "Ain't seen nothing yet ."

THE BEGINNING

Prologue
Bongovia: The Future

*There would come a time when the world would be
controlled by men of honor.*

This, however, would not be that time. It would, instead, be a time of deception and of denial. It would be a time of power and of subjugation. It would be a time of cruelty hidden safely beneath a veneer of civility. A time of belief and trust rewarded by betrayal. A time of cameras mounted in the trees, watching... forever watching... as you walk silently in the park, confident of your safety, this is what you had wanted, and yet somewhere beneath that confidence a refusal to ask this one simple question: what could have been gained, what may have been lost?

It would be a time of great restrictions and of unjust imprisonment, and somehow an even greater indifference toward the suffering of others. A time of hypocrisy and sanctimonious judgment. A time of paranoia and watchfulness. Of repressed desires exploding uncontrollably at regular intervals compelling the need for definition as evil or ungodly. It would be a time of religion, which had been once revered and respected, now contorted into the unkind face of religiosity: a faustian mask demanding acquiescence to its vision. A time of metaphor and obscurity, of black and white, of good and evil, of thoughtlessness and deviousness. A time lacking in subtlety and governed by subtlety, when all seems to be known yet nothing is clear... it was, in short, a time like every other time that will have gone before.

Bongovia came into being, not with a bang but with a whimper. There was no war which precipitated its inception, only one which followed it. And that one seemed so distant as to not affect the daily workings of the lives of most citizens. It occurred outside their normal experience, rarely involving those they knew or cared about. Admittedly, shortly after the establishment of Bongovia there had come about some internal conflicts, when the evolving philosophies of Bongovism came into dispute. Those who had held with the original precepts of tolerance and passivity were supplanted by the more aggressive believers in Bongovistic dominance. Their argument went something like this:

How can we be tolerant of those whose philosophy it is to be intolerant of us. Therefore to preserve tolerance in this world we must not tolerate intolerance.

In an ironic twist they also found it difficult, therefore, to tolerate those who were in fact tolerant of all people because, by definition, that would make them tolerant of the intolerant. And, inasmuch as tolerance and passivity do not engender great material power, the decline of the classical Bongovians to the neo-Bongovians... or Bongovists, as they preferred to call themselves, soon became historical fact.

Bongovians had tended to include within their world view, the philosophies of those who had come before. They intrinsically believed that Bongo was not a new god, bringing salvation to the universe, but just another way of expressing eternal truths which only a select few may actually comprehend at any given time, and that others would only come to, once they had achieved a certain enlightenment. They referred to the stories of Bongo as metaphor, and felt that their deeper meanings were lost when literalized. They offered logical proofs that the stories were not meant to be taken literally. How, after all, could the Great God Bongo be surveying her dominion when reality had not even been created yet? Upon what road did he walk? Upon what hill did she stand in order to do all of this surveying? How, in fact, could any act be accomplished before the beginning of time, when every action requires the compass of space and time within which to be manifest? The Bongovists countered that the glory of Bongo cannot be comprehended by mankind, and only absolute faith in His word could lead to salvation. Bongovians felt that blind faith and dogma were antagonistic to the nurturing of the mind and the spirit, and they further added that Bongo had never claimed to be an exclusive god, but an inclusive one. To prove this assertion they cited many previous doctrines – the Buddha, Dionysus, Pythagorus... the Gnostic Christ, to name but a few – and demonstrated how these prophets had all historically vaunted identical philosophical concepts and wisdom to that of Bongo, long before the Ninth of April, Nineteen Ninety-Seven. But, and as proof that genius doesn't need to be restricted by logical thought, one clever Bongovist, named Justin Turtle, explained it this way. He figured it as a given that belief in the Great God Bongo was the salvation of the world. Therefore the truths that Bongo brings must be unique... or else we could all have been saved without Bongo. As it is therefore impossible for Bongo's words not to have been original, any historical pre-echoes of His thoughts must have been put there (in order to confuse those who possess insufficient faith) by someone who is, not only antagonistic to Bongo, but also has the ability to travel through time. This then would have to be the Devil, Satan, Beelzibub, Lucifer, Cacodemon, Dybbuk, Apollyion, Old Nick... whatever you prefer to call him. And so the term "Satanic Impersonation" was introduced to describe a type of imitation which occurs before the existence of the thing it is imitating. This concept, along with others, such as "Circular Logic" (which insisted that "if Bongo says something then it must be true because Bongo said it was, and everything that Bongo says is true") had many a Bongovian scratching his or her head in exasperation. Of course they tried to reaffirm the idea that there was no other thing than Bongo, therefore no Devil, or dark destructive power could exist outside of Bongo. But the Bongovists were not having any of this kind of rarefied or subtle intellectualizing, which they considered wishy-washy and, quite frankly, somewhat demonic.

Most Bongovians went quietly the way of the obsolete, philosophically preferring to live out their lives, peacefully, in their own way where it was possible, but largely keeping their mouths shut and not rocking the boat. They knew that change comes when it comes, and not when it doesn't. But others of their persuasion voiced their complaints loudly and made a public nuisance of themselves. Still others chose violent rebellion, stating that Bongo had never said that one shouldn't defend oneself.

The vast majority of these 'rebels' were crushed mercilessly by the newly formed Bongovist security troops, but some few still prevailed in dark and underground places and grew, eventually, to be a constant thorn in the side of the new authoritarian establishment, and an unwelcome whisper nagging annoyingly at the conscience of society.

Regularly, in posters pasted up secretly at night, and also with spam e-mail, the Bongovians would appeal to Jason Cyllabus Novedi, the High Priest of Prickly Bog, to speak out against this ravishing of the holy word. But the High Priest was not saying a thing. He seemed now nothing more than a ceremonial head of the Temple of Bongovism. A legend more than a man. Perhaps... some believed, he had never actually existed.

Chapter 1

Six shadows slither silently across the compound yard. The moon, a thin and waning crescent, damns with faint illumination the glinting metal edges of the vehicle that is parked so provocatively close to this ripped and tortured wire fence. Dust rises lightly at every padded footstep, acknowledged by neither eye nor ear... nor sense of touch. Each mind attuned intently upon its mission. Trigger fingers poised and gripping, with avid anticipation, the very means of that mission's accomplishment. No breath is wasted, no movement labored; simply the precise unerring drum of events spurring on their phantom steeds towards inevitability. Close by, a host of crickets supply the unseen backdrop, whilst somewhere in the cold distance, a morbid howl disturbs the colorless sky, and sends transparent veils of liquid emotion bleeding – one across the other... one into the other – merging thus, within celestial pools of unfathomable measure.

A window shade flickers. A spark amidst the silhouettes of the buildings within the compound. Their hulking blackness slumped together as if the coldness of the night (and not the pen of the dreamer) had drawn them so. Nervous fingers smear a dewy circle of clarity within the misty frame, and a distant face appears. A man's face. Unrecognizable as it nears the casement. Lighted from behind. Its features caressed by the obscuring darkness without. Something distracts him from inside. A small and feminine hand drapes lightly its presence upon his naked shoulder, and as he turns to greet its owner he is unmasked somewhat for one brief moment. A glimmer of light upon his cheek... upon his nose, brings shape to life and some state of familiarity is born – yes, you know him; he is you! But then the shade is released and all is moony darkness once again. And you begin to wonder— was I mistaken?

Were you?

Deluded by your own need for permanence. Driven by an unresolved narcissism to believe that you will not pass gloriously from this plane, but instead will crumble away out of memory, expendable, interchangeable, replaceable. You will not have changed the world.

And yet, still... six shadows growing ever closer approach a door beneath that blinded window. Black gloved hands signal strategy. A lock is deftly picked. And the sound of twelve feet creaking up the narrow staircase raises no alarm but is submerged beneath the groaning of the mattress springs above, where she lies beneath him; virginal and sweet., the essence of a symbol of a dream you dreamed forever. Her tiny rounded limbs... so youthful, so naive. She stares at only him— I want no other man but you— her eyes declare. No other. Her legs held open wide accept his honor. Proudly. Gushingly. His chest flicks lovingly across her softly pointed breasts. Their lips embrace. Their union is complete.

With a crash the door frame splinters and breaks apart. Six men scurry in, surrounding the carnal bed. Eagerly they point their heartless weapons toward the object of potential fulfillment. But sadly they wilt. Sadly they suffer just one more frustration in a life filled with such— What is there to hope for in this? What end is there for us? Who will remember our accomplishment when we have none to show?

He is not there, but just that one step ahead. The bed is empty except for the naked temptress who was paid to betray him. The spy – cold as ice, her reputation – she lies there, blissfully writhing within the throes of ecstasy. Lies there smiling, eyes closed, rubbing her legs together upon the sheetless, soiled, blue and white striped mattress. A prisoner, she – of *his* seduction. Unaware (even now) that he is gone.

Amid the darkness of huddled buildings, where once a window shade had flickered... suddenly glass shatters, exploding outward, the fragments... the shards, propelled by flames and smoke billowing, circling, expanding, extracting life from where it stood or lay. Dispatching it into the coldness of the night. Burning light into the blackened air, as particles of roof collapse upon seven twitching skeletons who lie within that place, their nervous systems charred but connected still, for one last flash of an instant of a moment, within which eyeballs scan that final inferno before their lidless agonies are forever numbed. Forever (we assume) their torment: to feel no feeling, yet to yearn eternally for the single flash of an instant of a moment of the Hades which their memories will evermore recall.

A winding string of black smoke rises from the glowing embers of their grave. An almost naked man looks back from the surrounding country to whence he came. He measures his escape. He is not turned into a pillar of salt, but he is cold in the unforgiving dawn. He wonders, on such occasions— could survival be worth the price?

But he knows, also, that in the end there is no choice. One must survive until one no longer does. The game is afoot, and one must dance the dance the drummer dreams. One must play whatever tune is dealt.

Chapter 2

Dominic Devine was an unkempt man. But not for the obvious reason (sloth). There was always a rationale to his actions, or inactions as the case may be. He had always believed that contrived presentation somehow devalued the object to be presented. To this end he never gift-wrapped a present, believing that the gift must speak for itself. In fact he rarely gave gifts, believing that the gift itself was a contrived presentation of his feelings, his admiration, his respect, his... love. So much better, then, to bestow the sentiment itself in its purity. To give love. So much better also to present himself unwrapped – well, naked was impractical – but without costume or plumage which might deceive, might characterize in some false way who he was. The costume was for the actor, the clown, not who *he* was, the *real* Devine. And so, plain shirt, beige pants, sometimes stained (he often looked like a sloth). Not only to others who might not understand his commitment – although Dominic couldn't remember anyone ever having actually commented on his appearance – but to himself, when he looked in the mirror. Or, for that matter, as he looked around his apartment, where clothing lay strewn awaiting eventual gathering for the journey to the laundry, where newspapers and books and bills and letters were piled upon each other in great disorganized heaps. Things that he couldn't find were there. Things that he'd forgotten he was looking for. And in the sink, dishes and more dishes (sometimes grease-stained – no... always) and forks he couldn't find, and spoons that he wasn't even looking for. At least every second day he would wash the entire amount but usually not long before eating and so, very soon, a new collection would begin.

His father had been a bit of a peacock, Dominic felt. As dapper and lean to the end, as Dominic was squat and creased from the beginning. He'd taken great pride in his appearance and his health, and he'd valued his possessions, perhaps sometimes, to the exclusion of the needs of those around him who needed to be valued. Dominic did not loathe his father, but he may have resented the fact that his father had never done anything to justify being loathed. He would alternate periods of nagging— you need to do your sit-ups, Dominic— or— that's enough ice-cream, Dominic— with periods of total disinterest in his son's affairs. And yet... somewhere within that nagging he had imparted the notion of a belief in his son's ability. An expectation (and that's not necessarily a bad thing) of achievement... notable achievement at that. Maybe not success, but some type of greatness, and we know that those two familiars often travel separate paths.

This *may* explain the way Dominic felt about himself (sloth or no) although there may well have been any number of other reasons why, but still, he had always felt that he was destined for greatness. However, that morning when he received a letter from the Popodell Publishing Company, confirming that very fact, it nonetheless gave him quite some cause for surprise. It read like this:

> *Dear Mr. Devine,*
>
> *Our staff of editors have conducted an extensive evaluation of all the manuscripts submitted in our nationwide talent search, and your novel, "The High Priest of Prickly Bog" has been judged to possess exceptional merit. Our company prides itself upon the relationships it fosters between editorial staff and writers. Therefore it is of the greatest importance that we develop a personality profile of each young member before any contractual commitments are finalized.*
>
> *In this regard we are hereby establishing a telephone appointment for you on the 28 December between the hours of 10a.m. and 4p.m. You must call 5348-384-9273 at that time (calls will not be taken at any other time) and answer some questions which will help us to determine if your personality is compatible with ours.*
>
> *It is critical that you make this call as it will determine the strength of your devotion and ambition.*
>
> *Once again, calls will not be accepted at any other time. We look forward to hearing from you.*
>
> *Sincerely, George Burgess.*

And of course all of this would have been fine but for one simple fact. It was now the seventh of January and Mr. Devine (that is to say, our Dominic) had missed the crucial date with destiny.

It cannot be— he thought, as a rather irritated lump rose in his throat— That's simply not *fair*.

He checked the date on the letter, thirteenth of December— Yes but— although it did occur to him that one could date a letter the twelfth of never but that doesn't mean that's when the letter was mailed. He checked the post mark— Aha! Oh... fourteenth of December. I wonder if that can be forged. Or... could the Christmas mail have slowed this letter down so much? Or... could someone be playing mind games with me.

Well of course it seems a bit like paranoia when you start assuming that every little thing that goes wrong is some kind of a plot to get you. Little you. But then again these conspiracies do have the effect of making you bigger... in your own mind, if nowhere else. A little self importance can't be bad when no one else is paying much attention. What's really confusing is when you do get a taste of attention, a little tease... combined with a major attempt to mess with your head. It makes you think. Know what I mean? Although not necessarily about the essential subject. Namely how much of this crap has been fabricated by your own imagination. And so you make grand sweeping judgments about the rest of the world and about the place you do... or should, occupy within it.

You know what the trouble was. It was his novel. "The High Priest of Prickly Bog". It really *was* exceptional. It *should* be published. It could have important consequences upon society. It was revolutionary. It would change the way that people think and relate to one another. It would teach them respect. It would show them how to become comfortable with themselves. How to lead a life of honest creativity. Who knows, it may even put an end to war... and poverty... and suffering of every sort. And he... yes, our Dominic Devine, would finally be given that credit that he so richly deserved. He would finally be recognized as the savior of our... hold on a minute... savior? Okay, this was getting a little over the top. Especially from a guy who couldn't even live with anyone else because he was so obsessive-compulsive about how the toothpaste tube ought to be squeezed, or the cutlery placed in the tray after washing, that he would constantly be instigating the most moronic domestic altercations. Yeah, *he* was going to teach you all how to live in peace with one another.

I mean, he knew that these things didn't really matter. He had written it all down in his novel. He knew that objectively there was no right and no wrong. At least this is what he claimed to believe. Jesus Christ... this is what he preached. Albeit in an ironic sort of way. It's just that he couldn't see the irony of it when someone was actually irritating him. Look... Dominic Devine was not a stupid man. He didn't really believe that he was going to be the savior of the world. Let's face it, he thought that the world was impossible to save anyway. Not that he believed that it was going to "Hell in a Handbasket" as some do. He just thought that "Hell" is here already, as is "the Handbasket", as is – to be perfectly fair to him – "Heaven". Or not... the lot of them!

"When I was a young man..." he would tell top heavy party beauties, their cleavages winking as they inhaled with boredom, "I used to be rather grandiose". His accent sometimes claiming membership within a rank not usually given to one of his financial background. His hand gestures sometimes causing concern regarding the potential spillage of Claret or Barolo on expensive newly purchased crepe blouses predestined, often as not, to be returned to the local boutique the following day, refund in full, party being over.

"Oh?" they would mouth just before sucking on a lipstick stained ™Virginia Slims.

"I used to think that I could change the world. That my generation was going to make a real difference. I was considered by some to be exceptionally talented. They said I was a natural leader of my..."

But of course by this time they had already wandered off and were busy ignoring some other old fart, or for that matter some muscular toy-boy who prattled on about the benefits of tanning machines over the actual sun, high levels of ultraviolet and so on. And they... these same waxen pouty lipped ™Slims sucking cleavage winking self appointed beauties would be wondering to themselves— If 'women's lib' couldn't change the world then why the hell am I smoking this fucking thing?

As for Dominic, our Mr. Devine? Well, he was still saddled with the twin problems of getting his book published and acquiring some *god damned respect* (which, in the interest of causing the least possible offense to true believers of every hue and dictum, lest they take it upon themselves to come after me for my ungodly arrogance, will simply be referred to as GDR henceforth). After all, there was precious little of that to be had in his present line of work. Children these days were hard to impress. Admittedly, he picked up fairly consistent work from the greasy fellow who ran the 'Burger Meister' fast food establishment. And then there were the occasional private birthday parties. But still, the idea of amazing a five year old by pulling a coin out of her ear is hardly cause for self congratulation. And the big shoes and baggy pants really don't seem to make them laugh anymore. Not when multi-ethnic costumery can be witnessed promenading down Main Street every day of the week. Even the word 'clown' had taken on a derogatory meaning. That's what you call your loser brother-in-law when he's trying to touch you for a twenty spot that you know you'll never get back. But there was a whole tradition to clowning, as ancient as civilization itself. The mythical archetypes of the 'Commedia' constructed by the collective unconscious of thousands of generations; to fulfill age old needs and desires; to act out the pomposities and heroisms, the wretchedness and humor of life, and those who dwell within. It was a need, he felt, to understand oneself. To be understood. Who was he?

—Who am I?

—I know who I want to be: Scaramouche! That's right. All dressed in black. Swinging across the stage. Helping those in need. Bringing justice with the wave of a pointed sword. Restoring balance to its rightful perch."

But sometimes he would feel (although he'd never admit this to himself) as if he were one of the other characters. Pulcinella, perhaps... crass and cruel, lasciviously drooling over the passing flesh of virginal innocence incarnate. Consuming but never caressing. Unable ever to really touch deeply, because he would always push just that little bit too hard for intimacy. Or the pompous doctor... opinionated... so filled with his own importance that he couldn't even arrive at the most obvious diagnosis despite that evidence which was staring him right in the face. Lessons learned in childhood, they were, from fathers and mothers who we try so desperately to resist, but in the end, somehow... become. But then didn't they too wrestle with their archetypes, and act out the play?

Act out?

Sure... like children act out. Act out their loves – Inamorati, a capricious romance, thoughtlessly foisted upon future generations until their life becomes your life, their needs... (what once were) your aspirations.

—Be a clown!

—I know what I want to be, God damn you!"

And he had studied well. It's not so easy being a clown. It takes hard work and talent. He knew them well, those characters. They represented each of us in some way or the other. One's body type, one's basic nature. It was really more the science of understanding human psychology than anything else. But it was also philosophy and anthropology and dance and acrobatics, all rolled into one. 'Roly-polgy' he called it. But Arlecchino and Pantalone didn't go down big in the suburbs. Not like Coco and Bobo and Bilbo and Dildo who, with their squirting lapel poppies and their big red rubber noses, like the proverbial Dangerfield got no GDR. What the hell.

Now this book, however, "The High Priest of Prickly Bog," well, that was another kettle-of-fish altogether. This could be his... er, 'clowning' achievement, so to speak. He had put everything he knew into it. And (he believed) he knew everything that it was necessary to know – plus a few other things as well. Anyway, he'd put into it everything which possessed true value (he felt). Amazing, isn't it? A book which contained all the knowledge that one would need. You wouldn't have to go rooting through encyclopedias for the essential details regarding how to live. You wouldn't have to read the Bible from end to end in a vain attempt at discovering enlightenment, or the Torah or the Q'ran for that matter. And some people really 'just didn't like' the style of Gibran's "The Prophet," all that poetic nonsense, you know what I mean... flowery. But here it was. All the crap cut out. Just the real deal. No muss no fuss. No mess no fess. And entertaining too. How many books, after all, have a story line, these days... that you can follow? Well okay, lots – but, you know what I mean. It was an idea. Hell, it was a damned good idea. A book with everything you would ever need to know. Someone would surely buy etc... in droves. I mean, how could it fail to be a huge success? An instant and enduring classic.

They're going to love me— he thought— All I have to do is find some way to get it out there. He picked up the telephone and dialed— Let's see now... five, three, four, eight, three, eight, four...

"I... am... sorry," it was a machine, "the... number... you...

have... dialed... five... three... four.... eight... three... eight... four... nine... two... seven... three... has... been... disconnected... no... further... information... is... available..." he hung up and sat unmoving as a truck drove past his house, rattling the frames of the windows. One of them was slightly open. It was a cool morning, but when the heat came up it could get uncomfortable in there with no way to control it from his apartment. Not that he'd ever complain about too much heat – he *had* lived in cold places before.

He stood and walked to the window carrying the phone with him. Before he slid the window shut he noticed two people, one floor below in the street, passing by at a painfully slow pace. A tall fat man was restraining himself from deserting his companion, a thin old woman with what Dominic described to himself as 'hag-face.' She was complaining about something, it seemed. The sidewalk in front of her, that she prodded with her cane each time she took a step – it was all uneven! She clung to his arm. Dominic thought he perceived a look of frustration on the tall fat man's face – why was the fire house so far away?

"It used to be closer!"

"It's where it always was, they haven't moved it in the fifty years I've been alive."

"Ah, you don't know nuttin'! They moved it before you was born."

"Sometimes I wish I hadn't been."

"Where haven't you been?"

"What?"

"You said you haven't been?"

"Haven't been what?"

"I don't know! You're the one who said it!"

The window made a little bumping sound as it shut. The tall fat man looked vacantly in the direction of the sound, but he was wondering to himself where in the world one could find a little GDR. The old woman prodded the ground ahead of her and took another step.

Dominic stared at the phone in his hand. He went over to the dining table where the letter lay enticingly open. He examined it once more. There was a letterhead that he'd payed no attention to before...

with an address... and, there it was... a phone number. A different phone number. He dialed it.

"Good morning," a human (sort of) answered, "Popodell Publishing Company. How can I be of assistance?"

"Oh... well..." he hadn't actually expected to get through, "I... er... I received a... er... letter from you this morning and..."

But she cut him off. "Do I know you sir?" Her voice was sharp and intimidating, though he felt no personal animosity coming from her. But still... it seemed an irritatingly odd question, nonetheless.

"W-well... I don't think so."

"Then I doubt very much that you received a letter from me, sir!"

"W-well... I, er... didn't literally mean you..."

"And in fact," she continued, "even if I did know you I would still doubt very much that you had received a letter from me this morning as I have not sent a letter to anyone in the last seven years. I know the mail can be slow, but seven years... even with this lousy postal system, seems unlikely."

"Yes well," he was starting to get the hang of this conversation now, "talking of slow mail, someone at your company by the name of... er... George Burgess did send me a letter which took over three weeks to..."

"George Burgess?" she interrupted again, "he's in our other office. I have no information about the project in which he is involved."

"Well, could I speak to Mr. Burgess?"

"I doubt it," she replied in a deceptively friendly, even conspiratorial tone, "He has a secretary who won't let anyone near him. Sometimes..." and here she substantially lowered her voice, "I think that he doesn't really exist!"

Dominic sighed in desperation. "In that case," he requested, "could you please put me through to her?"

"Who?" (Was she trying to provoke him?)

"The bloody secretary, of course!"

"Oh! You mean *him*," she replied. "Well, you don't need to get like that about it – and by the way, we don't go in for that kind of language around here... and anyway," she continued, as Dominic tried his best to regain any possible form of dignity or composure, "I *told*

you, they're not *in* this office, you'll have to call 5348-384-9273!"
And she hung up.

The number seemed to have a familiar ring to it. He checked the letter again. Yeah sure... there it was. The original number. His eyes focused on the words, "Calls will not be accepted at any other time." But for some reason, which he really couldn't understand, he dialed the number again. Maybe through some magic (the magical suggestion of the officious receptionist perhaps) the line would be reconnected. Stranger things have happened. Why not?

But then he heard the message machine again, "I... am... sorry... the... number..." He slammed the phone down. Hard!

He picked up the receiver again and touched it lightly to his lip as he thought about it for a moment. He dialed. Only seven digits this time. Local number. He waited awhile as the gentle, high-pitched purr-purr emanating from his phone's earpiece indicated that somewhere in the city another phone was signaling to be answered.

Finally, it was. Mechanically.

"Marvin. Hi! Listen, I'm having a problem with trying to get in touch with someone... oh, it's me, by the way, Dominic. Anyway... there's a bit of a mystery here, and I thought you might be able to help me out, er... with some of your dubious contacts. Apparently someone is interested in publishing my book, which – by the way – I accidentally left at your place the other night, I hope you didn't use it for kindling or anything, I'll pick it up tonight if you're around – but anyway – this er... publisher guy, appears to have... well, disappeared off the face of the earth. I know you love a good mystery. Call me as soon as you can, er... bye!"

Chapter 3

Now, a bog is sort of like a swamp. And a prickly bog, one might assume, is a swamp surrounded by something... prickly? Thorn bushes, or nettles, or some such thing. But the town of Prickly Bog was neither anywhere near a bog nor did it have an abundance of prickly things, unless of course you're describing the personality of certain residents, and in any case, not more than any place might. In fact it was a rather modern, characterless looking town, set out in the middle of nowhere, filled with thousands of condominiums inhabited, for the most part, by employees of an immensely powerful computer and electronics conglomerate called JCN, which – owing to the messianic founder's habit of encouraging them to convert to his own personal belief system – was known secretly by some of them as Jesus Christ Nuts. However, and you may have guessed already, this is not what JCN stood for. Neither did it stand for *god damned respect...* in any language, for, although they had been generously furnished with these sanitized habitations, a suitable deduction was made each week from the employees pay packets, in compensation for their quarterage. Suitable, inasmuch as it kept them in a perpetual form of indentured servitude until they had payed for their accommodations in full.

Taking into consideration the fact that a period of some thirty years or so might possibly elapse before the final accomplishment of such a purchase, and also the other fact that this town had only been in existence for a period of approximately fourteen years, it may well be possible to deduce that no such property owner had, as yet, emerged from this system. And even if one did, it would be difficult to leave the job or to sell the dwelling, as there were no other jobs available in the area. Well, precious few anyway. JCN, it seemed, had wrapped up a pretty nice little monopoly for itself. Of the few independents which did still exist, there was the supermarket, which required check out clerks occasionally, and the 'Burger Meister' employed the odd 'Maestro Burger' assembler. Now, the 'Maestro Burger' was a top of the line concoction which consisted of about half a pounds worth of various animal fats and waste materials ground together with some mineral polymers and compressed into a flat patty which was then singed on either side and served inside a 'bun' made of aerated grain and foam rubber, all topped off with a viscous fluid containing red dye #3406 and some artificial tomato flavoring... and (if you wanted) some chopped onions. Chopped onions were the only 'natural' food available, although the word 'natural' had been redefined into legally acceptable terminology several times in the preceding years, and thus may or may not reflect the meaning of the word as we know it today.

But even these two enterprises were under negotiation for sale to JCN, which would probably eventually absorb them and convert them into something more modern, more appropriate for The Mall. The Mall offered various other delights to capture the heart and spirit of the JCN employee. There had been a boutique called 'Fashions Galore' based on the type of outfit that the ancient motion picture actress Honor Blackman might have worn in her roles in such classic celluloid literature as 'The Avengers,' or 'Goldfinger.' It was (to say the least) a foolhardy enterprise – thought up by a member of JCN's middle echelon marketing and development team, named Tony Barnes – and it went under after a grueling first year. Barnes was disgraced, as it had been his third attempt at one of these so-called concept boutiques, none of which had lasted more than a year. He became despondent after this hat-trick of failure, and soon took to not showing up for work, which was quite a taboo amongst his conformist peers. His 'friends' and colleagues, who were really one and the same were sent to see how he was doing, but he refused to let anyone in the house. They all returned with stories of a strange odor emanating from his apartment. Eventually of course, police were called in, who broke down the door and discovered Barnes sitting in a pool of blood sucking his thumb. He'd killed his grandmother, who had lived with him for so many years, and of whom he had taken such good care, according to the neighbors. And he'd also killed (and eaten a large part of) his dog, which it seemed had been (quite blasphemously) named Bongo. During the following days of interrogation, when the police asked him why he did it, he repeated over and over again that Bongo had told him to. At first they assumed that he meant the divinity of the Temple of Bongovism. But when a neighbor, whom they later questioned, remarked that she'd heard him calling the dog by that name on frequent occasions, it left them in a state of some confusion. God? Dog? Could it be— they wondered— some sort of conceptual dyslexia? JCN Enterprises was rather disappointed by this outcome, which they considered a personal failure. So, naturally, they quickly covered up all record of it ever having occurred.

Anyway, 'Fashions Galore' was replaced by a scuba equipment store named 'King Canute's Mistake,' which came on the heels of an announcement that an artificial lake was to be built close to the town, with sandy beaches, and parkland, and restaurants... the whole works. Some courageous souls actually patronized the place and purchased diving equipment in that very gung-ho, JCN manner which was so common amongst them. But the months went by and eventually even the most deluded converts started to realize that it may well have been their mistake (not King Canute's), as it was starting to look like this project would never happen.

Then, of course, there was the perennial 'Mall Shoe Store.' An uninspired name for sure, but then nobody ever shopped there. Perennial because for some strange reason it went out of business every winter and then reemerged with a fresh 'grand opening' every spring. Somebody at JCN had decided that it wasn't worth buying and that it would, one spring, simply *not* 'grand open'. It certainly didn't present any competition in terms of potential employment (in other words, keeping control of the workers – which was the only thing that really concerned the JCN authorities) as the place was owned and operated by a family of suspect genetic origins. The words 'inbred' and 'trashy' being often used to describe them, carried aloft by the type of malicious rumor that spread so easily amongst JCN employees. A family who lived in a trailer on the outskirts of town, with clothes hung continually from sloppy lines which allowed them to drag in the mud. Who took turns working at the shoe store. Who didn't belong to the Temple of Bongovism. Who resisted all attempts at conversion. And how they achieved their miraculous yearly rebirth was nobody's business. They made no sales as all the other inhabitants of Prickly Bog sent away for their shoes through the JCN 'Greentrees' catalogue. 'Greentrees' shoes featured real leather trim parts and offered a substantial savings – up to seven percent – to those who could prove that they were active members of the Temple of Bongovism by producing canceled ticket stubs for the last four Sunday services.

Well, yes it's true the church did charge an admission fee for the services, but it was very reasonable... really! And the founder, one Jason Cyllabus Novedi, who incidentally was also the founder of the JCN computer corporation, just despised the idea of collection plates or donations by mail. Churches that used those tactics— he asserted— were run by some type of con-men who just wanted to fool you into thinking that you were getting something for nothing. No, what he offered was an honest service at an honest price. It was the tradition of capitalism at its best. The work ethic of the heartland. Family values, you know the story.

But then this wasn't heartland sort of country as *we* think of it nowadays. I mean, no rolling green hills, or amber waves of grain for that matter, or anything vaguely resembling that picture postcard ideal.

Let's face it, this country hadn't actually ever been like that. No, that was just an illusion created by a ™Walt Disney cartoon. A painted representation of places on this earth which actually *do* look like that... I know! I didn't believe they really existed myself, but since then I've actually seen them with my own eyes. They do exist. But not around Prickly Bog (and not around here, either).

There, they were mostly just something people dreamed about. In the future, I mean, because that's where Prickly Bog was... and Jason Cyllabus Novedi... and the Church of the Great God Bongo, which had all started as a... oh, but let's not go there. Not yet anyway. Let's see now, the future... oh yes, there would exist all kinds of stuff that we've never seen. Meanwhile, all kinds of stuff that we find common? Well... gone! Farms. The farms were all gone. There were things *called* farms of course, by changing the legal definition of the word. But now, I wonder... what word would spring to mind to us, from the present, were we to experience such a farm? Oh yes, now I remember... factory.

They actually *manufactured* such things as dairy products, and also grain-like substances. Although there *were* animals sometimes employed in the manufacture of said products, who had been deprived of their GDR so long ago, and to such an extent, that they no longer resembled anything that we would know to be a living creature. In fact it was not certain in anybody's memory if GDR had actually ever existed, or whether it – like Santa, or JC... the other one, without the N – was just a myth perpetrated by the advertising companies in order to give people hope when the work ethic starts to sag. For it is written (on whatever it is that they write it on up there) that a man without hope is not a good consumer. And, whereas a man who gets no GDR can still hope for it, a man who does get it, needs no hope. This of course, also makes him a bad consumer. (For those PC types who are offended by the use of the term 'man' when referring to people in general, let me add that this prescription applies equally well to woman.)

Prickly Bog was not so special, however. In that time, there were many such towns in the area, and many such corporations, several of which were owned by Jason Cyllabus Novedi. Others, by different people or groups of people. It was perfectly possible for *anyone*, regardless of race, color, or sexual preference to become an owner. Although certain psychological characteristics would, of course, be necessary to become one, as at any other time in the history of mankind (excuse me... humankind). What was not possible, however, (also as at any other time) was for *everyone* to become an owner, even had they all magically and simultaneously come into possession of the necessary psychological characteristics. There was simply only so much room at the top. Nonetheless, everyone could own their own domicile, at JCN anyway. Well okay the word 'own' had taken on a sort of temporary meaning of late. For instance when traveling, one might stay at a hotel by 'buying' a room for a couple of nights. Not that a lot of people were traveling around regularly... sometimes for the company, perhaps. But more often, the concept of ownership applied to where one might live... or certain methods of vehicular transportation. Everything had a time limit on it. You know, never say "forever." I mean, how could you actually keep something forever, anyway? Impractical. But they all had their own ways of doing things... the towns, the corporations. They were all different from each other. Some were based on religious precepts, such as Bongovism. Although Bongovism had been designed, initially at least, to act as a foil to those traditional dogma (or was it god, ma?) by injecting a sense of freedom into one's spirituality. But, although its written tenets did offer a *potential* for freedom, and, although they were still paid lip-service by the community of the faithful – which included pretty much everyone these days – one could see, were one to examine the matter with unbiased eyes, that its original spirit of rebelliousness had been lost somewhere along the line, and the basic human need to stereotype, to reduce to the lowest common denominator, to normalize, as it were, had razed that religion to the level of so many others which have fallen by the wayside before it. Fallen yes, in the eyes of their originator, whilst at the same time (and for, in fact, the same reason) being exalted on high by the idolatrous hordes who clawed at it and sucked it dry of all meaning in order to quell their wants. Nothing fails like success.

Some corporations were based on political principles. You know, democracy, equality, etc. etc. Some were based on philosophies – Plato, Descartes, Proust, Kant, Engles, Marx... and they resembled those philosophers' ideas as closely as Hitler resembled Christ. Some on scientific principles – Pythagorus' theorem, gravity, E=MC squared... yeah, but it was all bullshit. Because ultimately they were all just like each other. Someone at the top had control, and the rest did as they were told.

"Why? Why?" you ask? "Why did they do as they were told?"

How about patriotism, regionalism, parochialism, provinciality, chauvinism, racism – call it what you will, but 'conformity' describes it the best.

And, "why," you ask, "is conformity so powerful a tool of control?"

I don't know! Bongo said it's why we all like to dance together. When we vibrate at the same frequency we become one again. We become one with Bongo.

"But conformity," you say, "is not the same as oneness." It is a false oneness, because someone's buzzing is askew. Someone is not joining in with the other children in this dance, but stepping outside of the circle and using this power for their own demonic means. "But isn't that Bongo too?" You ask.

Maybe, maybe... again, I don't know! Why are you asking me these things, I only write what I see. But I'll tell you one thing: stepping outside of the circle is nothing more than elitism; simply thinking that one is above all others; believing there is no need to be fair. You're right, it's *not* oneness. But Bongo isn't just about being one. Bongo is also about being fractured. Accepting the other's truth... even when the other will not accept yours. But that... that is hard to do. How can the other one also be Bongo when they insist that you are not?

"So then how can one bridle the power of this false oneness, this conformity?"

There are many ways, but fear... that is the strongest. Fear and hatred. Fear, hatred and an almost obsessive devotion to ones... I don't know... country? I know what you're going to ask me next.

"From where can this fear be imported?"

From abroad.

"A broad? Do you mean a woman, a girl, a chick, a babe, a bird, a hoochie coochie mama... like your mother or your girlfriend?"

Well, they can play that game too... but no! *Abroad*, silly. Out of the country. The other. The one you hate. Foreigners. You know. War! That's what I'm talking about. War!

They needed the war, you see. It created the permanent crisis. You cannot criticize 'your own' in times of crisis. And if there were no actual crisis? Well then crisis must be manufactured. An attack upon our civilization? Yes there had been such attacks, but not in a long time. A couple of the more militant Bongovian sects had banded together a few years ago and done some damage with home made bombs. A few of the more suicidal insurgents had driven cars and heavy lifting machinery into buildings, killing a lot of people. Nonetheless, the actual damage they had done paled in comparison to the way their acts were exploited by the authorities. The war took on much greater significance after that. Hundreds of perfectly peaceful Bongovians, and foreigners, were rounded up and never heard from again. Everyone took a deep breath that the danger was over. But that wound was constantly reopened by those in charge, in order to gain support for whatever action they desired to bolster. The war, for example – which in turn, of course, became the rationalization for further internal oppression. We must stand behind our leaders. They have our best interests at heart. Anything less would be treason during this time of crisis.

That's what made them so much the same, the towns the corporations, the provinces, the states. They were all complicit in one thing. Their need to control their communities. Some of them would have liked to control each other, but military might was expensive, and if you use up too much of your cash you start to lose control. So pick on someone easy. That'll do the trick. You can get the other states to help you out. It's good for everyone down the line except, of course, the poor bastard who's getting beaten up. But hey, everyone gets a turn to get beaten up. Well, everyone who has no power, anyway.

And it was brilliant, in a way, because they used the religion, philosophy, science... whatever, to invest a dogmatic morality upon their purpose, and so ingrain the idea within the consciousness of the population, that nobody could ever believe their leaders would be so evil as to flagrantly employ something as horrific as war, in the pursuit of their own selfish designs.

"Boy you're cynical!" You say.

I suppose it's alright to believe that the other guy is doing just that same thing? But what exactly is the difference between them and us?

"Listen here you ungrateful treasonous bastard! We believe in country, Philosophy, Mathematics, Bongo... whatever! You can't compare us with those heathen scum. Now get back in your hole and do your patriotic duty, or go live with them if you love them so much!"

But I don't love them so much. In fact, I think they're just like you...

The war!

And so the war continued. It was always there. Some people were sent to it, some came back, some did not, but all in all not enough to really anger the masses. It was a delicate balance. A fine tune played on an old guitar. The war. It stoked the engines of industry. It stifled the murmurs of criticism. It motivated the desire for cooperation. What could be bad? And sometimes you could pick up cool stuff after destroying someone else's ten-thousand-year-old culture. Neat!

And at some point it became even more sophisticated than that. Because you didn't have to have a war with another country. They came up with concepts to be at war with. They... who are they anyway? Well... actually they... were very expensive PR companies who were hired by JCN, at first... later on JCN simply swallowed up the most prestigious and useful ones and turned them into subsidiaries, or departments.

Anyway— they figured— why be at war with someone, or something concrete, when there is the potential for victory or loss. That means it could come to an end. A concept, on the other hand is a much more vague thing, and it is much harder to determine whether one has ever defeated it or not. As such, it can be utilized indefinitely.

For example, it became noticeable to many at one point that people were losing the art of common courtesy. That's right, they were getting ruder. What could be done? Some fine young Miss Manners type at one of these PR companies came up with the idea of a "War on Rudeness." Who, after all, could state that rudeness was ever completely defeated? Let's take this concept one step further. People are always getting sick. Let's have a "War on Illness." What about dirt? Some people just aren't clean enough. It's insanitary. And it smells bad. "War on Dirt," I say. We're going to show them what's really clean! Bring it on! What about obsessive compulsive behavior? Can't be good. Bang! "War on Obsession." Bang! Bang! "War on Compulsion." That could go on for ever. And so could the list of things that one could come up with. If you took drugs they didn't want you to take. Wham! "War on Drugs." If you didn't take the drugs that they wanted you to take. Kapow! "War on Not Taking Your Medication." Etcetera ad infinitum. But... the best one they ever came up with was... get this... Evil. Ha-ha-ha-ha-haah! "The War Against Evil." Now, *that's* enough to strike terror into your heart.

In this way JCN and the Church of the Great God Bongo colluded with the other states to preserve a condition of permanent discomfort amongst the populace and a commensurate feeling of gratitude to their governors for the safety afforded by the restrictions imposed within the community, for their own good, of course. War demanded certain special conditions. Everyone understood that. As long as they were at war with someone or something they would just have to put up with not getting every little freedom they felt entitled to. It was tough for everyone but, "we all have to pull together." "Let's not criticize each other." "Join up." "Stand by your group, flag, country, religion, whatever." Which was strange, because it was almost completely opposite to the teachings of the Temple of Bongo. Those taught you that you were free to think in any way that you pleased

The other states were different, yes, in some superficial ways; but in crucial areas they were very much like one another. And, although there were power plays amongst them, and constantly shifting alliances, most of the time they just cooperated with one another. It was easier. They were so closely connected. Conceptually, psychologically... yes, physically, touching each other. Side by side. Back to back. On and on.

Within the confines of that same urban rental sprawl they went on and on... until it ended. And then, an even more desolate landscape took over. There was nothing for miles and miles. No houses. No farms. No condos. No factories. No offices. No malls. No shoe stores. Not even any natural landscapes. No mountains. No rivers. No valleys. No grassy savannahs... it couldn't even be called a desert. But in the middle of all this expanse of... nothing, there were a cluster of houses, hulking together as if drawn so by the cold night air, surrounded by a wire fence with a large gash in one side, an open wound revealing the place where an ominous looking black van lay parked in a ditch. And now, as the late morning sun brought clarity to this picture, one could still see the smoke rising from this topless building, like a headless chicken refusing to die; standing (or should I say running) there, a living monument to its own stupidity. And leaving its footprints in the dirt, not unlike the single set of human ones we see in this picture, trailing away out of the rubble and clutter, an escaping phantom memory, out into the wilds of nowhere. And nowhere, a half naked shoeless man (where's a shoe store when you need one?) limped away, his toes bleeding and sore. He was thankful at least for the slight warmth of the sun as it strengthened but he wished for comfort and rest... and anonymity. It was his fame which plagued him so. There was nowhere in the world that his face was not known, and so he would retire, from time to time, to here (nowhere), in order to escape this curse. Everywhere he went people loved him. Everywhere he went people hated him. There was no middle ground. Sometimes they cried from their love. Sometimes they sneered in disgust. They followed him around to present him with pieces of their lives or to take pieces of him for their own. They stalked and hunted him in an attempt to capture and display their trophies, when friends and neighbors happened by. They stalked and hunted him to revenge the loss of a sister's virginity. They sought comfort within his embrace, or sought to be the one to comfort him in theirs. They longed for his approval... and his condemnation, whilst they also had the need to approve or condemn his actions and his beliefs. One thing was for sure, no matter what they felt for him, love or hatred (or some combination of the two), they had all allied their sense of self identity to the myth of his being. And that inseparability tormented them in their need for independence yet warmed them in their need for belonging.

Here he crawled amongst the noontime rocks and underbrush. The physical embodiment of a disembodied spirit. Was he... or wasn't he... Jason Cyllabus Novedi? Yes... and no. That spirit was the common denominator of the desires of all who believed in him. It was not a concrete thing. But it was real, and it was powerful, and it could have moved mountains had it so required. Whereas he... the physical Jason Cyllabus Novedi, was having a problem getting past a large stone which was blocking his access to the highway. There he was hoping that he could hitch a ride from some kind and discreet soul who might be sympathetic to his dilemma.

It was not a well frequented highway but after a fair amount of time waiting by the side of the road, caressing his swollen feet, picking his nose, licking chapped lips, imagining the twin luxuries of cleanliness and satiety... a cloud of dust appeared upon the distant horizon signaling a vehicle heading in his direction. After a few minutes, however, the dust had not reached him and in fact changed course and seemed to be heading away from the road. Someone must live out here, in one of the infrequent shacks that can occasionally be seen when speeding past in a company limousine. Eventually the dust cloud disappeared into the distance and Jason Cyllabus Novedi took his place once again by the side of the road, and dozed a little in the sun and dreamed a half a dream of a garden where he used to walk and sit by a pond, filled with golden fish. Fish, who knew nothing but the pond. Fish, who tried not even to escape the prison of their lives, their whole lives lived out in this little thing, this little world, this little pond. But yet who dreamed of being somewhere else. Here perhaps. And as he sat and slipped in and out of his reverie he was jogged awake by the sound of an engine creeping into his consciousness from behind. A small block. A V8. An ancient gas guzzling, lead polluting monstrosity that towed in its wake another ghost from out of his dreams. From out of the past, from where he came... from where we all come, through slit eyes, half awake he saw it as a child sees it and points, a four year old...

points, and says, "Bel... jun" pudgy baby fingers curled and not quite aimed correctly at their mark, "No silly," his mama says, or maybe his aunty says, "no silly, not Bel-*gian*... Bel *Air!*" A vision of rolling beauty, turquoise and white. Two-tone paint job, big fins with chrome edging, Three-hundred and fifty cubic inches of Ram Jet V8 rumbling past, "™Chevrolet... Bel... Air". And sure enough as he opened his eyes, here... now... he saw it, this anachronism pulling a huge cloud of dust behind it, approaching him as so many things in his life did, from the wrong direction.

He jumped up and started to wave it to a halt. It was just as he remembered, or dreamed, or whatever. Same colors, same year... nineteen fifty-seven ™Chevy Bel Air. And it was being driven by the last remaining virgin in the land. The last one who had never even seen, let alone been ravaged by, the great Jason Cyllabus Novedi. Although, according to the strict tenets of his personal mythology, she could not exist. No woman, they said, could have escaped his devouring rampant phallic excesses. And yet here she was. Driving this behemoth, calmly... meekly even, proceeding in this antique conveyance, towards a town called 83047. Here she was, right in front of his lying eyes. Here she was, the reality of what he wouldn't dare to dream.

She was going there to bail out her father who had been arrested last night on a drunk and disorderly. Apparently, this had become a regular occurrence since her mother died... oh, fifteen years ago. It was a fact he refused to accept. And after he'd had a couple, he'd tell anyone within earshot, including his daughter (*their* daughter), "She's run away to the big city, the real city, 'cause she don't give a shit about me no more... nor you neither. And there she finds ample employment driving a taxi cab by day, and every night, taking her clothes off in drinkin' establishments for the amusement of strange men of all types and professions. Sailors, and judges and... undertakers I wouldn't doubt. But she'll return, one day, mark my words 'cause thain't no love there.

And you can't live with no love. And anyway she's just doin' it for us, me and my little girl... our little girl... so she can come back and bring us all the things we ever wanted." And then slowly he would turn his moistened eyes to the heavens and then to the floor and with a slight warble in his voice he'd continue, "But you know something? The only thing we ever wanted... was for her to just come back."

And so she'd drive to pick him up, Jocelyn, for that was the virgin's name, but not so anxious now as she had been the first time that she'd had to retrieve him. That time she had gotten up in the middle of the night to go get him. She'd driven all the way to 83047... in the middle of the night she went, only to find him comfortably crashed out in a nice warm jail cell, oblivious to any inconvenience he might have suffered as a result of being there or, for that matter, any that he might be imposing on those around him. But these days it was different. Last night the sheriff called to assure her that her dad would be well taken care of, and even given a good hot breakfast by the time she got there to pick him up... "and sure, anytime would be okay – as long as it was before noon." He was a sweet enough man, the sheriff, to treat her dad so well, but then he'd gone on for a while about his personal life and asked her many questions about hers. She wasn't sure if she liked policemen very much – something about the rigidity of a nature which *believes* in the law... respects it, as if it were something more than just somebody's idea of how things ought to be. But he *was* sort-of funny. He entertained her even as she tried to put the phone down. Goodnight... but then he'd come up with some other (truly) interesting topic, just as she was pulling the receiver away from her ear – he knew more than she would have expected of a cop – and still, she would listen... answer... allow herself to be drawn in... but all the while, she would resent his unsolicited intrusion into her life.

On one occasion, he'd regaled her with the story of his attempt to have the town of 83047 officially renamed, 'Nottingham' – so that he, of course, could be the 'Sheriff of Nottingham.' His laughter, as he related this tale, satisfied Jocelyn that his sense of humor was acceptably wicked. Well apparently— as he told it— that day at the town council meeting, there was (as usual) a complete absence of any other topic up for debate. So the name change was proposed and seconded, and, after a lengthy discussion, which took in every possible scenario regarding the consequences that such a change (or, for that matter, a lack thereof) might engender within the community – with particular reference to the economical, political, social and (not to mention) psycho-spiritual ramifications of the idea – it was, eventually, unanimously decided that the naming of the town should go forward immediately. Large wooden signs would be painted with beautiful gold lettering complete with flourishes and curlicues, in a style reminiscent of the 'Age of Chivalry,' of knights in armor, of Robin Hood and Maid Marian. These would be posted at either end of the town. Everyone was terribly excited at the thought that this simple change might help their little town stand out amongst an otherwise banal sea of numbers. Perhaps a yearly festival with an heraldic theme might be conjured up, with wizards, and jousts, and drinking establishments open all night, which would bring in visitors who would spend their money here. The new 'Nottingham' might become a Mecca for tourists and holiday makers, known and respected throughout the land.

It was a dream, however, which did not sit well within the jaded subconscious sentiments of those very same denizens of 83047 who, in their superficial, childlike exuberance, had believed that such delightful chance might actually grace their ineffectual history. So it came as no surprise to anyone that, once the signs were painted and positioned in their respective locations, it was discovered (within a relatively rapid twenty-four hour period, mind you) that the name of the town had been misspelled, '*Nottinghang.*'

If we cannot even get the sign right— was the unspoken

consensus— how can we deserve to even hope for more. Needless to say, amidst the general embarrassment of the townsfolk, the signs were rapidly removed, and no utterance was ever again heard regarding names, or heraldry, or even (Bongo forbid) the Knight's of the Round Table. To this day the town is still known by its postal code, 83047. Although Sheriff Duco, that very same proposer of its nomination, in his dry and prankish way, satirically attempting to evoke the discomfort of his compatriots, does occasionally (and publicly) refer to that town as 'Hangman's Humiliation.'

Jocelyn was never sure about her own feelings, but she was anticipating (with some satisfaction) this excuse to connect with Sheriff Duco. Perhaps he would prove himself, in some fantasy future, to be more human than policeman. Perhaps he would prove himself a tolerable distraction. And anyway, there were precious few men around where she lived, let alone ones who still owned all their teeth. Her father's small farm was a rarity now in that area, as was any social event that she might attend. They lived an isolated life out there most of the time, and young maidens they do get weary of their father's attentions and hanker, sooner or later, for the hard feelings of a softer kind.

The farm was a pretty run down affair with only the two of them to work it, which of course recently, meant only one... her. Jocelyn maintained a little vegetable garden which actually produced more than enough for the two of them. There were some chickens, and a she-goat who, in return for sustenance and domicile, gratefully shared her regular lactations with the humans. What vegetables and eggs that they could spare provided a valuable commodity when it came to trading for other necessities: clothing, soap, reading materials and the like.

Romance was a little known commodity in her life, and Jocelyn was a romantic. This was a trait that she had inherited from her father, and so she could not hate him for his misery which was, after all, a consequence of his romanticism. And although she chided him for his

41

drunkenness, it was the drama of his getting drunk which had introduced Jocelyn to an element of adventure in her life. And although he had caused her so much pain and done her so much damage, still it was the romance of his loss, and of his embitterment, which led her now toward the town of 'Hangman's Humiliation' in her nineteen fifty-seven ™Chevrolet Bel Air.

But her journey was to be interrupted by an unforeseen event. By the side of the road a half naked man reclined like an iguana next to a rock, and raised a fist, thumb protruding, the gesture of the hitcher, as the blue and white automobile approached. Jocelyn's heart shuddered when she saw him. Not because she recognized him for the icon that he was. She didn't. Because, not only was she the last living virgin in the world, but she was also one of the very few people who had never seen a picture of Jason Cyllabus Novedi. To be quite honest his very existence had hardly touched her life at all, not directly at any rate. She may very well have heard his name mentioned in idle chatter from time to time, it would be difficult not to, but she would have been unlikely to remember it if called upon to do so for herself. No, her heart shuddered because she found within herself a conflict. It could be a risky proposition to stop for a man who looked like this out in the middle of nowhere. These were dangerous times and she had been warned of the tricks that a felon might concoct. On the other hand, she was not one to refuse a soul in distress, and it was that very same frightening demeanor that made this creature seem so in need of sympathy. There was no way to reasonably assess the verity of the situation, and so she feared the inevitability of the decision that she must make. In the end she did that which she would always do when evidence could not be provided either way. She gave the situation the benefit of the doubt and pulled her car to a stop.

Chapter 4

Marvin was a dark skinned man. He lived in a rather seedy part of town, but his apartment was plushly furnished if not altogether in the finest tradition. Still, it offered all the comforts of home, and then some. It reminded Dominic of a brothel he had once visited – which had, in fact, been a rather pleasant experience – and so he always felt somewhat cosseted and reassured by his visits to Marvin's. In fact Marvin had toyed with the idea of pimping, at some point, and had even gone so far as to having a couple of questionable looking women living at his place for a time. They would pull the occasional 'trick,' when the need for cash outweighed the need for dignity, bringing their 'Johns' back to Marvin's place for twenty minutes of stiff and artificial prurience. But he never made any money out of them, in fact, he even felt guilty about charging them rent (such was his calling as a business man). They cooked him a meal every once in a while and took turns with a blow job now and then, but to tell the truth, they weren't such good blow jobs, and he was relieved when first, one of them left, and fairly soon after, the other.

Marie, the second one to leave, an Irish girl, had endeared herself to Marvin, despite his assertions to the contrary, and he had felt, along with his relief, a certain sadness at her departure, which he never admitted to. She may have, in many ways, been just as unsuitable for polite society as her friend Abby, but she had a refined and anarchical beauty, which was perfectly complemented by reams of natural red hair. She attracted many a young man, not strong enough to thwart her domination. One such weakling was a rich man's son who promised her the world, if only she would give herself to him. The marriage didn't last long before he was emotionally annihilated by her vigor. The boy's overprotective parents, trapped within their own habit of controlling and coddling their child, bought her off. She agreed to an annulment and the abortion of their unborn child and – after pocketing a fair bit of change (she wasn't greedy) – vacated the sniveling wretch's life, leaving him to find solace, someday perhaps, in the arms of some vacuous debutante, more suitable to the requirements of Mater and Pater. Marie returned to town after less than three months of living at the fabulous country estate. "What the fuck," she thought, "it was a nice long free vacation" – she could be a tough bitch at times – and she bought herself a little apartment with her amoral earnings, and got herself a job as a stripper during the day, and a cab driver at night. Once in a while she would come over to Marvin's and screw his brains out... never sleeping over. They were not jealous of each other's independence. They had their own lives to live. Dominic Devine reckoned they had the perfect relationship. He was wrong. There is no perfect relationship.

Nowadays Marvin got by mostly shifting small quantities of Cocaine or Marijuana. Recently L.S.D. was making a comeback. The kids were harking back to the revolutionary stance of their parents. They had missed the excitement of those hippy days, but what they didn't realize was that, more than just excitement, real changes had occurred back then (and real payments extracted). Maybe not the changes that they thought were occurring, but something actually took place. This apparent revival was nothing more than a shallow impersonation of form and fashion. A 'virtual reality' sixties where things only happen in the digital domain, and they can be deleted and reentered in order to create a more 'authentic' organism. It was not a necessary thing as the original had been. It was no longer necessary to make changes, they thought. Changes were making themselves. And so they buried themselves within their computer games and let 'Change' wreak havoc and pillage and rape the changes that their parents had given blood to make.

That's what Dominic thought. But maybe he had never quite left those times behind in his mind. He still, after all these years, aspired to the Bohemian way. He reveled in the type of underclass characters who frequented Marvin's environment. What's that you say? Reverse snobbism? Snobbism is snobbism. Some are better and some are worse. Alright, Devine was a 'Scum-hag' if you want to put it that way, but he also found a type of humanity in those people which was either not available to the middle classes or so repressed beneath their fear of the unusual that it seemed to have disappeared completely.

Luca sipped from a can of 'Olde English'. His day job was spackling and painting for a contractor, but right now, by being here, he was shirking his evening job. He ran a small electronics repair shop where he hardly ever charged for his work. Mostly he would sit around drinking beer with a couple of homeless guys who had come in from the snow, or the rain, or the darkness... or the light, and he would tinker with a black and white, twelve-inch ™Ferguson. He liked to fiddle with things, it kept his mind busy. He didn't feel it would be wise to just let his mind think about whatever it wanted. As Dominic listened to him explain this he got an uneasy feeling that Luca may well be right. Most nights Luca partied at his shop, but tonight he'd come to return Marvin's cassette deck and maybe snort up a line or two. He put down his beer-can and inserted a cassette into the machine. Marvin rolled a joint.

Peggy and Joe sat in the corner watching T.V. They were an elderly couple who worked at a magazine stall at the corner of the block right next to the subway entrance. They didn't really interact with anyone else in the room, or for that matter, with each other; not on this occasion nor any of the previous ones in which Dominic had encountered them. It was difficult to determine exactly how they communicated. Non verbally. Psychically perhaps. Once in a while Joe would get up and walk to the kitchen for some more cheese or something, or to the bathroom to relieve himself. But Peggy, who had a facial tick as a result of years of ™Thorazine treatment – sometimes her head would snap alarmingly around for no apparent reason, (otherwise) never seemed to move.

Dominic had never seen Peggy and Joe arrive... or leave. Sometimes they were at Marvin's place, and sometimes they weren't.

Marvin was (sort of) the 'Godfather' to his little crew of followers which, admittedly, waxed and waned with the seasons, but always survived (like Marvin) to see a new one in. He was an inspiration to Dominic Devine. He lived the life that Dominic imagined, or wrote about. Marvin *was* Scaramouche. He would tell Dominic about this woman he had fucked when he was thirteen years old. "She was thirty-five at the time," Marvin would say, "but sexy as hell." Dominic would wish that *he* could tell people that he'd fucked a thirty-five year old woman when he was thirteen. He sometimes wished, when he heard Marvin talk, that he could have fucked a thirteen year old... when he was thirty-five.

"I mean," Scaramouche would say, "what's the fuckin' difference?"

"Well, don't you feel," Dominic would ask guiltily, "that it might be wrong for a grown man to take advantage of a child that way?"

"Are you a fuckin' sexist?" the reply would come.

"What? What do you mean, sexist?"

"I mean," Marvin would say, "Do you think the thirty-five year old woman that I fucked when I was thirteen, was taking advantage of me?"

"Possibly... well, no... I suppose... it's the way you put it. You said *you* fucked *her*, not *she* fucked *you*. It implies that *you* took advantage of *her*. I suppose it *is* sexist. The male fucks the female."

"So what you're saying is," Marvin might respond, "that it's okay for the fuck-ee to take advantage, but not for the fuck-er?"

"Is it? I'm not sure."

"Well, what *I'm* saying is, that it didn't do *me* any harm. I would never give back that experience for anything. You see Dominic, it doesn't have anything to do with who's older or who's younger. People take advantage of each other everyday. Some people are stronger than other people. Some people are smarter than other people. Some people are more devious than others. But they have relationships with each other all the time. Do you think they're taking advantage of each other? Of course they fuckin' are. What's that got to do with it? Nothing! The real question is, are they *abusing* one another? Any two humans, or animals for that matter, could have an abusive or a non-abusive relationship with each other. My relationship with Cleo..."

"The thirty five year old," Dominic would inject, for clarity.

"correct... er, was a non-abusive relationship. I took advantage of her... she took advantage of me, and we both agreed to those terms. Quite frankly I think she gave me so much more than I could ever give her. Over a period of six weeks she taught me a lot."

"Sexually?"

"That... and other stuff. In fact we discussed this very same issue at length. I mean she had no guilt, you understand, about what we were doing. But we both knew what kind of trouble there'd be if anyone ever found out about us. That was my first lesson. The world isn't a rational place. Things are taken out of context. People make stereotypical judgments about stuff they have very little information about. You know what she told me once – and I have always remembered it… and lived by it – she said, "there is only one rule in the universe: you can do anything that you can get away with. But… *You* have to define 'getting away with it' for yourself."

"How do *you* define it?"

"Me? Guilt! If I don't have any guilt. And I don't mean, if I don't *feel* any guilt – that's just repression! You've got to know yourself. You've got to have that inner dialog, man. Freedom. That's where that comes from. Converse with your own sweet self. Cleo taught me that!"

"How did she do that?"

"Man! She hipped me to the weeed! Heh, heh, heh!"

And he would throw a joint at Dominic that he'd been rolling all the time that they were talking. And Dominic would laugh, and the two of them would laugh, and laugh, and light the joint, and smoke, and squeal "weeed!" in high pitched voices and laugh some more.

"So what do you want me to do?" Marvin winced slightly as he exhaled and passed the spliff to Luca, but he was speaking to Dominic Devine. "You want me to find out who this George Burgess character is… or what?" The smoke came out of his mouth in little puffs, one for each word, like the smoke signal translation of what he was saying, for the hard of hearing Native American. But Dominic took them to have a hidden meaning that he was unable to decipher. Halfway through his exhalation Marvin sucked back the same smoke that was already on its way out. He looked at Dominic quizzically whilst holding his breath.

"Well…" Devine was non committal, even a little mealy mouthed as he sometimes tended to be around Marvin. "Only… if er… you're, like, interested. I figured it would be like er… one of those mysteries you're always interested in. You know, Holmes!"

The acid was starting to come on now and Dominic could definitely see a little Sherlock in Marvin's lanky and hawk-like profile silhouetted as it was now by the evening light coming in through the window. The allusion must have titillated him as he posed, almost, with his chin resting on his fingers and considered using a pipe for the next round of weed.

"Yo, Homes!" Luca looked up slightly through heavy heavy lids, he handed the roach back the way it had come. Dominic Devine waited for his host to correct this error in procedure, but instead he took the offering and just ate it.

Marvin switched on a lamp beside him and examined the letter again. "This guy ain't in town, man. It's gonna be difficult to get a fix on him." The other two men just nodded. In the corner of the room Peggy's head snapped round suddenly for no apparent reason. Her eyes caught Dominic's gaze for one brief flash, then she turned back to watch the T.V. news. Some black guy, apparently, was roaming around the ritzy part of town raping lawyers' wives, and nuns, or something. They had a drawing of him on the screen. It could have been anyone with a black hood.

"Homes... it's you!" Luca, pointing at the T.V., burst out laughing.

"So what do you think he's up to?" asked Dominic. "I mean do you think it's a scam of some kind?"

Marvin was looking at Luca. "Asshole!" But he laughed.

Dominic repeated himself, "Could it be a..."

"Yeah, yeah... I don't know... maybe."

"But how can they scam me if I can't even get in touch with them?"

"Maybe they lettin' you sweat!" Luca really didn't know the story well, but he pitched in anyway.

"Maybe you'll get another letter," said Marvin. "Why don't you just wait and see? Maybe all your questions will be answered. Maybe there is no mystery."

"No... no..." Dominic was watching patterns on the carpet as they started swirling around one another. He was shaking his head in disagreement. "That would be playing their game. They're just doing this to get me all antsy, like the electrician here said."

"I ain't no fuckin' electrician!"

"If I allow this to proceed according to their game plan then they have the advantage

"Antsy?" said Luca with a rat-like grin, and looked over sarcastically at Joe in the corner. Joe raised his can of beer toward Luca and grunted with a sort of smile on his face. Luca turned back this way. "Get your own fuckin' beer," he mumbled.

But Marvin could identify with Dominic's logic. His lifestyle had trained him to be suspicious of everyone. He'd run a few scams himself, and people who cheat others always think that someone is cheating them. He knew that scams always involve manipulating the ego of the mark in one way or another, and Dominic Divine's ego was so ripe for manipulation, especially as far as his book was concerned.

But then Luca, who appeared to have dropped off, suddenly spoke. "Hey look at this man... what if it's fuckin' true?"

"What do you mean?" said Dominic. Luca's voice had left a trail of echoes in his consciousness, and he wasn't sure that he understood the question. He wasn't even really sure if understanding the question was appropriate to the situation.

"Well... what if them fuckers actually like you're piece of shit book and want to publish it?"

The two just stopped and stared at him. Even Peggy and Joe turned to look. Time seemed to halt for a moment. There was no sound. The four faces were a photograph... a black and white photograph staring back at Luca as if he wasn't there.

"Look! You think this crap is worth reading, don't you?" Luca pointed straight at Dominic's chest. Dominic didn't know what to say. "Well? Don't you believe that some asshole would think that it was good enough to publish? I mean that's why you fuckin' sent it to them, ain't it? I seen a lot of shit out there man. Your book gotta be at least as good as that! I mean... you did write it 'cause you wanted it to be published, didn't you?"

This question, as it repeated itself over and over in his mind and slowly exposed its simple significance upon him, stirred a battery of emotions from within his dry unwavering universe. And the intrusion that he felt at this idea infuriated him in some way that he wasn't able to recognize just yet. "Yes but..." he retorted in an attempt to deflect its implication. "That's exactly what they *want* me to believe, so that I'll feel frustrated and desperate."

"That's if it's a scam," said Marvin, "... which it probably is."

"Yeah..." said Luca, almost (but not quite) resignedly, "probably... but... what if it fuckin' isn't, you stupid cock!" He aimed this epithet at Dominic even though he was technically responding to Marvin's comment.

Dominic looked at him, and then at Peggy and Joe, who were obliviously engrossed, at this moment, in some kind of a glitzy variety show airing on one of the Spanish language stations. Their faces were illuminated by the image of a standard poodle on roller skates which was humping a leggy dancing girl, while a short man in a crimson and violet leotard rotated a hula hoop around his waist and sang La Paloma in falsetto. Dominic's gaze drifted incoherently from this spectacle to Sherlock Holmes and thence back to the rat-faced Luca who by now had actually become a rodent of some kind, sniffing around the cushions of the sofa looking for crumbs.

"I suppose," said Marvin, "that we could consider that as an outside possibility."

Outside possibility— thought Dominic Devine, unable to put any value judgment on the phrase. "Yes... yes, but... but," he said because he had unconsciously, in many ways, been trying to evade that possibility ever since he'd received the damned letter in the first place, "if it isn't a scam... I mean if everything they say is true, well... don't you see? It's... it's totally unfair. I mean a mistake like that couldn't possibly happen. I mean it's too contrived to imagine... that... that the one thing which they absolutely insist must happen would be the very thing that would coincidentally go wrong. It's a cheap plot device. It's too... Hollywood." There was a diagram of parallels and connections hanging like some futuristic hologram right in front of his eyes. He wasn't sure if he was explaining himself the way that he thought he was, but cogs and wheels clicked visual perfection where only *he* could see them. "I don't believe it!" he concluded.

"Truth is stranger than fiction," said the rodent. "let's see now... you don't believe that your destiny could have come so close as to tap you on the shoulder from behind, and then run away before you had a chance to grab it by the fuckin' balls and make it your fuckin' bitch?"

Marvin looked at Luca with a renewed respect. Dominic just stared dolefully at his own brown shoes sitting beneath him in the darkness; the laces tied and untied themselves at will. The rat continued. "It's true though... it's hard to imagine that fate would be guilty of the same kind of tricky manipulation that the fuckin' ad companies do. No win situfuckination! The fuckin' carrot dangled in front of the cocksuckin' donkey's arse. Motherfucker can never reach it! Tell me something, er..." He snapped his fingers several times while looking to Marvin for support.

"Dominic," Marvin prompted.

"Yeah Dominate, er... tell me something. Do you believe in luck?" Dominic stared blank faced for a moment. He wasn't sure exactly what he believed in right now. "Speak English?" Ratty taunted. "I say luck... not fuck! I didn't axe you if you believed in fuck!" He was grinning at Marvin as he spoke.

But Marvin wasn't smiling. "You make your own luck!" he snapped. "That's what I believe!" And he walked away towards the kitchen.

"No!" said Dominic, attempting desperately to gather his resources for the retaliatory skirmish. "I don't believe in luck. Good or bad. I believe that when you are ready for things to happen... they happen."

"Just like that?" spake the rat bemused.

"I don't believe that fate draws near and then pulls away. I don't believe in the likelihood of things happening. They either happen or they don't. I don't believe in chance, or odds, or random or arbitrary occurrences. I believe that fate moves surely, unhesitatingly to its appointment... and... it always gets there by its appointed route."

"Through rain or sleet or dark of night." It was Marvin returning from the kitchen with a can of ™Guinness Draught. There was a slight hiss as he popped the ring pull open, and he poured the creamy black stuff into a long clear glass. Dominic peered into the glass as he approached. It looked like a microcosm of the deep unmanifest potential of the universe. Here and there a bubble of life, rising... rising surely, lifting itself up to the surface where it can see, and itself be seen, and become blinded to its own deeper potential, forgetful of what it once was and essentially will always be.

"Exactly!" countered Dominic. "I think people who gamble are playing with an illusion of possibilities as if they all exist equally. In fact they don't all exist, equally or otherwise. Only one possibility exists in reality... or at least in any reality that any one of us might experience, and that is the one which will actually happen."

Luca just breathed for a while.

Finally he spoke nodding his head gravely. "Heavy Dominate! You a heavy dude." Then he looked at Marvin. "So? You think it's a scam?"

"Yeah," said Marvin.

Dominic Devine leaned back in his seat imagining himself the conquering hero. Papa Joe looked up from the T.V. set. Its light, flickering on his upturned features and his Mama's down turned ones, made them liquid and blue and prone to change, lengthening their chins and noses alternately like the chins and noses of the everlasting parade of freaks who passed before them everyday, on the street and on the box, whose existence passed for normalcy, whose currency was religion and dogma and belief... such everlasting belief. Amen. Papa Joe looked up from all of this and grunted in a voice that Dominic Devine had never heard before, "Hey! What's that? Guinness? Hey! Can I have one of those?"

"Go get yer own mother fuckin' beer!" the rat replied.

Peggy didn't so much as twitch.

Chapter 5

Jason Cyllabus Novedi limped across the gravel. Jocelyn instinctively jumped out of the car to assist him. She wasn't pretty, Jocelyn. Not in that 'pretty girlie' way, anyway. That was the first thing he would notice. But then there were so many pretty girls around, and he'd certainly had his share of *that* type. Most of them were tiresome after the first few minutes. Even if they were intelligent they seemed to rely disproportionately on the emotional effect they had on men, and it was always difficult to find out who the hell they were before he got bored with their pretense. She certainly didn't look like she was pretending anything, but then, you know, some pretenses take longer to establish themselves. Some pretenses only show themselves with intimacy. It's not that she was ugly – far from it. He saw, immediately, a beauty in her which had been hidden from him for as long as he could remember. She was healthy, for one thing. There was beauty in that, not least because of its rarity thereabouts. Her skin was supple, and it had color. And her eyes glinted as if an independent mind functioned behind them. Another rarity. She wore no make-up, and sweat – from sitting on those vinyl seats – adorned her back and armpits. It exuded a mildly musky odor that he was soon to experience. It was her natural perfume.

His grimy hand leaned upon her arm. But the grime looked new and not a part of him. No vagrant this, she inferred. His body was strong and lithe beneath the rough veneer, and he seemed not to be diseased in any obvious way. There was no smell. Could this be a deception? she wondered. But his feet were really bleeding, and he was acting in a non-threatening and even grateful manner. She opened the passenger door and guided him squarely onto the seat.

"I'm sorry," he remarked, 'I'm getting your fine upholstery all dirty."

No— she figured— this man is not out to rob me. But she wasn't one who showed her most positive feelings easily. Positivism was something her father had always considered saccharin and insincere. The tradition of their house was to attack and antagonize people as much as they could possibly stand, in order to display affection and prove acceptance— I wouldn't insult you if I didn't care. Although in truth she and her father had been known to insult many for whom they did not care.

"Don't worry," she replied, "I'm going to make you clean it all up..." but then she took another look at this pathetic heap slouching beside her and her voice softened, "later on... " she capitulated, "when you're feeling better." After all she did not know this man. How intimate could she allow herself to be?

"Oh, I'm feeling better already," he replied. He did not know yet, this game of communication. But as she pulled the befinned conveyance, gravel crackling beneath them, back out onto to the open road, he felt a stinging sensation in his feet that he had not noticed before.

She did not look at him for a while but drove silently, wondering what her own thoughts might be. Wondering, indeed, what *his* thoughts might be. But not allowing herself the one thought that she wondered about the most. This could not be a mistake. From the corner of her eye she began to notice his left fist clenching and unclenching repeatedly on the seat cushion. On the pretext of scanning the road behind her, she glanced in his direction momentarily. Water was running from his eyes down unemotional features staring straight ahead. Tears? she wondered. But no. Should she question him? Would questions provoke something in him that she had not yet seen? Did she want to see that which was, so far, hidden from her? How to broach these things? what to say?

"Are you... er... having some kind of ...er... problem?" She was trying desperately to sound callous and nonchalant but one of the words injected a little unintended squeak into her tone.

"I'll be okay," he answered as he cleared his throat.

She was quiet for another moment. "I can take you to the hospital in 83047."

"No!" he shot back. His hands, both of them, clenched hard on the seat. But then he let go, " ... not there... take me home!"

"Home?" She considered this for a minute. "Where's home?"

He stared at her in amazement. "You don't, er... know?" He seemed surprised, "Prick... Prickly... B–Bog," he stuttered unintelligibly. Then he cleared his throat again, and repeated it more slowly this time. "Prickly Bog."

Her eyebrows raised at this. She sort of whispered it to herself. "Prickly Bog!"

"Well... not f–far from the Temple, anyway... just north of it." He peered at her for some sense of recognition, but she did not know what his look meant. She hesitated, swerving slightly to avoid a pothole. She licked her drying lips and scanned the rearview mirror.

"Do you, er... do you mind if I ask you, er... what you were doing out here?"

"Jogging!" He had figured that she would ask him that question sooner or later. The slight smirk which accompanied his answer did not charm his host in any way.

"Well, Prickly Bog is a little out of my way," she said. "but maybe the sheriff can arrange some transportation for you, but first I have to..."

"Sheriff?" He snapped.

"Yes!" she responded equally harshly. "Duco. Sheriff Duco in 83047. That's where I'm heading now."

"No!" He jerked the steering wheel from her hands and aimed

the car at the side of the road. She hit the brakes hard, bringing the vehicle to an undignified halt.

"What the hell do you think you're doing?" She was breathing heavily with the shock of the thing. She turned off the engine and, pulling the key from the ignition, reached for the door handle. But he beat her to it.

"Let me out of here!" he yelled, and reached for the passenger door handle himself.

At this her motivation changed, and she leaned across him suddenly, her left hand grabbing his right to pull it back, preventing his escape. Her body was facing him now, chest to chest they both breathed heavily now; she could feel it upon her forehead. Her hand still held his, a little gentler now. "Are you wanted... by the police?" She questioned in the softest of tones.

It was finally dawning on him that she really didn't have a clue as to who he was. "Baby..." he pushed her away from him gently by the shoulders and back to her position in the driver's seat. "I am wanted by... everybody," and he started to laugh.

But his laughter became giddy and silly and she started to feel irritated by it, as if he were making fun of her. As if he were using the fact that he knew something that she didn't, in order to belittle her. She even felt rejected, a little. He had pushed her away. What did that mean? Not that it mattered to her. And now this silly laughter. It was childish, boyish, even. It almost charmed her for a moment in the midst of her anxiety, and would have, but then it changed, becoming more incessant... hysterical, which reignited her irritation, until – that is – the laughter, hysterical as it was, turned into a peculiar kind of sobbing. Not crying, but a lumpy gurgling sound. After a while she sensed the wetness of her own eyes in response, and began looking sensitively at his bleeding feet. She found herself touching his shoulder and saying to him, almost as if she were begging, "Let me help you... please!"

With absolutely no warning he ceased the sobbing. The tear streaks still lay inscribed upon his grimy face like a river splitting into a million streams, but other than that, all signs of hysteria had completely vanished. He peered through the windshield as if the answers to his questions were dancing past his field of vision, but those answers themselves were nothing but the roots of further questions.

"So..." he finally spoke, "What's he, your boyfriend or something?"

"Who?" She seemed destined to be baffled by him.

"In 83047... whoever it is you're going to see?"

"Ohhh! I see what you mean. N-no... that's er... my father"

"You're father?"

"Yes."

"Daddy's girl?"

"My father..." she just couldn't get what he was implying, yes... I'm going to meet my father!"

"Duco? The sheriff?"

"Oh... no..."

"He's your father?"

"No, no, no!"

"I didn't know he had a daughter."

"No, no... not Duco... do you know sheriff Du... no, my father is in... well, oh yes... I see what you mean.... no Duco is not my father, it's just..."

'He's your boyfriend?"

"No! He's not my boyfriend either! And what if he wa..."

"So what's your father got to do with..."

"*Wait !*"

She had had enough. This was the most confusing and frustrating situation. She needed to regain control of it. "First of all, this is none of your business... and... and..." But she couldn't really think what else to say.

"So he's not your boyfriend?"

"Right! That's it!" She slowly replaced the key in the ignition and started up the engine. "And if he was, it would be none of your business! And I've had enough of you, so if you would like to get out I'll be saying goodbye!"

"Well, who's your boyfriend, then?"

She reached across him once again, but with her right hand this time, and opened the passenger side door. With her left foot on the brake she revved the engine repeatedly, looking straight ahead. Jason Cyllabus Novedi looked her up and down slowly. Finally he lifted himself out of the car. He slammed the door shut. She drove away, over the crest of the road, and disappeared.

Chapter 6

Dominic Devine headed home down past the canal, clutching jealously to his vest, the precious manuscript he had recovered tonight. Despite all of his concerns, it had sat safely on Marvin's sideboard, awaiting his return, for no more than thirty-six hours at most. He looked around as he walked, examining his environment, almost as if he expected a miracle to suddenly occur (it was not an unusual condition for him). He noticed that the canal water was sludgy and dull, and greasy opalescent rainbows shimmered right beneath the surface of decay and grime. Tethered up and down the waterways, floated brightly painted barges which reminded him of Gypsy caravans from technicolor movies. There were people who actually lived on some of them. He wished that *he* lived on one.

He'd worked a party on one of them once, owned by a seemingly wealthy woman, who (Dominic felt sure) *must* own a real house as well— Big one, probably. Maybe a couple of them. She must live on the barge most of the summer— he fantasized— Probably so that she could get away from the hubby for a period. You can drive them around, you know...barges. People do. Up and down the canals. These canals connect to rivers, and the rivers... to other canals. Apparently you could travel hundreds of miles in one... if you could afford the diesel fuel. If you had the free time.

She had plenty of time, he decided. No children. She liked to do favors for people. You know, to fill her time. Her friends... who may not be so wealthy. May not have as much time. Kids. They take a lot of time. Eat a lot. Need entertaining. Parties and such. Birthdays. What better place for a birthday party? A barge painted like a Gypsy caravan from a technicolor movie. So she'd hired him – Dominic, the clown – for a party. Some less wealthy friend whose child was having a birthday. He went down there... one of these barges right along here, which one was it now? Anyway, so he'd gone down there, all dressed up in the clown outfit, nothing fancy, nothing classical... or renaissance or anything like that. Usual stuff, red nose, big shoes, white face... it's Dominic the clown, children, doesn't he have a funny nose!

She was nice looking. Sexy... for an older woman. Still, she was probably younger than him. But not one of those bimbo types, like all the older guys usually go for. There were books on the shelves... in the barge, yes! Literature. Real stuff. No Barbara Cartland romances here. And philosophy. Carl Jung. Child psychology. Why would she need that? He wondered. Too smart maybe. But *very* good looking. Body was nice too. Trim. Good boobs. Nice. Wouldn't kick her out of... in fact, he was kind of thinking – what with the husband not overtly in the picture, and all – about asking her out, maybe. But then he'd thought — maybe not. Not with the nose and the white make-up on. Although to tell the truth he probably wouldn't have the confidence even if he were dressed normally. She was so... so much more than he felt he deserved. He didn't know how she'd accumulated her wealth, whether from hubby... or daddy... or made it herself, but wealth... just wealth itself... it lends an air of accomplishment to those who have it, doesn't it! Anyway, she had an air of accomplishment – wherever the hell she got it – and he didn't! And not only that. She looked so good, like she went to a gym or something. Whereas he... well he did have a bit of a spare tire these days. Okay, he'd had it for the last twenty years, then. He'd *never* been in shape. Couldn't *imagine* what the inside of a gym looked like.

There was a time when he would tell himself that he was going to start exercising soon. He'd feel guilty when he saw those TV commercials— Special offer if you act now! Summer's coming! Nineteen ninety-five a month— He'd start nervously flicking the channels up and down... out of guilt. But then slowly he stopped feeling the guilt (like a fish no longer feels the water). Although it would spark up – subliminally, at least – every once in a while when he'd meet someone (like her) to whom he was attracted. Funny, isn't it? He was never attracted to someone who was in as bad shape as he was. I suppose it just wouldn't have made him feel guilty enough.

She dressed well too. Successfully. With class. And... a sense of style. A little different, but not so different as to seem, er... different. Not to attract the attention of any but those with a subtle eye. Even in casual gear. Jeans, what have you... and a sweater. But a good sweater. Tasteful colors. Maybe a scarf of an ideally complementary hue. And the jeans with life still in them. Worn to just the right degree. Beautiful leather shoes. Previously owned by the Shah of Iran's grandniece... or whatever the fuck.

Whereas his clothes were all falling apart after years of misuse. Not that he would know what to buy himself if he could afford to. He wore plaid shirts mostly, or denim... blue, with beige cotton pants, even in the winter, like now. Long johns underneath. Probably made of some awful artificial fiber. Clingy and staticky in the cold. Itchy and harsh indoors. He was always uncomfortable. Too hot in the summer. Too cold in the winter, like now. He paced the embankment in his new shoes, though. Brown leather. Classic style. Well... newish anyway. Last year. New for him. Not much wear yet. First expensive pair he'd ever bought. The soles had collected rock salt off the ice. Like now. Patchy... ice, that is. Another six inches on the way – snow, that is – and deposited it on his living-room floor... rock salt – that is – wetly. It's still there now, it occurred to him as he examined the barges, and considered how large they might be inside. Living-room, bedroom... same room anyway. Studio, they called it. Study... he could call it. Why not? Or library. Books? Plenty! On floor, on bed, on table... dining, that is. Studio? I suppose that covered it, just about. Dining – slash – bed – slash – living – slash – dressing – slash – make-up... studio. Bathroom was separate... of course, that is.

Wonder where that rich-bitch lives— he thought— it was one of these canals here. And then he laughed at his own language. Rich-bitch. He persuaded himself that it was just a habit he had taken on in the course of hanging out with Marvin and the infestation of street people who frequented his residence. Even Marie. She had no compunctions about trashy or misogynistic language. She thought that things were just the way they were, and that people were either decent or crap. And Dominic, like her, ascribed his own usage of certain verbal forms a meaninglessness that denied deeper associations. Not that he didn't accept the existence of deeper associations, just that they didn't necessarily apply to him.

But you had to watch out these days, when talking to some of those hyper-fems he knew. You had to be careful what you say with them. Sometimes he would provoke them on purpose (another party trick that he'd learned from Marvin) just to see how committed they were. It was always the most strident ones, he felt, who crumbled completely when it came time to criticize one of their 'own' (by which he meant anyone they had to associate with on a regular basis). Because their anger and self righteousness was too vitriolic to be maintained for more than just short bursts. So it could be shot, by a process of subtle manipulation, long distance, at an unfamiliar 'enemy.' But it could not be used in conjunction with any analytical or constructively corrective method.

On the contrary, they would rather believe that he was joking – which he was – but, even if he hadn't been... they would. Okay, not all of them. Who *is* 'them' anyway? When we define, we generalize, by definition. And nobody is a generalization. Fair is fair, as they say, a rose is a rose is a rose... fair, or else. Supposedly then, fair is fair be it rosy or not. So... not all of them. Bad show. (Not fair... lumping them all together.) Some, then – shall we say... would.

It was definitely one of these canals. She seemed a bit of a hyper-fem herself, actually. Capitalist Bitch. He considered the phrase. Wasn't that a contradiction in terms? Contra-dick... he thought... one who is against Nixon, no... a Nicaraguan terrorist's penis, hmm. Oxymoron. Let's see... an idiot who uses pimple cream on his... no, an idiot who breathes as if... still, money is money, fair or not, and a rich-bitch isn't half the bitch a poor-bitch is. Not that she lives on the barge. Probably has some ritzy place in town. Another one in the country. She can get away from her hubby in a number of ways. He didn't even know if she was married. Must be. Probably. Maybe not. No... probably was.

He stopped. Amazing! This was it! Here it damned well was! He was standing right next to the very barge itself. No wait a minute! Maybe not. It was a while ago. But no... no... this was it. He was pretty sure. *Looked* just like it. But then what did he know. No... it was. The very barge. He couldn't believe it. Can't be— he thought. But it was.

Suddenly he was shivering with the cold. This stupid fantasy he'd been having for the past month about coming down here and running into her... it was too close. He wished that it was summer. His fantasy had been that it would be summer. It looked better in the summer light. And yet, here he was. Standing beside it. It was definitely the same barge. He remembered it now. There had been this bright red panel encircling the boat with some kind of a gold scroll work painted upon it. Traditional. Gypsy like... even. But unique amongst this mooring. Enough to distinguish it from any other one around here. About six months ago, it must have been. Took him this long. But he'd thought of her often. What was her name. Something with two Ms... Manley, Mirabella, no... Marina, no... Miranda. That's right, he remembered now, because when he first met her he said "You have the right to remain silent..." but she didn't laugh. Heard it before. Miranda Manley. Manly— he thought— not in appearance, anyway. But maybe so. Maybe in character. Strength. Maybe that's what scared him about her. Maybe that's what attracted him to her. Maybe that's what kept him away for six months. Maybe that's what brought him back here to this embankment... to this canal... to this barge, now.

Someone was home. There was a light on inside. But why— he wondered— would she be there now? It was a weekday. Why didn't she go straight home to hubby, straight home after work? Where did she work? In some fashion house? He looked down at himself again, down at his clothes. That's really me— he thought— fashion plate. What the hell am I doing here? skulking around like a prowler; prowling around like a stalker, in the dark. Watching shadows dance around on Venetian blinds. Hmm... Venetian... on a barge... on a canal. Appropriate. But what if somebody sees me? What would she think if she saw me? What if the hubby is in there with the rich-bitch? What if I just walk across this plank and knock right on the door? What would it be like, to open that door, from the inside, and see *me* standing there? The fashion plate? Depends, I suppose... if it were she, Miranda Manners, the rich-bitch... or hubby!

What, on the other hand, if it were me in there – fashionably attired, trim and healthy, of course – partying up the proverbial storm, champagne, cocktails... all that jazz, and some *other* 'Bozo' comes a knock-knock-knocking at her door. What if I were in there seducing her nicely, that lovely piece of ass, just getting ready to make a meal of her succulent little breast like a tasty chicken morsel... baked all crispy, like? Juicy and plump. Tweaking her nipple with my finger and thumb. Tasting it with my tongue. When all of a sudden... knock-knock-knocking at my old barn door, knocking at her old barge, knocking at her gypsy barge door. What then?

But... what if she were alone? All alone and friendless. Doing the dishes after a lonely dinner. Thinking about masturbation.

Fantasizing that some stud would show up out of the blue and do it for her. Wondering whatever happened to that sexy fashion plate of a clown I hired several months ago for my poor friend's underprivileged child's birthday party. What a hero he was, helping the needy. Just like me. So good with the kids. Some people just 'got it'. And he's one of them. I'll bet underneath all that make up, and wig, and red foam-rubber nose... he was a hell of a handsome devil. And as for the manual dexterity with the juggling and the card tricks... why I'll just bet that he could handle parts of me in a most satisfying manner. What hands? What fingers? I can only imagine.

Yes! he thought. What if? And he felt emboldened by the possibility. Nothing ventured nothing gained! Jesus Christ, now he was quoting his mother to himself. That drew him back a little. But no, this is one occasion where mother was right. Okay, just do it... now quoting sneaker commercials? But he did have some kind of an inner support group urging him onward. Go for it! Go for it! Go for it! Go for it! They drummed upon his inner sense of rhythm. And he began forward across that gang plank – holding on at all times to the notion of what it meant to walk the plank – and he knocked proudly upon that door.

But as he stood there waiting for an answer, bending and unbending the corners of the overstuffed manilla envelope he held, it suddenly occurred to him what he had just done. And the beating of his heart turned into a booming becoming louder and louder, and eventually drowning out all other cheering sections that his mind might have produced. And now he just felt completely dumb struck. She wouldn't even know what he looked like. What was he going to say— er... excuse me but... no, er... you may not remember me but ... no, er... I just happened to be passing when I, er... no, er... no, er... better still... Miranda darling... no, er... how about this... remember me? Dominic? Dominic the clown? And then I could pull a gold coin out of her nose – not that I have any gold coins— and he started rooting around in his pants for loose change. But just when it all seemed like it might be perfectly hopeless, it changed and became perfectly pointless. A man answered the door.

Not a particularly attractive man. Not a rich looking man, either. He was wearing an undershirt and a pair of pyjamas, and Dominic could see that he was not in any kind of great shape, no better than Dominic himself. In fact, his appearance was not dissimilar to Dominic's. He thought that maybe this was the wrong place. Ms. Miranda Rich-Bitch wouldn't be caught dead with a loser like this. Of course that meant that neither would she be caught dead with Dominic Devine. It almost gave him hope to see this schlubby little fellow here. But there was a paradox. If he was her lover, then it means that she *would* consider some loser like Dominic. But, if he *was* her lover, then she didn't need Dominic Devine. In an instant his mind went through a thousand ways in which he could be just that little bit more 'right' for her than *this* one. And then he came back to where he was. Should he ask for her by name? It could create an embarrassing situation. Maybe this *was* hubby, or the mailman, or the electrician. Or maybe this actually was the wrong place. Perhaps it was the right place but she had sold it to someone. How could he get the answer to his questions without totally making himself look like a prick? But as things have a way of happening, you get all sparked up about something that never comes to pass.

"Psst!" came a voice from the embankment. Dominic, and the man inside the barge, who had to crane his neck around the doorpost to do it, both turned to see who it was.

Dominic turned back to the business at hand. "Oh... er..." the man now turned to attend to him. "Er... excuse me, er..." he continued.

"Yo!" Came the voice from the embankment, "having a party in there?" An old vagrant emerged from the shadows and started toward the gangplank.

The man in the barge looked sternly at Dominic and, without losing eye contact reached down behind the door for something that Dominic could not see. "What do you men want?"

"Oh, no... " said Dominic, pointing at imaginary things. "He's not with, er... well, you don't understand... you see I, well..." then he turned to the vagrant, who was just taking his first rickety steps onto the wobbly plank. "Look! Go away!" Then he turned back to the door and said, "I was just, er... just looking for..."

But at that moment a woman from inside called out, "who is it?" Her face appeared briefly in the dull glow from within and Dominic Devine thought to himself that she looked rather like Miranda Manley. Not as he had remembered her of course but, most probably, closer to the way that she actually was in real life. Sans make-up, sans hairdo, sans party-dress. An ordinary woman. A little tired perhaps. Who sometimes got a little grumpy. Who sometimes wished that she lived alone. Who, mostly, was glad that she had someone to be with. Who felt, on occasion, that she had no value, but who reminded herself, and was reminded from time to time by those who loved her, that she did. And in the end, what more can be said of anyone? And as their eyes met for that one brief moment, Dominic believed that they had revealed all this to him.

"I don't know!" the man yelled back at her. "That's what I'm trying to fucking find out!" He turned back to Dominic. "Now!" He produced the metal bar he had been hiding, "what the fuck do you two want?"

"Yeah!" said Dominic, "is Barry in?"

The man took a deep breath and spoke very softly. "There is no Barry here! Now fuck off of my property!" He shut the door on Dominic's apologies.

"Yeah! Sorry about that. Must have the wrong place." His voice trailed to a whisper as he turned away from the door, looking above and below as if searching for something, and resting his gaze finally on the gangplank ahead. But the stupid old bum was already halfway over. "Get the fuck out of here you stupid old..."

"What?" said the old man, his bottle hanging in one hand at his side.

"Go on now! Turn around!"

"Okay, okay chief! Didn't mean no harm." He started looking at the plank behind him. It didn't seem wide enough to turn around on. If he could just get to the barge and then turn around, it might be safer.

"C'mon! C'mon!" Pushed Dominic, and he stepped up onto the end of the plank. "Move it now! These people don't want you here!"

The old man mumbled as he tried to turn. "Don't look like they want *you* here either, chief."

That pissed him off. "C'mon now!" Dominic gave him a little shove to get him on his way. But the drunken old fellow was unbalanced enough as it was, and the shove just served to send him toppling into the canal.

"Oh fuck!" Dominic was immediately contrite. He knew that it wasn't really the old man he was angry at. He ran across the plank to the embankment side and, he leaned over the edge trying to grab the old geezer with his one free hand. "Are you all right? Are you all right?" he kept on yelling. But he couldn't reach him; it was too far down. The old man was splashing about in the mucky, polluted, icy stuff – which at least seemed like a good sign that he was still alive. There were some grey stone steps nearby which led down to the water. Dominic ran to them, and then down. But he almost fell into the drink himself, losing traction on their nasty slippery surface. It occurred to him to place his manuscript down on the embankment well away from the edge. He moved a little more carefully now to the bottom step where he called out to the 'drowning' man. "Hey! Come over here! I'll pull you out."

Well, the old fellow did finally work his way over to the steps, and as Dominic was pulling him out, spluttering and cursing in a loud voice, the door in the barge opened a crack and they heard the man with the metal bar shouting, "I've called the police! They're gonna be here in five minutes."

"Quick!" said Dominic as he pulled the tramp up onto his feet. "Let's get the fuck out of here!"

The old man stood there dripping torrents of slimy water examining his hands as if he wanted to make sure he hadn't lost any fingers. "Where's my bottle?" he said.

"Never mind your fucking bottle, the guy just said he's called the cops!" Dominic was grasping at his shoulder. He considered running for it and leaving the old coot to his fate, but he felt somehow responsible for him now, and he knew the police weren't likely to handle him with a great amount of sensitivity.

But the old man was leaning out over the water as if he could see something. And maybe he could. Maybe one of those glints out there on the surface of the water was his bottle. Half filled now with canal sludge. He turned to Dominic. "You think he really called the police?"

"Na!" said Dominic. "Not really."

"Well?"

"But he might have. So come on! Let's go." He tugged at the old man's soaking wet coat. If he'd have let go of it right then, the old codger would have probably fallen back in. The thought of being arrested, or even just harassed by the law, did not seem appealing to him. What if it came out that he actually knew Miranda Manley? He might have to explain his whole motivation for being here in the first place. The threat of such embarrassment almost made him drop the old guy in again… but still, Dominic felt some sort of camaraderie with him. They were in this together. It's not as if everything had been going so well for our Mr. Devine *before* this old bastard showed up on the scene.

"C'mon," he prompted more gently this time. "I'll get you another one of those."

"Yeah?"

"Really."

"Really?" The old man was licking his lips. "A full one?" It looked as though a tear of gratitude was dripping from the old man's eye, but it was probably just filthy canal water.

"Yeah." Dominic was walking away when he stopped… and returned quickly to pick up the fat wedge of papers he had almost left behind. The old man took one last loving look out to sea, as it were, and then walked complacently up the steps behind his new found friend.

Chapter 7

Just as Jason Cyllabus Novedi had concluded that he was a gonner, a previously empty patch of road on the crest of the hill (at which he had been gazing despondently) was suddenly occupied by a speeding, blue and white, nineteen fifty-seven ™Chevrolet Bel Air convertible. It descended the hill and zoomed past him for a few hundred yards, but then turned once more sharply, screeching those huge rubber whitewalls as it pivoted radically around its own axis. Moving slowly now, it approached him, and finally pulled up on the gravel beside where he limped, looking rather sullen, and pretending not to be aware of its existence. But he couldn't help laughing out loud when he turned towards the car and caught sight of its driver looking up at him through that enormous expanse of curved windshield. Her lips were moving but he couldn't hear what she was saying.

"Wha-hat?" He cupped his hands to his ear to signify his inability.

Slowly she opened the door. Pulled herself out of the seat. Walked around to where he was standing. She spoke begrudgingly. "You *knew* I'd come back, didn't you?"

Still chuckling to himself — whether out of amusement or simple relief, he couldn't tell — he answered her. "I don't know about *that*! But I'm sure glad you did."

They'd been driving along in silence for a while but he couldn't hold out any longer. "Sometimes," he said, "I can't tell if I'm incredibly lucky… or if I'm incredibly unlucky."

"Do you mean," she asked, "that sometimes incredibly lucky things happen to you, and other times incredibly unlucky things happen to you?"

"Well... " and then he did a double take. He was impressed with her question. She had not assumed (as many people might) that she understood him perfectly. She wanted to be sure that she truly comprehended his meaning. Most people— he believed— *think* that they understand everything, or at least they *act* as if they think they do. They seem afraid to ask questions about what they don't understand, just in case— he supposed— they be thought of as stupid. It sometimes takes an intelligent person to ask a stupid question— he suspected. It certainly takes an honest one. And intelligent people *are* honest (at least to themselves, one would hope), especially about what they know, and (even more importantly) don't know.

"Er, no... not exactly. Although, what *you're* describing might actually be easier to assess. I could, for example, simply tote up the times that I felt I was lucky, and compare that with the total of my unlucky times, and see whichever numbered the greater. Then I would discover if I was more lucky or more unlucky... or normal, for that matter, if the numbers were equal... assuming, that is, that normal people have an equal amount of good luck and bad – which I'm not so terribly sure about. No... what I mean is a somewhat more difficult message to decipher. It is in fact the very same occurrence which, to me, tends to be both lucky and unlucky."

"For instance?" she prompted.

"Well... for instance, like falling out of a plane and breaking every bone in your body, and then later, when you are recovering in the hospital, finding out that, seconds after your fall, the plane exploded killing everyone on board.

Jocelyn was amazed. "That really happened to you?"

"To me?" he answered. "No, not to me... but I'm sure it must have happened to someone... sometime." She looked disappointedly at him. "Well, you just asked me to give you a 'for instance'," he explained.

She grunted some sort of an annoyed acknowledgment.

"Is that what you *wish* had happened to me?" he asked, feigning offense.

"You look as though it happened to you *today!*" she scolded.

"Don't you believe my jogging story then?"

"I don't believe a word that comes out of your mouth."

"Ouch!" He reclined with a pouty smile, crossing his arms behind his head. And then, after a few moments, "well, here we are..." he looked around at the scenery as it seemed to, simultaneously, whizz by close at hand, and yet float languorously off in the distance, "we hardly know each other. You know absolutely nothing about me – which I find quite surprising," he added under his breath, " and I know precious little about you – other than that your father is a convict..." he saw that she was just about to protest but he cut her off with, " *and...* your boyfriend is the sheriff of 83047..."

"He is *not* my..." but then she just moaned with sham frustration, "oh, never mind."

"And despite the lack of familiarity," he continued, "you choose to chide me as if we were an old married couple." He ruminated upon the idea momentarily... "I think I like it."

Her lips remained critical but her eyes glancing sideways smiled at him.

"So what *are* you going to do with me?" he asked eventually, "... hand me over to the law?"

"Not if you don't want me to," she replied, and then added, "why, is there some particular reason you might be hiding from the police?"

"No," he said (so) casually, "no particular reason." He waited. "So then, er... what *did* you intend?"

Jason Cyllabus Novedi waited barefoot in the back seat of a two-tone, turquoise and white, nineteen fifty-seven ™Chevrolet Bel Air convertible (top up), until his new found virgin savior returned. Presently, the street door to the sheriff's office opened and Jocelyn appeared hustling a short, plump, elderly figure before her. A young man with shaggy blonde hair followed her outside onto the steps. He was wearing a light tan uniform that Jason had had experience with in the past. The leather plackets were going a little too far he'd always thought, although some of the brassy elements he could tolerate as being representative of the genre. If not creative, then at least backed by tradition, boots... you know, well polished. And every time that Jocelyn turned to walk away, the young man – young-ish anyway – would say another thing, and she would stop, and turn, and resume their conversation a little while longer. All this while, her father, who was standing down a couple of steps closer to the street, remained silently looking this way and that, as if expecting another getaway car coming from any one of a number of possible directions.

At one point Jocelyn pointed toward the car and all three of them turned to look. Jason knew that it was too late for him to hunch down and pretend that nobody was in the car. The sheriff, using his hands to shade his vision from the sun's glare, peered squinty eyed at Jason's silhouette in the back seat. He knew that he couldn't be recognized from that distance, but still, Jason wondered, could his virgin savior be possibly betraying him?

Of course there would be no actual danger to him if she were. In fact Jason would probably get the royal treatment if he simply presented himself to the sheriff. It's just that there was a certain amount of embarrassment quotient inherent in this awkward situation that he just didn't think it necessary to put himself through. Yeah, but she didn't know that, did she? So it could still be considered betrayal nonetheless.

But eventually the party split up with no betrayal apparent, and the young woman and her father took leave of the handsome trooper right at the door to his office, where he stood and watched as they departed. And still one more time, as she approached the car, he called out after her and took a few paces forward until he reached the edge of the steps, and stood in a pose not unreminiscent of a ballet dancer. The grey wall behind him confetti'd, in wisps of some airborne pollutant and the whole scene lit – as the noon time sun will – from above, he stretched one arm forward and up as the opposing leg reached behind him to offset his balance. Jocelyn responded hastily over one shoulder with a smile and a wave, and hurried on purposefully to the car.

Now, what— wondered Jason Cyllabus Novedi, to himself— will I say to the father?

Fritz D'Orion introduced himself as the car rumbled away. "You've heard of The Picture of Dorian Gray... well, I'm the picture of D'Orion bald and fat... with a little grey around the sides, while another one who looks like me runs around laying claim to my once prized leanness and my rightful head of hair." And he laughed out loud as he leaned over the seat to shake hands. That was when he noticed Novedi's feet... and his general condition. Jason had covered himself with a tattered old (and very small) plaid blanket that he'd found in the back seat, but it would have been clear to any imbecile that he had no shirt on underneath, and Fritz D'Orion may have been a drunk, but he was no imbecile.

Jocelyn's father eyed him suspiciously, while yet trusting to his daughter's judgment. "My little Joss-stick didn't mention your name Mr. er...?" And then he looked a little closer but he could not believe what he thought he was seeing. "You, er... look awful, er... familiar." And he cocked his head at an angle in order to rummage more easily through his recollective files. And his pudgy sweaty fingers drummed a tattoo upon the vinyl backrest of the front bench upon which he sat. "Mr. er...?"

Novedi snapped out of his daze. Should he let on? "Er... my name is Ja..."

But then Fritz got it, and quickly interrupted, "Mr. Jay! Good to meet you." His eyes were flicking rapidly from one side to the other

"Jay?" said his daughter.

"Yes!" urged her father.

And then she said it happily again. "Jay. Yes you look like a Jay. A Blue Jay. I shall call you Blue for short. Tell me your real first name isn't actually Blue. No! That would be *too* silly. But still..." she giggled like a schoolgirl, "appropriate don't you think, with that awful voice, a taunting voice, taunting my black and white pussycat around the back yard. That seems like you. You like to taunt."

"You have a black and white pussy...cat?" taunted Jason, in a blatantly lascivious manner.

Fritz D'Orion cleared his throat gruffly. "Ahem! Mr. Jay," he repeated, and then to his daughter, "why, you seem to know this fellow very well, my darling, and yet you have omitted the mentioning of his existence to me in the past."

"I'd never met him before today," she replied. "I found him hitchhiking in the middle of nowhere... looking like that."

Fritz was not fatherly. He did not scold his daughter for her recklessness, as she had never scolded him for his. It was a deal they had made when she was small. Unconsciously maybe, but all the more binding for having been so. As far as she knew, this was how people were. Not all people, maybe... but people. In this she may well have been right.

"What happened to you my boy?"

"He was out jogging," replied Jocelyn.

Jason's eyes caught her's twinkling back at him in the rearview

74

mirror. But then he resumed his attention toward her father. "I had to leave somewhere in a hurry," he admitted truthfully.

"He didn't want the sheriff to see him," added Jocelyn. She was braver in her verbal notation of the obvious now that she had an ally, and also in her attempt to garner answers from this hitcher. Her father noted her last comment in the way that he scrutinized Jason.

"It's alright." The man in the back seat seemed to be reassuring them. "I'm not wanted by the police or anything like that." He was reclining now and starting to fade slightly. He'd been up all night between one thing and another. His speech was starting to become a mumble. "I just didn't want to be interrogated... and bullied, by the handsome sheriff..."

"Ha-hah!" Fritz turned to look at his daughter. "That would be a reference to you, no doubt."

She tried to pay no attention to this remark, but eventually it played on her mind until she just had to respond. "Look! Why doesn't everybody leave me alone?"

"We-hell," said her father (he was the only man left awake in the car at this point), "Steve Duco's a nice enough boy, but... no, I gotta say, he's been very fair to me..." and sometimes he wondered why that was, "but... well, he's not exactly a challenge, is he?" His daughter glanced at him and clicked her tongue. "Well, I mean..." Fritz continued, "he's no Einstein, is he? I mean! Just take a look at his chosen profession." And he voiced the last word almost with disgust. "Policeman."

Jocelyn raised her voice now to attack pitch, almost. "Look! For the last time! There is nothing between him and me!" And she accelerated the car by another ten miles per hour, as her father nodded humbly in agreement beside her. "And anyway," she continued suddenly, "what's wrong with being a policeman? Someone's got to do it."

"I suppose." Fritz looked into the distance, but he spoke as if he had a gut full of bile regarding this issue. "They are the lackeys of the established power structure." He glanced in the back to assure himself that their guest was indeed asleep, and he continued, though more quietly perhaps. "To serve and protect; that is their motto. That's right, to serve and protect the wealthy and the powerful... from losing that which they have stolen in the first place. To serve and protect a singularity of thought. To maintain order at any cost, no matter how soul suffocating it might be. To force unquestioning obedience of all who disagree with their... their..." and here he laughed a little and almost whispered the end of this recitation that Jocelyn had come to know by heart after all these years, "their *lack*, I suppose, of philosophy... by the way..." he too, seemed to be losing his thread now, as he turned toward his daughter in an altogether more jovial tone.

"Could we stop at the liquor store on the way back? We're out of Scotch." She cut him with a sideways expression. But he was prepared. "Your sleeping friend here! We shall need some for him... for medicinal purposes, you understand."

Chapter 8

Henry took another swig of Scotch from the bottle in his hand. He was freezing, but that's the great thing about booze... you don't give a shit. He was dripping canal water all over the bathroom floor, but he didn't give a shit about that either. He'd already dripped a nice big puddle in the living room, and dragged some fairly decent tracks through the corridor, and his new friend (the one who'd given him this bottle) was mopping all of that up right now. He'd probably mop up *this* mess eventually.

Dominic tapped gingerly on the bathroom door and pushed it ever so slightly open. "You can take a nice hot shower if you want." In actual fact he was rather hoping that his visitor would. Although that still left him with the problem of the clothing. As yet unremoved. Wet and dirty. Dirty and stinky and wet. Stinking wet... and stinking dirty. Hanging, as of yet, upon his dirty, stinky, wet frame. Though not a flabby or sick frame, Dominic observed, in fact rather lean and lithe for one of his advanced years. There were wrinkles hidden behind that mess of hair and beard, around the brows and eyes, but within those eyes a sparkle dominated the order of things and brought a sense of lightness to what must have been (to say the very least) a difficult period in the man's life.

A short while later, as a reasonably well rinsed Henry – attired solely in Dominic's fleecy, though not very attractive, tartan bathrobe – lay down upon some strategically positioned cushions on the living-room floor, Mr. Devine thrashed a pile of assorted garments in a soapy solution in the bathtub. Thrashed, it must be said, in a maternal caretaker sort of way, but creating within that tub something that was starting to look rather like the canal the clothing had been immersed in previously. In light of this phenomenon, Dominic couldn't help but wonder if it were the canal which had polluted the clothing or the other way around.

To tell the truth Dominic was glad that the old goat had finally dropped off. He'd been rambling on about the angels before, who had taken him to the future and brought him back again. Dominic had laughed internally, it sounded a bit like his book. It set him to wondering if one could copyright story ideas. What if someone else uses the same premise in *their* novel? I mean if some crazy homeless bum can fantasize infinitely, wouldn't he eventually come up with any story that you could possibly write? You know, like the monkeys accidentally typing up Macbeth, excuse me, 'The Scottish Play'... anyway he'd been going on like that... "And *you*," he'd said, "*You* were there! Or should I say, you *will* be there," he'd made strange magical gestures with his fingers, and squinted his eyes and raised his eyebrows alternately for extra effect. "Not you, of course," he'd continued, "... not you, the man, for this will be after you and I are long gone from this earthly plane... no, but *you*, the idea... the spirit... the... the *concept* you."

Dominic had always tried to engage this kind of craziness by asking questions. If you take people seriously— he thought— maybe they begin to make more sense. But as in most such cases, the man hadn't really connected logically, and had seemed to ramble on at his own rate regardless. Preachy rather than communicative. "You had taken the big risks! You had payed the big prices! I am the prophet of doom! I am the prophet of salvation," he had spluttered through almost foamy lips— more like the prophet of sal-*i*-vation— thought Dominic. "Our meeting was no coincidence. I have seen the future and I have returned... to be of assistance to one who is coming to clear the way for 'He who will'. That's you, by the way."

"Me? Why me?" Dominic had asked.

"Why you? Why me? Why anybody? Why? Why? Why? I don't know. It doesn't matter why. What is ordained, is ordained, *because*... that is why. The future is the past. The past? Well..." he thought about it for a minute, "well... that's even before the present, so it must be... long ago. Doesn't *seem* so long ago, does it?" He'd tapped his nose, and looked knowingly at Dominic. "The past... it doesn't *seem* so long ago... eh?"

"How far into the future did you go? I mean, how many years?"

"Nah! It didn't seem so long ago. You see I recognized you," and here he whispered and turned from side to side as if someone might overhear, "from the statue... in the town square..."

"Oh yeah?" Dominic had pushed further. "What town was that exactly?"

But the old geezer seemed to get annoyed and started to raise his voice. "Right... what town... very funny... *the* town! Don't hand me that crap! Where the buildings are not buildings, but stars. Where the streets are not streets but blazing infernos of chaos and hydrogen gas. That's what that Dante fellow was talking about, by the way."

"You mean 'Dante's Inferno'? Wasn't that about hell?"

"*No*! Don't be *stupid*! It wasn't at all about hell – *yes*... yes it was... okay... so it was about hell. Yes... okay... it was." Here again he'd done some magical finger and eye contortions and lowered his voice to a whisper. "Do you think..." he had challenged, "... that angels would take a man to hell?"

"How can you be sure they were angels?" Dominic had asked. "Even Mohammed was fooled one time."

"No, no... Mohammed was never fooled. You're talking about that 'Satanic Verses' thing. You know, people go around talking about things they don't understand. There is value to ancient traditions, and they shouldn't be messed with. It is not what comes out of your mouth that I am concerned with. God speaks through the pen, from the burning bush to the... the..." here he'd almost stuttered the word, "A-poc-rypha. It is your writings that speak the truth."

Dominic wondered, as the tubful of scummy water drained away for the third time (only light grey now) whether he was starting to look like a writer... that even someone with so hampered a vision as this old man, could see it so clearly marked upon his countenance. He was flattered. And even though the old man's rantings irritated him somewhat, he was charmed... seduced even, by the notion that someone thought that his writings might be the word of God.

You're losing it Devine— he thought— you're good... inspired, maybe, but you're letting some old drunk get you all hyped up. It's only coincidence that there is an angel in my book. He accidentally hit, in his rantings, upon the word of God. It's a joke. What I'm writing about is metaphor. Hey, what's-a-metaphor you? I don't actually *believe* the things I'm writing. This guy *believes* the crazy ideas that he has. It's a totally different thing. If he actually read my book he'd probably be very disappointed. Who knows what kind of crazy scenario he has going on in there. That's his reality. For *me* the angels are just fiction. Not part of my reality... even though... I suppose, that I wish they were.

But if wishes were horses, then beggars... well they'd no longer be beggars by the time they'd mounted up. And their bridles and stirrups and reins would be made up of dreams. And in some ways they are real. As real as dreams are, to those children who dream them. And their nightly wanderings do become the journeys of their lives. And simple suggestions become the prophesies that direct their futures— you stupid idiot, you'll never make it, you're not talented like that, you're too fat, your hair is the wrong color, you can't draw, you're not the right body type, color, sex, sexual orientation... whatever— such simple suggestions, such incredible power.

But to be told that your writings are the word of God, whether you overtly believe it or not, whether the person who says it is credible or not, somewhere inside that's got to flick a switch, push a button, if only a little one. There's power in it. No matter what. Canned power. Power in a jar. Power you can keep in the freezer until the day you come home powerless and hungry.

It was hard to sleep that night. There were no walls to divide them. There were no separate rooms. The living-room *was* the bedroom, and the old bastard snored like a pig snoring, lying there, not all that far away. Dominic tried stuffing his ears with toilet paper. He tried rolling the drunk onto his side. He even tried waking him up several times. And he would stop for a while. But sooner or later that little *zizz* would start up again, growing stronger and stronger until it had, once again, worked itself up into a mighty roar. Vibrating the walls. Vibrating the furniture. Vibrating... yes, even, the very foundations of his domain.

The other thing that was keeping Dominic awake was how he was going to get rid of the guy now. Once you take someone in off the street... they get used to a little warmth, a little comfort... now how are you going to tell them they have to go back out there? I mean, why can't they stay just one more night? And then why can't they stay just one more after that? How could he justify this sudden turn around of his generosity... or lack of it? Throwing the poor bum out in the street like that... with nowhere to go... when you have so much...

His mind was spinning in turmoil when he finally fell asleep that night, and it was spinning in turmoil when he finally awoke the next morning. Of course, spinning in turmoil was the natural state of Dominic Devine's mind most days, and so it was probably not an amazingly notable event for him. This was one reason, therefore, that oftentimes, the things that came out of his mouth were not very interesting to those who heard them. Whereas the things he wrote… well, they were, after all, the voice of God. Almost as if the simple act of writing could transmute baser verbiage into a golden rule. The simple act of organizing one's thoughts could alter, in retrospect, the very nature of those thoughts. At least the nature of Devine's thoughts, until they did in fact become divine th… well, you know, that editing and stripping away the unnecessary can help one to discover… rediscover the essential truth hidden within. No crap. And in that way, the tumult of a mind in turmoil can be a good thing (okay, so there *are* no good things, *or* bad things, just things upon which we place our judgment)… can be a thing, then – any kind of a thing with any value whatsoever – but a thing that can be a boon to creativity… whatever value one may place on that. Good? Bad? A boon, yes. A tong, with which to pick up the burning truth… so as not to burn yourself, you understand? Now, does that have value? And if so, is that value,

1) Good?

2) Bad?

c) Whatever?

Whatever… the point is this: *Henry's* mind was not spinning in turmoil. *His* mind was like a steel trap. His thoughts were efficient, cohesive, single minded. It's true that he may not have been a dot more intelligible when he spoke than was Dominic Devine, in fact, let's face it, he was a lot less… *but* – and this is a big but – he knew what he knew.

I know.

That's a cliché.

But I can't help it

Clichés help to eliminate the turmoil in one's mind. They keep one's thought patterns pure. And that's a *fact* (albeit a clichéd one), and therefore not required to hold to the very highest standards of truth, whilst at the same time maintaining possession of the most absolute of truths. But truth is not the issue here. Rather, it is the events which will comprise our reality as they are about to unfold, in short… what is going to happen.

And that is a *fact* which shall be laid bare through the prophesies of one whose mind is:

1) spinning in turmoil?

b) like a steel trap?

"Chicken placentas!" Henry seemed to be enjoying them nonetheless. "Don't usually eat these," he said, "but... when in Rome..."

This isn't Rome— thought Dominic Devine— I wish he *was* in Rome... or in Constantinople, or Mongolia for that matter... anywhere but here. But, even though he was thinking these things it was still, he felt, somehow gratifying to be helping somebody out. And Henry, despite his gruff manner, was surprisingly appreciative.

"Noovell, then?"

"I beg your pardon?" said Dominic.

"The eggs. Noovell Koozeen?"

"Oh... I see. Yes... er, no... hardly. No, I er... there was just some curry left over in the pan. I er..." he half laughed in embarrassment, "warmed it up for lunch yesterday. Get it at the little Paki place by the station. Don't always... heh... wash the pan after I..."

"Caffay-oh-lay." Henry smiled a wicked smile as he raised the cup to eye level.

"Well, I have this little milk steamer..."

"Hard to imagine, I suppose," Henry continued, "that one such as I, with my seemingly degenerate lifestyle and my ragged attire and my, let's say... proclivity for the hard stuff, could indeed appreciate the finer things in... you know, but it wasn't all that long ago that I was... well, and in fact even as we speak... somewhere, I am still appreciating the finest things that money can buy, for you see..." and here he looked around him – despite the fact that he was presently seated at Dominic's plastic topped kitchen table with the holographic Jesus printed on its surface, who had eyes that open and close depending on your point of view, that Dominic had picked up cheap at a local garage sale because he really loved it, and also because it was cheap – and his eyes, Henry's that is, like a conspiratorial Judas, surveyed, this side and that, the ugly glossy yellow kitchen wall behind him, it's dust painted imperfections gleaming in the morning light... in order to insure no eavesdropper might hear, and he beckoned Dominic, who wasn't really listening anyway, to come closer, "... you see, they made a little mistake and put me back a touch too early."

"They?" inquired Dominic quietly enough to insure privacy.

"The Angels."

"Ah! Yes! Yes I see... the Angels."

"Yes... that's right. They brought me back to a point from before they had actually taken me in the first place, er... if you get what I mean."

"They brought you back from...?"

"From the future! God dammit man aren't you listening?"

"The future... of course, of course... I see now. So in other words there are two of you running around right now. There's you... and the future you."

"Jesus fucking Christ man, I *am* the future me. The *other* one is the past me. Well actually he's the present me. Although I can see how it would be a little confusing. Let's put it this way. There's the rich me, and the poor me. Can you guess which one stands before you now?"

Dominic smiled insecurely at him. "Ah – ha... so, er... tell me, is it common for the Angels to make mistakes of this nature?"

"Well... strictly speaking, of course, it's not really a mistake... 'cause I had to meet *you* at this time."

Oh-oh, here we go again— thought Dominic— but it's my own fault for asking him in the first place. I just wish he wouldn't involve *me* in his fantasy.

"One might assume, in that case," Henry continued this path of logic, "that the pick-up time may well have been the mistake. But hey, the Angels work in mysterious ways, you know, and anyway to *ass-u-me* their intent, as they say, is to make an *ass wipe* out of *uranus* – or is it my anus... anyway, this was my sacrifice for the Angels. My duty. For I was – and still am – a rich man, enjoying a hell of a breakfast... somewhere, at this very moment." He wiped his eggy plate with some english muffin and stuffed his mouth with the result. "And I would lose it all again in order to be of assistance to the next savior of our planet." He licked the fingers of one hand and with the other he pointed at Dominic, our very own Mr. Devine.

Oh good Lord— thought Dominic Devine— Now I'm never

going to get rid of him. But then he had (what he thought was) a splendid idea. "Why don't you go to your house then, your... past house," he said, "and find your former, er... your rich self, and explain everything to him? I'm sure he wouldn't mind sharing his wealth with you. After all, it would just be like insuring his own future, wouldn't it?"

But Henry was already shaking his head. "Couldn't possibly work," he said.

"Sure it could!" Dominic was trying hard to egg him on.

"Couldn't!" said the old man categorically.

"But why not?" asked Dominic. "You would do it for you, wouldn't you?"

"Of course I *would*," said Henry. "But that's just it. I didn't!"

"Didn't what?"

"Well it's *me* isn't it? The rich one. It's *my* past isn't it?"

"Yeah. So?"

"So, I remember what happened."

"Yeah? What happened?"

"Nothing!"

"Nothing?"

"Nothing! I never had a visit from myself."

"You never..."

"Never saw me standing at the door asking for a hand out. Never received a phone call from myself. Neither did I ever receive a letter, a telegram, a fax, an e-mail, an F.T.D bouquet of chrysanthemums, a strippergram, morse code, smoke signals, drum beats, a telepathic communiqué from the afterlife... or any other form of communication which might have led me to believe that another me existed simultaneously on the planet surface. Therefore, in knowing my past, I also know my future. At least that part of it anyway. I know one thing for sure, beyond the shadow of a doubt, that before I will ever meet a past me... my past me must surely have met a future me."

"Pheeoow!" Dominic whistled. "The old 'time loop conundrum,' eh?"

"Whatever. But I also know this for sure, that no matter how hard I try to meet myself, I will never make it... Because I never did. Nope, in fact I can't even remember any odd or unresolved experience which might possibly have been me trying to get in touch with myself. So, and in conclusion I must thereby, er... conclude, that it's just not worth the trying."

"And the most likely reason, I would conclude," argued Dominic, "that you never did meet yourself in the past, was simply because you never thought it was worth the trying."

"Huh?"

"Because you sat around here on your arse convincing yourself that it was impossible!"

"You may well be right," said the old man, "for that is indeed what I intend to do. And anyway, what's done is done, even if it hasn't yet been done... or will not be done. And if what will not be done happens, perchance, to also be my destiny, then I would truly be a fool to rail against it. Would I not?" He smiled a wise and knowing look at his host as if expecting approval for his understanding of sublime verity, as if he knew he had passed the test.

"Oh this is fucking ridiculous!" said Dominic Devine. "I can't play this stupid game with you all day. Listen, I have to get to work now and I'm afraid you're just going to have to be on your way."

"Oh! That's alright, that's alright chief." Henry arose quickly from the table. "Yes! I er... don't mean to be upsetting your equilibrium. But I must remind you that our meeting was not an accidental one. And if you will allow me just fifteen minutes of your precious time, before I go away forever, to deliver a message which your destiny has bid the Angels transport me backwards through time to recite to you, and which I am sure you will be glad to receive, and after which I will never darken your doorstep, nor shall you ever see me again."

"Oh..." Dominic whined, "must you?"

"Firstly, allow me to formally introduce myself. My name is Henry Lewis, known in another time as Jason Cyllabus Novedi."

Dominic's eyes nearly bugged out as he stared in disbelief at the old bum. "Y-Your name is... *Henry Lewis?*" he sighed deeply, finding himself unable to move or think any further. The old man sat back down in his chair and began to recite this story.

"I was born fully clothed. This is possibly why, I suppose, I've always had a well developed sense of style..."

Chapter 9

Actual chickens made actual clucking sounds out in the yard. Fritz D'Orion and his daughter, Jocelyn – in answer to Jason Novedi's question (considering how much real eggs were fetching on the black market these days) – did not feel that they owned them, and therefore could *not* sell them for a million dollars. They felt bad enough about stealing the birds unhatched offspring, every once in a while, and callously consuming them. But still, the chickens themselves were free beings – living, thinking entities – who were entitled to choose wherever they wanted to live. The eggs, the D'Orions rationalized, were just payment for sustenance and living expenses.

"It's all a bit primitive though, isn't it?" mentioned Novedi, dressed now in a plaid shirt borrowed from Fritz. "Chicken placentas. I mean, actually eating them. What's this white part? Sort of gelatinized amniotic fluid? Probably doesn't contain all the right nutritional... er... nutrients, you know, like the 'eggs' at the supermarket."

Fritz and Jocelyn looked sadly at each other shaking their heads negatively. Their appearance suited the room in which they sat. Brown— thought Jason— wood... old wood. Not fine wood – polished and lacquered to bring out the reds and the golds like a rich man's library, and with a luster to provoke a hand's caress – no, not like that at all. Old wood, brown... and yet browner still. Flat... and splintery, without aspiration. The walls, the floors, the table too, their eyes... brown. Sadly brown, to him, Novedi. But he didn't really know them. And he didn't really know brown, either.

"Those don't have any egg in them," said Jocelyn.

"Probably more sanitary that way though, eh? I mean... without." He was thinking of his own apartment high atop the JCN office tower. Just a short escalator down to work in the morning... or early afternoon. Or whenever. It's not as though they needed him much. Most things took care of themselves, or Rigby took care of them. White. Mostly white. He stayed home a lot. Hah! Home. That's a joke. But... sanitary, mostly. White. With black shiny surfaces. Easy to clean. Well, maybe not easy to clean, white leather sofa, white rug... but easy − at least − to tell if it was clean or no, eh? Anyway, *he* didn't have to do it. A plump lady came in everyday— What's her name? Silly. No Sissy... Celia... Rigby had hired her. Jason had given up hiring cleaning staff. He'd hired several nice looking young women, one after another. It never really worked out. They didn't tend to clean much. Not once they'd figured out how to distract him. It was pretty easy, really... for them. Rigby got annoyed. "Every time I come over this place is filthier than it was the time before," he'd said. And then he said it again the next time he came. One time he showed up at the apartment and Jason had xeroxed a quote from the 'Catechism of the Great God Bongo,' and left it lying on the dull smudgy surface of the highly styled and extremely expensive black coffee table. This is what it said:

If you want to complain about your problem - go ahead, complain.
If you want to do something about it - go ahead, do something about it.
Whatever you prefer.

So Rigby did something about it. He hired Cicely... Felicity... whatever. She was a little surly. Jason always thought of her as older but, truth to tell, she was probably younger than him. Plump and a little unattractive, that always seems to confer age upon a person. Still, she cleaned up well enough. Windows too. The place always seemed very sanitary. Nothing left lying around for long. It always smelled of some kind of disinfectant after she'd been there. She knew where everything was supposed to be, and she put it away. Jason could always find what he was looking for. Home? Not exactly. That was the one thing that he couldn't find.

But this place – the D'Orion residence, with its brown, splintery, almost impossible to clean surfaces, and its undoubtedly unsanitary examples of wildlife of all kinds wandering about... randomly, with no sense of order or purpose, the kind of thing that would usually make him feel rather anxious... yet still – it seemed like a home. Not his, admittedly. He felt like an outsider, despite their tremendous hospitality, but that was down to time, or the lack of it... and mostly down to the fact that he didn't know how to belong to anything; which seems strange considering that he was responsible for such a 'belonging' cult. How did it get like that?

The smell of the eggs frying in the pan in butter... from cow's milk, was starting to reach his nose. There was something tantalizing about it. And yet it was heavy with flavor and aroma, and that disgusted him slightly. He hadn't always been like that. Before he came to Prickly Bog he had eaten real food. Mama Myrtle used to cook some good stuff every night. And so it tantalized him. But, since he'd been here, the food had progressively gotten worse and worse, and he was beginning to lose the habit of flavor, beginning to lose the habit ot taste. And so it repelled him. But on the other hand it made him think of how things had been... and how things could be again. And it tantalized him, and it tempted him, and it made him forget, for an instant, the fears he had, of everything that threatened him, or disgusted him. He inhaled that bouquet of splattering grease and succumbed to its seduction, banishing, simultaneously, his reservations, to a place just outside of his inner festivities, where they could peer in upon his abandon with wagging judgmental fingers, and suffer the indignity that their own morality had bestowed upon them. Yes. It smelled good.

"But I'm an adventurous spirit," he commented. "Never let it be said that I didn't try everything... at least once. You know? When in Rome..."

"What's Rome?" asked Jocelyn.

"I don't know," Jason lied. And then he carried his deceit even further. "It must be some place, somewhere. Er... my father used to say that, every time he did something that he didn't usually do." His eyes flicked back and forth. "I don't really know what it means.".

"It means," explained Fritz, "that you go along with the local customs, even if they are not yours... do as the Romans do, is the full phrase."

"When in Rome do as the..." Jocelyn was mumbling to herself. "Oh, I get it!"

That was enough for Jason. "Alright then," he said, "I'll have an egg."

As they ate, all was silence except, of course, for the necessary sounds of cutlery clinking on the side of the plate, or the sound of chewing, and sometimes even the sound of digesting. Occasionally, Fritz would belch... rather loudly. After one of these occurrences, Jason started mumbling to himself, "when in morning dew..." or, "when in doggy doo..." or, "when in 83047 doo." Jocelyn would watch him until he caught her eye, and then she would turn away quickly. At these points Jason would smile to himself, and Fritz would become aware that he had missed something.

"When in Xanadu..." said Jason.

"Did Kubla Khan a stately pleasure-dome decree ..." chimed in Fritz.

And then there was silence once more as all three sat redundantly, their appetites – for physical nourishment, at any rate – temporarily satiated.

"So..." Jocelyn finally spoke. "Mr. Jay... Whatever-your-name-is! What are we to do with you?"

"Well... Your Majesty," (her father tittered at Jason's retort) "you could take me home. Er..." he hesitated momentarily, "I would be willing to pay you, of course..." he searched her face expectantly for some sign of an answer, "...er, for your time... er, fuel etcetera." He looked over at Fritz who was looking at the floor and cleaning his nails. Suddenly something slammed and Jason Novedi caught sight of Jocelyn's back as she stormed out into the yard, sending chickens flying off in every direction. He could see her out there, through the ripped and dust caked screen door, just standing there with her arms crossed. Standing there, and staring at the hen house. Staring at the goat pen. Staring at a puddle with a tire track going through it. Staring at the mud splattered upon shiny blue and white paintwork. The screen door still shivered from its recent movement. A corner of the wire mesh flapped from where it had become disconnected.

"You should never offer a woman payment when she wants to do you a favor," said Fritz.

Jason turned back to him. "What?"

"It makes them feel like a prostitute. Specially that one. One who's a vir... well, you know, one who's never..."

"I didn't actually mean *money*. That's not really what I was offering."

Fritz just sat there nodding. He reached up to the sideboard for a bottle of scotch. He took a sip, wiped off the top and offered it to Jason. Jason took a swig and stood up. He looked for a moment at the old man, who gestured for his bottle back, and then (having returned it) moved quietly out into the yard.

"Look..." he spoke from behind her. Her frame twitched, but he didn't know whether frustration or impatience was the cause. "I didn't mean to offend you... in any way, so... if I did... well, I think... maybe you, er... misunderstood my, er... intention, yes... my intention..."

She remained still.

Nervously his hand reached out to touch her elbow. "Er..." He was just about to speak when suddenly, out of nowhere, without any warning... whatsoever, in fact, in the blink of an eye, and out of the total blue... her demeanor changed, completely, from silence and repression, to a hysterical, tearful, bleary eyed, frothing mouthed shriek.

"*Who the fuck are you?*" she yelled.

He stepped back.

"*I want to know exactly what has happened to you, to bring you into my life!*" Her voice was harsher than he had heard it before. It was filled with the distance that defensiveness brings. It was not plaintive or begging. It was threatening. And her body confirmed this hypothesis. Finger pointing accusingly towards him, her legs stood strongly spread apart in an attitude of balance and readiness for combat. "*Upsetting my life! Upsetting my father! Causing problems! Telling lies! I mean...* I don't know *what* you've done..." (was she softening a little?) "... or are *capable* of doing! I don't know *why* you're running from the police... or, or... even if you *are* running from the police." She took a little breather and dropped eye contact momentarily. But then, quickly, she marshaled her forces and came in for the kill. "I want to know *everything* about you! And I want to know it *now!*"

Her lip was quivering as he stared open mouthed at her, and her body swayed slightly as if she fought to maintain her posture, but her eyes were still and deadly now, as she examined his features for any sign of impending revolt.

"Everything?" he asked simply.

"Your *life* story!" she threatened one last time.

There is a bench.

There are holes and cracks in this bench, and dried chicken shit all over it. Once it was painted green, and that color, however faded, still graces the majority of its surface.

He takes her quietly by the hand and leads her to that bench. He sits her down upon the chicken shit and the faded green painted protruding nail heads. He sits beside her. He brings into play his other hand and cups hers tenderly between both of his. He inhales deeply. Her eyes, in response to his sudden attentiveness, are scanning the floor. He waits for them to meet his. They do. Then they look away again. Then they look back, why shouldn't they? It is obvious to both of them that something is in the air. Something of importance. Something that may – or may not – change their lives forever. In this way, of course, it is a lot like many other things. She moves her free hand to her mouth and coughs, once, into it. She is ready to hear what he has to say.

He inhales lightly to speak, but stops... and starts again. She does not know this but it is not his way to be so... so inhibited. There have always been plenty of words to say. They have gushed from him like a river overflowing its banks. He has used their power to create, to control and manipulate, to frighten and to force his ideas upon the weak and inarticulate. And yet, maybe sometimes, they have not been the right words. This time, for the first time, he decides to know what he is going to say, what he is thinking... *before* he speaks. It does not occur to him that it is in fact that exact thing which makes this moment so important. He is only aware of a change in plan, something which must be taken care of. His mind wanders back in time and, as he starts to relive the experiences which have created him and brought him to this place, his mouth begins to emit the peculiar fart like noises known to us as... language.

"I was born," he said, "fully clothed..."

Chapter 10

I was born fully clothed.

This is probably why, I suppose, I've always had a well developed sense of style.

I understand that this does not necessarily follow, but the clothes in which I was born were a particularly stylish set of togs.

As you can well imagine, my parents took this rather alarming occurrence as a sign that I was destined for greatness and, in order to position me where I could be of the greatest service to the world at large... and also in fear for their own peace of mind, they immediately abandoned me. They deposited me – in light of my unique incongruity, still wrapped within that swaddling attire – upon the doorstep of an unrenowned fashion boutique just before opening time on a Wednesday morning (a scant two hours after my arrival on this planet), and ran away, never to be heard from again. It was a cold midwinter's morn, the twenty-first of December, to be precise, and I was fortunate to be discovered upon that doorstep before I froze my little arse to death.

The man who found me, the owner of the boutique, not one to miss an opportunity, copied the unusual cut of my garb and by spring had come out with a collection of apparel that positively wowed the swank and a la mode. Within a year he had acquired an impressive reputation as a designer, and amassed for himself a small fortune. Of these riches I saw not one shilling although, in all fairness, I suppose one should take no credit for that in which one has had no creative, or designing hand. Jason Lewis, for that was my benefactor's name, did not however subscribe to that virtue – a common foible within his calling – and in turn, as soon as he found me, handed me over into the care of his maiden sister, a woman with whom he would never again communicate for such time as she walked this green and bountiful orb.

My "Mama" Myrtle, as I referred to her, was a devoutly

religious woman. She spent at least *some* time in the local church every day and prayed for guidance at the drop of a hat (fashionable or not). And she must have been granted that guidance because, unlike many of the devout I have known, she was an extremely honest person... to others, and also to herself. She, for example, informed me, as soon as I was old enough to understand it, that she was not my biological mother, and hence treated me more as a friend than as a child. She knew my strengths and my weaknesses as a good friend should. She allowed me my strengths and supported me in my weaknesses – and even helped me to overcome some of them. All in all my abandonment by my parents may well have been an extremely lucky thing. I have no way of knowing this for sure, but I must bow to their judgment in this matter, the only matter, in fact, in which I have experienced it. I know not if any other judgment they would have made, had they decided to keep me, would have been as lucky for me. I know not whether they would have supported me as my Mama Myrtle did, or whether they were religious people, or, had they been so, whether they would have imposed their beliefs upon me. But Mama Myrtle never did, other than by example of course, which in its own way can be quite an imposition.

We lived in a small apartment which was stark and featureless. It therefore possessed a strong and unique character, except for my room which was brightly colored and seemed at all times to suffer – or perhaps I should say 'benefit' – from an extreme sense of disorder. When I think back on it now I seem to remember loud and exciting music always playing in that little room of mine. This, despite the fact that I also remember that I had no access to the means of any such musicalization. Strange, isn't it, how two contradictory facts can cohabit within an otherwise logical reality. The rest of the apartment, if I remember it correctly, was always completely silent.

Sometimes, when I was in the mood for neither total silence nor excitable volume, I would go outside and sit upon the stoop of our building and watch the snow falling on the people as they walked past. The snow, of course, would have fallen on me too were it not for the cheap black umbrella I held aloft, alternating one hand (to hold its crudely seamed shiny plastic handle) with the other, which would then immediately resume a warm and comfortable location buried deep within my trouser pocket. This process, when in a seated position (as anyone who has tried it will doubtless be aware) requires a particular contortion which tends to pull the seam on the crotch of the trouser into the crack of one's anus, thereby causing a slight amount of discomfort. In this way I learned the tragedy of life: that a little pleasure is always accompanied by a little pain. On the other hand it is quite possible that I was actually learning the glory of life: that a little pain is always accompanied by a little pleasure. It is hard, sometimes, for me to speculate clearly upon these lessons. But I remember one thing, my umbrella, which normally was useless in any kind of weather accompanied by even the slightest gust of wind (owing to its proclivity for turning inside out) stood me, nonetheless, in good stead when those infinitely variable, feather-like, crystalline structures floated down from the heavens, looking like nothing so much as the angels' dandruff.

Angels were, my Mama Myrtle had assured me, the messengers of God, and as such never suffered scalp conditions, or any other health problems for that matter. On the contrary in fact, they radiated the golden glow of perfect health and spiritual temperament at all times. That's what the halo represents— she told me— and the angels must be respected as the perfect beings that they are, and if ever one should speak to you, he must be believed as though his words had come straight out of the gospels. However— and her tone would always soften at this point, for she believed that all dialogues should end in the purity of love and acceptance— however, and of even greater importance (to her at least), was the fact that they were, surely, very kind beings, and unlikely to begrudge a little humor at their own expense.

I turned twelve years old on the day that I was first visited by an angel. At least he said that he was an angel… and I was taught to believe angels. I was standing in the back yard of our building, looking at the freshly washed sheets that my Mama Myrtle had recently hung upon the line. They were blowing back and forth on the breeze, and I was speculating as to why it was that the light they reflected was white, when originally it came out of a blue sky. She had gone upstairs to take a cake out of the oven, which she was baking for my birthday. I had told her that I would join her momentarily. I had just turned to enter the building, when I heard someone behind me calling out my name. I do not know how he got there, as there was no other way into the yard than through our building, but I was forced to believe the evidence of my own eyes and ears, and, by their authority, accept the validity of his presence. He was a very tall man, with a very beautiful face. He told me that his name was Mastroianni, and I asked him how Sophia was doing. He didn't laugh. But, I must admit, he didn't seem to begrudge me my little joke. I considered this a positive sign, and I asked him why it was that I had been granted the opportunity to converse with an angel, when nobody else that I knew seemed to have been equally blessed. He told me it was because I was destined for greatness. I asked him how he knew that, and he asked me if I had ever heard that I was born fully clothed. I told him that I hadn't heard that one. Well, he assured me that it was indeed true. And I, well... I was taught to believe angels.

The following year another angel showed up. He told me that *he* was Mastroianni, but his face was different... not so beautiful, and he was about six inches shorter. Now, I'd heard about people getting their face changed with an operation, and I'd heard of people getting taller, or fatter... or even thinner. But I had never heard of anyone losing six full inches of their height before, and I didn't believe that this could actually happen. Well let me tell you all something, I now have it on good authority that it *can* actually happen. How? I don't know how. But I do know that it can, and what's more, I believe it with all my heart. The reason that I believe it...? Well, I'm getting to that.

You see, on the following year, I was visited by a still shorter... and uglier Mastroianni. And each year after that he became shorter and shorter... and uglier, to the point of grotesqueness, until that is, the day of my twenty first birthday, which was the day... that my Mama Myrtle was laid to rest.

She had passed away at the last stroke of midnight, just long enough to see me all grown up. And I sat guard alone over her, all night long. It was the first time that I had ever felt so truly alone, and the darkness seemed to last forever that night. But the morning arrived eventually, just as it always will, and in the cool early hours, after notifying the proper authorities about my Mama's condition, I attempted to bake that cake which was our ritual every year at this time. I didn't get too far though. They came to take her away whilst I was mixing up the batter. I just pointed them to the body. When they were all gone I continued my mixing, but the bowl slipped out of my hand and hit the ground instantly smashing into a thousand pieces. So I just sat down on the kitchen floor, in amongst the spilled batter and the broken shards of that poor departed crock pot, and I cried a deep and never ending howl such as I had never done before in my life. And I mourned the tragedy of the loss of my childhood, and awaited expectantly the pleasure which I was sure was to eventually accompany it.

After a few hours of this I went down to the local cemetery where she was to be expeditiously buried next to the graves of her previously departed family members. There was one space reserved... for her brother (you remember) the fashion designer. He was unmarried and unlikely to perpetuate the ancestral line with his progeny – it was a lifestyle choice. Anyway, there was to be no continuation of the family name. Therefore, even though I bore no blood kinship to them (I had never even been legally adopted) I decided at that moment to go forth proudly bearing the family name of my Mama Myrtle Lewis who had given me so much more than I could have ever possibly expected out of life preceding our first meeting.

This funeral was also the only time that I would ever get to meet my 'uncle'... my rich and exalted 'uncle,' the famous designer, Jason Lewis, who had been informed of Myrtle's passing, and who, along with me – and a stray dog which had casually wandered in from a neighboring property – was the only other mourner present. The priest mumbled a few abbreviated sentences and sped off rather sharply... followed by my 'uncle' Jason, who had not actually acknowledged me in any way during the entire (though admittedly brief) ceremony. I waited with the dog, who seemed an amiable enough animal, until two dirty men filled in the grave with mud, and erected a lopsided stone at its head. There had been no one else there before, but I was not surprised when a strange three foot tall man stepped out from behind the head stone, like one of those television magicians you sometimes see. I guessed that it must be Mastroianni. I was not incorrect. The dog barked at him, but Mastroianni simply raised his arm and the dog calmly went and lay down at his feet.

"Welcome to your new life," quoth the angel. "I bring you tidings of tremendous import, which may endow you with a not inconsiderable profit."

Anyway, to cut a long (and very dull) story short, he gave me some tips on the stock market, based upon which I invested my meager inheritance. To my utter surprise they paid off, and I discovered that I could support myself quite comfortably on those earnings alone. In the following years I was visited by a sequence of increasingly taller and taller Mastroiannis, each of whom augmented my financial advice to such an extent that, very soon, I found myself in the embarrassing position of being an extremely rich man. My life truly seemed to be unnaturally charmed for many years, and I found myself constantly troubled by these two uncomfortable questions:

1) If I was indeed destined for greatness, then when on earth was greatness scheduled to arrive? Surely the acquisition of large quantities of capital could not be considered greatness in itself, specially in consideration of the fact that I had taken advantage of some rather influential connections in order to attain said wealth, and not actually done anything to earn it myself, as it were.

My second question was this:

b) Was three feet the minimum height requirement for angels?

If so... why? If not... why then did the angels' height start to increase again after it had initially been reduced to that particular stature?

On my fortieth birthday a huge seven foot six inch basketball player of a Mastroianni showed up at my mansion. 'Security' was all set to eject the intruder. They had discovered him prowling around the grounds, a black man dressed in soiled and shabby clothing, and they naturally mistook him for a vagrant attempting to steal from me. His skin was blotchy and broken out in places, with toxic looking pustules, and scabs, and scars, and he exuded an unhealthy odor from his pores. Fortunately I happened by just at that moment, having coincidentally stepped out of the house for a breath of fresh air – although I no longer believe that anything is coincidental as far as the angels are concerned. I recognized him immediately having, after all these years learned to distinguish angels in all their guises. He accompanied me on my walk around the garden. It was just as well that we remained outside, because within an enclosed space his rancid perfume may well have been a little overpowering. However, his demeanor and tone of voice did not in any way reflect his outward appearance and he spoke to me soothingly and gently. And he revealed to me, finally, the details of a great mission which I must undertake. It was the very mission for which I had been born under such strange circumstances all those many years ago.

He instructed me, in fact, to put all my affairs in order, as I would not be returning from this mission. And I know that this seems surprising to most people, but that idea did not bother me in the slightest. After all, the only things in life that I had ever acquired were money, and possessions, and I cared not for either. There was, in short, nothing to return to. I suppose that, instinctively, and in preparation for this moment, I had never developed any bonds or friendships after my Mama Myrtle died. For that matter, I had never had any other friends even when she was alive. We two had had no one but each other, and that was just the way we liked it.

But that life is behind me now, and is framed in my memory,

within the cold easiness of solitude. I was neither ready for the challenges of relationship, nor its comforts. Mama Myrtle bequeathed me too much to be lived up to. She was rational in all things, and she taught me to give and accept criticism, without an attachment to the emotional hysteria which normally accompanies it. This, in my subsequent experience, has proven to be a rare thing to find elsewhere, and the absence of which, I have come to believe, is responsible for the majority of humanities problems. I would not, however, contend that I have always acted perfectly in this regard myself. Nonetheless, I informed Mastroianni that my affairs were in order and that I was ready to go at any time.

The angel passed his hand before my eyes and, as I blinked, he was gone. So was the whole world as I knew it. In its place a different world; one that I would come to know in a way that I had never known the one before.

It was the future. I was in a large and unwelcoming looking urban environment in the middle of the winter. I was not dressed for the winter. I was penniless and homeless and, even more importantly, I still didn't know what my mission was. On the other hand, things had always come to me before, and I was confident that whatever I needed, or needed to know, would make itself available to me, all in good time. I remember wandering the streets of that city for long hours. Traffic flowed... and stopped... and flowed around me in every direction. People passed me by without noticing my presence, which was really not so different from the way my life had always been. I had never made much difference to the world. Even with all the money I had acquired, I was still an anonymous man, and I would hazard the guess that it was a rare occasion on which another soul ever accorded me a second thought. But, despite this recurrence of strolling anonymity, which I felt that I was undergoing, I found that the longer I stayed here, and for the first time in my life, I started to... vibrate, no... bubble up with this... fire, yes fire, of... potential. It was an amazing feeling. Suddenly, energy for... I didn't know *what* was to come. I felt myself a burning ball of pure hydrogen. I was a star, just bursting, waiting to go super nova. I felt no hunger. I felt no cold. I did not feel weary or uncomfortable. I did not feel lonely or afraid.

Eventually I stopped outside of a bookstore which had a rack of discounted books set out on the sidewalk. As I browsed, a small novel caught my eye. The photograph on the back cover was of a man who looked a bit like me. In actual fact he didn't look anything like me. He more resembled... the first Mastroianni that I had ever met. No, really... it didn't look like him either. But something, whatever it was, made me pick up that book and start to read.

The book?

It was called "The High Priest of Prickly Bog." The picture on the back was of the author. A man named Dominic Devine.

I stood there, out on the sidewalk, in the cold and the slushy snow, reading for about forty-five minutes. I was totally dumbstruck. It was the story of my life. I mean literally! It had my name in it... Henry Lewis, and it told of how I was brought up by my Mama Myrtle. It even mentioned Mastroianni and many other intimate details about me. But, despite these amazing coincidences, there was something which struck me as far more important than all of that. Here was a book which seemed to be speaking of a different way in which we could live our lives. Of other choices we could make. In these times, when the possibility of self destruction surrounded us like an army laying siege to our lives, and our society teetered upon the precipice of its own limitations (which, incidentally, made it rather similar to mostly every other period in history) people needed a way in which to balance themselves. In a time when race was turned against race, gender against gender, belief against belief... people needed some common ground in which to cultivate toleration. They needed something which eliminated the sense of self importance brought on by the fear of the 'other'. They needed the great non-discriminator. This book! This book, I was convinced, held the answers to my questions. Not only did it tell of my past, but it foretold of my future. Suddenly my mission had become clear. This book *was* the mission, and I needed this book in order to fulfill my destiny.

The problem was this: I had no money.

It didn't matter if this book *was* on the discounted rack. They couldn't discount it enough for me. I had nothing which I could trade for it. (I hadn't even worn my watch that morning when I'd decided to go for a stroll in the garden for some fresh air.) I explained my situation to the desk clerk inside the store, a youngish fellow with clumsily chopped black hair the consistency of a horse's tail. But he was not sympathetic to my need. I tried to explain to him how important it was that I have the book; how I believed that it was the sole reason for my being in this particular place at this particular time. I showed him that my name was printed inside the book. But he asked me how *he* would know if that was my name or not. Of course, I had no proof as to my identity. But even if it *was* my name— he simply explained to me— that was no concern of his. *His* job was to take money for the purchase of any book in that establishment based upon the price which had been allotted it by the management of same. I became frustrated with his rule bound mentality and I heard my own voice begin to rise and become edged with anger as my arguments no longer concerned themselves with the book or my need for it, but rather a critique of the young man's personality, and my belief in his need to mature, and learn to make complicated decisions without adult supervision. I may even have mentioned that I felt he would be better off if he removed the broom stick, which it seemed to me was most likely lodged inside his anal cavity. This was probably the wrong approach as it did nothing to bring the clerk around to my position. There was obviously nothing more to say. I stood there uncomfortably, alternately staring at the man, and at the book. I didn't know what to do next. My feet were tapping and my shoulders began to twitch. The clerk glared at me with a challenging look. I was nervous and desperate and I began to sweat. As I allowed the pages to flicker back and forth through my fingers, my eyes landed several times on that photo on the back of the dust jacket, and possibly the solution to my dilemma.

There was a short biography beneath the photograph which I had already read, but which (only now) seemed to apply to my situation. It explained how after many years of frustration at not being published, the author, Dominic Devine, resorted finally to a criminal act in order to achieve his purpose. Apparently, he had held a gun to the publisher's head until a contract was signed. In this contract he agreed to serve a jail sentence for this act of terrorism, but the publication of the book could not be invalidated for any reason whatsoever. These terms were agreed upon in front of television cameras with the whole world watching, directly after which Mr. Devine was taken off in handcuffs. The publishers immediately set their lawyers to work on breaking the contract, which they probably could have done easily, considering the fact that they had been coerced to sign under threat of violence, but several other publishers quickly sent in offers, understanding that huge public attention had already been brought to the book and hence a market had already been created for it. This served to convince them that the contract they already held was of considerable value and it would not be a good business decision, coercion or not, to invalidate it.

It seemed appropriate to me, therefore, that I should make off with the book in a criminal manner. I felt that by doing so, I would be following the example of the author. And, as I may have mentioned before, I have found that for myself a good example can be a powerfully motivating force.

So I ran for it!

And as I ran – for some reason I do not fully comprehend – I shouted, "*I must have this book!*" On further reflection, I suppose, I may have reasoned that, if I were to explain my actions, then those whom I offended with my thievery might somehow understand and be less angry with me for them. That concept had always worked with Mama Myrtle. Perhaps though, now that I come to think of it, that wonderful rational woman had actually done me a disservice with her great gift of rationality... by not preparing me for a predominantly irrational world. I tend usually to believe that in nature all pairs of opposites eventually balance each other out evenly. But I sometimes think that the rational half of this universal equation must be hiding behind the furniture somewhere... or the architecture... or perhaps some other place. Because, personally, since my Mama Myrtle died, I have found that quality exceptionally hard to find.

And so my ploy to gain sympathy did not work, neither did my attempt to flout the law... or maybe it did. It may, in fact, have been quite fortunate for me, because the luckiest outcome that I could ever have hoped to avoid was forced upon me without regard for my protestations.

I was arrested and sent to jail!

But jail may not be such a bad place when your destiny awaits you there, however unrecognizable it may at first seem.

I took an instant dislike to the serpentine, slithering creature who already inhabited the dank and gloomy accommodation to which I was assigned. My cell mate, namely one Rigby Delaney, was small and thin with as untrustworthy a countenance as I had ever come across. At first I responded tersely or not at all to his chatty overtures, but after a while the boredom and his persistence drilled tiny apertures in my defenses. My elation of earlier on had deflated since the disagreeable turn of events which had brought me to this consequence, and now I felt myself a dark lost soul trapped within a confinement of my own making. And this reptilian flatterer, this sycophantic co-dweller, Rigby Delaney, was my only companion. And eventually, he became the only friend that the universe would allow me. Without his constant dialog, I would have suffered for lack of entertainment. Without his ceaseless attentions, I may very well have gone completely insane.

He told me that he had been arrested after perpetrating a 'change scam' at various local groceries. It was a simple enough ruse whereby one would confuse a young and inexperienced cashier with a series of money transactions all done simultaneously. If done correctly you could walk off with the groceries and a little bit of spending money and they'd never realize it until someone balanced the receipts at the end of the day. It was a small time confidence trick, and most shopkeepers wouldn't bother to call the police, even if they *were* to deduce which actual customer was responsible for their shortfall. (I must confess that I took a wicked pleasure in the fantasy that one of his victims might have been the very bookstore that I had visited not so long after my arrival.) Apparently, Mr. Delaney had not been focussing adequately on the job at hand on the day that he was taken into custody. He argued that he had been tired and hungry at the time, and so he carelessly allowed himself to take risks which were not his normal practice. Maybe he had perpetrated one too many of these 'scams' in stores in this particular neighborhood, within too short of a time period. Whatever the reason, the police had acquired a suitable description of him, and picked him up entering a laundromat, where he was about to ask for change for the telephone.

Oddly enough, after word of his arrest had spread throughout the small community, there were several stores which he had never even visited that turned up short on their receipts that week... to the tune, all tolled, of several thousands of dollars. He was charged with the theft of all that money. Well, he swore to me that he had not stolen half of it, and Rigby Delaney, despite my earlier misgivings about him, was a man that I was quickly becoming compelled to believe.

He even confessed to me that in days past he had actually perpetrated some rather impressive 'scams' and amassed for himself a small fortune, but that was all gone now, misspent alongside his youth. And he told me that he longed, once again, to do something substantial. But this time it would be something that was of use to all people, something for which he could be proud to be remembered, unlike the many misdeeds of his past, for which he now was truly ashamed.

At one time, for instance, he used to sell nonexistent land to unwitting 'patsies' (I think that was the word he used), or at least, he said, he wasn't sure if the land existed or not... or perhaps it already belonged to someone else. Then again, there was the church which he'd founded. He remembered that church with some pride. There was much prosperity to be gained from religion... and not only prosperity, he claimed, but social perks of a more intimate nature, in short... women! The fairer sex seemed to possess the proclivity to want to do just about anything for a preacher man. They would cook for him, clean for him, and of course... the usual. And these were not just single women. Married women too... when their husbands were out. And sometimes they would send their daughters over, to be 'touched' by the holy spirit. On one occasion, he reminisced, a married woman, of pleasing proportions, actually brought her daughter along with her to his ministry so that they *both* might receive the blessings of the Lord together, and the Right Reverend Rigby Delaney was only too happy to oblige them *both* with the very special gift of his own 'divine' spirit... over and over again, until he was completely satisfied... that the devil was exorcized. But the best part of it was that, when her husband drove over to the church to pick up his family, the Reverend Delaney, or so he claimed anyway, succeeded in extracting a substantial donation for his church from that poor cuckolded bastard. And as he told me this, he laughed a little, in such a manner as to make me believe that he had garnered no actual satisfaction from it, and yet was trying to convince himself that he had.

"You must be shocked," he asked me in that dry and reptilian tone of his, "to hear that I could be capable of such evil. Such desperate evil. And believe me my friend... my dear friend, it was truly the product of my desperation." And he continued in that way assuring me that he was in fact a changed man, that he presently despised his former self, that he would never again be capable of such despicable acts. Now that I come to think of it, he may have held certain beliefs about me which were not altogether accurate: that my morality would lead me to despise his former actions with as powerful a vehemence as he himself seemed to. And he seemed to want *me* to believe in his miraculous conversion, whilst at the same time, *he* was finding it difficult to do so. I didn't have the heart to let on that his story, although mildly interesting, didn't particularly move me to outrage, so I just shook my head and clicked my tongue as he spoke, hoping that this would suffice. But in any case, I am a trusting soul, and found no reason not to take him at his word. In fact, he added, putting aside his outrageous behavior, it was indeed the *technique* of his actions which he now remembered with pride and not at all the evil intentions of same. If only, he surmised, he'd had the chance to put his tremendous talents to use on the behalf of good. Well, just think of all the great things he could have achieved.

I told him – as I supposed he wanted me to – that it was not too late to change. And I offered myself as an example. I revealed to him, finally, the nature of the events which had brought me there. How I had discovered the 'word' of Dominic Devine in a second hand bookstore, and all the trouble it had caused me. How I now felt that it had become my mission to spread that 'word' to the world. Quite frankly I was surprised to discover how easily he believed some of the details of my story. Time travel, for instance, is not a concept I would personally have found easy to digest had I not experienced it myself... nor angels, for that matter. But Rigby Delaney seemed to be a man within whose experience all manner of magical and contradictory events could exist simultaneously with an uncommon tolerance for each other. For this, if for no other reason, I came, eventually, to feel an intense and abiding closeness toward him.

And even more. As we talked I saw this... gleam come into his eye, which I felt, surely, must be the power of goodness gaining ascendance within his soul. And by the end of our dialog I had come to conclude that Rigby Delaney was a changed man. That a... miracle, yes a miracle had transmuted him into a finer element. A golden likeness of his former self, but with a new found connection to his soul. And he pledged this new soulfulness, along with some of the other talents that his old disconnected self had possessed – his amazing salesmanship, primarily – to my cause, promising to 'wash me up' and deliver me, sparkling clean, into the hands of my destiny, my public, my congregation. And, before I even knew it, I had trustingly delivered my fragile future into this stranger's guidance. And only in rare moments did I ever think to even question that decision of mine. But whenever I did he would quickly assure me that he was utterly born again in spirit and morality, and that he knew now that he could never ever use the sanctity of our crusade in order to profit personally, as he once might have done. He would never embarrass or betray the worthy ideals to which we aspired. He would uphold and honor with all due dignity the name of Dominic Devine, the originator of our (as yet) unborn persuasion.

And I believed him when he said these things for one very important reason. And that is, well...

I am a very trusting person.

That was more than fourteen years ago. And Rigby Delaney, at first anyway, was true to his word... in more ways than one. Firstly, he managed to somehow procure bail for the two of us, and within the next few weeks, he had finagled a compromise with the judge, whereby we were required to pay only minor fines for our offenses, which my new friend even payed for himself, out of his meager savings. Not only that, but Rigby Delaney took care of all my other living expenses temporarily, including furnishing a little start up money for some interesting investments I felt disposed to secure. The intricacies of the stock market had not changed so much in that future time from the way I had known it, and I was able, fairly soon, to duplicate a fragment of my previous accomplishment, even without the aid of the 'insider' information which I had been used to receiving from my special source. Delaney himself was no slouch when it came to setting up businesses of all stripes, and he seemed to possess a genius for the arcane arts of advertising and promotion. I encouraged him to take advantage of his talents, and I invested, myself, in many of his ventures. All above board, of course, and – at my insistence – all serving some kind of ethical purpose. We invested, for instance, in several types of cottage industry, in small, out of the way places. We wanted to help downwardly mobile areas rebuild, which they did... modestly it's true, but still in ways which positively affected the community in question. A small organic foods farm, providing fresh and nutritive provender to their neighbors. A women's craft association exclusively employing single mothers to carve or paint such beautiful gift items as they may, which could then be marketed to affluent connoisseurs of fine artifacts, thereby affording equitable remuneration to the previously mentioned... er, women. Rigby and I set up an organization for accounting and packaging and delivery of these goods, and others with which we were involved. And the profit which we obtained from these enterprises, although small at first, was enough to support us in the furtherance of our ministry, to whit the 'word' of Dominic Devine and the Temple of Bongovism. And as our ministry spread, so our business interests multiplied, and that growth was itself powerful enough to drive the ministry to even greater heights. Within a few short years we had created an entire system of socialized, economically self sufficient communities, which were almost entirely free of poverty, free of violence, free of crime.

Now, as the figurehead of such an organization – according to Rigby Delaney anyway – the name Henry Lewis just didn't carry enough cachet. I required, he claimed, a more magnificent appellation... a more resplendent handle... a more glorious moniker... I needed, in short, a better name. I remembered a story in which the three initials of a well known computer conglomerate had been shifted one place forward in order to achieve the name of a famous fictitious computer. I decided as a sort of literary joke to shift the same initials one place backward, and I ended up with the letters J.C.N. Now all I had to do was to figure out what they stood for.

The 'J' was easy. That would be Jason, my uncle's name. But also it was for Jason and the Argonauts, whose mission to find the fabulous Golden Fleece was a spiritual quest worthy of imitation. I had loved that story since a child, and I identified with it's hero in his weaknesses, and in his strengths.

For the 'N'… I remembered a young woman who had caught my eye one day as I strolled beside the river. I had cautiously introduced myself to her, taking great care not to intrude where I was not wanted, but she seemed to tolerate my presence. We chatted pleasantly for a short time, at the end of which she took her leave handing me, before she left, a piece of paper torn from a checking deposit slip upon which she had hastily scrawled her name and telephone number. Now her family name was Noveck, but her handwriting was such that for several days, when I would wistfully examine that scrap of paper, I would incorrectly read the name as *Novedi*. Now this word intrigued me and I kept on trying to imagine what it could mean. It seemed to be some sort of Gallic or Latinate translation for the ninth day of the week. An interesting concept. Or, if one preferred, adopting musical terminology it may well be the second day of the following week. The idea tickled me.

As for the 'C'. The word Cyllabus just popped into my head. I have no reason why. I had never seen or heard of it before. I know not what it means.

Rigby Delaney felt that a new look was also called for, I had been dressing all this while in the cheap attire common to that era in which I presently found myself. He insisted that I personally design my own wardrobe, and, based upon some sketches of mine, had several new suits made up for me at the finest tailors in town. I remember with fondness the day these suits arrived at our residence. Delaney personally attended my bathing and dressing ritual. He handed me the shampoo at the given time. He sprayed me down to rinse. He placed the towel upon my back to dry me. He blowdried and styled my hair. He ironed my shirt until it was a crisp and gleaming mirror of perfection. He shined my shoes and held my jacket up for my outstretched arms to enter. And after I had examined myself, I turned from my reflection to encounter his benevolent scrutiny. It was then that he called me – the first time that anyone had ever done so – Jason Cyllabus Novedi.

So there I was. Jason Cyllabus Novedi (the listener gasps), powerful magnate and religious leader. I purchased a tract of wasteland which was called Prickly Bog, and upon this mire I built a town. My intention had been to allow people a place where they could control their own lives. Where they could think and breathe without fear of assault. A place free of pollution. Free of intimidation. Where they could fulfill themselves spiritually, in their own way... or not at all, if they so chose. Where fresh and natural harvest would be made easily accessible. Where lost arts and artisanship would be rekindled. And so with Rigby Delaney's invaluable service, I propelled this dream into existence.

And for a while it seemed to me that all was going as planned. But perhaps I was not diligent enough in my husbandry to notice the slow change which had occurred in my design. Because at some point, I realized that I was no longer in control of the direction that my Great Empire was taking. I had let slip the wheel of leadership, and it had been taken up, enthusiastically, by my friend... my partner... my cohort in this adventure. And, as grateful as I was to be rescued from my laxity, I felt nonetheless, that we had turned toward a course that was not of my choosing. It was of his. And it suddenly struck me that, maybe, I had misjudged the depth of Rigby Delaney's conversion from criminal to saint, inasmuch as it now seemed to me that it may never have actually happened. Old habits die hard, and old instincts return, and it soon became clear that Mr. Delaney had – brilliantly, I must admit – tied everything up legally in such a way that my own hands might just as well have, literally, been bound.

I tried to confront him on this issue, but he was always too busy to talk right now... a meeting or some such, to which I, of course, was never invited. But don't worry— he would constantly assure me— nothing was amiss, and everything would be explained to my satisfaction eventually. This went on for about six months, and I suppose that I was not strong enough to insist upon clear communication. Maybe I was ineffectual, or maybe I was simply content with my lot. My life had reverted to pretty much the way it had been before I came here. I spent my time doing pleasant things. Playing musical instruments. Painting. Reading great literature. Learning enjoyable facts about things which did not affect my life in any way. And yet... there was this dream. This reason for living. This mission which had been halted. I felt that I was letting someone down. Who was I letting down? Was it the people of this time, who had a right to the freedom that Dominic Devine and the Great God Bongo had dreamed into existence for them? Was it Mastroianni, my guardian angel, who had been with me all my life, and who had brought me here to fulfill this noble calling. No! Well... okay, yes, it was them too. But mostly it was me. Me, that I was letting down. And god damn it – I wasn't going to let that happen. I marched downstairs to Rigby Delaney's office, but I caught up with him in the hallway, just as he was about to leave the building, and I grabbed him by the throat, and I pushed him up against the wall, and I told him, "you will speak to me now!" There were some workers who had gathered around, possibly to come to his aid, he signaled to them not to get involved. And then he convinced me to let him go, and I followed him back into his office.

He spoke quietly, despite my volume. He told me then that he had total control of all our business affairs, and that my hysterical behavior only proved that I should not. That he had no intention of letting me have any. That I would only destroy everything if he did. That I could not be trusted. And as I listened to him say these awful things about me I entered some strange kind of mental zone, in which I split myself into all these different parts. One which was enraged, and wanted to beat this verminous creature to death. One which was depressed, because it actually believed the awful things that he was saying. One which was filled with guilt, for having let the other parts down. And my head echoed with the clash of those things that battled within and without. Finally, however, I managed to pull myself together, and I threatened to expose him for the confidence artist that he was. I told him that I believed that he was cheating the people we had pledged to serve. Using them for his own gain. I said that I would discredit him and have him arrested and thrown out of Prickly Bog forever. But he knew that I had no proof. He denied that he was cheating anyone and told me that I was having hallucinations. Further proof of my incompetence. Moreover, if I tried to do anything which would threaten his position he would have me killed. Then he walked calmly out of the room closing the door gently behind him. I believed him.

During the following years, I did my best to stay out of his way. My life continued on as before, pleasantly enough with everything provided that I could want for myself. I learned how to survive in a world where there were some people who hated me, and would have killed me as easily as I believed Rigby Delaney would have, and there were others who loved me and would have died for me, had I expressed it as the merest whim. But they all felt the way they did for reasons which were counterfeit. I was an illusion, as were all my supposed actions. I had become no more than a trademark. JCN, a stamp on a product. Nobody knows me. To that extent I am as anonymous as I ever was. I sometimes wonder if I will ever complete my mission. I sometimes like to convince myself that, in some unknowing way, I already have. It is hard for a man to admit that he has not, in fact, ever achieved anything.

Chapter 11

"This is fucking amazing," said Dominic Devine.

"This is amazing," said Jocelyn D'Orion. "So... *you* are the famous Jason Cyllabus Novedi? How do I know that you're telling the truth?".

"How could you know that story, I... I... don't understand." Dominic's mind was swirling as if in a dream. Some kind of crazy magic was at work here. It excited him with the potential of new worlds... new realities... new possibilities but, at the same time, it scared the hell out of him. He didn't trust his perception of what had just happened. He couldn't. He couldn't trust Henry Lewis, that's for sure. Fuck, he didn't even think that he could trust his own mind at this point. How could this be happening? How could a total stranger pop out of nowhere and recite for him, word for word, a chapter out of his own book, which had never ever been published – not yet anyway, not in this time – and of which he possessed the one and only copy of the manuscript?

Jocelyn was excited, but she couldn't figure out why. She had heard of Jason Cyllabus Novedi, but she certainly didn't have any respect for him... or his corporation, or his town.

"If you don't believe me ask your father. He had me pegged right away."

She looked uneasily at him. "Yeah?" She spoke softly.

"I was rather amazed..." he added (almost narcissistically, she thought), "that you didn't, er... recognize me, that is."

"Ohhh..." she lengthened the vowel unnaturally whilst at the same time turning up her nose. "Excuuuuse me!" And then she added in a very matter of fact way, "I have no use for celebrities. I'm not plugged into 'pop' culture."

He ignored the taunt. "But you must have seen my face on the television. Those bastards follow me everywhere!"

"Oh, poor you" she intoned facetiously. "No. I don't own a brainwashing device. I like my brain a little dirty. And anyway, I have too many *real* things to do!"

"No, I er... see. " There was a little pause. "Well... you're probably right."

"Thank you so much for allowing me my opinion." But then she seemed to retreat a little, and she touched his cheek lightly. "I suppose..." she said, "it turns out that you're not as bad as I thought." Her eyes were so beautiful, marked with a sad and natural darkness beneath her lower lids.

Jason peered into their watery green depths. "Not nearly," he agreed genuinely.

Dominic got up hurriedly from the dining table and went over to the cabinet where he had stowed his papers last night. Nothing seemed to have been touched. Anyway, he remembered, the old man had been taking a pee when he put them away. How would he have known where they were... or *what* they were, for that matter? Dominic tried to visualize how this could have happened? It hardly seemed likely that the old man could have awoken in the middle of the night, guessed somehow that Dominic was a writer, rummaged through his things, found the manuscript amongst all the other papers and junk, perused it meticulously to find just the right spot, and then sat down and memorized eighteen pages of it in one sitting, and recited the entire thing perfectly the next morning. But then where else could the old bastard have got access to it?

The proposal that he had sent out to publishers and agents didn't contain more than the first thirty pages. This chapter was definitely not included. Only a few very close friends had even heard parts of the book... sometimes he would read to people. But no! It was impossible. What this man had just done was totally impossible, unless... well, unless his story was... no, but that was ridiculous. It was a dream. *There is no such thing as time travel*! He knew it. I know it. You know it.

Yes sure, odd things happen once in a while. Someone on the radio says a word just at the same time as you happen to read it on a magazine page. Peculiar coincidences. Sure... someone calls just as you think of them. Strange coincidences with names... numbers... colors... people knowing other people whom still other people didn't know that the first people knew. But, actually thinking that he, Dominic Devine, could write a book – a novel, fictitious – that would predict someone else's life, and such an implausible one at that. No. That was unimaginable... okay, not unimaginable, but certainly unrealizable. I mean, just the prospect... the consideration that this would ever really happen was sending our Dominic into quite a tailspin.

The trouble was this. He really wanted to believe it. It was, after all, a magic thing. He just loved it. He loved the very idea that something so unbelievable could manifest itself somehow. But even more, he loved the fact that it was he who was at the very center of this magical occurrence. That meant, of course – if it were true – that there was something magical... something amazing about him.

"But then, what was all that fuss about the eggs this morning?" he asked, as if suddenly accepting the validity of the old tramp's story.

"That was a joke," replied Henry Lewis.

"That was a joke," replied Jason Cyllabus Novedi.

"So you have eaten real eggs before?" she asked.

"From chickens," he said, "just like these."

"But I still don't understand how you got here?"

"The angels," said Henry Lewis.

"The angels," said Jason Cyllabus Novedi.

"The angels?"

"Yes. They saved my life. They brought me here... to you. I have learned to trust their judgment. "

"You are altogether too trusting," came the listener's reply. "For that matter, so am I. Every molecule of my cynical being tells me that your story is utterly crazy. Unbelievable. There are no such things as angels that whisk you off into the future and back again... and yet... something inside of me wants... needs... to believe you. Somehow your story makes me feel... complete. I hope you are not deceiving me. I hope that everything you say is true."

The story teller looked a little ashamed. "Yes," he said. "It's true. Every word of it. And now, I must go."

Henry Lewis picked up his things to leave.

"So, what am I supposed to do?" asked Dominic as he walked the old tramp down the stairs to the front door. "Go and stick up the nearest publisher?"

"You will do," replied the oracle, "what you will do." And then he turned once again to gaze intensely into Dominic's eyes, like a crazy mad thing. "There is no doubt about it. There is only one future for you. And in that future – whatever it might be – it will already be done." And with those final words he walked out into the snowy morn, and he disappeared slowly from sight like a phantom. Dominic Devine, as he stood there, saw it himself. Saw him physically disappear, as he walked away, into a blizzard of the angels' dandruff, which had begun to fall at some ungodly hour that morning.

Jason Cyllabus Novedi bid a duplicitous farewell to his new friend Fritz D'Orion. It was as if they had some kind of secret code between them which Jocelyn was not privy to. Fritz had laughed when his daughter protested his silence regarding Jason's true identity.

"What're you complaining about?" he'd argued, "It wasn't *me* who lied to you."

At first Jason had felt that he was getting double-crossed, but Fritz liked to tease as many people at a time as he could get away with. He knew that his daughter was too quick for that.

"A lie of omission." She pointed an accusing finger at her father. "You didn't tell me the truth!"

Jason went outside and positioned himself quietly in the passenger seat of the Bel Air, where he patiently awaited his temporary chauffeur. Jocelyn silently rebuked her father one last time with a cold, cold stare, and then emerged through the ripped and creaky, swinging screen door, into the late afternoon sunlight. The anxious chickens nearby clucked with violent alarm in response to its crashing movement, just as they always had, and then returned to their incessant pecking at invisible particles upon the earth.

Jason wondered about their intelligence: the fact that they just never learned that their alarm was as unnecessary as it had been the last time. Or maybe they were intelligent enough to understand that some day it might be necessary. But perhaps, on the other hand, this behavior is not even a function of intelligence. Fear is, after all, an emotion, is it not? Sometimes fear and intelligence can be hard to differentiate. I mean, *either* could be the motivation for getting out of the way of an oncoming train, for example. Is it unintelligent to be fearful when you are safe? Because, you know, you *will* do (he wondered... how did that saying go?) what you *will* do. There is only one future for you. What will be is what will be, and this you will surely see. In other words, if it's going to happen, it's as good as happened, and there's absolutely no reason to fear what's already happened. And then again if it's not going to happen? Well...

It's a balance, isn't it? On the one side you have extreme paranoia, or – as it's known in the business – Chicken Shit Fear (CSF). On the other side you have what has come to be known as Total Lackadaisical Fatalism (TLF). Certain ethnic groups tend to exhibit a predominance of one characteristic over the other. The CSFs tend to get a lot accomplished but are never able to enjoy the fruits of their labor because they're too busy laboring further in order to distract themselves from that which they fear. Whereas, the TLFs never get anything accomplished (why bother), and therefore have no fruits from... no labor... to not enjoy. It seemed to him that when one is ruled by either of these emotional extremes it would be difficult, if not damned nigh impossible, to attain for oneself any GDR. As in most things in life, the intelligent way... and, the emotionally stable way... was to ride the fence straight down the middle. A line to balance upon. A shade of grey. Or was that just another extreme. Another lack of flexibility. Another easy place to get stuck. In the middle... with you.

Not one shade of grey, then – shall we say – but the entire spectrum from black to white. And let's not forget infrared and ultraviolet, and whatever lies beyond. But then, that may be too many choices to be making all the time. Tell you what, let someone else decide. Easier that way.

The ride back to JCN headquarters passed mostly in silence. There were the few odd directions he had given her, but apparently he had decided it wiser not to test her further. Within that emptiness certain thoughts went through her mind, try as she might to suppress them. What kind of place did he live in? Would he invite her in when they arrived? She would of course refuse, she decided. Would that then be the last that she ever saw of him? Not that she really cared, she insisted. In fact, as far as she was concerned, she wasn't even really thinking about these things. They were just... remote possibilities that someone (not her) might consider if, of course, that someone were far more impressionable, far more desperate than she. And in fact, as far as she was concerned, there was nothing more than the scenery upon her mind (as well, of course, as the usual necessities of visual comprehension which piloting a vehicle require). Only the gravel burning up the ground beneath her rubber. Only the splintered telegraph poles whirring by stroboscopically, whilst far distant sentinels of corroded steel and wire moved hardly at all, but followed their progress, falling back only slowly, and after miles of transit.

As they entered the town of Prickly Bog he directed her again but no more than was necessary. She'd been here a couple of times before, but not recently, and not enough to know where she was going. They came shortly to a place where an ugly corrugated metal fence hid what lay immediately behind. There was a crude iron gate, but it was set at such an angle as to not reveal the interior. What she could see was that there was a tall building inside set well back from the perimeter of the property, but only the higher floors were visible from her viewpoint on the street. Maybe if she could just get out of the car and take a little look around...

"You can let me off here," he said.

She pulled to a halt beside the gate. "Will you be safe now?" she asked genuinely.

He raised his eyebrows as if to scoff, but then he thought for a moment looking at the muddy carpeting beneath his feet. His right hand reached for the door handle and opened it slowly. "More than likely," he answered with a serious tone, looking her straight in the eye for the first time since they had entered the car. Then he leaned forward to gaze up at the sky through the windshield.

"Oh yes." she said. "The angels."

"Oh!" He caught the reference. "That's not what I was, er... I mean I've never actually seen them since, er... well anyway, er... thanks for the lift." He got out of the car nervously and slammed the door shut. Jocelyn glared at him momentarily and then hit the gas hard, performing an aggressive U-turn as he stood there watching. She pulled up beside him again and jerkily rolled down her window.

"So what about that reward you promised me?"

He walked slowly over to the car wiping sweaty hands on his pant legs. "Sure," he replied lazily, and with the slightest smirk upon his features. "What do you want?"

She looked at him with complete contempt. "Nothing!" She spat it out. Her back wheels spun in the dirt beside the road shooting dust in all directions, including his. There was a little chirp as they gained traction on the asphalt and the car sped away. She watched him in the mirror as he grew smaller and ever smaller. Even when he had become a tiny dot, she could still feel his eyes upon her, burning into the back of her head. Begging her and commanding her. She could tell already, that from now on in, she belonged to him. What she didn't know, however, was if she would ever see him again. Something magical had just occurred, whether or not she could bring herself to believe in it. Regardless of what she had always imagined would be her destiny. Regardless of what she had always wanted. Destiny holds no reverence for mortal yearnings. If nothing else, learn this: we get what we get — there is no other truth. And so she accepted it, because she could feel it... inside of her, and that was the only way she had of knowing what was real.

Chapter 12

Marvin was having a good old laugh. "So this bum gets... what? Taken to another dimension by Martians to save the Universe from exploding." The surface of the coffee table in front of him was littered with broken peanut shells. His finger traced an arc amongst them.

"Not Martians... angels," said Dominic.

"So what's that? Angels? Something from fuckin' *God*, right?" He took a sip from a beer can and waved his fingers around in the vicinity of his brain. "I forget that shit from when I was a kid, man. Something from fuckin' heaven."

"Well, I'm sure that they're not literally that. I mean... if his story *were* true it could be that something..."

"*True? True?* Some fuckin' refugee from a mental institution tells you some cock and bull story about flying through space and you think it might be true?"

"Not space. See? Now you're getting the whole thing mixed up. Of course it seems stupid when you put it that way. But there could be other ways of describing these occurrences which make them seem more plausible. Symbolic ways. Ways that have more to do with the subconscious mind."

"Oh yeah?" Marvin wiped the wetness from his mouth with the back of the same hand in which he held his beer. Cheap domestic brew, it sloshed around inside as the can moved to and fro, and flattened rapidly, losing what meager effervescence it had once possessed, and gaining, in return, the vulgar tang of saliva and aluminum.

"Well I know," continued Dominic, "that the old tramp was describing everything as if it had literally happened to him, and maybe it was all just an illusion... "

"Maybe?" his friend interrupted.

"... well anyway, in this, er... fanciful illusion that he may..." and here he glared challengingly at Marvin like the proverbial turning worm, "... or may not have imagined somewhere within the deep recesses of his twisted little mind, he has yet managed to recite for me, word for word – or at least as close as I could remember, anyway – an entire chapter out of my unpublished, unseen, unread, untouched-by-human-hand… novel. Now, how do you think he managed that?" But before Marvin could say a word Dominic took the opportunity to resume the roll that he was on. "Somehow, on some level, this fellow has experienced that very story which I wrote…"

" Or *think* you wrote," Marvin joked, spitting out microscopic bits of peanut as he laughed. "Maybe *he* wrote it, and *you* memorized it."

Dominic continued undeterred. "I mean, either he actually lived through it just the way I wrote it, or possibly he had some kind of deep telepathic link with my mind. Either way… it's fucking amazing. Personally, I find the telepathy theory more plausible than the time travel. I mean, I just can't believe that such a thing could possibly exist. Also then you'd have to account for the fantastic coincidence of me writing about what he did, without having known about it, and – and… why would he, even then, I mean how could he use the same words? Exactly? No… but whatever it is, this whole experience shocked me so much, that I find myself increasingly more open to almost *any* new idea."

"Bullshit!" said Marvin, cracking another peanut shell. "I say he read it at your house last night while you were sleeping."

"Yes, yes, but even if he did read it, how could he have set it to memory so quickly? So perfectly? No, no, I'm telling you, what he did, it's… it's impossible."

"Maybe he's one of them guys with a, watchamacallit… " Marvin snapped his fingers several times, "… photographic memory. You know there really are people who can do that. I saw one guy like that on You Bet Your Life. Right? Now it may not be common…" he spoke as if he were addressing a retarded child, "but we do know that it's possible. Whereas time travel, mental communication, well… now isn't the 'possible' a bit more 'plausible'…" and here he framed the operative words by using the first two fingers of each hand to draw quote marks in the air, "… than the 'im-possible'?"

"Well… it's true, of course," Dominic seemed to begrudge him this concession, "and in any other case I would agree with you, but…"

"But what?"

"Well, the thing is this. None of my papers had been touched.

I'd swear to it. Also, he was so drunk... I saw him polish off a bottle of scotch myself, and that was on top of anything he'd had before I ran into him. He fell off to sleep long before me and when I woke up he was still snoring. In fact his snoring was so loud that he kept me up half the night. I only slept for a couple of hours. He wouldn't have had enough time to do everything he had to do. I know he didn't see me put the book away. How would he have found it and left all my papers just as they were? How would he even know that it *was* a book? Or that I had even written a book?" Dominic was staring down at the floor shaking his head slowly.

"Maybe..." Marvin was racking his brain for an answer, "maybe he just stumbled on it, you know, rifling through your things. And then ... and then formulated his cunning plan after putting it all away neatly."

"Yeah... I don't think so. Because, well... for one thing he was starting to tell me stuff the night before. Before we even got to my house. He said how he'd been sent to see me, specifically... and how I was responsible for some major thing that was yet to happen." Marvin hardly concealed a little titter. "No," continued the author, "if this was a cunning plan he'd have to be some kind of evil super genius in order to come up with it off the cuff like that. No... you'd have to work on something like that for a while. Plan it out. Know your subject..."

"And I suppose," said Marvin, "that the idea of him being a super genius is less likely than angels coming out of the fucking..." Dominic looked like he was starting to get a little agitated but Marvin wouldn't let him interrupt regardless. "Alright, alright!" he added. "So let's say he got hold of your story someplace you left it before."

"No, no," said Dominic with an irritable tone. He had been deciding whether to reach for a peanut from the bowl, but became distracted from his undertaking by having to answer this. "I didn't leave it *anywhere*."

"What'chu talking about? You left it over here the other night! You know, you oughta be more careful with that thing. Who knows who else's place you've left it at."

"I didn't leave it at anyone else's house. I don't have any other friends. And assuming that you didn't have that bum up here in the last few days..."

"I have a lot of bums up here regularly," Marvin joked... almost as if to say— you're one of them.

"... then nobody could have seen it," Dominic continued unassailed. "And hey, anyway, why *should* I be so careful with it? It isn't a secret document, or anything like that. It's just a novel that I'm writing."

"Yes but," added his friend with a vicious sarcasm that wasn't uncommon to him, "a novel that will change the world!"

"Ha ha!" said Dominic. "Very funny!"

After a brief pause Marvin looked over at him and said, "So?"

"So what?"

"So where else did you leave it?"

Dominic almost shrieked in response. "*I didn't fucking leave it anywhere!*"

"Alright, alright, calm down," (his confessor's design... to lull). "So what do you want to do now? Go stick up your nearest publisher?"

"That's funny," said Dominic in such a way that Marvin tilted his head inquisitively. "That's what I asked the tramp just before he left." He looked over at the bowl of peanuts. They called to him.

"And?" prodded Marvin.

"He told me that I would do, what I would do, and that nothing could stop me – or something like that. That the future has already happened – or something like that. I don't fucking know. Anyway, I think that what he meant was that I don't really have to do anything. That whatever is going to happen to me... is going to happen to me."

"Very Zen." Marvin spoke sarcastically. "Sounds like the typical fucking attitude of fuckers who never get anything done. And you wanna know something else?" Dominic shook his head. "There's one serious logical shortcoming to that philosophy."

"What's that?"

"That is, that the future *hasn't* already happened. That's why it's known as the fucking *future*. Not to be confused with the fucking *past*, which *can't* be changed. It's just semantic bullshit to say that you can or can't change the future. Of course you cannot, by definition, change something until it already exists, because there is nothing, so far, to change. That doesn't mean that you can't cause things to happen. But you've got to be willing to make the decisions that have to be made.

125

You've got to be willing to take risks. If the future was set, then there would be a way to know what it was. If we knew what the future was, there would be no risks. Without risk, there would be no fear. Without fear, there would be no need for confronting fear. Without confronting fear, there would be no way to overcome fear. Without overcoming fear – the fear of change, which we all have to some extent – there would be no growth. Without growth... well, there would be no future, 'cause time is a vacuum..." here Marvin paused for a second, and turned slowly to look and point a fateful finger at Dominic Devine, "... time is a vacuum which pulls growth into it."

"And along with it." Dominic stretched his arms upward and yawned. "I suppose you're right," he said, seemingly unimpressed by Marvin's antics, "Of course you understand that what you're telling me is that I should go stick up a publisher and be prepared to go to jail in order to get my book published?"

"I'm not telling you to do anything at all. I just believe that... well, let me put it this way... one time I heard this shrink on the radio saying that it was better to just hold back and do nothing rather than do the wrong thing... that might fuck up the situation totally. And for a long time I believed that was a good way to be... probably 'cause I fucked up so many things in my life just by doing one wrong thing. But eventually I started to realize that if you practice that philosophy all the time, you end up doing nothing all the time – 'cause no one can ever be completely sure that they are making the right decision – and you start to lose confidence in your own ability to make decisions. You don't make any mistakes, but you *need* to make mistakes... in order to learn. You never find out which of your judgments are right and which are wrong. And, worse than that, you never get any fucking thing done. What I'm saying is this: I now believe that doing even the wrong thing is better than doing nothing."

Dominic did not reply at first. He had been contemplating whether, if he were to start eating peanuts now, he would regret it later when he sat down for his lunch. He had the strange feeling that he'd been insulted in some way, but he couldn't quite figure out how. Marvin's voice had held a perfectly ordinary tone and yet... he went over the last few sentences again in his head, and then he got it. "Are you saying that *I* never get anything done...? And that if I were to make a complete and utter asshole out of myself, or get myself injured or killed, that I couldn't possibly be worse off than I am now?"

Marvin just shrugged and walked off into the kitchen.

"That's nice," said Dominic, ungratefully behind him.

After a while Marvin looked in on him again. "Resisting growth," he said, "is a form of self destruction." He disappeared momentarily and then appeared again adding, "I'm not saying that *you* are any more guilty than anyone else is. You can decide that for yourself."

"Thanks very much," said Dominic Devine. He reached down for a peanut and cracked its beastly little shell.

Chapter 13

Jason Cyllabus Novedi did not understand that the way one feels is the only thing that really matters. He thought that his mission was the most important thing. In a way, I suppose he was right. But then his mission, of course, was not at all about the thing that he thought it was about. It was, in fact, about the very thing that he did not know it was about. To be succinct, his mission was simply to find out just how important his feelings were. Okay so maybe that wasn't entirely it. Maybe it was partly about that and partly about something else. His belief in angels was a part of it. Some might have called him naive, but there was always a truth to the things that he believed in, and he was honest enough with himself to recognize the flexibility of truth. Who's truth, after all, will not be swept away eventually, as time – and other people's versions – distort it irreparably? For example, when I say to you, "this is my heart, and the blood that pumps through it is red," how can I be so arrogant as to assume that you see the same thing that I do?

Rather, I should acknowledge that you – facing the opposite direction – *must* see the exact *opposite* view of that which I do. Like a face punched in a sheet of metal and suspended between us. I see the features as concave. You see them as convex.

"Concave schmon-cave! Convex schmon-vex!" You might exclaim. "What the hell is the difference? It's the same face, isn't it? It sure looks the same."

Look again. The shadows.

The shadows are reversed. At least, those are the words that I use to explain the way that I think you see it. Because you and I shall never ever see anything from the same angle. The reason for this is that our heads are in two different places – no two heads can occupy the same space at the same time – or maybe it's just that they are screwed on in a different way. Close maybe, some are – or similar – but no two exactly alike. Know what I mean? Yeah well, even if you do... even if you agree fully with what I'm saying... that's not exactly what I'm saying.

Beware, beware the agreeable. Beware, beware the honest intention. Beware, beware the vulnerable. Beware, beware, beware the naked man.

Jason Cyllabus Novedi was not the naked man. He was armor clad and armed to the hilt. Which was not the fault of his Mama Myrtle. She did by him just as well as could be expected. He'd been traumatized, as young as he was, before he even came to her. She just taught him how to defend himself in the same way that she had learned to defend herself. She was a master of the art of emotional self defense. Her technique was deceptively simple. She kept out of trouble in the first place. So did he.

Maybe the most important thing for him, was to learn how to get *into* trouble. It appeared, on the outside anyway, that he was in a lot of trouble now. But he wasn't worried, because he knew that everything had always turned out okay before. So as far as he was concerned, he felt that trouble hadn't really troubled him as yet. And the way one feels is, after all, the only thing that really matters. Except, of course, for Jocelyn D'Orion. Her image troubled his mind (which was so untrained at being sensitive) in a way that he could not even discern yet. But anyhow, there it was, rubbing away and chafing up a nice little raw patch smack in the middle of his unconscious mind.

Now, why should such a thing bother him? Why should this woman, of all women, disturb him so? Less than twenty-four hours ago he was responsible for the death of another woman, and also of six men. Admittedly they had plotted to murder him. But even so, this is not an act which leaves one unchanged, and Jason Cyllabus Novedi had never killed a human before. Neither had Henry Lewis. Furthermore, the woman had been his lover... perhaps not for very long. Sweet little thing, she was. Short... and short lived, as it were. But it was only her physical substance that remained with him in his mind. It was the only part of her which had penetrated his emotions. It was the only part of her which she had given. But her mind, he knew not more than that it was where she stored her betrayal. And it did not possess volume enough to conceal that deceit. She had conspired, that little beauty, with... *someone*, to assassinate him – the High Priest. The Prickly Priest he had become. When threatened his thorny back had stood erect and skewered his assailants. Those poor bastards didn't see it coming. But he felt no sympathy for them, neither did he feel animosity. And the fact that he felt nothing for them was noteworthy in itself. He couldn't hate anyone. He had not learned how to do that. He didn't really care what their motivation might be for attempting such a thing. He had simply done what he had done in order to survive. Plain and simple. He assumed that they had *not* been laboring on behalf of their own interests, and that indeed, *someone* had put them up to this adventure. He believed also that he could most likely guess exactly *who* that someone might be. But he didn't hate *that* person either. It really didn't matter who or why. What must be must be. And not even because it was necessary. It's not as if Jason was the type who would carefully weigh up the pros and cons, the morality versus the necessity, so to speak. That was not how he did things. He just did them. He was not an evil person, or sadistic in any way. He did not enjoy watching others suffer. He was without affect in these matters... without judgment. It was not a quality that he possessed. He had never loved anyone in his whole life – no, not even Mama Myrtle. And when she died he didn't miss her... although he thought of her often, and fondly. And at her graveside he didn't cry. But then... there were always the angels. The god damned angels. Maybe they were the ones who took his feelings away. Took away his soul. Or maybe the opposite was true. Maybe they were the remedy to his unfeeling. Maybe this was the reason for the mission they had assigned him. To lead him back. To restore him to his feelings, like a king to his throne.

"You know something? I don't like the way you're talking to me! I'm juggling fifteen things over here, and I've got this prima donna to mollify... what... yes, of course legally I've got it all tied up, but there is such a thing as public relations, you know."

Rigby Delaney was sweating, and it wasn't that hot. His feet were up on the desk, and his tie was undone. One floor below the JCN penthouse apartment the late evening sunlight was dying, and the long shadows of his feet upon the opposing wall were fading slowly into nonexistence like the rest of his office around him. It seemed a metaphor of what the man on the other end of the phone line might do to him were he to lose his edge. Rigby responded, as he always did in situations of stress, with bravado. He was always amazed at how that con would work on people you would think were far too intelligent to be duped by such a lame trick. Their weakness was that they couldn't believe that anybody would even try to put something over on them. Therefore if you had an attitude and sounded like you were lying, well... you *must* be telling the truth.

"P. R. yes! If it doesn't matter, then why do we bother having a figurehead? A logo? A brand identity... yes that *is* what he is... we need the punters. The punters have to be carefully greased. They are, after all the ones who pay for the product.... I agree, we don't necessarily have to improve the product, or in certain cases even *have* a product, as long as there's the illu... what? Oh... yes, yes I see what you mean, but it doesn't matter what threats you come up with, 'cause none of us is as powerful as we think we are. I can control him, but only if I do it a certain way... well of course I can make him disappear... but... but... no, what I'm saying is that it makes things more difficult... what... no, you're right, not impossible… no, I appreciate that… yes, a hierarchy, but it doesn't just go one way. You're responsible to those above you *and* below you… what… hmm… hmm… I get you, I get you… yes but listen to this, you need me just like I need him… no… no…. no, I'm not talking tough, I'm just saying that we all need each other. Now look, this thing will work a lot better for us, and for the state, which is the most important thing, if we don't fight amongst ourselves. Let's not forget, there is a war on. I know it's hard for us to remember that, sitting in our luxury towers, as we do. There is danger abroad, and the product we must cash in on is the hope of salvation, just like every other culture, every other civilization that came before."

He lit a cigarette as he hung up the phone. While he was talking he'd been breaking the tips off of every stick in the packet. There was a pile of them sitting at the bottom of his waste bin, and there was a small piece of wet tobacco caught on the end of his tongue. He tried to remove it with the same hand that held the butt, and, after several tries involving that little breathy spitting sound one makes in such a situation, he finally did.

Why do I fucking bother— he wondered— I do all the work and those bastards reap all the profit. I mean, what's it worth if I don't come out of this with a substantial measure of power and prestige? And it was true that Rigby Delaney was responsible, more than any other single person for the empire that he'd created out of the name of Dominic Devine, and his creation, The Great God Bongo.

But when it comes down to it no one could do such a thing all by themselves. He had needed Jason to be the living figurehead, to be the High Priest. He had the charisma… the spiritual aura that people would go for. And also he wasn't too bright. A little self obsessed, maybe, but that was good. That way he kept his mind turned inward and didn't focus on what was taking place around him. Just as well, because he wouldn't have approved of what was going on, that's for sure.

And then there were the other people who had to be involved. Frederick Greaves had supplied most of the know how and the contacts, it's true, but now he was acting like he ran the whole show. Giving orders. Issuing threats and ultimatums. Who the fuck did he think he was? Maybe he'd had some power before, but it was nothing compared to what Rigby Delaney had delivered him on a platter. But was he grateful? He wasn't the only person who could have somebody eliminated, you know!

There were a lot of things that needed to be taken care of. Just like in any other state. He'd had to delegate authority to various departments, each with their own leaders and leadership problems. 'Communal Services' handled roads, water, electricity, transportation, fire departments... that kind of thing. The department of 'Control' was the police and the courts; prosecutor and public defender included. The 'State department of Protection', one of the most important, and highly funded departments dealt with the military and the ever present war, which continued so constantly – yet so distantly – that for most of the populace it was an inevitability which they assumed would carry on forever.

The ever popular department of 'Sickness and Injury' was perennially one of the biggest moneymakers. It was a convoluted but somewhat brilliant scam. There were so many different ways in which the punters got taken, that they didn't know if they were coming or going. And god forbid that one ever actually needed its services. The cost of saving a life could result in payments that would destroy a life. Not that it was unheard of for them to accidentally kill people (and quite regularly for that matter) who came to them initially suffering from some insignificant condition. It was a well kept secret that in rare times of emergency, when the system was unable to function for one reason or the other, the death rate would actually go down five to ten percent for that period, and then resume its normal rate when the emergency was over. These accidental deaths... amputated limbs... side effects of unnecessarily prescribed medicaments... were not registered as such but instead were ascribed, in a clever though cowardly manipulation of reality, to an imaginary disease. It was called 'iatrogenic' disease.

Incompetence was rampant as was the arrogant belief of the incompetent that they know best. They disguised the barbarity of their methods behind the sheen of polished chromium and the prestidigitation of a high tech three card monte game. Find the queen. It was a mind numbing task to decide which way to look. The cost of treatment was determined by the cost of the practitioners' education, and insurance coverage. The insurance coverage was dependent upon the ability and performance of said practitioner. Their ability was determined by their education. The education was provided by the department of 'Teaching and Learning,' whose institutions were sponsored by various corporations within the department of 'Sickness and Injury.' They were also, of course, funded by the deeply inflated payments of the students themselves, although the students were not there to express – or to even have – any kind of discriminating opinion. In fact the most important thing they learned there, was to believe in the system. It was important that both the punters and the practitioners believe in the system. The Insurance and Chemical corporations funded, and therefore controlled, not only the manner of learning, but also of its substance. This small investment at the early stage assured them profits down the line. The punters were assured that under this superior system they could choose any kind of treatment they wanted... as long as it was approved by the department. But the department only approved treatments which were profitable. And those treatments were vaunted widely by the department of 'Communication.'

'Communication,' obviously, meant media of all kinds: paper, electronic... even word of mouth, and was basically all propaganda of one sort or another. Oddly enough they had decided to keep 'The

Intergalactic Temple of Bongo' as a separate department even though technically you could say it fell within the job description of the former. But I suppose it was to maintain that image of purity which might become tainted were it to become too closely associated with the profit making enterprises, which all the other departments were. The church, despite its membership fee, was a completely non-profit organization, and had to be shown to be so even under the most microscopic investigation. People had to believe also, that they supported it willingly, just as they believed that they supported the whole society willingly. 'Communications' profited financially by advertising the salable output of (you guessed it) the department of 'Product Services.' Each department consisted of many subcontracting organizations which were appropriately called Corporations. For example, 'Product Services' included corporations entitled 'Food,' 'Clothing,' 'Automotive' and 'Entertainment,' which is not to be confused with the 'Entertainment' corporation within the department of 'Communication.' One had to do with purchasable items – T.V. sets, sports equipment, children's toys etc. – while the other was involved with T.V. programs, sporting events, cinema etc. Sometimes, as in the case of video games, or computer software for instance, there were petty disputes between the rival chiefs of competing corporations as to who should control what, and then one of these items would end up, for political reasons, residing in what seemed to most people, an illogical placement. Sometimes these disputes could become quite vindictive, and on occasion had been known to lead to the deaths of parties involved.

Usually, however, payoffs were made, which would solve the immediate problem to the satisfaction of, at least, whoever made the biggest payoff. Contracts were awarded on the basis of this kind of payoff. To put the best spin on it, it was a kind of a bidding system. Except it wasn't so much that you'd bid the lowest cost for a program, but you'd bid the highest payoff to the official directly responsible for the allocation of the contract. Admittedly this didn't provide for a very efficient use of resources, but the cost would simply be handed down to the punter – the taxpayer – and everyone was happy. Most of this 'bidding' activity got filtered off along the way long before it reached Rigby Delaney, but he didn't mind. He figured it must be going on. That's how you keep the wheels greased. But he didn't really care what was happening below, as long as each department was handing in the stipulated profit margin at the conclusion of each cycle.

Once in a rare while someone would accuse someone else of corruption. At that point, if the accused was an indispensable part of the organization, they might be furtively reprimanded... for being discovered and endangering everyone else, and the accuser would be dispatched in any one of a number of ways. Conversely, if the accused official was dispensable enough, they could be made an example of, proving once again the fairness and incorruptibility of the system. The accuser, if considered adequately corruptable, might then be rewarded by being drawn into the system, or promoted within it. On the other hand, if they were considered too honest for such a position, and therefore dangerously likely to draw attention to every little impropriety, they might simply 'disappear.' This would occur at some later point in time, so that it would not seem to be connected to the original circumstance. In earlier days, Delaney had often stemmed these antagonists by undermining their reputations and, sometimes, destroying their livelihoods. Journalists, for example, might lose their jobs on the basis of alleged disloyalty... or incompetence... or simply misrepresenting the facts. This did eliminate their immediate threat to the system, but it tended to leave too many disgruntled and dangerous bottom feeders swimming around in the recesses of the pool. What would happen, one wondered, if they were to all join forces and collaborate with one another against the system's corruption? They might have the potential to instigate a meaningful vigilance within the average punter.

Anyway, a better method had been devised. With the war ever present, laws had been quietly enacted which provided for the internment of those who might constitute a threat to the state, without the benefit of legal assistance or in fact even a trial. This not only contradicted the 'innocent until proven guilty' law, which already existed on the books, but was even worse than the alternative 'guilty until proven innocent' law of certain neighboring states, which so often had been criticized for their barbarity. Bongovian law was worse inasmuch as it didn't even allow the accused the ability to try to prove themselves innocent. It simply defined them as enemies of the state, and as such, undeserving of the right to a fair trial. But, as the authorities rationalized, in times of emergency, harsh temporary measures must be employed in order to guarantee the safety and liberty of the populace.

In this way, 'permanent' came to be called 'temporary,' and 'imprisonment' came to be called 'freedom.' One may find it well nigh impossible to believe that a civilized and well educated citizenry could swallow such a kind of topsy-turvy cart-before-the-horse arse-backward circular logic, but for the purposes of this story you may be well advised to suspend your disbelief. This, after all... is fiction.

Then there was the war.

The interminable war.

It required so much of Rigby Delaney's time. It was like a fire that mustn't go out. It must have fuel supplied at regular intervals, and be stoked constantly. It was absolutely crucial to maintain that flame, in order to motivate the population behind actions and expenditures, which could not otherwise be justified. Of course, there was always someone around to fight with if you really needed them. But it was more than simply getting into a fight. It had to be a just and honorable fight. It had to be an enemy who threatened the very nature of our culture... our lifestyle. An evil enemy. One who desired above all things to deprive us of our divinely inspired... sacred freedoms. One who thoughtlessly, illogically, just simply and wickedly did not want anyone to be happy. In total contravention of the teachings of The Great God Bongo, this evil and unrespected adversary did not want to let others live as they wanted, but wanted to control and intimidate others, and make them do as he wished. Make them worship *his* god. Make them as evil and crazy as *he* is. The bite of the Vampire will turn *you* into one.

It wasn't easy. Delaney soon discovered that people who have been so heavily conditioned to be reactionary don't have a very long attention span, and that means that they get bored with the same old demons and boogeymen very quickly. So, within the department of Communication, an ultra secret division which reported only to Rigby Delaney had to be created. These people were very clever at demonizing (admittedly) *already* dangerous and crazy people, and at provoking them into actions which could be categorized as being at war with the state of Bongovia. In fact— he suggested— let anyone who criticizes the nature of our just and fair society be rendered as disloyal, and sent to join the ranks of the enemy.

Surely some of these things were a help to him in his work, but as you can see, there was a huge amount that he had to be on top of all the time. Did Frederick Greaves really believe that he could be intimidated? If Rigby Delaney wasn't around to coordinate this beautiful construction— Rigby Delaney believed— it would all come tumbling down like a house of cards. There was no one else who knew all of its workings as he did. But Frederick Greaves knew something that Rigby Delaney didn't know. He knew that after a structure such as this is built, it takes on a life of its own. It becomes organic and no one can know all of its mysteries. And no one is indispensable. Frederick Greaves came from a class of people who had been the masters of their own destinies (and other's) for millennia. It wasn't important to them to know how a thing works. It was only important that it works... for them.

The white stone angel didn't *look* much like Mastroianni. Not like any of the ones Jason had met, so far anyway. It had wings and a beautiful placid face. It looked down from its brilliant marble pedestal, set amongst the palms and ferns of the roof garden Jason had built and nurtured all these years, atop the JCN Enterprises tower. He hadn't received a 'visitation' since he'd been in this world, and after all these years of their absence it was slowly dawning upon him that his previous confidence at business dealings, was in no small part dependent upon their regular occurrence. It was possible, he considered as he strolled now beside the goldfish pond, that he could no longer rely upon the changelessness of life as he had once known it. That the good fortune which had, in the old world, always lingered conveniently within his province, anticipating his slightest appetite, had somehow now slipped its leash. It seemed to have passed on in a way, that he was only now realizing, that things did. And yet for some reason, he wondered, could it be that losing his 'luck' might possibly be the best thing to have happened to him?

Rigby Delaney had called a little while ago. He had seemed coy and hesitant and couldn't seem to make up his mind as to why he was calling. He asked if Jason knew any good cold remedies at first, and then changed the subject to the new color scheme at the main Temple of Bongo in town; how well it complemented the gigantic portrait of Dominic Devine, (copied from the photograph on the book jacket – the only picture of him which existed) which was displayed upon the wall behind the rostrum. Jason conjectured that it was Delaney who was behind the attempt upon his life, although he knew nothing of the people to whom Delaney answered. Not even the fact of their existence. But he did seem to recall that it was at one of Delaney's little get-togethers that he first met that whore. No, he shouldn't say that. He'd felt something for her. She had a way – Marina, that was her name – of making him feel that she was affected by him. That he could educate her. Open her life to new meaning. She would become excited at small discoveries, and it had pleased him to see her so. Specially if he believed that he had led her to them. The nature of black holes... the prophesies of Nostradamus... the uncanny and persistent recurrence of the number nine when totaling the sum of any of its multiples. Maybe, just possibly, she hadn't known about what was going to happen. Maybe she had been as much of a dupe as he was intended to be. Maybe she was supposed to get killed as well, according to Delaney's plan. Jason, for one split second imagined his hands around Rigby Delaney's weasly little neck, his face turning purple through lack of oxygen, but then the image faded. No— he thought— she was in on it. And once he had made that decision, it distanced him from the emotion that he pretended not to feel for Delaney. But it allowed other perceptions to interfere with the sense of survival he so desperately needed right now. There was this other thing that was inserting itself where it wasn't wanted. Something was rubbing unsympathetically on his insides, chafing him sore, and he couldn't make out what it tasted like, what it smelled like, what it looked like. Oh yes, it looked like... Jocelyn, that's what it was. But what did *she* have to do with all of this?

No matter how hard he tried to superimpose what he felt about Marina upon Delaney, he just couldn't figure it. He couldn't picture Rigby Delaney in the role of some cheap whore who would seduce him and then try to murder him... actually, when he thought about it for a minute the description didn't sound so far off. But still... to actually kill someone you had grown so close to in so many ways. The difficulty was not so much in the reality of the situation as in what Jason was willing to accept. He couldn't understand his own hesitation in wanting to kill the man. After all, people kill each other every day. At this very moment someone is killing someone somewhere… whilst somewhere else – or even sometimes in the same place – someone is causing another to be born. Insemination. Ejaculation within the confines of a fertile playground. More than one in fact. The population increases. It's nature. Just like thoughts popping in and out of Bongo's head. It is each thought's responsibility to linger on for as long as it possibly can. But, he wondered, must that automatically include the elimination of another, or can the population increase?

He seated himself upon a white painted wrought iron garden bench and observed the goldfish as they scattered this way and that. Why had his mission failed? He wondered. And for the first time, suddenly, he was aware of acknowledging its failure. This idea made requisite the asking of various other questions. In what way did it fail? How did he know that it had in fact failed? What had he hoped to achieve in the first place? How much of it had been his own vision, and how much had been implanted by Rigby Delaney in order to further his own greedy ends? How subtle are the differences between success and failure? And is the human mind even capable of detecting such subtle differences?

Everything had always seemed so simple to him before. There was right and there was wrong. Why must it all seem so complicated now? He began to doubt the entire plan. Was it possible that organizing the population into such tightly controlled communities might not be the solution for the Human Condition? Maybe some undesirable effects were necessary to life. Maybe the elimination of crime had side effects which no one had anticipated. Maybe it was a valve which released certain pent up societal energies that could be dangerous, if not allowed to run somewhat free. Or… what if the criminal, for example, served some other sort of purpose in society? The receptacle of everyone's hatred, possibly. Without their existence, he wondered, where then would all that hatred go?

What about the impoverished and the disenfranchised, the disabled and the aged, the crazy and the sick, the stupid and the frightened and the weak? Once this procedure of elimination had begun, where could it possibly end? Who among us could not, at one time or another, be described by any or all of these terms? Who has never been criminal? Who has never been evil? Who is not sad and pathetic, at least some of the time? Maybe if all the sad and pathetic moments of our lives were eliminated, then our sympathy for each other would become unused, and it would atrophy and wither away until we had none left to give. Suddenly, sympathy seemed more to Jason Cyllabus Novedi than just a utilitarian device, necessary only to dispense to others who were in need. He thought of it now as a quality which possesses its own inherent beauty, within which there is a joy simply in the feeling. And Jocelyn's face, oddly enough, came to his mind − he didn't know why − but somehow it reinforced his new found conviction regarding the intrinsic worth of this particular sentiment. It was, he was beginning to realize, a way for us to connect with each other's pain. And that pain itself is a necessary and beautiful thing that we cannot... must not, do without. That loss is a tragic and wonderful experience which colors our story with the redolence of loneliness. That loneliness, itself, possesses that bitter tang which somehow tastes, all at once, sweet and musky and sour and salty. And that all these flavors and the beauty which they yield had never, in all his life, availed themselves to him, despite the many lonely years he'd known, because he'd simply been unable to acknowledge his loneliness.

And now that his mission was dissolving before his very eyes he found himself, somehow, relishing the sadness which that dissolution brings. Gone were the dreams whose rainbow arcs he'd followed so faithfully before, with their model towns and their blessed churches housing pure and absolute belief, the believers in their commonality giving endless love to one another and a tireless caring born of a perfect god. That was, it now occurred to him, not only a naive and impossible dream, but also, in all probability, an undesirable one.

Gone was the choking, controlling grip of the Prickly Bog Temple of Bongo. A church which he had started, based upon the ideas of a veritable 'John the Baptist' of a man named Dominic Devine, who had come before. Based upon the principles of decay and rebirth, which had so appealed to him when he was first introduced to them. Of nonjudgmentalism. Of tolerance and flexibility. Loss and grieving and pain were at the core of all change, it stated... and change is inevitable. Where had these ideas become perverted? He wondered. What would Mr. Devine – whose picture hung in grand state every Sunday morning above the bleating congregated flock – have thought about this nefarious shambles? He who had written in his holy scripture, "Create each moment anew, for no two situations will respond exactly to the same set of rules." He who had incanted, as the police dragged him manacled from the offices of a certain publishing house, namely the Popodell Publishing Company, "You don't have to believe what I believe, just believe that I believe it." How and when, Jason Cyllabus Novedi now wondered, did that turn into, "We must all believe the same thing?" For this is what appeared to have happened.

Was it *really* Rigby Delaney's doing? Or was Delaney (just like the criminals whose demise he had inadvertently strategized of late) merely acting out the darkest fantasies of the populace he beguiled? The Intergalactic Temple of Bongo was long established, and well in control now, but did that make its words the truth – even if everyone seemed to believe they were? Maybe so... but Jason thought that its truth was lodged on some rather flimsy foundations. And such a structure – even though it may never actually collapse... many such flimsy truths have persisted throughout the aeons – would quiver until perpetuity, its vibration announcing shamefacedly its guilty secret, like some ringing mark of Cain... the bell of Cain perhaps.

But even Cain and a bell cannot point a vocal finger at any given individual, for truth cannot be put to flight by one liar shouting in the wilderness. It takes a myriad liars pointing a myriad pealing tongues at reality to turn a falsehood into truth. And even worse than that, it takes one who lies to himself to believe another's truth without challenge, without doubt, without responsibility for all that belief implies.

So... who then was responsible? "You cannot con an honest man," came the resounding response. It did not justify Rigby Delaney or his actions, but it stopped just short of vilifying him above the horde of co-conspirators. It sought mainly to spread the blame, a little thinner perhaps, but over a wider net. It takes a village. By this same token then, Jason Cyllabus Novedi was also a guilty man, as — I suppose — are you and I. Let it not be said, however, that within these pages is encouraged participation in the popular version of the guilt sharing game, wherein the participants all console themselves with their mutual status and declare, "Hey, if I'm no worse than anyone else, then why the hell should I change?"

It is hard to say whether this kind of conformity is the cause or the product of competitive thinking, but one thing is for sure: if competition is the only motivation we can scrape together in order to accomplish or even establish our goals, then there is no wonder that we cannot abide solitude, or any form of introspective thought. Still, Mr. Novedi-slash-Lewis had encountered much of introspective thought in his time. After all, he felt alone most of the time anyway. Odd isn't it, that those who exist at a distance from society tend more often to be the ones who feel urged to take on the responsibility of changing it, of nurturing it, of helping it to grow... and sometimes, perhaps, of helping it to turn upon itself in a destructive manner.

But he was a man who could be the loneliest when he was with other people (the feeling of incongruity heightened in their proximity), and blissfully fulfilled when mantled in solitude. Alone, with the perfection of his thoughts. Their accord. Their ability to differ graciously. To agree to disagree. So much so, that sometimes he blocked out extraneous influence so that he would be unaware of the proximity of others. He was not aware, for instance, that at that very moment Rigby Delaney stood directly behind the bench upon which he was so innocently seated.

Delaney's small frame was partially obscured by large palm branches which swept across his meager chest. Within the humid atmosphere created by the mass of surrounding foliage, his watery eyed gaze was fixed unmovingly on the back of Jason's head. His thin white face was visible to whoever might look in that direction, with its pencil moustache and shock of black died pommade slicked hair. As were the shoulders of his dark widely spaced pinstriped suit, and finally (interrupted by some leaves and the image of a Jason Novedi seated thoughtfully upon a white painted wrought iron bench) the cuffs of his trousers, incompatibly, resting atop grey and silver running sneakers.

Jason leaned forward. He rested his elbows on his knees. His face upon his hands. He was thinking of his long and tortuous relationship with Rigby Delaney. It was the only one he had known. He must, therefore, be forgiven for being unaware that all such relationships possess a convoluted and meandering nature. That man, he realized, probably knew him better than anyone. If not because of their friendship, then at least because of the innate understanding of human psychology required by a confidence trickster. In the days right after they met, Rigby Delaney had fed him, clothed him, looked after him, and coached him in how to speak and act in public as befits a leader and a statesman. He had tried to guide Jason in his manner of dress, but he quickly realized that Jason possessed an innate flair for unusual but sophisticated attire which automatically gave him the look of a leader, the character of a prophet. One who has come to make the way clear. One who comes in answer to the prophesy of one who came before. An even greater one whose very word will become the fruition of all human potential.

There were many charming and endearing things about Rigby Delaney, not least of which was the way he looked. It was phony and overblown in such an obvious way that its very naiveté endeared him to Jason and many others who took the time to get to know him. He was funny and quick witted. His humor could be quite sharp and merciless but it always seemed that it was aimed at those who deserved its barbs. Yet he was discreet, and rarely allowed these musings to be revealed to anyone who might be offended. This facet may have been guided by a sympathy for other's feelings, but more likely was a pragmatic attempt to not create enemies. But his charm was inconsistent, and certain things about him could be off-putting, even to his own detriment. This was true in particular for those (Jason had once believed) who could not recognize his inner goodness.

Jason smiled now at his *own* naiveté. Inner goodness indeed! But it was not evil that guided Delaney, so much as a lack of understanding. There was the feeling that he would someday end up the victim of his own thoughtlessness. It seemed a shame. Jason felt sorry for him. It would be easy to forgive him almost anything because he seemed so pathetic in some way. As much as he controlled everything else, he didn't seem to be in control of himself. Still it would be hard to forgive someone trying to kill you. Even harder if they succeeded. If not impossible. Having had his life threatened in such a way had certainly frightened Jason Novedi, no matter how cavalierly he seemed to have dealt with the threat. But he still found it hard to believe that Delaney would have considered such a plan. Hard to believe, because he knew that somewhere in the deepest recesses of his mind Delaney had acknowledged their friendship, and still held it close to his heart, as a child will with a special gift.

Sure, he had threatened to kill Jason, but nobody ever took him seriously about these things. He was always so full of hot air. A true bullshit artist. Always threatening this and that, to kill somebody, or to kill himself because he just couldn't take it anymore. Then five minutes later he was back in charge and pushing everyone around again. As far as Jason knew, he had never actually been responsible for anyone dying before. Still... this latest thing had been scary, and he felt concerned enough – for the time being anyway – to want to stay the hell away from Rigby Delaney.

All the same, it made him laugh to think of the way Delaney interacted with people. He could seem so serious and self righteous about an issue one moment and then all of a sudden, right in the middle, pull out a completely self contradictory joke that would absolutely crack everyone up. He was a man who could be inconsiderate, and downright nasty sometimes, but then – let's face it – which of us is never so? He had a funny little walk, those tiny black shoes tap-tapping as he moved. Such peculiar little shoes. Round toed with no seams or ornament. Plain, and perfect in their plainness. Shined (again) to perfection and gleaming, as was the pocket watch whose chain straddled proudly the belly of his waistcoat. Fingernails manicured regularly, and outfit, the cartoonish (maybe even clownish) zoot-suit, ever pressed and tailored and brushed free of dust and lint, his trouser legs falling just so, in conformity with the distinctive step of those feet, whose smallness – even for a man of his considerably reduced size – was out of all proportion to the rest of him. And yet he covered ground faster than any long legged man Jason had ever seen.

No, Rigby Delaney was not a man who could ever stroll leisurely through a garden of roses, never mind actually take the time to smell one. He was obsessed by whatever it was that occupied him at that moment. And something always occupied him at all times. It sent a shiver up Jason's spine to think that it was his own untimely demise that seemed to be occupying Rigby Delaney's mind at that particular moment.

And it was at that particular moment that Jason Cyllabus Novedi looked down and noticed – not a small, round toed, perfectly polished black shoe (which he would have recognized immediately as Delaney's), but (and equally tiny) – a very contemporary looking, silver and grey, running sneaker, poking sneakily... sneaking, in fact, er... pokily... out of the bushes right behind his bench. The was a slight delay in his mind, a fractional silence, and then suddenly... he jumped out of his seat, holding tight to his heart and breathing like a steam pump with a faulty hose.

"Oh my *god*, Rigby!" he yelled. "You nearly gave me a fucking *heart attack*!" Delaney just stared at him with a contorted expression. "But then," he continued, "I suppose that would have made your job so much the easier." Delaney said nothing, but a slight wheezing sound was emanating from his lips. "Well?" Jason pressed, having regained his breath to some extent. "How are you going to do it, now that your plan to scare me witless didn't work? A bullet in the head? A knife in the back? Strangled by a rope with a knot in it? Push me off a cliff? Electrocute me in the bathtub? Tie me to the railroad tracks? Leave me in a car with the engine running? Poisoned steak and kidney pie? Bury me alive? Bore me to death by telling me over and over again the story of your life of iniquity and your subsequent conversion? Or... would you rather kill me with kindness, you lying, mother-fucking, cocksucking bastard?"

Now I'll admit it is indeed quite possible that Jason Cyllabus Novedi did not in actual fact manage to say all of these things in the time allotted – although it is somewhat likely that he was thinking them – because, as he stared at Rigby Delaney's face, he became aware that the man was not even listening to him. In fact, that wheezing sound emanating from his mouth had grown to quite a hiss. And eventually that hiss brought forth this single whispered word: "Invest…" And then a large amount of crimson fluid flowed out, following that word, hitting the pristine white wrought iron garden bench, splashing thence upwards in tiny droplets over Jason's lawn and flowers, and into Jason's field of vision, some of them coming to rest upon his lashes. And then that tiny body, whence sprang this stream of life stuff, slumped forward over the backrest of that white painted bench, revealing a large red hole in the back of his exclusively tailored, double breasted, black and white pinstriped jacket.

There was, after that, one more final gushing exhalation of blood and air, and then, alas, did poor Delaney breathe no more.

Chapter 14

I should have made Rigby Delaney a machine— thought
Dominic Devine— you know, like when Jason finds his dead body, there
could be a little red light flashing from inside the wound. Sort of the
way they did with 'The Terminator,' or 'Robo Cop'... or Mr. Data,
from 'Star Trek.' The anthropomorphosis of the machine; isn't that
what it's all about? It's as if we've needed Robots and Cyber-men, ever
since... well, ever since we had the huge automobile boom, in the
fifties... maybe longer. Maybe it was the industrial revolution that did it.
Steam power. Man-made power, that's the point, isn't it? It's what
makes us like... god. Anything that isn't organic at its root. Ha ha— his
accidental pun amused him— root... organic... but no, it's *us* were
trying to figure out, isn't it? By talking about the human mind in terms
of 'ram' and 'hard drive' we think that we can learn to understand
ourselves (at least as well as we can a computer, anyway). But if we could
actually create a computer that had consciousness, it would mean that we
had learned, somehow, to trace back to where consciousness comes
from. And if we could do that, then maybe... we could know who we
are.

Ah, but it's too late now to change a character. The book is
already written. Although, I suppose, since it hasn't been published yet,
it couldn't do any harm to play with certain... details. It would be
insignificant to the story really, but then, what would be the point? What
would I be saying? Am I trying to leave some way open for Rigby
Delaney to come back to life? Would this be one of those Death –
Rebirth – Transformational – Symbolic type of things – like 'Little Red
Riding Hood'? And even so, why a mechanical man? The 'Tin Man.'
The man with no heart. Or maybe he shouldn't be completely
mechanical. Does he need to be part human? You know, so that we can
identify with him. So that we know that he is really us, but corrupted...
yeah, that's right, us, but corrupted by technology. So that we're not
really, you know... to blame.

What are we feeling so guilty about? Are we ashamed of our
own progress? One step forward, two steps back. Okay so I might be

exaggerating, two steps forward and only one step back. There is definitely progress, but what a laborious process. It is possible that we are afraid of that mechanical monster within us who drives us ever forward. He is a severe taskmaster, but like that old wolf, or like Judas Iscariot, he's a necessary part of our biography, and not at all something to be ashamed of. But hell, never mind. Delaney's dead, and that's where he's going to stay. Too bad though. It's a shame that they didn't get to know him better... he's based upon such an interesting character.

Meantime I've got a different kettle of fish to fry.

That bum (who calls himself Henry Lewis) has created quite a situation for me. One that I find difficult to ignore. And now, after having had that long conversation with Marvin about it, I feel like I'm being forced to understand something about myself (finally, I suppose) that I've been avoiding for a long time. It's that... well, that *I'm* the only one who's responsible for my own inability to succeed. There are certain risks, it's true, which I have taken with my life. After all, I'm not a corporate type... or a factory worker for that matter. I've lived, basically, from day to day, seeding nothing away for myself. And, occasionally, from woman to woman, unwilling to make that permanent commitment. And yet my lack of commitment to external forces – relationships, nationality, occupation, cultural groups, etc., of which I'm actually proud because I see them all as limiting definers – although it grows stronger all the time, has not brought with it the subsequent and inversely proportionate gain in commitment toward myself, my success, my happiness. It makes me wonder whether one needs to trade something important (freedom for example) in order to gain something equally important (security maybe).

Or could it be that I've been merely building up a head of steam, so to speak, in order to get this thing off the ground? Could it be that the time is drawing near for me to seize my own future... and that these *crazy and magical events* – surrounding that awful man, Henry Lewis, who I had the bad sense to dream up out of whole cloth (or maybe from my own destiny) – well anyway, could it be that *they* are the harbinger of things to come? The proverbial 'kick in the pants' that I am needing, at this very moment in time when I am needing it.

I suppose that Marvin sees me as a bit of a useless bastard. He seems to get so much 'done.' At least the way *he* tells it. But no... I'd never thought of it that way before. I suppose it's just that I feel so anxious sometimes, you know, about my own involvement in things, that I don't clearly observe those around me in order to gain an insight into their feelings or attitudes. Not something a writer should admit, I suppose. I wonder if that is the mark of a successful writer – or a successful man for that matter – that he listens more than he speaks. Perhaps not.

But for me, and those others like me, who have the misfortune to be haunted by their doubts – not evolved enough to accept them entirely, not limited enough to deny their existence – what of us? What about me? Where do I fit into this interplay? What line do I tread? Where does my path lead? What signs do I follow? When am I allowed to rest the weight of my unknowingness, and upon what rock? Whom shall I trust? My devil... or my angel? My dark side... or my light? My forgivingness... or my condemnation? Is it enough just to ask the magic question, like some latter day Parcifal upon his quest (Whom serveth this Grail?) without knowing the answer? Is it enough just to remind myself of the truth, occasionally, without anchoring it to my memory? How can I let go of the need to do things that keep me so paralyzed... so unable? How can I begin to realize their needlessness and allow them to mutate into the things which I need to do? Why does time always invade my space and push me into the tiniest little sliver of a corner where my elbows bang against metal edges? Bang their funny bones, sending shivers of hysterical pain throughout my universe. Sometimes I can see why, in Marvin's eyes, I am nothing more than a fool. I am a fool. Every achievement of mine, what few there are, have been nothing more than the foolish luck of one who knows nothing. I admit it! I admit it! I effing admit it already!

But sometimes, something *has* to be done... just to get the ball rolling, if nothing else. Even a thing as seemingly simple as acknowledging one's own responsibility for a given situation, has to begin with a painful shove against apathy. I mean, it's not about total passivity, is it? It's not so much that the Universe will do it for you – you will have to do it for yourself – but there is a sort of partnership, inasmuch as you need to know the Universe... understand it... in order to appreciate where it will succumb to your investment, and conversely, where it will resist. You know, the path of least resistance. The Zen butcher who never needs to sharpen his knife because he knows the path through flesh so well that he never strikes bone. Unlike me. I'm striking bone all around (if you'll pardon the expression). My knife is getting really dull.

How dull is your knife, Rodney?

My knife is so dull that it couldn't cut through sh... well, never mind, it's dull enough.

Here! Did you ever give it a really good shove only to find that you'd ended up in the wrong hole? Well, then you know what I mean. Admittedly, sometimes the journey has its own appeal. Sometimes the journey becomes the destination. Sometimes the journey was in fact the destination all along... and you never realized it. But then again, who wants to end up stuck forever in the wrong hole?

And that is exactly where I seem to be. I feel like I've been ploughing away at that secondary hole for quite a good long while now. And, whereas it may have its own reward (all journeys can claim as much) and whereas each journey may indeed be necessary in its own way, there does come a time when one starts looking forward to bigger and better things. One does, in short, get rather fed up. And so the time has come for me to face up to that painful stab at my apathy, and to take that risk that I've been avoiding for so long. The time has come to either shit or pick my saggy arse up off of that porcelain convenience upon which I have rested my proverbial laurels for so long, and, in the words of the old negro spiritual (or was it a sneaker commercial)... simply, *do it!*

"The time has come," the walrus said, "the time has come, the time has come, the time has bloodywell come."

Dominic Devine pushed his bedcovers away. The clock beside his bed informed him that it was 10:55 am. It was not abnormal for him to rise at this time. His right hand fondled the penis, erect, beneath his flannel nightshirt and he considered momentarily where this action might lead him. Astray possibly. He reconsidered and released the member. Masturbation had been occupying too large a portion of his time of late and he wondered if it might be functioning as a distraction from the accomplishment of his necessary duties. Instead, he rolled over onto one side and reached the edge of the bed. A small accomplishment, perhaps. One foot reached down slowly until it rested, finally, upon a grey plastic slipper – the left half of a pair he had purchased for two dollars and seventeen cents about a year ago. They were cracking and discolored already, and had absorbed, permanently now, the odor of his feet. He blindly inserted first one toe, and then the others, lifting the slipper up to a visible level only to discover that it was in fact on the wrong foot.

Soon, however, he was shuffling in them – correctly situated left and right – across the stained and bubbled up linoleum kitchen floor. The steady sound of water running, echoed loudly enough from the toilet to accost his hearing several steps ahead of his actually reaching the bathroom. He lifted the top of the porcelain urn, made heavier by a stack of poetry and writers trade publications, a couple of well used and now useless emery boards, and the mustache scissors he no longer needed. He immersed, slightly, the tip of an index finger, and tapped the ball-cock which, having been acknowledged, deigned to rise with the rest of the late birds, and ceased immediately its night long nagging trickle. He replaced the top of the urn and lifted the plastic imitation wood toilet seat, and attended to his own nagging trickle, allowing it to patter, golden and hollow-sounding, upon the surface of the water in the bowl. The slightest strain brought puffs of wind chirruping and moaning from out of his rear. The feeling of emptiness— he thought— is a wonderful thing.

He sat at the table pouring black liquid – after its hissing had signaled completion upon the flames – from the tarnished metal percolator into a large ridged glass jam jar he had rescued from the recycling system years ago. Scalded milk from copper pan, and sliced Italian bread... toasted lightly... smeared with sweet brown aging banana and maple syrup, supplemented his wake up brew.

I should have made Rigby Delaney a machine— he thought as all those flavors blended upon his tongue... between his teeth— there could have been the most touching moment when he felt his very first human feeling. You know, tears flowing from his silicon lenses, and tears – as we all know – could rust the tin man in his tracks. It could happen just as he was about to murder Jason Novedi... and that one split second of hesitation – where he considers the meaning of life – would be his undoing, because Novedi would then seize the opportunity to remove the computer chip from a little door behind his ear, rendering him utterly useless. Utterly human... and useless.

But what am I saying? That being human is useless, and that you have to think like a purposeful machine in order to get anything done? Whatever happened to 'the journey'? Although, sometimes I think... we do think too much.

But no! That's not the problem. Delaney is a human. He has a very human inability to feel the things that need to be felt – not because he could not have been programmed in any other way – but because, indeed, some previous human had actively programmed him that way. Although, to be perfectly fair, perhaps it was not their intention to do so. Perhaps they simply knew not what they did. Jesus! Perhaps they themselves had been improperly programmed by their own previous human. And even though (according to the law) ignorance (of the law) is no defense... in my book it constitutes a pretty serious inability.

The truth, however, of this particular situation departs somewhat from that particular line of theorizing, and creates yet further complications to our plot, inasmuch, and to wit: Rigby Delaney had not actually been trying to kill Novedi! No, not at all. He was, in fact, trying to warn him... of something. "Invest," is what he'd said. But Novedi couldn't understand what he meant. This is funny — thought Dominic — whenever he's been told to invest before, he's been given precise instructions as to what to invest in. And the reader will be just as much in the dark as Novedi is. Their minds will travel back in time to that meeting with the shortest ever Mastroianni who appeared behind Mama Myrtle's tombstone. But they, like our hero, would of course be wrong, and just not understand what that warning meant. Rigby Delaney wasn't telling him to invest in anything.

Dominic Devine considered the similarities between himself and his protagonist.

I wonder if – on some subconscious level – I could also be misunderstanding a warning that has been sent, magically, through the ether... to me. Perhaps a little detective work is in order. Sometimes a great mystery, after it has been explained, is revealed to be nothing more than a common or garden everyday event. I used to consider myself quite a dab hand at those murder mysteries. Conan Doyle. Agatha Christie. John Dickson Carr. On many occasions did I deduce the killer, and often his method, some twenty or even thirty pages before the authors revelation. With Carr though, I must admit – as hard as I tried – it was less often... but then maybe that's exactly the problem. Maybe I'm just trying too hard to figure it out. You know, it occurs to me that the difference between Jason Novedi and me is that he never tried to figure anything out in his whole life, and everything seemed to work out fine for him. That is until he started to question things, analyze them, make judgments... that's when all his troubles began. Why couldn't he just leave it be? Things were going alright. He had everything he needed. Why get involved? Go with the flow. Maybe that ought to be the watchword for the day. Don't make waves. There are so many out there already. Me... on the other hand, I think about everything. Motivations. Consequences. Relativity... no wonder I never get anything bloody done.

Well that could be it, then... my warning, you know. Don't delay! He who hesitates is a useless arsehole. A lazy bones. A card carrying good-for-nothing. Time waster. Bone idle. Without any definable purpose. Going nowhere. Achieving nothing. A total Doolittle who will most likely come to a sad and meaningless end.

Loser!

There is only one thing for it then. I must go where my fate beckons me. (Drags me kicking and screaming – more like!) But no, if I were to just stop resisting... and let it happen... then there can be only one future for me. Why must I see it as a crazy idea? It could work. It's really very simple. People always see the simple ideas that other people succeeded with, and then think to themselves— why didn't *I* do that? It's just one afternoon... and then it will be all over. I will be renowned. The price? I would gladly pay it if ... if I could be *sure* that this would work. But *can* I be sure... No! Don't do that! You see! Always thinking! *Stop* that thinking! Look to the goal... but what if somebody gets hurt? What if I get... Nobody's going to get hurt! *Idiot*! Just stick to the script. Later on you'll explain how it was all a publicity stunt. Look! You'll say, "look at this gun... it's a toy. No bullets. I wouldn't hurt a fly. Couldn't! Couldn't possibly hurt anyone... aside, of course, from those who have been very close to me, those whom I purported to love, who owed me no attrition, who had done me no harm and had, in fact, blessed me with their many kindnesses... and how did I repay them?"

But!

There is no one now who answers to that description. I come alone. Unable to do damage. I cannot hurt... and, of course, by that time they'll all have a copy of the book. And, having read it, cover to cover, they will know. They will know me. Me! Humanist. Philosopher. Vegetarian. I wouldn't hurt a chicken! And they will want to know more. There'll be interviews, I'm sure of it, and articles. A biography? Possibly. Fan club? Fan magazines. "Dominic Devine in prison. A martyr for his art." An 'Artyr,' perhaps. "Mr. Devine, is it true that the only color socks you have worn since you reached puberty, was pink? How does prison food fit in with your strict vegetarian diet? Are you allowed writing materials? When will the next book be out?" I could organize the inmates, battling bravely for their rights. Prison reform. Group therapy. Royalties could pay for a reform center for ex-cons... or the homeless... battered wives... unwanted pets. We could grow our own vegetables... organic (roots), in our own backyard. We could turn abandoned urban slums into a beautiful garden. A paradise. *God!* — he took several deep breaths— how my name shall be revered. Who else will have accomplished so much? And it could all start with this simple step.

He noticed there was about a half an inch of roach sitting idly in his ashtray at the far corner of the table. He slid the ashtray towards himself, lifted the tiny spliff deftly between thumb and forefinger, and was heading for the stove to obtain fire, when the clack of his mailbox, and the flutter of envelopes falling on the hallway mat, distracted him from his purpose, and demanded his most immediate attention.

The trouble is— he thought, as he veered his course and shuffled his feet, in those grey plastic things out towards the origin of these new sounds— I don't know *who* I should stick up. I mean, I've sent so many letters to different publishers, I wouldn't know which one to choose. I must make the right decision. Don't rush this. It might take a while to decide.

Fantastic! More delay tactics. Certainly he could spend the rest of his life evaluating which was the perfect publisher to go and threaten with a gun. I mean, it's an important decision, isn't it? If he delayed it long enough he could arrange it so that he never actually got to do anything, while at the same time convincing himself that he was hard at work on his project, and doing all that could possibly be done.

Oh yes, this could take forever. Decisions, decisions – failing, of course, a sign from God – and those kind of things only happen in the movies... or in novels, we all know that. But he should have known, he should have known. Strange events were taking place... and this was real life. Because there it was. There, right under the telephone bill and the bounced check notice from the bank. He could see the address and logo printed in the upper left hand corner of the envelope:

Popodell Publishing Company
317 Northcroft Ave.
Little Hurst, 2853-10

Chapter 15

"What am I?" they all chanted.

"You are what you are!" the priest asserted.

"What am I?" as one voice they inquired.

"You are what you have always been!"

"What am I?"

"You are what you will always be!"

"How did I become what I am?"

"By water!"

"How do I become what I am?"

"By air!"

"How will I become what I am?"

"By fire!"

It was only the second funeral that Jason Cyllabus Novedi had ever been to. This one was somewhat better attended than the first. In fact a huge throng of mourners had managed to pack themselves through the gigantic front portals like a host of surrendering sardines by the time he arrived. "Intergalactic" by name... intergalactic by nature, the temple had been a mammoth undertaking to construct, and it stood there now a monument... a cathedral (literally), not so much to the Great God for whom it was named, but to the need in its congregants for belonging. More immense than any other physical thing in their lives, it symbolized, commensurately, that which was of highest importance to their emotional survival. Friends, family, fellowship. All the effs.

The entrance was a great square archway set into the towering facade of the structure, a simple monolithic design of an almost colorless grey. The Intergalactic Temple of the Great God Bongo seemed almost carved out of the surface of the colorless grey sky behind it. There were no statues or carvings or decoration of any kind, to mar its perfect symmetry, which spoke eloquently of an unvarnished truth; an immense and structural truth. Unlike those curlicued and gargoyled flying buttressed monstrosities of yore, this establishment could stand on its own two feet. It needed no outside help. Its walls were six feet thick. Its doors were always open... both of them. In fact, it was not possible to close them. They bore no hinges. They had been permanently affixed to the walls and the floor in an open position. They were heavy and black and studded with thick brass diamonds, whose design feigned function, and eschewed the pattern which was its only object. But there was one purpose which they achieved with a stunning efficiency: staying open. They would never close. Not ever. No sir. Not never.

The multitude who now squeezed themselves over that threshold could witness most of the glorious interior from any vantage. Again, the height and simplicity, and the same invisible grey matter of which the outside walls were composed. No transepts, no nave, no small chapels built off to the side. Just a thin stained glass meridian encircled the very top of a simple but imposing and perfectly oblong basilica, and provided a dull golden glow from above, onto the tops of the walls – whose height was in the same ratio to their length, as their length was to the sum of the two, and whose width was in the same ratio, again, to its height. Perfectly oblong, that is, but with one exception. At the back wall, behind the huge and theatrical altar, a concave (when viewed from within) semicircular indent employed a central location amidst that surface, to house a massive three dimensional representation of the deity. A "steel" sculpture ironically dominated by the geometry of the "golden" ratio. Two spheres which intersected each other's centers, and a pyramid whose triangles were projected following the same math. The two heads of the Great God Bongo possessing the communal – and magical – third eye.

Just below that, but still above the altar, hung a huge painting. It was the largest portrait of Dominic Divine in creation. A strange portrait; an exact duplicate (though greatly enlarged) of the photograph found originally on the dust jacket of his novel, "The High Priest of Prickly Bog." It was the type of photograph that professional photographers take for publicity purposes, knowing nothing, or very little about their subject. The type of photograph which represents its subject in a way that they have never actually looked. It was, in short, a head shot. The head slightly angled down and to the left, but eyes focussed directly at the camera lens. The shoulders held high behind the head, in the suggestion of a shrug. A slight curling upward of the lips on the near side, but not enough to be considered a smirk. Hair coifed into a style it was obviously uncomfortable with. Black turtleneck gave a clean and serious appearance, which Dominic Divine had never previously enjoyed. But to be fair, at least they had refrained from the tweed jacket with leather elbow patches cliché, and the nut wood pipe cliché, and the seated before a library bookshelf cliché, which were typical of the traditional 'literary' author head shot. Mind you, in his jail cell, where the photograph had been taken, we must remember that, even though somehow a hairdresser was acquired, options were otherwise limited.

The point to be reiterated, however, in case it hasn't been made clear enough, is this: the picture didn't look anything like Dominic Divine. Not at all. Not the slightest bit. It was not a well known fact, but there had actually been instances, when he was alive, that even personal acquaintances had inadvertently picked up copies of his book... from a discount rack admittedly, scanned the jacket, glanced at the photograph and assumed half consciously that it must be some other Dominic Divine whose book they had just replaced upon the shelf. So it must be of some interest then, that now... here... in this "Intergalactic Temple," where all these thousands of people "literally" worshiped at the feet of his head shot, as if he were almost a god, *almost...* that these people would never have even the vaguest idea of what he actually looked like, how his voice sounded, his speech mannerisms, how he walked, how he scowled when he was angry, how he picked his nose, farted, masturbated... or what kind of a bastard he could be, when he was being a bastard. And one might respond that those things don't really matter in any substantial way. If we read a man's writing we get to understand his soul, and therein lies the truth behind the things that we believe about him.

So then it may be of even greater interest to discover that the vast majority of these people, assembled here within these temple walls, had never even read "The High Priest of Prickly Bog," but preferred, instead, to rely upon the interpretations of the truths revealed within its covers, as bestowed upon them by the founders of their persuasion; namely one Rigby Delaney and one Jason Cyllabus Novedi. And now this funeral represented the reduction of these choices by one. But still, who's to say that Mr. Novedi's interpretations were not faithful to the spirit of Mr. Devine's teachings? Or, for that matter, that they were not even more truthful than that which was originally recorded within that scripture?

The odds of faithful interpretation, as anyone who ever played the "telephone" game can attest, are low. Also known as the whispering game, it has to do with the transfer of information from one, to the other, to the other, and down the line. If each generation does not actually deteriorate the information, it does, at the very least, alter it. Let us hope then, that in the final analysis, our second theory – the one suggesting that greater truth can be achieved through the use of interpretation – is correct.

"My friend... Rigby Delaney," said Jason Cyllabus Novedi, "is dead." The pungent smell of Frankincense pervaded the heavy atmosphere. His arms gestured eloquently before their eyes. No matter how many times he'd quoted Antony's reluctant and self effacing concession, he knew how to hold them in the palm of his hand. But still he demurred, for the breathing... and the moment. "In the few years since this temple has been in existence," he played it down, "some small number of our flock have departed our society this same way. And yet... you have not seen me here, presiding... in such a capacity, on any previous occasion.

"Certainly no disrespect for those who have passed this way was intended, or ever felt. But rather, it was the proof of the belief I hold so earnestly within myself, that death is no 'thing,' as such, but just one way in which we... witness, the change... the natural change, which all existence must meet in every passing instant. And inasmuch as death, when compared with almost any other change, can cause the greater grief, can provoke more stabbing pain... it is, however, a quantitative rather than a qualitative difference. And in some ways, perhaps, it is not the death so much, but the loss... the bleakness and permanence of it, which stabs at the heart so desperately and wrings the tear-filled lament from out a deeper place.

"But be of joy my brothers and sisters, for I bring you good news. My friend... my brother... Rigby Delaney, along with all of those who have gone before, is not dead... are not dead. I know – I contradict myself. But I tell you, as long as the subsidy which they have built into our society exists, as long as there is a place within our hearts for them forever... then forever... will they live... in our hearts. For most certainly, within this small nation of ours, a bond has been created. A bond of such great permanence, that it can outlast even death. A bond formed of the very fabric of the essence of the nature of that which is reality. And we shall call this substance... 'love.' I speak not of that trifling emotion with which schoolgirls infatuate themselves, nor even the deep and abiding devotion of a parent for a child. But I submit now

– for lack of any better word in my vocabulary, and in order to describe the very glue which holds our universe together – the word 'love'."

He took, now, a deep breath and surveyed his congregation. They stretched hundreds of feet back into the distance, to where a flood of undiluted daylight was gushing in at the foot of the temple, above their heads, and through the open archway, rendering a hazy viewpoint from his location. "In our world... in our life," his voice intoned, " I believe that there is a separation between things, which is only right and proper, as we require dualities and divisions to help us define and categorize. But sometimes, it is in our nature to consider that very separation, that... pulling apart, as evil, and the bringing together of things... as good; hatred and love. And, whereas these emotions do not in themselves define a universal truth – for they are just the illusions into which we immerse ourselves from time to time – they do, however, supply a clue as to the nature of that other thing to which I presently designate the appellation, 'love.'

"I say again, there is a place, outside of these realities within which we have confined ourselves; where we are not known by our separateness, for there is no separation. And 'knowing' is a different thing altogether than the thing we understand it to be. There is a place, I tell you, outside of time and space, where all things come together, and are together, and will always be together. And that place, even though it is not here, is ever close at hand. So close is it, in fact, that a mere thought can provoke it to envelope our consciousness. And that thought, I humbly offer you... is best described by a term, recklessly used throughout the centuries, which yet maintains its power in all its simplicity. The word... my friends, my brothers, my sisters, my children... is 'love'."

Silence rung thickly in the emptiness above their heads. On some level they must have understood the meaning of his words, if not necessarily on a conscious one. And similarly, perhaps even *he* could not necessarily (on a conscious level) comprehend the subtlety of the concepts to which he referred. But then reality is such a fickle thing, filled with loopholes and metaphor. With each metaphor bouncing off another one, each symbol off another symbol, reverberating and stirring up such a fuss as to seem a solid and definable whole. Whilst, all along, its liquidity keeps us bobbing and weaving tentatively through the serpentine path of its constant variations.

"But then why— you may well ask— have I come here today? And I shall answer that, despite all these things I have said to you, Rigby Delaney…" he waited until the resonance of that name amongst those high grey walls had diminished to a whisper within the minds of his listeners, "… is dead. And I have come here to tell you why."

Maybe it was the way his voice took an edge as he spoke those last words. Maybe it was the look in his eye. Maybe there had been clues coming for a long time now which a blind man, five miles away, turned in the opposite direction, could have seen quite clearly. Or maybe it was simply that they all, who were still his congregation, remember, at that very moment entered with him, for just a split second, that place where all things do actually come together. Whatever it was, each one of them realized, at that moment, that all this was about to end. Somehow they knew that Bongovia itself had not long to endure. That the Intergalactic Temple had run its course. That J.C.N. Enterprises was about to collapse. That its surviving founder, Jason Cyllabus Novedi was about to go away and disappear from their lives forever, permanently, and never return… not ever. Not never. That their lives, in short, were about to fall apart.

Her feet slipped into shabby sandals as Fritz D'Orion snored in the other room. They were the best she owned, and it was going to be warm again today – she knew it somehow – and the rings on her toes ached for self expression, little crowns on little piggies gasping for air…

needing to shine. Who doesn't? And the air today was thick with ominous clouds of protoplasm, and by nightfall a hard rain was sure to have washed away the husks of the corporal. She could feel its proverbial flood licking her piggies now. It tickled, and it threatened, as tickles often do. And, as tickles often do, it pleased whilst carrying the seeds of displeasure.

She'd heard (or seen) it somewhere, she'd told her father last night – Okay! Okay! She knew exactly where... on the radio of her nineteen-fifty-seven ™Chevrolet Bel Air. On that show, you know, with the two idiots. Cox... and Wolfgang Von Whatzisface – that Mr. Novedi, yes him, the actual High Priest (hah!) was going to be appearing, in person, live, at the 'Temple' today. "Get therr errly ferra goood seat," the Scotsman had advertised. And that is exactly why she was slipping into sandals, sneaking down the stairs, silently turning the backdoor key, on her way to meet a man from the believer trade. Her motor revved distantly causing a flutter in her father's sleeping eye, and then she was gone, heading for an appointment with inevitability, the consequence of all deeds. And in her mind thoughts of her future, and her present, and her past, flickered in technicolor precision across a mental canvass, evoking memories... yes, and tears. Memories not frequently recalled. Memories of death. Memories of loss. But not of love – she was, in the end, 'the last remaining virgin' – she could not remember ever being loved. And yet a child – not loved either... not born, even, but lost, somehow – had been conceived, somehow, within the last remaining virgin... how? Conceived and lost. The magical child, not ever made manifest. The mystical miscreation of a love unconsummated. Nonexistent, in fact. It plagued her and haunted her, that god damned foetus. She'd been so young. She'd had to deal with it alone. She'd had to dispose of it alone. No family, no friends... her father? Fritz? She did tell Fritz. He was pretty drunk at the time. He'd grunted some kind of acknowledgment, and on a more sober occasion had asked her if she'd taken care of that... 'thing,' and nodded at her affirmation. But he'd never mentioned it again. Never.

Ah yes, it was hot out, but the wind whipped at her beneath an open top and cooled her with the same rough hand which had always consoled her trials. She dreamed to be free of her secrets, of her ghosts, and she was drawn, in rejection of her every instinct, toward a temple of worship. A place, she'd always believed, where the promise of a brighter future was dangled enticingly before the glazed eyes of the easy marks, to distract them from the hand which probed the pocket. But she went, despite the risk, despite the danger, or maybe because of it – she'd met this man, you see, and she believed (as believers often do) that she could trust his intentions. She knew him (she thought) in some special way. She knew his secrets (she believed) as no one else did. And just the image of him, dusty and barefoot and totally defenseless, wandering deserted terrains, made her think that she might easily bare her soul to him, and he would not judge her. She believed also (as believers very often do) that she might, as a result of all this soul-baring, be accepted, somehow, into the bosom of the divine (whatever that means) or, at the very least, come to a place of self acceptance.

And yet in no way would she have admitted (even to herself) that she could ever entertain these thoughts which proliferated within her fancy, as she parked her car, as she entered silently the steadily filling temple, as she took her seat along with a multitude of others, to wait and watch as the High Priest of Prickly Bog delivered his final sermon.

"Rigby Delaney was my friend," he continued, "my closest friend, for fourteen years." (Rigby Delaney was his only friend, ever.) "Without him, none of this would have been possible. This... temple, this... nation of Bongovia, these beliefs which we hold so dear.

"And so it is hard for me now to question whether the thing that he made possible for me... for us, all of us... is really the same thing that I had intended in the first place. Of course, nothing ever goes exactly to plan, but when you find yourself facing south, and your intention was to travel north, well... perhaps it seems ungrateful to speculate so, upon the passing of a friend... and perhaps it is true that I may well not have been clear about exactly what I did want, at the beginning. But the achievement of early goals has, for me, brought much of our final purpose into greater focus. And if mistakes were made, then let them be toward the betterment of our understanding. Because mistakes have most definitely been made.

"My mistake was to allow others to carry my burden for me. Out of fear, perhaps – or just plain laziness – I entrusted to the hands of Rigby Delaney the day to day management of an organization which he couldn't possibly understand how to run... at least, not according to *my* standards. I say this fully admitting that, if run according to my standards, this enterprise may never have succeeded in the way that it has. But then my standards have *never* rated success by *that* measure. Had I never gained one single follower, but simply lived my life in the way that I believed... would I not have truly achieved the greatest of all possible successes?

"But it is possible that I had no confidence in my own judgment, and I allowed myself to be seduced by a dream of something more glorious, than realistic. I, as most of you have also done, allowed my dream to be sidetracked by the rolling mechanical monster of propaganda, which convinced me to discard my tolerance and follow in the secure footsteps of an unthinking but powerful majority. I have not been a leader. I have led you only where you were already going." He waited until the coughing died down.

"And why, you may ask, have I done this?

"Because, I suppose, it was easier than doing the hard work which true leadership entails. Easier, perhaps, than taking responsibility for my own actions. Easier... than owning up to my own failures." The crowd began to murmur slightly. Legs were crossed and uncrossed. Adults began to fidget like children. The children, noticing this, sat up and began to pay attention.

"What's this? You say. Why is he talking this way? We have the greatest nation ever. We have found the truth. Equality. Freedom. The Great God Bongo would never let us down. We are the perfect success story.

"You want to know what I say?

"I say that we are like ostriches!" He noticed his voice had taken on a strained and condemning tone. But he liked it, so he continued in that manner, "with our heads buried up our... our heads buried in the sand... believing in the illusion of stability, believing in the illusion of our own invulnerability... while inches away a lion sits, licking its lips, deciding which part of us to eat tonight.

"And yet, unlike that lion, who sees this stupid bird, with it's head stuck in the ground, and takes a big bite out of it's arse, knowing simply, that it is his nature and his need to do so, *we*... cannot face the violence within ourselves. And so we must always find an excuse, or a *scapegoat*, on whom to blame our dirty deeds. And then we hang *that* poor bastard as if *he* were the guilty one!"

This time, an actual gasp was expelled by several of those gathered therein, who then (after gasping) all held their breath, collectively. They were not used to *this* High Priest. He had changed, they thought, since his withdrawal from the pulpit several years ago. He'd been so much easier to revere in his absence. But they were, of course, wrong. He had not changed... much. He had simply learned to speak the truth. The problem was...

"The problem is," he continued, "nobody really wants to hear the truth. They just want to be reinforced about what they already believe. We all do it for each other. It's a sort of mutual masturbation!"

Before they even let out a breath, this time, they had sucked it back. Sucked back the same stale air, and held it tightly within their lungs. Like the same stale thoughts they held tightly behind their throats. Thoughts of anger, and jealousy, and the dangers which encircled their cosmos at every living moment... and the separateness they felt which induced them to cling together, the way they do, knowing that they cannot ever be close enough.

"But there is a place..." his voice had regained its composure, "where all things come together. It does not deny the place where there is duality and separation. These two places can coexist within us, if we can create the space for them, if we can open our hearts, if we can open our minds.

"We haven't done this yet. We have listened *only* to those who would tell us what we wanted to hear. We have been victims, yes... but we have been victims of our own dishonesty. We have been robbed... but we have been complicit in our own mugging. We have been sold a bill of goods, we have been suckered, conned, bamboozled, flimflammed, led up the garden path... we have, my brothers and sisters... been betrayed!

"You see, it is not freedom to have the choice between eighteen different colors of the same flavor. It is not the truth just because you see the same view of reality from a hundred different sources on your hypnotism box. It is not democracy when you vote for the same man wearing three different suits. Rigby Delaney bought and payed for each of those suits. And Rigby Delaney's suit was bought and paid for by his masters... as was mine. There was no honorable motivation behind our government's policies. There was only profit. They made it seem as though *we* would be the ones to profit. And so we went along. Well... you can't cheat an honest man... but a greedy one is putty in a swindler's hands. We didn't care who the endless war destroyed, as long as we were convinced that our safety and comfort were ensured. And it comforted us to be told that a great good was being exported in our name. And when we found others hating us, it made it easier to accept if we believed it was because they were simply evil, simply stupid, simply crazy... and ungrateful for all the wonderful things we've done for them. I tell you, my brothers and sisters, it is *we* who have been stupid, crazy, and ungrateful. And our actions have been responsible for as much evil as anyone we might criticize.

"But still we cannot see it!

"Why can we not see it?

"Because to see it is to admit our own blindness!"

He stopped dead.

He slowly scanned the gathered throng. They attended him, a sea of blank expressions glowing dimly in the gloom. Unsure, uncomfortable, and unable to understand... why was he saying all of these awful things.

"Rigby Delaney," he stated it for sure, "was a crook!"

They gasped.

"Yes he was!"

They gasped again.

He pointed upwards and sort of shrugged his shoulders, "A petty crook, really... and fairly harmless, I suppose... if we hadn't all been sustaining him in his misdemeanors. But a lot of damage can result from some simple lies. And his crime was not so different from ours. He, like us, just did not consider the consequences of his actions. Sometimes I think we commit our legacies of turbulence and destruction to the wind without so much as the blink of an eyelash. We elect those leaders who promise us a better life, with little concern for the suffering their policies may inflict in some foreign place. As long as our garbage is removed, we ask ourselves, why should *we* care where it goes? If the energy we consume results in the contamination of future generations... why is it *our* job to look out for others?

"And these may well be valid questions to ask, but questions often have answers. And we may grin like idiots who think they know the answers, but all the while our acid feelings, and the products of our constant waste, seep into the universe encircling it with a toxic aura which must eventually come back to haunt us. We must live, in short, in the world which we have created.

"And so, this message I wanted to deliver – which has become, over the years, so lost in politics, and the need to control others; which, I believe, was the original message of Dominic Divine – was really quite simple: Do not feel guilt about those things which cannot be changed, and you may find that you will become able to distinguish those things which can. Do not try to change the world for others, they must make their own mistakes. Help them only when they call for your assistance. In this way you change your own world more dramatically than you could have imagined. Our generosity returns us greater rewards than our small mindedness and our bigotry. Yes, there is risk in generosity, but there is no such thing as 'no risk.' Without risk we have stagnation, wherein lies a much greater danger waiting to explode. And when it does... well, the Great God Bongo does not help those who don't help themselves.

"This is how Rigby Delaney employed our assistance to corrupt this society. For we pretended to ourselves that we were blameless of any iniquity, and some of us..." Jason's gaze, as it swept the room weighed heavily upon the eyes it trapped, and made them sink in defeat, in denial, in resentment, of their invaded sanctuary, of their discovered complicity, "some of us... are still pretending. Rigby Delaney believed in that old aphorism 'you can't con an honest man,' and all he had to do was talk to any of us, at any time, to be reinforced in that belief. I will admit, for my part, my own dishonesty and move along.

"But he went one step further, you see. In order to carry out his plans, he involved men of power who were more honest in their deception than you or I. Men who may be almost... admired, for their singularity of purpose. They do not feel guilt – or so they claim – for the things they do. They convince themselves that their kind of order is in our best interest, and they will stop at nothing to achieve their goals. Once they were involved it didn't matter what Rigby Delaney's original intention was, he had already sold his authority away. They were more dangerous than he could ever have imagined. More so than even *we* can imagine. Because, you see, if they were to have their way, even the small freedoms you have left today would be removed. These miserable lives of self-imposed slavery, which I see now define the character of Bongovia, would no longer be *self*-imposed.

"Perhaps that would be a good thing, because then you would no longer be able to deny it. It would be forced to your attention." He gazed blankly about the room for a second, wondering if he were saying the right thing, but then he continued. "However... no one wants *that* to happen. The point is this..." and, as he spoke, he saw her sitting there. Jocelyn. Yes, the one he'd been trying not to think about but couldn't stop thinking about. Whose strange and unacceptable beauty had touched him in a place he hadn't realized existed. Whose innocent bedevilment had poked and prodded at his 'level of discomfort.' Whose knowing smile had kindly understood him in a way that hurt and caressed at the same time. What the fuck was she doing there? Right there in the third row. She'd been there, in front of his face, the whole time. How could he have not noticed her until now?

She looked straight up at him displaying a cryptic Mona Lisa smile. He began to speak again, still watching her, as she watched him... watching her. "The point is this. Rigby Delaney, just before he died, gave me a clue as to who his murderer was. The very last word he said before he died in my arms was— invest!" But in his watching her watching him, what Jason Cyllabus Novedi failed to notice was the dark suited gentleman with heavy shades who walked up the central aisle towards the podium. Yes, the same one who pulled a 'forty-four'

^{TM}Magnum out of his jacket, pointed it at Mr. Novedi, and let fly five leaden missiles in his direction – the first two of which imbedded themselves, with a splintery cacophony, into the heavy wooden podium before him, leaving the third, fourth and fifth to, more accurately, enter his chest. He also failed to notice how that very same man then fled back down that very same aisle, waving that very same 'forty-four' ^{TM}Magnum in front of him, which miraculously parted the throng of worshippers, who had clogged his egress, like ^{TM}Moses parting the ^{TM}Red Sea. The same man who ran down the temple's front steps and disappeared into the awaiting black limousine, which swished silently away, unhindered and unmolested by the more than adequate security and police force which surrounded the building.

No one inside had moved, except of course for the one woman who now bent hysterically over the prostrate body. Jocelyn saw rivers of life leaking in thick dark torrents across the altar floor. Everyone else remained in dumbfounded stillness where they sat. Eyes staring with shock, perhaps less from the shooting than the speech which preceded it. They were not sure, at this moment, whether they approved or disapproved of this action taken. Either way, out of subconscious complicity, or... out of fear, no one chased or tried to stop the assassin.

Let us look down on them from above for a moment, as if we were indeed the Great God Bongo nesting in the eaves at the pinnacle of that magnificent cathedral. We see them – first one, and then a few more – slowly... silently vacate their seats, as if they had been choreographed, by some divine power, to do so. They file in dribs and drabs up toward the altar, where those more forward ascend its majestic trinity of steps and gather around the body of their fallen priest, whilst others stare on from the level below, feeling (perhaps) more comfortable in this position, their hats held respectfully in two hands clasped together. The denial of emotions already starting to solidify within the memory. The mythologysm of truth taking seed upon the wings of the angel which martyrdom creates. It would be easy now to forget that last speech. It would be easy now to remember him as he had always been. It would be easy, also, to remember Rigby Delaney that way now, as they had always thought of him: the right hand of the savior. And these two – Novedi and Delaney – might be finally released to go and join the spirit of Dominic Devine, somewhere up there in the ether, and create the new Holy Trinity of the Intergalactic Temple of the Great God Bongo. A faith which, contrary to the most recent supposition of its founder, one Jason Cyllabus Novedi, is destined to continue for a thousand years, growing ever stronger, firm in the knowledge of that which is rigidly and oppressively right and true – despite the fact that it never actually happened. And the six foot thick colorless grey slab sides of that building where this myth began, proclaimed proudly, without even words, their commitment to the myth, the whole myth, and nothing but the myth, so help me Bongo.

Chapter 16

"It says exactly the same thing! I mean... exactly! Word for word!" He showed Marvin the two letters, "except of course for the most important thing. Look!" He pointed at the dates. "The date they want me to call them on, is one week later than in the first letter."

"That's good," said Marvin, he was flicking through the channels on his remote.

"No! It's *not* good," Dominic emphasized by slapping the letter. "This new date was still three days *before* I got this letter."

"Oh yeah..." Marvin didn't seem terrifically interested in the whole story at this point, his eyes reflected silent daytime soaps. "So call it anyway."

"I did," whined Dominic. The number was disconnected just like the last time. I was going to call this regular number again, but I didn't want to have to talk to that stupid receptionist who answered before." He clenched his fists in unconscious mimicry of 'Yosemite Sam' who flashed momentarily across the T.V. screen. "Ooh, it makes me so exasperated, I wish there was something I could do!"

"There's always something you can do," said Marvin, "but you've got to stop wishing... and start doing." The remote landed on the coffee table with a disgusted 'thunk,' and it's owner retreated to behind the kitchen counter.

The remark stung like a jab in the ribs. There were times when he really resented Marvin – but then Dominic was a man who was easily manipulated (and motivated) by his own resentment and guilt. These manipulations, however, had never led him to a place of satisfaction. He had not discovered, as yet, a method by which he could foresee the inability of his actions to satisfy, and therefore, preemptively choose an alternative course.

He fiddled with a scrap of paper in his hands which he'd been twisting and untwisting for some time now. "Can you get me a gun?" he said suddenly, loudly trying to overpower the mechanical grinding sound which had, just that moment, begun to issue from the direction of the kitchen.

Marvin ceased thrusting carrots through a small plastic funnel, and clicked off the juicing machine. "Huh-huh-huh," he almost laughed. He turned his drooping head deliberately in the direction of Dominic Devine. "And who d'you wanna shoot?" He smiled. "Not me, I hope."

Dominic sat on a hill. The days were getting warmer now, and the first buds appeared on the leafless trees. In town, all the snow had melted, but out here, away from the hectic friction of people and machines, slim white patches of winter's fading spirit still drained slowly, as they warmed, into the profane and thirsty earth.

Below him and to the left, a small river wound intriguing silver threads through clumps of dry and rugged foliage. Here and there its sparked reflections were synchronous with the chirps and rattles and barks of woodland creatures who greeted one another, or warned off predators, or chose simply to express their individuality.

A wisp of cloud provided the deliberate flaw in an otherwise perfectly open sky, but the sun, like a gleaming, round, yellow robot, chased behind it, biting snippets from its lazy tail. It did not protest, but gracefully gave itself up for consumption. There would be more clouds tomorrow. They were welling just beyond the day's horizon, and as always, time would ensure a balance of all things throughout infinity. But for right now, in this place, there lived a blue, blue sky undaunted by future or past, secure within its moment. Dominic could have learned from its self confidence, but instead he reveled in sentimentality, recalling another hill... on a tiny tropical island, atop which he had sat when he was a much much younger man, escaping from his older sister and her entourage of friends, whose company had been forced upon him in order that he be allowed to travel with them to that place. And as he thought of the past, his hand unconsciously searched his pockets for the cigarettes which would have been there that day, but from which he had long since abstained. As if, in his mind, the polluting, addictive smoke somehow complemented the green and freshly awakening countryside. His fingers touched the missing cardboard box where it would have been located, but finding (as solace) only cold, hard, deadly metal, retreated quickly in their failure, back out into the chilly air.

His arms consoled each other by crossing to hug his body,

warming him behind themselves, and protecting him from the unsympathetic judgment of the dawning season. Spring, he thought, should have brought him to a rebirth of thinking. Spring should have guided him away from the stagnation of the past. And that is exactly what he believed it was doing. But, he was wrong, yet again, and in fact these thoughts he conceived were connected to the past by a stale and pungent twine.

That cocksucking bastard! Who does he think he is anyway? It's not as if *he's* some big success in life. You know what? I should never have told him anything about my personal shit! He's not a good friend when it comes to being supportive. Whenever I have a problem, he just ridicules me in that smirky, smug way he has of talking. You know, like he knows everything... like he's just perfect. That's why I hate to ask him for anything. Like money, for instance. He makes a lot of it... well, more than me anyway. So what? Okay, okay, so he's lent me some cash once in a while, but he knows I'd do the same for him... if I had any cash. Anyway, what makes him so superior? Dealing drugs isn't exactly something to be proud of, is it? But meantime, he looks down on *me*!

I know the work I do may not be great literature or anything, but shit... it's supposed to help people feel good about themselves. Yeah, I know, drugs do that as well, but... you know what I mean, in a constructive, lasting sort of way. I really believe that in my own little way I could make a difference. The problem with Marvin is that he doesn't even care whether he makes a difference or not. I mean, I'm trying to be creative by offering up some deeper part of myself. He, on the other hand, is just keeping it all for himself.

Okay, so I haven't got my novel published... yet, but shit, at least I wrote one. Completed it, from beginning to end. Do you know how much time and commitment that takes? I think that *that's* an achievement. I mean how many people could actually write a novel? Okay, millions of people have. But, you know what I mean... what percentage of people? Right? Probably pretty low. Anyway, *I* think it's an achievement. It's easy to criticize, isn't it? But I'd like to see Marvin write a book. Fuck, I'd like to see him *read* a book. Oh sure, he's got shelves full of them; all about psychology, and Sufi mysticism and shit. I've looked at some of those books. They're mostly full of pictures anyway, with superficial little captions underneath… which he quotes endlessly, as if they were products of his own great wisdom. Or maybe he gets his witty little aphorisms from the fortune cookies at that disgustingly greasy little Chinese place he loves to frequent… or from those "somebody done somebody wrong" songs he listens to on the country station… I don't know. Is that what I'm doing? Am I singing one of those songs myself? Am I just looking for somebody to blame so I don't have to admit to my own inadequacies?

Or do I just need a fuck?

And at that moment, for some strange reason, his mind drifted to thoughts of Marvin's girlfriend, Marie. And as it did, two things seemed to happen to him simultaneously.

1) His heart seemed to soften, and…

b) His body seemed to harden – not in that way! (I know how your mind works.) It hardened with rage.

That's what I'm talking about. It's as if all the anger in his spirit, in one fell swoop, decided to transmigrate into his physical form. I don't know why it did that. All I know is that he wanted her, and he couldn't have her. And what's more, he blamed Marvin for the fact that he couldn't have her. Which was rather silly, when you consider the nature of that particular couple's relationship. They were, ostensibly at least, not jealous of each other's dalliances, and so… theoretically, Marie would have been perfectly free to fuck Dominic's brains out, if she felt like it. Almost as if he were bragging, Marvin had told him, a million times— We don't have to own each other. We don't have to limit each other. We're separate human beings with separate lives. Jealousies are such petty things.

Well, Dominic didn't really want to hear all that bullshit. Because, in that case, who *else* was she fucking? It certainly wasn't him. And it just made him even more resentful, even more insecure, because, when you think about it, it really meant that Marie didn't have the slightest interest in Dominic Devine. But, of course, that made him want her even more. It made him want to hold her tightly. It made him want to rub himself up against her body. Put his hand up underneath her skirt and in between her legs. Spread her thighs apart, and shove his cock inside her glorious wanton cunt. Man, he was horny!

Being horny was the least of his problems – he could jerk off right there on the top of that hill, if he wanted, and take care of that – but he was a lot of other things too. He was frustrated, for one thing, and not only in a sexual way. His whole being was frustrated. His whole being couldn't get what it wanted to get. It couldn't see what it wanted to see. Couldn't hear what it wanted to hear. Feel what it wanted to feel. Fuck what it wanted to fuck. It couldn't be what it wanted to be, dammit!

But so what?

So here he was, sitting on a hill, with a piece of metal substituting for a cigarette pack, in his pocket, thinking about sex, and friendship, and books, and... murder. And down there in the valley, a single melting drip of brownish water fell from the underside of a flat piece of pockmarked ice, down there where the light was strange and filtered, where traces of mud and grit and acid discolored the porous white surface, like venial sins (they had taught us as children) discolor the perfect surface of the innocent soul.

And it dripped down into a crack in the earth.

And it traveled down deep where it was moist.

And it joined, down there, with a river of its brethren, who washed over worms and roots and rocks, and mingled resolutely with a stream of conscious water bleeding kindly where they ran and played and slept for fortune had embarrassed their possessive souls despite incessant diff-er-en-ces was not buried nor coerced in anyway except for safety's sake – for saving grace – for saving face it always unto one an-other was believ'd a sep'rate thing and never could remember where it started in the firstest place by getting lost and then resuming getting lost and then returning getting lost, getting lost, getting lost...

Fuck! Where was I?

Oh yes! Now I remember.

So here he is, sitting on a hill, and he pulls this gun out of his pocket. He examines the several chambers. There are bullets in there. Five of them, alright? Real. Live ones.

Chapter 17

Universes were spinning in and out of focus.

Spinning one way for a time, until they teetered deliberately to an intemporal halt followed, without suspension of activity or motivation, by an immediate reversal of direction, and then accelerated at an equally measured pace until they'd gathered enough momentum to be considered spinning once more. Meanwhile, outer universal rings spun counterpoints of color, speed and direction, and inner ones pulsated on and off, energies leaping quantumly from one to another. Ghostly figures evolved from their midst, pointing warnings, extending invitations, beckoning him forward, and simultaneously rejecting his advances.

The angels, the angels... where are you now? How have you abandoned me in my moment of death? Are you gone? Do your wings no longer shield me from this fiery storm? Have I not attended to your bidding without complaint or challenge? Have I not yet been sacrificed enough? Will you not bring me now to my final home? To join with the everlasting sea, a wave... a crest... a grain of foam upon that infinite liquid pasture. Home, back to the fold where I belong. How this sad shell hath ser-ved thee I cannot know... and neither would I.

Jason Cyllabus Novedi did not see his entire life flashing before his eyes.

For his life... was not his life, but something that someone had once written in a novel somewhere a long time ago when he had had another life. *His* life. His *real* life.

He reached out for his real life now, and a garden began to grow up around him. His garden, where angels lived, white marble ones, just like the ones in the book he'd read, which was about his life. Just like the copies he'd had made. Copies of the ones he saw now, which were so similar in every detail, that *these* ones seemed like the copies to him now. But even these angels were not real. Not human flesh, nor divine substance… no, not even marble sculpted into form. And these trees too, and these bushes, and these flowers… like the inner rings of spinning universes, pulsated on and off, came and went, becoming alternately real… and then spectral… and then real again.

Once again he experienced that moment – whilst thinking that he had been brought back to the reality of his own life, where it had all started – that very moment… when Mastroianni had clapped his wings and sent me flying through time and space to god-knows-where. And there I was spending years and years, fourteen years altogether… but no, that didn't really happen, it was just a dream, just a fantasy. I am here, still here, in my garden. I was taking a stroll, and then I felt weary. I sat on this bench to rest, and I must have dozed off. I am forty years old, not fifty four, and I have done nothing, achieved nothing, I have been nowhere. The garden is my home. It is where I want to be. Where I have always wanted to be. Safe and warm and comfortable. Unthreatened and unthreatening. Oh Auntie Em! There's no place like… Holy shit! What the fuck is this?

These holes in my chest!

How did they get there?

Oh yes. I remember now.

And then…

It was as if a giant hand from space, had landed with eerie grace… upon his shoulder, and whipped him back out of there.

Suddenly, all the trees were disappearing, and the bushes and the flowers, and that little pond with those ridiculously expensive Japanese goldfish (half of which froze to death in the winter time), and his little white wrought iron garden bench, the copy of which Rigby Delaney's body had slumped over in his final (and possibly finest) moment. But the original of the copy of all these things, the reality... his real life – which had disappeared fourteen years ago, and then started to reappear just a minute ago right after three leaden missiles had burrowed themselves (totally uninvited) into his chest – was now disappearing again.

Honestly! It was all a bit too much!

Although, what replaced it was no consolation prize. Meaning, of course, that it was just as good, if not better, than what was presently disappearing. Yes, there were those condoning white veneer walls, and there were rubber tubes filled with blood and plasma flowing this way and that out of large glass jars, inverted and suspended from chrome covered frames. And yes, there were these three holes in his chest, enshrouded in bandages, more bandages... and yet more bandages. And also yes, there were the strains of vapid muzak washing thinly through the crackling, uninspired sound system lodged in the contradiction of an acoustically tiled ceiling. And even one more yes, a moving, jumping line of techno light described and monitored his unstable heartbeat for all the world to see upon an otherwise perfectly black oscilloscope screen.

But something else was also there, which made it all worthwhile.

Someone else was there who made it all worthwhile.

She smiled down upon him from her transcendental position above his head, looking for all the world like the last living virgin... and cried too, a silent stream worming softly down her cheek to a place where it formed a little lake, and then just seemed to dissipate into her pores, like the end of the Nile evaporating into desert air. Hmm... the Virgin of the Nile. It did not fall, that tear, and land upon his sheet, but it... evolved, somehow, some part of it recycling back into the body whence it came, and the remaining part acquired a spectral presence, only to reemerge someday in physical form as a... cloud, or a dew drop... or, perhaps, an ice cube in somebody's scotch and soda.

"How long have you been here?" his voice creaked through parchment lips.

"That's a funny question!" Jocelyn sniffed a little as she spoke. "Most people in your position would ask how long *they* had been here, not..."

He tried to push himself up on his elbows, looking cautiously around the room. There was what appeared to be a glass of water situated on the bedside table, a swinging affair, positioned temporarily so as to be out of his way. He reached for the glass across what seemed an interminable divide. She got there first and transported it the remaining distance to his hand.

"Why?" he asked. "How many people have you personally witnessed in this situation?" He took a sip of the water and looked at the glass oddly. "I hope no one's been soaking their dentures in here overnight."

Jocelyn took the glass from him and replaced it where it had been. "You know what I mean," she responded, turning her face away from him slightly, and then quickly turning it back, as if she might have given something away. "Anyway, let's have no more stupid discussions now. How do you feel? I'm sure you don't have enough energy..."

"I agree," he interrupted, lightly touching her hand, as it rested beside her on the edge of the bed where she sat. "Let's not... but what do you mean— I don't have enough energy? Energy for what?"

"For stupid discussions," she said, "come now... rest," and she put her finger to his lips.

"Alright, alright," he mumbled in submissive acceptance, as he allowed her to help him back down onto the pillow. "I feel awful anyway." He was gripping her hand tightly now. "Just tell me one thing... did they get him?" But she just stared uncomfortably into his eyes for several long moments without saying anything.

"Never mind," he said. Jason knew the answer. "It doesn't really matter. The person who hired him to do it is more important, anyway."

She began to speak, but he stopped her with a scolding forefinger. "Listen… these people are very dangerous, and you have got to be very careful…" he hesitated a brief moment, "in fact, I think you should leave here right now, and do not come back."

"Oh, shut up!" she said.

"I mean it!"

"This is like a scene in a grade B movie," she replied. He wondered aloud how she knew what a grade B movie was. "It's just an expression! What difference does it make?"

He stopped and took a deep breath. "Look, I know it sounds terribly clichéd, but it's the simple logic of the situation. Somebody is trying to kill me, and therefore being around me is a dangerous place to be."

"Life is a dangerous place to be, but if you don't want me to…" said Jocelyn.

"And I love it that you feel that way." Seeing the quizzical look in her eyes, he added, "I really do, nonetheless… oh, by the way," he tilted his head in apparent consideration of the possibilities, "is there a cop outside this door?"

"Two."

"Good. Although, why that should make me feel any safer, I have no idea. Nonetheless…" he waited until she met his look, "I must tell you that I can't stand people who get all paranoid at the drop of a hat, who think that every situation is an invitation for a major accident to happen. You know, the type who think that if something *can* go wrong, it *will*… and you're just the opposite, you're so brave, you make me feel great, just being here… really, I – I really appreciate having you near…" he looked down at her hand, and touched it more softly now.

She felt something well up inside her. "You do?" she asked, completely without agenda for once.

"Yes, I do... and I don't want to lose you to some overpaid hit-man."

"I would never leave you for a hit-man," she said, gathering herself, "no matter how much money he made."

"You wouldn't?" he asked, his wide open eyes seemingly mimicking her authenticity.

"Shut up!" she said, unsure as to whether she should be embarrassed or not.

Feigning wounded indignation, he stressed, "I mean it!" She softened again for a moment until, that is, he pushed his luck by adding, "Shrew!"

"Bozo!" she said.

"Listen, could you do me a favor?" His face remained impassive, but somehow it could not repress entirely the tension held within."

"Well?" she asked.

"Could you get the doctor in here right away with another dose of whatever pain killer I'm on, 'cause this is starting to hurt like a motherfucker all of a sudden!" He looked down at his own chest.

"Oh!" she stammered a quick acknowledgment, and hastily got up, backing her way to the door. Opening it, she called to the policemen posted outside. They were lounging several feet away, with their backs to her, engaged in what appeared to be a humorous conversation.

"Excuse me," she bleated.

For an instant, one of them caught a glimpse of her out of the side of his eye, but he seemed unconcerned and returned immediately to his conversation. She took one more step, out into the hallway, so that she was forced to hold the door ajar with the heel of her outstretched leg.

"Excuse me!" she demanded, more assertively (if somewhat anxiously) this time.

It seemed to do the trick. They both stopped talking, although, as they turned to face her, neither attempted to hide the aggravation he felt at this interruption. This response, of course, infuriated Jocelyn, who still lived in that imaginary world where things ought to be the way that they ought to be. At times like these, she sometimes became distracted from her original goal, and set about correcting the formality of the situation. "Look! Are you two supposed to be on duty here... or not?"

They just stared at her for a few moments before one of them – the slightly less Simian looking one – finally spoke. "Can we be of some assistance to you ma'am?"

She placed her hands on her hips, and her feet in a firm, shoulder-width position, causing her to allow the door to creak slowly to a close behind her. She faced the policeman squarely as he approached her, and looked him straight in the eye. "Yes," she said. "I would like for you to go and call a doctor immediately. Mr. Novedi is in Pain."

He momentarily raised his eyebrows and let them sink again. "It is not my duty, ma'am, to go call a doctor," he answered pugnaciously. "My duty is to guard this door and to make sure that no unauthorized person goes into Mr. Novedi's room." At this point he made quite a show of looking her up and down before he continued. "Family member, ma'am?"

"What?"

"Are... you... a... family... member... ma'am?"

"Yes," she replied quickly. "I am Mr. Novedi's wife!"

Clearly taken aback, he snorted, "Excuse me, Mrs. Novedi, I..."

"D'Orion," she corrected. "Ms. D'Orion! I do not believe that women should have to give up their own name just because they get married."

"Excuse me, Ms... D'Orion, I was unaware that Mr. Nov... ahem, that your er... husband had taken a... I mean, that he was marri..."

But by this time she had already turned and marched back into the room, and he stood there looking at the door shut in his face. She must have supposed that if she left him without the ability to refuse, he would have to go do it, or at least cajole his cohort into doing it. On the other hand, if he wouldn't, it wasn't worth spending much more time with him, and she felt the need to get back in there and check on Jason. And not a minute too soon, as it happened, she caught him struggling out of his bed to clutch and push a red button hanging from a wire, typically located just out of the patient's reach.

"Get back in bed!" she snapped, like a head nurse would. But it was too late. He was already back lying down, and she wasn't sure she liked the way his eyes were rolling around in their sockets from the pain. "Look," she confided, unsure if he was able to pay attention at this moment, "You're going to have to tell them that I'm your wife, or they may not allow..." For a second his pain seemed to subside and he stared at her in amazement, "I – I had to tell them something, I..."

"No, no," he whispered, "I like that." And then his eyes started rolling again.

She put her hand behind his head and held it up a little. "I know that this is very difficult for you... er, in your present condition, but you're just going to have to stay lucid long enough to vouch for me. None of these people can be trusted to guard you." She pulled him up into a sitting position by his arms and held him like a baby. His eyes gazed up at her. "You suggested yourself that you couldn't even trust the policemen outside your door." She looked him straight in the face now, and noticed that his body was shaking uncontrollably. Her voice softened slightly. "You do trust me, don't you?"

He acknowledged her now, by lifting his hand to her cheek, and smiling. "Yes," he said.

"Well you *can*," she added matter-of-factly. And then she thought for a moment, "Is there anyone else who you trust? Someone I can contact? Someone who will help?"

"Yes," he whispered, "Mastroianni."

"But... where will I find him?"

"In the garden..." and he pointed toward a set of keys lying with a pile of his belongings on top of a dresser on the other side of the room. She let him back down, and went over to pick them up. "On the roof," he added hoarsely.

But before she could get any more out of him, the door burst open, and a short fat man, with the appearance (and costume) of a doctor, stormed into the room, followed by a tall and rather skeletal looking nurse.

"Who are you?" asked the doctor, rather harshly, "and what are you doing here?" The nurse looked on menacingly over his shoulder.

"I – I'm... Mrs... Novedi," Jocelyn nervously declared. The cop, who was now standing at the door, took notice.

"No you're not!" said the doctor. "Nurse Bettle! The medication!"

Jocelyn looked harshly at the doctor. "How dare you..." and she turned toward Jason, who muttered something incomprehensible. The nurse now produced a big syringe, and pointing it skyward, she squirted a tiny amount of liquid from the top. She handed it then to her master who, having concluded the preparation of Jason's arm, administered the medication.

"What is that you're giving him?" demanded Jocelyn.

Jason slumped into unconsciousness. The doctor turned his head toward Jocelyn as he absent-mindedly handed the syringe back to Nurse Bettle. "Not that it's any of your business – but it's a simple pain killer."

"A simple pain killer?" she repeated. "Then why did he lose consciousness?"

"Because he is tired," said the doctor.

"Tired? Don't be ridiculous! That drug just knocked him out!"

The doctor looked past her to the door. "Officer, would you remove this... er, person."

The policeman smiled.

Universes did not spin, and the garden where he sat was most definitely a dream. It was all loose and wobbly, the way dreams get sometimes, like a waterbed. But he was stuck here, for the time being, at least, and – as usual – there was not a hell of a lot he could do about it.

She, on the other hand, sat in a garden of sharp edges and thorn bushes. This one was real alright, just like life is (shaboom, shaboom). As real, at any rate, as a garden can be when it's sitting on the roof of a building. The second highest building in Prickly Bog, to be exact. After all the recent goings on – and without Rigby Delaney there to manage it – the Temple Headquarters was in total chaos, and people moved around it anarchically without questioning one another. So it had been a simple task for her to slip unnoticed up to the penthouse, and to ensconce herself within it and avail herself of its grounds. So here she sat alone upon a bench inside a roof garden which had been, for Jason Cyllabus Novedi, the only real thing left in his life – and there is something to be said for hard reality. It can be reassuring to know that certain things are reasonably consistent, even if they are the figments of one's own imagination. Consistency, of course, is a relative term, and that which appears to be consistent, when viewed from a wider angle, quickly dissolves into randomness. But then, that randomness, when viewed from an even wider angle, is seen to be part of a much larger pattern, which of course eventually breaks down into randomness as the viewpoint widens once again. Where this process ends, no one knows, and it is always possible that if we could see a big enough picture we might realize that there is in fact no process after all.

The white painted metal had been wrought into spirals and curlicues, which evoked foliage, rather than resembling it. The blood had been washed away from under that bench, and purity framed the summer dress she wore, ablaze with printed birds of paradise, and even more exotic flora, where parrots and macaws nestled, hidden behind tropical leaves. Yet in this authentic copy of a summer garden, where she sat, more temperate climes decreed its nature, and roses bloomed about the fish pond, and larches and weeping willows tickled the stone white angel when the wind moved them to brush his naked flanks.

How could she know that he was nothing but a facsimile of the one for whom she waited? The spit and image of his soul, which has no image and looks like nothing, least of all a block of white marble. What contradiction, marble wings. How could you fly, with such a weight? What contradiction, a cold hard soul. How could you feel, when so brittle and unbending? That creaking crunching noise behind her, was that his stone head turning to watch her more carefully? How could she know just how long she would have to wait for god knows who? How could she know, for sure, if this were even the right garden?

The angel Mastroianni had never been here. Only his image… and that looked nothing like him. Although, to be quite fair, his image had changed so frequently in the past that it would be practically impossible to imagine. In that case, one image is as good as another. And, as there was no sign of him in actuality, then perhaps, Jocelyn conjectured, it was his image that she should seek. And at that very moment of realization, as so often occurs, another realization came to her… that a sound had been quietly, but incessantly, puncturing the almost clandestine stillness of this Olympian retreat. As if silence itself was something to be feared, a place of defenselessness, where any sudden report could destroy what has been so painstakingly cultivated. And that dry, creaking, crunching noise of stone sliding on stone, eventually drew her attention back from her thoughts of love, and loss, and golden fishes swimming beneath reflections of the sky, and the clouds... and the silhouettes of the trees. Back to the craven marble. Back to the image of the imageless one. She turned to see what had been moving, and there was no one there. But it did seem to her that the stone angel was facing a particularly odd direction. Not clearly one way or the other – wouldn't it be better if he were facing the open area at the center of the garden, where the fish pond was located? Yes— she thought. Then his open angel wings would be aligned with the two paths converging from either side. As it was he seemed to be gazing down at nothing – well... a bush, actually. The one behind the bench, in fact.

But then, a different sound distracted her from this line of thought. Three chimes of a pleasingly mellow-toned bell emanated from some other part of the garden, and she was drawn, immediately, off in search of its location, as if she had been charmed away by its mellifluous voice. She followed a curving path which led in the direction of the source of the chimes, and she came, presently, upon a small clock tower, perhaps not more than ten feet high. It seemed to represent a steeple from a church, and all the facets, including the clock and, of course, the church bell, were there in generous miniature. There was a small door at the bottom, and several windows up the sides of the tower, indicating that the original structure, whose representation Jocelyn now confronted, would in reality, have risen seven or eight stories in height. There were even tiny gargoyles and statues embellishing the sides of the steeple, in a depiction of some sort of fable or myth. And, as she slowly circumnavigated the structure, she began to feel that she somehow recognized the story which was unveiling itself to her. She knew that she'd heard it somewhere, recently. It was indeed the story which Jason had recounted to her that day they sat beside the chicken coop on her father's farm. It was the story of his life. And there depicted quite clearly, in varyingly tiny statues, were the many Mastroiannis who had appeared to Henry Lewis, before he came to reside in this world. And it occurred to her that not one of them looked like an angel. Ah yes, Mastroianni – she remembered. And she hurried back to the site of the pure white marble seraphim.

She walked around him, observing him closely. She wondered if there was an opening into the statue, or a secret button or lever. She tapped upon his side with her car keys, but he was solid enough. She knocked upon the metal plynth with her knuckles. It rang hollow, but yet there appeared to be no opening. In fact... there *was* no opening. She walked around the statue again, slowly, as if she was paying it no attention (she knew that sometimes a peripheral viewpoint will discover subtleties of a kind which no amount of blunt focus can reveal) and she tried to take heed of the slightest inconsistencies which troubled her sense of satisfactory order. One such of these inconsistencies, she was reminded, was the apparently incorrect position of the statue upon its perch, and she found it hard to ignore the feeling that it should not be so placed. Time and again her gaze returned to his face looking doltishly down upon, of all things, a bush. Time and again she refocussed upon her search for clues, but there was something about this irritating angle which made her want to be in the place where his vision fell.

Finally she could stand it no longer, and she stepped in behind the white wrought iron garden bench, pushing her way through shrubs, and treading bushes and flowers underfoot, eventually crawling on hands and knees in the mud in order to align her eyes with the gaze of the angel. That was when she bumped her head on something caught amongst the twigs, something which should not have been there in the first place. It was a book. A book, in fact, which every *other* person who lived in Prickly Bog would have been instantly familiar with. But a book, nonetheless, which Jocelyn had never encountered. It was just about six inches in height, of a pleasing rectangularity, covered in rich red leather, with gilt edged pages and a silk ribbon for a page marker. Upon its front surface, embossed also with a gilt finish, was the triangle and two circles of the now familiar icon, and the title read, "The Catechism of the Intergalactic Temple of the Great God Bongo." So it was a prayer book then, she at first concluded, or at least it was, if one could judge a book by its cover. On second thoughts, it had always seemed obvious to her that one could not. And she was not wrong to suspect the obvious, because when she opened the book to look inside, she discovered that it was not, in fact, the catechism which it purported to be at all. It was, instead, a note book with blank lined pages, the first six of which had been inscribed by, what seemed to be, a fussy and meticulous handwriting.

The title in the middle of the first page was clear and capitalized. It read:

List of
INVESTORS TO JCN ENTERPRISES

The following six pages were filled with a series of numbers which looked to Jocelyn like some kind of an account of monied transactions. Each page was headed with, what she assumed to be, the name of an investor. These were the names:

Fredrick Greaves.

Vikram Chatterjee.

Anton Lebovsky.

Al Pomodoro.

Gustav Trondheim.

Tadashi Nakagawa.

Now, she had known a Freddy Greaves once. They had gone to school together in 83052. There was an unpleasant memory associated with him, which she couldn't quite bring herself to recollect. He was a year or two older than she, but she seemed to remember that he'd been held back because of low grades, and that by her last year she'd caught up with him and they'd spent time in the same class together... if only for that one year. But he was from a privileged background, and did not care (she suspected) to be seen in the company of such as she. Although he had dated one of her friends, Rebecca, a few times, and on one rare occasion they had, along with a bunch of friends, gone out to dinner together. It was faintly possible that Jocelyn had spent some time with Freddy alone, but only in private and hidden places. And, as we all know, that which is not recorded... never happened. And she could not, therefore, ever remember it happening.

She wondered if this could be the same boy. Of course he wouldn't be a boy any longer, but not all that old either, late twenties or so – like her, no... early thirties perhaps. Came from a wealthy family. Had a nice flashy car when he was sixteen. He wasn't such a bad type, she recalled – not the typical spoiled brat. But she didn't recall why she felt that. She remembered having had a little fantasy about him, but not that anything ever came of it. She blushed as if she still were that same innocent teenage virgin. It felt wonderful to have no past and nothing but a bright pure clean future ahead. When sexuality was just a thought (had it ever really been?). She was not a prude, Fritz had considered no subject taboo when she was growing up. She had known everything there was to know about sex... except, of course, what it feels like. And that changes everything, doesn't it? And if the desire for that particular frame of reference had not, as yet, thrust itself painfully between her self and her next action, then it had, at least, peeped in through her windows on occasion... rang her doorbell, perhaps, and run away like the cowardly little bastard that it was.

Fantasies? Well, for her at any rate, they were characterless. It's hard to know if this is normal (whatever that means), or a particular psychopathy brought on by some traumatic incident in her childhood. It was not young Freddy Greaves she lusted for, but an image of a body, which may, or may not have been anything like his in reality. An ethereal body of some kind, patterns of light beamed through color tinted celluloid. Not a real connected movement, but the simple belief that what you do not see continues on in the spaces between the things that you do. The wedding veil of reality, so to speak. The cloudy lens of romanticism. Now, whether this unreality of emotion is a natural thing or whether she had on some subconscious level not allowed the penetration of the memory of reality, is besides the point. Whatever the reason, time had passed, and Jocelyn had somehow not consummated the maturity of her femininity, regardless of what had actually happened. And she saw it as simply a matter of what is (or what isn't, as the case may be).

But Jason Cyllabus Novedi, on the other hand, not looking his best, admittedly, when she first met him (or since, for that matter)... punctured her bubble of subconscious sexuality, and prompted a revolution of sorts. Maybe it was something as simple as pheromones, or maybe − to rephrase that old saw − when the libido is ready, the pheromones will appear. But some part of her had suddenly started to understand a desire for a specific intimacy of a type of which she had been heretofore unaware. True, some other part of her denied it vehemently, and that only served to reinforce the impression that it was the same denial which she had been living under all along. But there is a difference between those two denials (if not qualitative, then at least, quantitative − insomuch as her earlier denial seemed to have been insurmountable, whereas the recent one was for her a more easily hurdled obstacle) judging, anyway, by her newly found loyalty to this relative stranger... and possibly even her (allegedly) pragmatic (though possibly Freudian) pretense of marriage to Mr. Novedi.

No, let's face it, something was, most definitely flowering within

Jocelyn D'Orion. And why is it so often the case that when such a gift is received, it is accompanied by the loss of the very thing whose removal renders the gift meaningless... a gift of the Magi. But she would not allow this gift to be taken away from her. She would fight to preserve it. Maybe that was how she knew that she really wanted it this time. The proof of one's motivation for change, she believed, could be evaluated by one's commitment toward the action necessary to accomplish it. Others, however, believed that only the accomplishment itself could be taken as proof. By this token, simply to take arms for one's beliefs does not in itself imply the desire for their fulfillment. Only the thing itself is its own proof.

Must we wait, then, before we trust her resolve, for our heroine to succeed in her endeavor, and reclaim the lover who would otherwise be lost through inaction? There is no substitute for winning... or losing. All else is merely in between.

Chapter 18

"Stick 'em up!"

It was like a scene from a gangster movie. It was an obvious pose. Nobody with even half a brain would be intimidated by that.

"You are a bad man!" Dominic spat the words out at his reflection. "You are a baaad man!" And then one more time, like a goat. "You are a ba-a-a-a-d man."

Oh forget it— he thought, as he slumped down onto his bed— I'm not such an idiot that I don't know when I'm fooling myself. This whole thing just isn't me at all. I'm not aggressive enough... of course I don't have to actually *be* aggressive, I simply have to *act* aggressive... I mean aggressive-*ly*. Let's face it, no one has ever achieved anything by remaining within the limitations of their own narrow definition of themself. After all, being successful is also not really *me* (strictly speaking), but we live in the hope that a change could occur, eh? Well okay, changes don't just occur, do they? Someone always has to initiate them... to make them happen. So maybe this gangster thing is just not me... yet.

"Stick 'em up!" He had swung violently around toward the mirror, and stood now motionless, a caricature of a poster of a villainous hero.

Can't be a *real* villain— he thought— the writer must be empathized with in some way, or they'll never read the book. A villain, but a hero. A cultural hero who stands up against the villainy of the establishment. I mean, I can't be seen as Adolph Hitler, can I? Who reads "Mein Kampf" these days? other than young 'Aryans,' of course, and there's not really enough of them to hit the bestseller list. A lot of Italian boys, incidentally... who are no more Aryan than my arse... well, actually my arse is, in fact, Aryan. But, you know what I mean, not blonde and blue eyed. No, the more eastern... swarthy type. I'd be killed immediately – if only for my personality. Ha! That's a joke. No, no, I mustn't be seen to have the type of personality that would make you want to kill me. They have to like me. They must empathize with the author... or else, all of this is to no avail.

But, despite his own apprehensions about himself, Dominic Devine *could* easily be empathized with. In many ways he was a loser, and all people have had their moment of loss. And misery, as we know so well, loves company. The paradox is that no true villain can actually be a loser. Once they have been toppled, they seem so pathetic, and therefore so much less villainous. More like us, I suppose. And if we empathize with them, we might start to understand their motivations. And then, god help us, we might even start to appraise some of our own behavior as having been villainous. No, we don't want to do that. It's better to see villains as glorious evil beings. So we deify them. They are godlike and omnipotent, and cannot be defeated... until, of course, they are. Well, they cannot be defeated, at least, by any normal, human means. Enter the hero. And the hero is often a loser to begin with. That's right, just like us. Some stumblebum who wanders around the country dressed in rags. A pure soul, no doubt, but still... his innate power has not yet been developed, or perhaps it is concealed in some way. In many cases his original motivations are selfish, and he is often only reluctantly drawn into the play. But at some juncture, his better nature is called upon, and at that crucial moment – when he has to choose between self interest and altruism – he chooses (against his own better judgment, of course) that heroic act which will save the world, which defeats the undefeatable, which returns order where there was chaos, which restores peace and harmony once again.

"Stick 'em up!" Oh, it's no use— he thought— this is not natural. Maybe my motivation is not honest. Maybe I have selfish reasons for wanting to be successful. Maybe I don't really want to contribute my gift to the world, but simply want my own glorification and aggrandizement. Maybe I just want *women* to want me... anyway, I don't believe that you can change anything when you don't really want to. I mean, I tend to have complete contempt for most of the people in the world, the way they behave, the way they treat one another... their stupidity! Why would I want to give of myself to people who I believe don't deserve me? Sometimes I see them all as the villains, and me... as the lonely, helpless victim. It's hard to feel sympathy for them when all I want is to be in a different world altogether: one where people are worthy of my respect... the kind of people who care for each other, and for whom I can care.

But at other moments I am reminded of those truths, which I have always known, but frequently tend to forget: that this angry and ferocious world of my experience may not exist outside of my acquaintance with it, and that (should I ever be inclined to reintroduce myself to my life in a more gentle and accommodating manner) I may well find, within myself, the power to transform it, and all of its many inhabitants – if not into the exact image of my desires, then at least – into something with which I could happily coexist until my time has passed. In short, that I might change this world – not for the world's sake, but for my own. A selfish motivation seemingly, but who could find dishonor in the guileless pursuit of happiness? Is it not *that* which we all aspire to? It is – or at least it could be – the universe of my own creation.

Courage, Devine. Courage!

And a surge of energy ran up his spinal column, until it shot straight out the top of his head.

"Stick 'em up!" he said to his reflection in the mirror. And this time his reflection looked like he really meant it.

"You don't need to learn how to shoot the damned thing!" The disembodied voice sounded thin and electronic, "you're only going to pretend to hold them up."

Dominic awkwardly cupped the receiver between his shoulder and his cheek. The hot bread burned his fingers and he rapidly dropped the piece he had torn off. "Yeah, but they don't know that I'm only pretending. What if somebody tries to retaliate or something?"

"I suppose you're just going to have to shoot them," said Marvin, sarcastically as usual.

"Don't be ridiculous," said Dominic, picking up the revolver from its spot on the table right next to the steaming Tuscan loaf, as he waited for it to cool down a little. It was great, he thought, how they sell them, pre-wrapped in foil, completely prepared with just the last ten minutes of baking left for you to do. This way, not only do you get a freshly baked bread, but you can con yourself that you know how to bake. "Listen, I want to make sure that I don't shoot anyone by *mistake*. Shouldn't I at least know how to handle the damned thing if I'm carrying it? I mean... aren't guns most dangerous in the hands of those who don't know what they're doing? Accidents happen!"

"That's when they're loaded, you idiot!"

"Oh… this baby is loaded," said Dominic.

"What the fuck are you on?" yelled Marvin. "Where did you get the fucking bullets? Don't tell me that asshole gave them to you…"

"Artie," interjected Dominic.

"That *asshole!*" complained his friend. "I told him you wouldn't *need* any ammo!"

"Yeah… I told him to fill 'er up." He snapped the chamber to try and open it, just like he'd seen them do it in the movies. It wouldn't budge.

"Fill – her – up? It's not your fucking car, you know! What… how many did he give you?"

"Give me? Sell me, you mean."

"Give you, sell you… just tell me how many fucking bullets you have!"

Dominic spun the chamber one more time. "Six."

"Now listen Dominic, I'm being serious," and Marvin's voice genuinely took on a different tone at this point. "Please do us all a favor and remove the bullets from the gun, right now."

"I'm not sure how it opens," said Dominic. "I've been tugging on it in every direction. I can't seem to find the catch."

"Sometimes," said Marvin patiently, "there is no catch, and you can waste a hell of a lot of time looking for it."

"Well, if there is no catch… and tugging on it doesn't work… then what's the solution?"

"If you eliminate those two options," asked Marvin, "what's left?"

Dominic Devine inhaled deeply and hummed a little as he exhaled through his nose. The sound vibrated his sinuses until they felt open and free. A slight whiff of Tuscan bakery entered his awareness. He took the chamber of the revolver and applied gentle pressure on one side, and then the other, until it clicked easily open. "I – I've got it," he announced proudly in a surprised voice. He could hear Marvin breathing deeply on the other end of the line. He pointed the firearm at the ceiling and whirred the chamber lightly. Five bullets fell out at first… and then finally the last one, which plopped and rolled and clattered and trickled busily across the worn and holographic image of Jesus, whose eyes seemed to follow it momentarily, past the steaming bread until it reached the edge of the mesa, where it teetered for an instant, as if trying to decide whether to commit to the long plunge, or not. Finally it fell, landing neatly, and safely... in Dominic's hand which had been waiting dependably to catch it just four inches below.

Dominic and Marvin took the short cut across the embankment by the canal. There before them, was Miranda Manley's barge. The sun was shining down and a man was working upon the deck, sweeping and tidying up, and such things. He was dressed warmly, and little white clouds of moisture demonstrated well the heaviness of his breath as he labored familiarly with his duties. It was not the same man who had answered the door the other night, and that entire incident now seemed to Dominic – in the bright light of day – as if it had been another lifetime. He had not related all of the specifics of that evening to Marvin as he had been somewhat embarrassed regarding his little fantasies toward Mrs. Manley, and he'd entered the tale at the point where the old drunk had fallen into the canal. The look on Marvin's face now made it clear that he was just remembering that part of the story.

"So where did you run into that old bum?" he asked. "On one of these canals?"

Dominic gazed around vaguely. "Er... yes, it must have been around here somewhere." But the amused expression that Marvin seemed to be trying to hide provoked Dominic to snap at him.

"What?" he said.

"Nothing," said Marvin, still half smiling.

"What's so funny?" pressed Dominic.

"Nothing," Marvin asserted as if he were actually annoyed, but then he couldn't seem to keep from smiling again. "I was just imagining, er... you trying to fish some soaking old souse out of this filthy drink."

"So?" asked Dominic. "What's so funny about that?"

"So... so it's funny!" Marvin turned and walked off at a faster clip than they had been going.

Dominic quickened his pace in order to catch up. The explanation didn't sit well with him. "I don't think that's so funny," he shouted after his friend.

"That's because it happened to you." Marvin didn't even turn his head. "Things are always more funny when they happen to someone else."

"I suppose," said Dominic, stuffing his cold hands into his pocket and skipping a little to catch up alongside the other man.

Shortly, they arrived at the cramped and dingy diner, which had indeed been the intended destination of this foray. The name, "Eric's Fried Food." had been sloppily hand painted in haphazard and dripping black letters above the large front window – partially opaque now, with age and grease – whose frame, in a style matching the wall around it, was peeling off (more than) several coats of faded and distressed paint of every possible hue, and shade, and pattern. The wall directly beside that window had, at some point in time, been the victim of a graffiti artist whose work, quite frankly, was more professionally rendered than was the official name of the restaurant. And Eric – if there really was an Eric – hadn't yet been motivated enough to erase this particular bit of vandalism from his property. So there upon his wall the emblem "Chick 37" had remained now for several years. No one knew who had painted it. No one knew what it meant. The number thirty-seven did not signify any connection with the restaurant, whose street address... was number fifteen. But its coloring was attractive, and its swirling font was provocative, and it piqued the attention of many a passerby. And not long after its appearance a surge of new customers began frequenting the establishment, which they now commonly referred to as "Chick 37." Moreover, in recent months, a set of pompous slummers from the ritzy side of the track had adopted the place, in a fit of trendy infatuation, and re-christened it "Chic Trente-Sept." But Eric – if there really was an Eric – didn't understand the importance of the graffiti to the sudden popularity of his restaurant, and still vowed – as he did every year – to, "clean that shit off when the spring comes." Fortunately for him, his commitment to anything that involved unnecessary work was presently about as flaccid as it had ever been. And his attitude only served to affirm the idea that even when ignorance isn't bliss... pure laziness can sometimes quite sufficiently substitute for it.

They seated themselves. No host (Eric or otherwise) had greeted them and, once situated, Dominic leaned back in his chair to survey the scene. The place was not well kept nor frequently cleaned. Years of spilled servings decorated the cheap linoleum covered floor, its original pattern having been forcibly subordinated by the myriad footprints of the long since departed. Although at no one sitting could this eatery have accommodated more than about twenty five patrons, its ancient scars provided enough clues to attest their abundant presence through the years. A crime scene of sorts... to the experienced eye, but Dominic, despite his chosen avocation, did not possess that eye when it came to reality, and missed now the opportunity to bathe in the stories which were presented there for his consumption. He noticed generalities instead. The interior decor, for example, exhibited no more finesse or ingenuity in its design than did the exterior of the building. Much less so, in fact, were one to regard with favor the graffiti, which paraded itself so proudly outside.

Although, in the 'unisex' bathroom, what was wanting in quality and comfort was more than made up for by quantity and content. On every inch of its thoroughly obfuscated walls and ceiling, meaning and humor juggled beside phone numbers and cartoonish depictions of macho members, and massive mammaries. The word 'cunt' had been scrawled four hundred and fifty-three times, at last count, in various sentences, jokes, put-downs, come-ons, teases, tall-tales, complaints and invitations. Several times it had been written, unexplained, just by itself. It seemed to have been nominated, by dint of its frequency (if nothing else) for the title of 'most revered offensive word.' Other words, 'cock,' 'dick,' 'balls,' 'tits,' 'pussy,' 'shlong'... also appeared many times over. Even the word 'penis' made a brief showing, although 'vagina' was notably absent. 'Cum' was up there several times, on one occasion actually spelled, 'COME,' and 'rub' was spattered about the entire surface with great frequency.

Strangely enough much of this graffiti was comparatively new. It had mysteriously appeared on the evening that a horde of young girls (well-off debutante types) had descended upon the place, causing quite a stir in the street outside with the working class male youths who normally habituate the neighborhood, singing Doo-wop on the corner where the Avenue meets the Street. The debs had parked their fancy foreign sports cars illegally, leaving tops down, seemingly quite unconcerned about theft or local ordinances. When taunted by the boys, one of the girls had spit at them and shown them her middle finger, whilst another had exposed a single breast in their direction. This last act had, of course, caused a total uproar amongst the rabble, and had kept them battling each other for prime positions before the grease-stained window – for as long as it took the comely tantalizer to consume her repast, anyway – in the hope the she, or one of her compatriots, would once again be similarly inclined as the night wore on. When the police finally arrived to investigate the disturbance, Eric – if there really was an Eric – was heard to say, "it's none of my business what happens outside of my business."

But tonight they didn't stare. Dominic could see no youths standing beside the street lamp as it came on. The "harmony" boys were sneaking into a concert on the other side of town, their souped-up 305 hemis parked, free of charge, upon the overgrown grass verge behind the parking-lot fence; chrome wheels crushing the twisted, rusting bodies of empty milk cartons, and ™ Del Monte pineapple cans, and ripped and spattered copies of ™ Hustler. No one would see them parked there in the shadows of the overpass (it was the one place the Hoi Polloi were scared to go). They'd be home late tonight, high as kites, when only their voices raised in impersonation would compete with their altitude. And the neighbors would open windows, and yell curses, and throw down bucketfuls of water, and threaten to complain to their families in the morning.

The yellowing lace curtain hung still in "Eric's" tonight, where only five other guests sat eating at this early hour. The air hardly moved, not enough even to evaporate the sweat from the faces of the diners. Despite the coolness of the weather outside, it was warm, and humid as a motherfucker in here.

At one table, two local women supported each other's past and future nagging of husbands who did not seem to understand, and were insensitive to their wives' needs, and didn't push hard enough in their careers. Apparently, these same men did not spend enough time with their children nor, for that matter, did they appear at the church on Sundays. They had no table manners and were never willing to try anything new. They slept in their underwear which sometimes they wore for several days in a row without changing. They drank too much beer and had, as a result, put on too much weight.

A young couple sat grimly in a dark corner, white knuckles gripping stiffly each other's hands. Their talk was hushed and serious, and Dominic had to pay close attention to discern the gist of their conversation.

"What could I do?" she was complaining. The boy did not respond. "It's not as if I *did* anything," she continued. "Anyway, I *hate* him! He's a jerk!"

"You *always* go out with jerks who you hate," he commented sadly, noting only unconsciously what this might say about him.

"Lunch!" she snapped, and then she gathered herself a little, "lunch." She almost whispered it this time. "It wasn't a *date*, or anything like that. We ate *food* together."

"So why'd you go to lunch with someone you hate?"

"I couldn't get out of it. We were in the elevator together. I was just making conversation. I said— what are you doing for lunch? And he took it as an invitation... arrogant bastard!" She paused briefly. "And then before I could say anything he was telling me how he couldn't possibly make it today – right in front of everyone... too busy, he said, and..."

"And so, naturally, you felt rejected, and then you had to have him."

She pulled her hand out of his. "No! I didn't have to *have* him," she said in a disgusted tone. "It's just that the elevator door opened right then, and he ran out shouting— tomorrow okay? Everyone heard him. And the next day he came over to my desk at lunchtime. Well... I didn't have anything else to do... so it seemed easier to just go than to make excuses."

"You don't have to make excuses," said the boy, "You could just tell him to bugger off!"

Her look conveyed disbelief and exasperation.

The boy continued more carefully now. "Well why couldn't you just tell him that you didn't *want* to go to lunch with him?"

"Well it wasn't *that* bad," she countered, avoiding the actual question.

"Not that bad? Do you often choose to do things based on the fact that they're not absolutely excruciating?"

"Oh come on!" She fumed for a little while, and then added, "you know perfectly well that this is not a big deal. So stop trying to make one out of it!"

He turned slowly and repositioned himself on his chair, sideways, so that he was almost facing Dominic directly. Although his stare caught Dominic's eye, it wasn't *that* which he was seeing. He was gazing at the mass of turbulent thoughts spiraling inside his head, never for one moment considering the fact that the eyes upon which he focussed concealed a turbulence all of their own.

Dominic averted his eyes and examined the ceiling where thick layers of paint obscured the patterns embossed upon the squares of timeworn tin. Squares with circles, and circles with four-leaf clovers, which had rusted and eaten themselves away in places, or just eaten through the paint, in lines which followed the patterns here and there. Brown and red ill-defined lines, and blotches, and holes, and paint, and no paint, coiling around each other in a serpentine snarl of anxious and unsightly confusion. What Dominic saw outside was the same as what he saw inside.

"So, what are you having?" Marvin had been examining the menu.

"What difference does it make?" asked Dominic. He absently picked up the menu and perused it perfunctorily. But, for some reason, he could not understand what he was looking at.

Marvin seemed confused. "I don't understand," he said, "are you asking that question in some sort of universalist-slash-existentialist way— what difference does anything make?" He shrugged, "or are you just trying to say that everything in this place tastes the same?"

"Like shit, you mean," said Dominic, slapping the menu back down on the table. "I don't know why you always insist on coming to this toilet. Honestly!"

"I didn't insist," Marvin calmly differed, "I suggested... and you agreed."

"I didn't agree," replied Dominic. "I didn't say anything. I just went along."

"Well, now you know where just going along gets you."

Dominic rested one elbow on the table, and his head in his hand. He looked around the room until his eyes came to rest upon the single other patron whose presence he had not as yet marked. He was a wealthy looking man of about forty. He was dressed casually, although in a stylishly conservative manner. Tweed sport's jacket, traditional and expensive but with an imaginative flair to its cut. Sensible brown shoes of supple and extremely high quality leather which yet projected a certain 'je ne c'est quoi.' He sported a neatly clipped moustache along with a little goatee. Some grey hairs peppered his whiskers here and there, in a way that might, by some, be considered distinguished, and a nifty looking shock of white bedecked the center of his coiffure – ladies of the more mature set had been heard to remark upon it approvingly. There was something familiar about the delicate way in which he raised the coffee mug to his lips, as if it were a tea cup of the finest bone china. Dominic wondered what a man of his obvious taste and dignity was doing in such a place... no less, of course, than he wondered what he himself was doing there. But still, there was something in this gentleman's mannerisms – as he cut his meat, as he perused the pages of his daily paper... even the way he looked – which struck a chord of familiarity with Dominic Devine. Recent familiarity. He tried to force the memory to his consciousness, as one will do, but, as usually happens, it was only when he let go of the matter and turned to address Marvin on a completely different issue, that it hit him, like an old boot, straight in the face. His eyes bulged so that Marvin thought that he was about to throw up. For a moment, Dominic looked like he was about to jump out of his seat, but then he seemed to get a grip on himself. He looked back at the man. Then he looked back at Marvin.

"What?" said Marvin.

Dominic tried to speak, but then he looked at the man again... and then at Marvin.

"*What?*" said Marvin.

Dominic swallowed hard, breathed deeply, looked back one more time at the man, who was still sitting there eating, reading, calmly unaware of having been observed, and said, "I take it all back, Marvin. This was the best possible place that you could have brought me to."

Chapter 19

Events were flashing by for Jocelyn D'Orion... as was the scenery. And the chemicals circulating inside her body were churning up a storm. The pace was picking up, and her lead foot was hammering that pretty blue jalopy like there was no tomorrow, crashing it over potholes, flying over crests and smashing down again several yards later onto rusty antiquated suspension components. She plied the ™Muncie shifter with dexterity to keep the small block V8 in its power band, although with such abundant torque, that may have been less necessary than recreational.

The radio was playing a strange combination of music by a band called "Bongo's Witness." One of the announcers, a Scot named Archibald Cox, was arguing about the record with his partner on the show, a man named Wolfgang Von Kuntz. They were debating the merits of the music in a comedic style which was not to her taste. She had heard them before on this station; she wasn't sure if they were a pair of idiots, or a very clever put on. They tended to feign a loyalty toward the Temple of Bongovism, but they would have had to have been stupid indeed to not realize how they burlesqued its dignity. The possibility that they were kindred spirits drew her back to their show every now and then, but right now she had no patience for their buffoonery. She switched it off.

She was heading for 83052, a town with which she was well acquainted. It was located a short half hour drive from the little family farm where she and her father had dwelt since her birth. And, as the telephone poles now stroboscopically flashed past her vision, they delivered an almost mantric effect upon her receptors, and caused her memory to return – beyond the events of the past few days – to a time when she had known young Freddy Greaves, and then... even beyond that.

She was born about fifteen years before Henry Lewis had even arrived in this place. It was, however, a not dissimilar world then to the one she observed around her today. Despite the influence of the Temple of Bongo, and despite the arrival of Jason Cyllabus Novedi, whose intention to rid the world of all injustice was a noble but not thoroughly considered one, the human tendency to pervert virtue (which itself seems almost virtuous, sometimes, in its resourcefulness) was quite as enduring in those days. Just as, in fact, it has always been throughout the course of history.

Her father, Fritz D'Orion, had always been of an iconoclastic nature, and this fact, combined with his not altogether unfounded suspicion of the Bongovian school system, had convinced him (at around the same time that his daughter was first gaining the use of language) to undertake her education personally. His tutelage continued until she was about fourteen, when a certain government official (after an anonymous tip – possibly by meddlesome and intrusive in-laws) took interest in the young girl's case and dispatched, forthwith, a truancy officer to resolve this unacceptable situation. After a brief and rather partial examination, the well indoctrinated young officer concluded upon the irresponsibility of the parent, and threatened to have the child remanded to foster care, were she not enrolled in the nearest appropriate government operated school immediately. Fritz, of course, was absolutely horrified, and balked vehemently at the suggestion, until his daughter pleaded with him to go along with it, explaining that she would rather have to go to school than lose him altogether. She added also that, perhaps, she wouldn't mind, quite frankly, spending some time with people of her own age for a change. But despite this demonstration of her balanced thinking in the matter, she could not know (young as she was) the effect that this sudden divesting of her social retardation would have upon her immediate future.

It is not our job here to discuss the psychological effects of repression and its abrupt release, nor to evaluate the quality of a young girl's upbringing. We shall not conjecture upon the details of her experiences, sexual, or lacking thereof. But we can admit, in fairness, that something which happened to her around that time, left an image upon her mind which would recur painfully throughout her life... or at least until such a time as she would learn to confront its implications. And yet none of this would hamper her intellectual and academic achievements. She could have been, in many ways, a model student. Her father had inspired in her that rarest of all traits, the desire to learn. But he had *also* imbued her with the dual aptitude to absorb large amounts of information, whilst simultaneously reserving judgment as to their truth. And in this way she was, arguably, the furthest thing from a model student, who is required to believe what she is taught without question.

As a result, the local authorities in 83052 – following the standards of the State and, in fact, not unlike beaurocracies the world over who cannot acknowledge the efficacy of any alternative system – kept her down (despite her obvious scholarly advancement) with the students of her own age. Later on, they begrudged her even *this* mild acceptance, and decided that, having been deprived all those early years of their 'blessed' patronage, and taking into consideration her argumentative and uncooperative nature, she would best be served by being remitted to the Learning Disabled Curriculum. The L.D.C., as it was commonly known throughout the system, was foisted upon a group of young people who displayed various differences (sometimes quite serious differences) from the average student. These young people were, as a result, largely stigmatized for their individuality by the rest of high school society. However, this situation played favorably for Jocelyn, who actually found more in common with *those* people (even the most alarming of them) than she did with the obedient thinkers who were regaled as the future cream of Bongovia. And in the L.D.C. she encountered the type of kindred spirits with whom she had not been able to consort in her previous class. Neither did she take any of this maltreatment personally, as she came to be convinced that she had not been any more abused by the system than (in one way or another) every other child within it. Certainly, the school authorities would have agreed, no child *ever* fell below the minimum requirements of acceptable treatment as defined by the official 'Child Abuse Standards Guide,' which incidentally, had been instituted by a previous (and some would now consider heathen) administration, at least twenty-five years *before* the new Bongovian age.

The story went like this: apparently, the incumbent administration at that time had held an investigation (coincidental, of course, with the campaign run-offs for their local elections) to examine the frequent allegations of child abuse within the school system. The investigative committee had concluded that, under the watch of their predecessors, a terrible regression in the treatment and education of children had occurred. And now, at the very end of *their* term of office, they were finally prepared to do something about it. Sweeping new legislations and penalties were introduced, affecting any and all who might have been involved in these barbaric and wholly unacceptable practices. Wisely, they set the new standards slightly lower than they had, in fact, previously been, thereby – in one fell swoop – ridding the system of all apparent malfeasance. And by manipulating the new regulations deftly, they cast those teachers who had originally complained about the problems within the system, as agitators and inciters of unrest. They weeded out all the troublemakers who were complaining that nothing had changed, and stabilized the school system decisively, going on to win the election once again. Yet more committees were created, security companies were hired, food suppliers were procured, money changed hands, things got worse. All in all it was a wonderful success for democracy.

But, despite these complications, and in consideration of all alternative choices, the idea of Jocelyn attending a school was probably not the worst thing for her. Even Fritz had to agree when he saw the pleasure that the company of her new friends brought to his daughter. He wondered secretly why no handsome young men ever came to visit, but he never complained about such a circumstance; when did a father ever? In the meanwhile, he had been growing slowly and increasingly aware of his own burgeoning alcoholism and, although he had never before been a man to shirk his responsibilities, he was now finding it harder to cope with even the most mundane eventualities of day to day life. He began to believe that his daughter's constant witnessing of his drunkenness would eventually affect her in a manner not entirely to her advantage.

It was true that his drinking had started shortly after her mother's departure, but Fritz would never blame the one upon the other. He had always thought he was, or at least should be, man enough to handle the sting that life's grim lessons inflict, and not depend upon the remedy of self medication in order to cope with loss, which is – he knew well – the one constant of existence. He did not need a woman to run his affairs for him, to wash his clothes, to cook his meals… to be the receptacle of his sexuality, his sympathy, his condemnation, his rage. And yet here it was, the bitter truth, that he was steeped in such sadness that he could no longer extricate himself from this morass of guilt and defeatism. But unlike tea-bags whose steeping empties them, humans steep themselves by building up such a structure of an image of who they are, that they can forget that the simplicity of change lies one brick at a time… one plank at a time, in dismantling that image – fluid thing that it is. Just the openness to see that they are not necessarily what they insist themselves to be could provide an emancipating insight. But Fritz

D'Orion lived within the turbulence of his own self image, which was that he was nothing without the presence of that which was not present. And no one was there to remind him of that which was so obvious... that which he, in fact, already knew, but was too blind to see. And so he continued on his downward spiral as his daughter grew, imbuing her with the antithetical merits of the cynical and the sublime. But inasmuch as clarity and blindness are both descended from an invisible ancestor, it was inevitable then, that in witnessing his blindness, Jocelyn developed her clarity, promising herself that she would never be so blind.

But clarity facilitates a frightening truth... that there is danger all around. There is danger in change, and there is danger in remaining the same. And sometimes, when her clarity forced upon her an impossible and frightening alternative, she clearly abandoned all attempts at perception and hid from that which she knew to be real. She blinded herself to her feelings, she blinded herself to the laws of nature, she blinded herself (even) to the rules of simple logic, choosing to believe that she was neither changing nor remaining the same. And eventually she began to exchange her ferocious compatriots from the L.D.C. with those of a more socially acceptable nature. Soon she was surrounded by a group of friends who were somewhat vacuous when it came to the subject of the human condition but, unlike her, they were (at least) honest in their vacuity. After all, they had been deprived of those marvelous character building opportunities which *she* had enjoyed: an abandoning mother, an alcoholic father, a life of poverty. And yet somehow she managed to make herself attractive enough – by feigning superficiality and maybe even believing in her own masquerade – to be accepted by such a group of people, and one in particular... Rebecca Burnside.

She hadn't spoken to Becky in years. The girl had sufficed well enough at the time, but when Jocelyn left the school environment and returned to live with her father on the farm, she no longer needed a friend who could offer nothing more than a rose colored reflection of her own thoughts. She discovered that her sense of integrity required a colder lens, without filters or pleasing distortions. There had been no falling out between them, but a gradual drifting and desultory separation of the ways.

Becky was the girl who had dated Freddy Greaves for a while, and she knew his family well (perhaps better than she knew Freddie). She and Freddie had regularly made wild passionate love – she had often told Jocelyn – by moonlight, right there beside the big swimming pool on the grounds of their huge estate just outside of 83052. Jocelyn sometimes felt that these confessions were designed to elicit reciprocity regarding her own sexual escapades. She skillfully avoided the trap. She'd convinced herself that sexuality was simply a topic that she did not feel it was appropriate to discuss. Becky eventually tired in her probing, but continued to harbor the suspicion that Jocelyn was secretly a raging inferno of lust and lechery, and her reticence to discuss it made her all the more suspect. It's possible that Rebecca Burnside had an instinct for life for which Jocelyn never really gave her credit.

Now Freddie Greaves had seemed a nice enough boy at the time. Jocelyn remembered him talking openly (and perhaps somewhat unsympathetically) about his family. She remembered the first time that it had suddenly occurred to her that coming from wealth did not ensure happiness. That the experiences lost – of having to rough it sometimes, or to make do with what you've got – and the invention which is mothered by those necessities, cannot be compensated for by all the amenity in the world. She appreciated her own father so much the more after that time. A "deprived child," is what she used to call Freddie... to his face. He seemed to like it. Perhaps it made him feel understood.

For all his family's wealth, Freddie never flaunted his position. If anything he seemed rather embarrassed by it. He dressed well, of course, but (to poor Becky's chagrin) he did not affect a materialistic posture by showering her with pricey baubles at every opportunity. She did not see the virtue in this particular behavior and complained of it often to Jocelyn. She would, however, immediately retract her complaint after she had been chided for her avarice— Was his company not enough? Were objects more important than human interaction? How superficial is such a love? She knew these questions well enough, did Becky... and when tested could respond correctly, chapter and verse. But to simply not be asked them... to not be reminded, just one time, for Becky, ah... that would have been a dream come true.

It's funny how that very quality which attracted Jocelyn to her, was the same one which ultimately drove them apart. Jocelyn needed someone who wanted to be asked the questions which she was starting to explore within herself. Becky needed someone shallow and self obsessed to mirror gratuitously... who would not delve, who would not probe. It's funny, too, how a questioning personality and one which hides from the truth can live together comfortably within a single entity. And so, although she was still afraid of change, still afraid of staying the same, these questions were knocking little chips out of the bricks which made up the structure of who Jocelyn thought she was.

They hadn't seen each other in what must have been well over five or six years. Becky hadn't appeared at the high school reunion two years ago, and no one there claimed to have heard from her... although, there were rumors abroad that she had joined the inner sanctum of a cultish political group led by an industrialist millionaire, about whom everybody was gossiping. Of course Jocelyn had had no idea about whom they were all talking at the time – she paid little attention to politics or who was running the country, she couldn't be bothered with it... and it couldn't be bothered with her – and only now, as she remembered the conversations of that particular occasion, did it smack her straight in the face as to what, and who, all that fuss was about.

In true melodramatic fashion she unthinkingly slammed her foot onto the brake pedal, sending the flabbily sprung muscle-barge of yesteryear (that's right, the Bel Air) into an angrily screeching diagonal slide, which left her – once she had come to a complete halt – with her bustle hanging down the slight decline of the dusty shoulder. Her left headlight and fender peeked dangerously into the slow lane now, and the truck which had been following slackened its pace to steer safely wide of this potential snag. Curious eyes viewed her from it as they rolled steadily past. A little boy in the back window was about to wave at her, but for some reason when he saw Jocelyn's smile he pretended to be wiping the glass. His mother's hand forced him back down onto the seat, but still he glanced tenuously over his shoulder from time to time as the vehicle faded to a dot.

Jocelyn reignited the stalled mechanism and pulled up just a few feet to straighten out the front of the car parallel to the road. She waited there a while, with the engine burbling, as she searched the glove compartment for a handkerchief. She wiped her face, where sweat and tears had coincidentally appeared in the instant of her revelation.

Was it possible— she wondered— that Becky could be living right there in Prickly Bog? Was it possible that Jason knew her? Could he know her well? Perhaps he knew her better than... well, this was going nowhere. Surely the Church of Bongo had centers all over the country. And who said that Becky had actually entered their 'inner sanctum?' It was, after all, just a rumor she had heard, and rumors have a tendency towards exaggeration. Let's face it, sometimes they can't be relied upon at all. But still... there were towns dotted all over the countryside which were owned, or partly owned, by J.C.N. Enterprises. There were factories and power stations everywhere now, comprising a trillion credit network which provided for the inhabitants of each region, and also recruited from them. The Church of Bongo was considered somewhat more consequential than a 'cultish political group,' even out here in the boonies... even in 83052 they'd read all about it in the magazines. Not to mention the fact that a couple of years ago the church had held a spate of large outdoor pop music festivals, attended by thousands and thousands of teenagers from every district. All the performers had represented in praise of the new order... the new spirituality... the new respect for even the lowliest of the lowliest. Following their attendance of these events, many of the local youth had soon set out for the big city in search of the new life which Bongovism promised.

But Jocelyn had kept herself down on the farm most of the time. She didn't read the pop-cult mags – such *piffle* – and spoke to her peers infrequently enough so that the celebrity names they bandied from time to time did not register deeply enough with her to educe connections. In her understanding, the culture of 83052 was still comprised of two distinct social groups. The local 'Waste,' as they referred to themselves, were lost souls. Their lives were going nowhere, and they could muster no motivation for change. They had already missed the turnoff for redemption and so they were beyond the call of religion. Then there were the "Nobs" upon the hill, who had led a privileged life from time immemorial. They also had no need for the call of religion. They were already redeemed, and therefore... above it.

She did not know which way to go now. Should she turn back towards Prickly Bog and start randomly searching for Becky Burnside? She had no evidence to prove – nor reason to assume – that Becky had actually settled there. She was already half way to 83052, where she could at least visit the Greaves estate with the probability of obtaining some information about young Freddie. But on the other hand, she could not doubt that Becky would become her willing ally in this affair. And she *needed* an ally right now.

She waited for a couple of cars to pass by before she made her U-turn, but in her backward observation, she did not notice the one that slowed down to a crawl after going past. The driver of that impossibly shiny and luxurious, long black phaeton tried to comprehend the meaning of this dance he saw reflected in his rearview mirror – re-reflected once again upon the mirrored lenses of his shades and thereby rendered true – in which she turned... and turned again. Turned firstly to return whence she had come, and then re-revised her turning plan to turn once more and to continue upon her way. To hurry back the way she had been going all along. But in her hurry she did not question why that powerful black limousine had pulled off to one side as she accelerated, allowing her to resume the lead and, once she had attained a distance of a suitable proportion, to then steal back upon the road and follow in her wake.

The white lines slipped ceaselessly past, in a never ending sequence of conceptual projectiles. Shot, like tracers from some hidden machine-gun, they were really nothing, going nowhere, fired from a virtual no-gun. Just painted concepts – walls, fences, rivers, mountains... these are real – but a color, visual? Yes. But only two dimensions. This is no object! This is no boundary! And yet Jocelyn, free spirit that she was, contained herself to remain ever upon the right hand side of those flashing bullets. Like a circle she had once drawn around herself, in wet sand, with naked toes. "Daddy," she had said, when she was five, "this is me," as he approached her circle. "No! Don't step inside my circle! *This... is... me!*" And she had lifted one foot and pointed a sandy toe at the circumference, while the other foot hopped, spinning her slowly around lest her pointer miss one tiny arc of that pie.

And if her father had never done one thing right before, he did it on that day when he stood aside and told her, "that's a beautiful circle Jossy. Maybe one day you'll invite me in with you."

But she just pursed her lips and said, "never!" And then she quickly released herself and spoke more sweetly to him. "You won't fit daddy. You're too big for my circle. Maybe somebody little... like me."

But the lines we have around us keep not only others out. They keep us in, caged like the metal beast, by the white lines on the highway. Doomed, the prowling blue Bel Air, to stay to the right, stay... forever, to the right. So that we may know exactly who we are, and who it is that we are not. We find our limits in the twin dimensions of graffiti we have drawn. We tell ourselves that we can do this, but we cannot do that. We can be one but not the other.

I'm a breast man!

I'm a leg man... I could never be a breast man!

And all we have to prove it is a line somebody painted on the street, or drew upon the sand... or scratched into our consciousness. We simply refuse to believe that the easiest thing in the world is to step over that line.

Really!

The easiest thing in the world.

Chapter 20

It was becoming increasingly clear to Dominic Devine that these are not the type of things which happen to somebody like him. Which is not to say that unusual or interesting things had never happened to him. It's just that not one of those unusual events had ever led to anything actually ever being accomplished. He felt a slight shiver as he examined his past... it was true, he had never actually accomplished *anything*. In fact, no one in his family had ever accomplished anything. They'd had plenty of big ideas, mind you... schemes... plans, which didn't so much go awry, as... peter out – quite rapidly sometimes. Like learning to speak Russian... or learning to drive... or writing a book. As if some immense jolt of caffeine had ignited such ambitions in a tsunami of artificial energy, only to leave them high and dry, as it drained away, exposing those pretensions as nothing more than pretense. His mother, his father, his elder siblings... none of them had ever completed any really meaningful task they had ever started. Even his little sister Damian had begun starting to show those tendencies. That was one of the reasons why he'd left before she grew too big; he couldn't stand to watch that inertia slowly enveloping her – or himself either, for that matter. But it might have been too late for him, anyway. You can't run away from the family which resides in your head; they're with you forever. The best you can do is learn to be yourself, despite them. But, despite his attempts to escape his family's influence, Dominic still believed, as he always had, that he would never actually finish the book he'd begun writing when he was seventeen. And yet, for some obscure and inescapable reason, it came to pass, that when he was thirty-nine years of age... he finally did.

Well then— some little rat-fink family loyal quarter of his diseased subconscious mind was assuring him now— you know you'll never get it published!

And yet, peculiar and mysterious events were conspiring – despite their frustrating nature – to persuade him otherwise. Was this a psychic... or just a psychotic episode, he wondered, or could he simply be dreaming? Perhaps it was that he was projecting his own needs, his own desires upon this unlikely tableau, so that he could give himself reason to believe in this craziness. Perhaps it was for his own insane reasons that he could see a similarity in that man's face where none actually existed.

"What the fuck are you talking about?" asked Marvin. "What man?"

"That man there!" Dominic whispered anxiously.

"Who?" asked Marvin blatantly, swinging his whole body around to look in the direction that Dominic had so covertly indicated with his pinkie.

"Shh! Keep your voice down," Dominic hissed. This only succeeded in briefly attracting the attention of the well-heeled looking gentleman seated at the table nearby, who absently glanced up at the sound... and then went back to reading the newspaper which lay beside his plate, neatly folded into a small rectangle, exposing only the relevant portion of the day's Stock Market report.

"What *about* him?" asked Marvin, in a somewhat more cooperative voice this time... although something about his manner suggested a mocking attitude.

"That man..." said Dominic Devine, "is Henry Lewis!"

"Who?" said Marvin.

"You know... the guy who came back from the future!"

"The psycho-bum?"

"Yes!"

"Yeah right!" added Marvin. "This guy *looks* like a bum... who gets drunk and falls into the river. Have you noticed that pinky ring he's wearing?"

Dominic glanced casually over and considered the diamond embedded in a gold band, perfectly chiseled and clear of hue – it meant nothing to him.

"That's worth about five grand," continued Marvin. "What d'you think... he found it in the fuckin' canal? Next to a fuckin' barge?"

This only succeeded in raising Dominic's hackles, which were already heightened to some degree. "I'm telling you," his voice was straining to maintain its quiet, "that is the same guy... I think. Anyway, it looks exactly like him... very much so. Well – sort of... richer of course, he was dressed like a homeless guy before. And he looks, sort of... younger."

"Yeah right," said Marvin. "One thing I know for sure. Nobody's feet ever got smaller... and nobody *ever* grew younger. This ain't the same guy who you saw fall in..."

But before he could finish, Dominic had stood up and was heading towards the rich man's table. "Excuse me," Dominic spoke, "would your name happen to be Henry Lewis?"

"It would," the seated man replied, seemingly surprised at this familiarity.

"Don't you remember me?" asked Dominic. But the man just shrugged his shoulders and raised an eyebrow. Dominic had the urge to continue with such reminders as— I was the one who pulled you out of the canal... you were at my home. But this man did look somewhat different, whilst at the same time being, most definitely, most positively, the same man.

"Wait a minute." Dominic needed to be sure. "Are you saying that you *are* Henry Lewis?"

"Indeed I am," said the man.

"And you don't remember meeting me last week?"

"I'm terribly sorry," said Henry Lewis. "Were you in Abidjan?"

"Abidjan?"

"I switch off sometimes... er, when I get back home," continued Lewis. "I sometimes forget the people that I met." He stood up and extended a handshake. "I do apologize, Mr..."

"Well, that seems strange," said Dominic.

"Would you care to join me Mr. er... ? Oh, I see you are with somebody... I just flew in last night and..."

"And boy are your arms tired," interjected Dominic.

Henry Lewis looked at him suspiciously for a moment, and then, realizing that it was probably a joke of some sort, he smiled absently. "Oh I see... yes. So... when did you return?"

"No... you don't understand," said Dominic, starting to become a little aggravated. "I was not in Abidjan. I met you *here*... last week. Remember? It must have been before you went."

"That's impossible, old boy," replied the other. "Been out of the country for six weeks." Suddenly he started frantically searching his jacket pockets, and then, just as suddenly, he relaxed, having produced from one a flat black plastic pouch. "Look," he said, "my airline tickets."

"Oh no," Dominic pushed them away without examination. "I didn't mean to imply that you were telling me anything but the honest truth." He was being quite sincere about this, and he turned and walked slowly away from the table with a confused look, mumbling something about it being *his* mistake.

"Yes but..." called Henry Lewis after him, "then how did you know my name?"

Dominic responded without affect as he regained his seat. "Oh... just a wild guess!"

Marvin still seemed dumbfounded as they walked back along the canals. He'd hardly spoken after witnessing the incident over dinner. His usual air of supercilious boredom was replaced by thoughtfulness and an apparent openness to this new and exciting idea.

"I can't believe it," he said.

"What?" asked Dominic.

"What all this seems to mean," he took a breath and continued, "you know, when you first told me this whole story, I must admit, I thought it was just a bunch of cock and bull. I figured you were just grasping for straws with that book of yours. But this guy... when he said that his name *was* Henry Lewis... I - I nearly fell off of my seat. First I thought that maybe this guy was pulling a fast one on you. Some sort of a scam, you know. But then I thought, well, how would he know where you were going to be tonight... you - you're sure it's the same guy?"

Dominic nodded his head. "The same, only... younger." He drew his hand down over his face. "There was less grey in the hair, less wrinkles, he was thinner... healthier looking."

"Healthier looking..." intoned Marvin, "yeah, yeah... but when he showed you his airplane tickets..."

"You see?" Dominic pointed an accusing finger at his friend. "You see? Now I'm not such an asshole as you thought I was!"

"I never said you were an ass... hey! Wait a minute! I don't suppose that it was *you* who set up this whole deal... just to make *me* look like an asshole? Maybe you paid that guy to be..."

Dominic stopped dead in his tracks. "I - I... swear." He held his hand to his heart. "This is *real*."

"I know... I know," Marvin was unusually soft and reassuring – like a mother. He took two paces backwards and put an arm around Dominic's shoulder. "I know," he said, "I don't think you could pull off a stunt like that, or..." he added quickly to avert offense, "or... would want to."

"Really!" insisted Dominic, offended nonetheless.

"I *believe* you!" his friend assured him.

There were parties aboard many of the barges moored up and down the canals at this time of year. People needed less than the slightest excuse to thaw themselves out from their hibernations. The sky was clear that night, and the moon was big and full and orange, and Miranda Manley, keeping vigil upon her colorful deck, pulled tight her shawl as she smiled flirtatiously at the stranger who passed by her station. He acknowledged her look narcissistically but resumed his conversation with his acquaintance. Dominic had affected his most intriguing facial expressions in an attempt to capture her attention, but it was Marvin she eyed as they walked past. And then it was too late, Dominic glanced back to see her turn suddenly the other way and wave affectionately at her dinner guests as they arrived. He consoled himself with a reminder of his mission. Soon he would be riding high... on fame, and she'd... well, he would be in jail, of course, but his words would be soaring high upon the best seller charts. And his name would be a household word, like Al Capone, or... Ned Kelly, or... yes, Robin Hood.

"So... are you going to do it?" asked Marvin.

"Do what?"

"You know..."

Dominic's eyes crinkled into a smile. "You mean..."

"Yes," said his friend.

"Stick up the publishers?" There! He'd said it. Put it into actual words. Breathed it, like Brahma, into the reality of the five senses. But still... as a question?

"Well?" urged Marvin.

Dominic pursed his lips and furrowed serious decision making brows. "Do you really think that Henry Lewis went into the future... and the man we met today was the same man... but from a different time?"

"Aw, come on!" said Marvin.

"I mean, do you really think it could be possible?"

"No, of course I don't think it could be possible," said Marvin, "and yet... and yet..." he stood there with his arms spreading around him like some sagging Jesus on the cross, too divinely detached to be disbelieved. "You're the one who's convincing *me*! Remember?"

"God!" Dominic looked up into the sky, his chest heaving with anticipation. "There's... just one thing that doesn't quite fit right for me."

Marvin stared at the ground, saying nothing.

"You see, just before Henry Lewis left my house, he said— you'll never see me again. But he must have known that I would... if, that is, this incident happened in *his* past."

"Oh, is that all." Marvin sighed the words, as if in relief. "There could be a *million* reasons why he chose not to tell you. Maybe he simply forgot. I mean, he had a lot of information to give you, how could he *possibly* remember everything?"

"Yes, that's true, but... during his entire story he never once mentioned that he had met me *before* his supposed trip to the future. And he was so clear about a lot of things. I – I just don't understand why he would leave out a thing like that."

Marvin walked silently beside him for a while. Finally he spoke. "Have you considered the possibility that he probably didn't realize that that was you tonight."

"What do you mean?"

"Well... you never told him who you were – your name, I mean. Isn't it possible that he just forgot the whole incident, as being... totally insignificant?"

"Hmm... but then, when he saw my picture in the book jacket... wouldn't he have recognized me then?"

"You mean, later on... in the future... when he sees your photo? Well, who knows what that photo looks like. It's probably one of those studio heads shots that don't look *anything* like the people they're supposed to be of. I mean, why would it bring back memories of some whack-job he met in a restaurant once? I doubt if he'd even put the two things together, let alone assume it was the same guy who wrote this *incredible* book. And then... after spending god knows how many years away, and then coming back to meet you... that one little incident is virtually erased by all the adventures and all the excitement he's lived through since then. Come on Dom, think logically!"

Dominic considered all the possibilities, and felt appeased by these explanations. But it is not easy to be objective when so flattered by the unspoken regalia of events. That history should choose one for its spokesman, that one should be remembered as having been needed to fulfill some consequential purpose... is as much as one may ask of fate. Take not that duty from me with the dry cynicism of your cold hard realities. Let me color them, let me flavor them, let me breathe the musky air of purpose upon this setting. Let me drip the humid fermentations of desire upon its foliage so that this green bower might abound within the jungles of fertile capability. For is not that what reality is? No hard metal frame of facts and figures. There are no facts which cannot be contested. Whereas our feelings... are our feelings... are our feelings.

Chapter 21

Her hand caressed, momentarily, the shining brass door knocker before she slammed it, only once, upon its target and then, following the briefest moment of indecision, released it to its own device.

She had driven up the crackling gravel driveway slowly, mostly out of fear for her paintwork, expecting to see the grounds a hubbub of servant activity: the gardner trimming the hedges... the chauffeur, stripped to the waist, hosing down the Bentley, 'shammy' at the ready... housemaids frolicking at the clothesline... but no such activity was evident. Knocking at a silent door seemed, to her, so much more invasive than being encountered along a garden path – so much riskier. What was she going to say after having disturbed these people from their most important duties? For whom would she ask?

When, after quite a while, no one had answered the knock, she dared to assume that the house was, indeed, empty. Unconsciously she had hoped that this would be the case, seeking to be freed of her obligation, having tried as best she could. Should she attempt the knock once more? Why bother, she rationalized, no one is home anyway. But as she turned to leave that place, she caught herself in the act of cowardice and, guiltily, she retrenched for a secondary assault upon her plighted duties. She returned, in short, to the shining brass door knocker. How could she, after all, ethically countenance any such retreat until she had irrevocably established that there was absolutely nothing more that could be done. Her visceral rationalizations were rendered gratuitous however for, just as she fingered that brass appendage, it was abducted impudently from her grip. The door, in short, abruptly opened.

"There's no need to make *quite* such a fuss!" She heard the crotchety old voice speaking before she could even see inside the darkened hallway. But her desire to defend herself was waylaid by the realization that these remarks were actually addressed, not at her, but at a little white dog which had begun barking when the door was opened. It now ran out straight towards her, yelping in a high pitched tone, and then backed up several steps only to charge once more. The little dog performed this maneuver several times, reminding Jocelyn of an annoyingly squeaky yo-yo. Finally, the owner of the voice she had heard, an emaciated silver haired elder, emerged into the light, and set about restraining his bantam canine familiar, by picking him up and vigorously stroking his head. The old man did not notice, that as he was doing this, a thin shot of golden fluid arced outward from the mollified yo-yo's nether regions, and landed square upon the toe of Jocelyn's sensible brown leather shoe. Still... it seemed such a *small* amount, that she chose not to mention it.

"And how can I help *you?*" he asked with a friendly twinkle in his eye.

"Oh! Excuse me I'm er... looking for Freddie Greaves... but I'm not sure if he er..."

"That's right, that's right," said the old man quite agreeably. "That's me."

"Yip!" barked the little white dog.

"Oh!" said Jocelyn, "but..."

"But surely," interrupted old Freddie Greaves, examining the sweet young thing up and down lasciviously, "you can't be one of *my* friends... can you?"

"Yip! Yip!" said the dog.

"Oh, well actually I er..."

"I knew it!" said he, expressing considerable disappointment.

"Yip! Yip! Yip!"

"Actually," she said, "it was a... younger man I was thinking of."

"Ain't it always the case," he feigned the common man's turn of phrase. "But never mind, never mind. It must be Junior yer after."

"Yes. Junior, that's it!"

"Well, he can't be disturbed. *Far* too busy, don't you know. What with his corporation... and family... and social functions an'all... no... *far* too busy." He walked back into the house leaving the door wide open behind him. His thin white legs were visible beneath the hems of Bermuda shorts. Jocelyn noticed that both his knees were bandaged, and he walked with a slight limp. Abruptly he stopped and turned to look at her. Still stroking the dog lovingly, he said, "he's too busy for *me*, I doubt if he'll see you!"

"Yip!"

"Shut up, Tom Tom! *Wha'* d'you wan'? *Who's* a lickle boy? *Who's* a lickle boy?" For a second he resumed a normal voice, "you'd better come in then." He put the dog down in the hallway and Jocelyn, having shut the door behind her, followed the two of them slowly toward the back of the house.

"Dada go get you num-num," he told Tom Tom. "Mmm... num-num... mmm."

"Yip!" said the dog.

A long black ™Bentley rolled sedately up the gravel driveway and parked just behind the ancient blue convertible. The window hummed as it smoothly raised itself shut. Within, the driver became obscured by the reflections of sky and trees upon its spotless glaze. His eyes, eternally secreted behind his sunglasses, portrayed those same reflections in a miniature form. His thin lips, pursed drily around a splintered matchstick, suggested burdens lying deep within his person. Life had not been kind to this man, and, no matter what profit he might wrest from it, he would always believe that it had somehow cheated him. Evil was the element which permeated his environment, and he was a crusader against its deadly influence. Morality had become his only motive for living; destruction his only rejoinder to its antithesis. But only the evil have true morality, and only the moral can be truly evil.

Old Freddie Greaves poured Rose Pouchong from what had obviously once been a fine teapot.

"My wife bought this on our honeymoon." He tapped it with a knobbly arthritic finger. "It fell on many occasions." His finger followed brown surface crack lines along their uncertain routes. "But it never broke... don't know why... she wouldn't use it, of course... had plenty of others. But when she died, I found it... in the cupboard... took it with me when they brought me here. Junior told me to leave it behind, but when he wasn't looking... I put it in my bag." His eyes twinkled in a wicked smile as he pushed the milk jug over to Jocelyn's side of the table.

"Sugar?" he asked.

"How long have you lived here?" asked Jocelyn.

"Oh, it's hard to say for sure, let's see... not long, not long. When was it now? Alfred came to visit me night before last." He noticed the inquisitive look upon her face. "Junior's brother, don't you know, three years younger... Alfred. He died in eighty-seven... fell off the balcony. That was when we lived in Sissingford. Oh, you know, when they had names for things... places, I mean. Sittingford... Audrey used to call it. She thought that were a far more logical name for a thing... place, I mean. Yes, eighty... or seventy-something. I don't remember. In the nineties perhaps... Alfred, who were only a child at the time, you understand, er... concluded that if Sittingford were the logical pronunciation of the thing... er, then Tittingford must be doubly logical... not knowing, ahem... you understand." He stopped and gazed at the floor momentarily. "Anyway," he continued laughing slightly, "Audrey told him to stop being so rude."

"Did you say," asked Jocelyn, "that Alfred came to visit you night before last?"

"Yes..." he stopped and suddenly smiled at her. "Not *that* Alfred. Yes... no! I'm not that old, you know. You see, I like to go walking down by the stream – of course, I can't now." He pointed at his bandaged knees. "I fell... right there." He leaned past her and pointed to the threshold of the room. "Banged them both!" His hand jerkily reenacted the movement of the ground towards his knees. "But I would go... down there by the reeds, we used to go fishing, Alfred and I. Anyway... I saw this boy..."

"Recently?"

"About two or three weeks ago, looking very much like... no, no, Junior and I were *never* close, anyway, he were too old then... ninety... seven... anyway so, looking very much like Alfred, and I said to this boy— your name wouldn't happen to be *Alfred*, would it? And he said— yes, it is. And I said— I used to have a son named Alfred... who looked very much like... er... and anyway, he took to visiting me, he came... let's see now... the night before last. Alfred. He came to visit me. Some time in the eighties it was. Yes... or the nineties, fell off the balcony... in Tittingford... and what of you my dear? Now where do I know you from? My memory..." he held a bony finger to his brow and smiled apologetically.

"I came here once, long ago," she said, "but, I'm here to see Junior."

"Oh, Junior can't be disturbed! He doesn't have time to see anyone! He won't even see *me* these days. He *won't* see you... you don't seem his type."

"Oh, I haven't seen him in years." Jocelyn wasn't quite sure how she should respond. "We went to school together."

"I doubt that!"old Freddie replied.

She didn't contest it. The old man seemed to be wafting in and out of reality, and it required quite a bit of attention to stay with him. "It's just that I'm trying to locate a friend of mine. Becky Burnside. She was his girlfriend for a while..."

"Oh yes," he said, "girlfriends... he has a lot of *those*. His *wife* don't like it very much... but he doesn't see *her* too often, either. He *won't* see you... I don't think."

"I just wondered," Jocelyn continued, "if he might know where she is. I drove all the way from Prickly Bog this morning, and it occurred to me that she might actually live *there*... but it's a big place, and I wouldn't know how to find her."

"Prickly Bog..." he savored the words for a moment. "A thing with a name... a place, I mean. Now *there's* a name. Eighty... seven it were, or ninety something... anyway, I think that's where Alfred moved to. Got married to some woman... of whom his father did *not* approve. Good for him, I say. Teach that bastard that he can't have his way *all* the time."

Jocelyn was getting rather confused now. "Wait a minute! I thought you said Alfred was *your* son?"

"Yes?"

"Well... how could he have gotten married and moved to Prickly Bog, if he died when he was a child?"

"Not *that* Alfred, silly girl!" The old man was getting a little irritated now. "I'm not *that* old, you know! I *do* know my own grandson!"

"*Grandson?*"

"Yes, Freddie!"

"I thought Freddie was your *son*... Junior."

"No, no, no." His agitation was increasing. "*Freddie*... is my son, Junior." He clicked his tongue in frustration. "Frederick... *not* Freddie. *Never* call him Freddie. He won't talk to anyone who calls him Freddie.

Even when he were a child, we were *never* close." He spoke the next few words under his breath, "I always hated that boy," and then louder, "but Alfred... now that were a different thing altogether."

Jocelyn was starting to get a little agitated herself. "Then who the f... I mean, who... is Freddie?"

But the old man didn't have to answer.

"Freddie is *my* son, Ms. D'Orion."

She spun around on her chair and stood up quickly, almost upsetting all the tea things from the table. An arrogantly handsome middle aged man was standing framed in the doorway. He was attired in a silver-grey business suit, elegantly fashioned from the finest silk. He looked to her like a man who commanded respect, if not deserved... then compelled. A man who got things done the *right* way, in other words the way *he* wanted them to be done. She imagined he might be the type who bothers rather less about the means... than the end. The type of person who, when shaking hands, might hold your's until *you* were ready to let go. And then, just before you did, just as your hand went slightly limp, he would lock it with a firm grip, rendering you his temporary prisoner. Suggesting his superiority. Suggesting your weakness. His presence made Jocelyn feel a little queasy. It gave her the irrational desire to rebel against him – for what reason, she did not know – but at the same time, she felt herself completely powerless to do so.

Standing just beside him, and back a little, a powerfully built, thin lipped man in a black outfit (possibly a uniform of some kind) peered at her through mirrored lenses. The kitchen was gloomy... and darker still the hallway where he stood. But neither did he squint nor search for detail amongst the shadows. His eyes saw only silhouettes of black and white, in dimness... or in the light of day. He needed nothing more, no shades of grey, from which to make his judgments. That was the kind of man *he* was.

Then spoke his master's voice. "I'm Frederick Greaves," it said. The little dog growled, ever so slightly, and moved to a safer place beneath the table.

Jocelyn spluttered and fumbled. "Y - you know my name," she said.

"I met you many years ago," he explained clinically. "You came here with... Rebecca Burnside, if I'm not mistaken." He seemed to spit the name out malignantly.

Jocelyn was impressed by the fact that he remembered her at all. She did not want to allow herself to be impressed by *anything* about this man, nor to let him recognize that she was. But she had obviously forgotten *him* completely... what he looked like anyway. (Obviously, if she had mistaken his father for him.)

"Then, Freddie... was the *third* one," she calculated distantly.

"Exactly," the old man cut in, seemingly quite pleased with himself. "Freddie the third."

"My son does not live here," Junior continued. "In fact," he added rather harshly, "I do not consider him to *be* my son anymore! He is not welcome here... and neither are his friends!"

"Oh... I'm terribly sorry," said Jocelyn. But Junior simply stepped clear of the doorway, indicating his desire for her to leave.

"I *told* her you were too busy to see her," said old Freddie. "I *told* her that you wouldn't see her."

"I... didn't know," said Jocelyn and, picking up her bag, she started hurriedly down the hallway. Its extra weight reminded her of that 'special' book which she was carrying inside it. When she'd got a few feet past the man with the shades, she stopped and turned back to address whomsoever might answer her. "Could you, at least, tell me where I can locate him?"

Junior simply shrugged and looked away. But his father, in a frenzy of inexplicable emotion, blurted out, "Prickly Bog! Prickly Bog!"

"Yip!" said the dog.

Already somewhat disturbed by this experience, Jocelyn, in attempting to resume her departure with as much dignity intact as she could muster, was shaken, yet one more time, by a loud crashing sound which pursued her from the kitchen. It was the sound of fine old china being shattered into a thousand pieces. She looked back to see Tom Tom whimpering beneath the table, and his decrepit dada, Freddie the first, his bandaged and arthritic knees, groveling down upon the tea soaked kitchen tiles, amongst the fragments of his departed memories. His eyes welled with tears as he attempted in vain to gather the delicate porcelain pieces, and reconnect them, one to the other as if, somehow, he might, through that travail, regain a life whose loss he would not ever come to comprehend.

The man with the mirrored lenses gazed down upon this scene with no compassion. But his mouth turned up at the corner where a splintered matchstick emanated from it, and Jocelyn thought that she could see the faintest smile.

Chapter 22

A member of the Little Hurst Council speaks:

People hardly refer to it as Little Hurst anymore. It's been absorbed into the Greater Lambden Area now, and the local government is very little more than a showpiece, ruled from above by the beaurocrats in Lambden City Hall. But they don't really understand Little Hurst, and they certainly don't understand the people who'd lived here from time immemorial. Those elitist bastards have been foisting an excessive influx of immigrants, of every species and hue, upon our beleaguered historic community. These people are showing up from all corners of the declining empire, as if they had some right to occupy *our* territory... good grief, we brought *them* civilization! Lambdonians don't want them mucking up *their* fancy neighborhoods in the center of town with their smelly foods and their foreign ways, and Lillerstians (some of the old timers still refer to us as such, and the term is starting to make a resurgence as Little Hurst residents are finding the need to close ranks against the outsiders), Lillerstians... well, we're becoming rather dismayed at the amount of property these backward outsiders are buying up and converting into homes and businesses, right here in the middle of this once venerated community. Businesses, mind you, which serve *only* the immigrants themselves... they don't *want* to fit in. Half of them can't even speak English, let's face it, most of them didn't know how to flush a toilet before last week – didn't have them in the villages they came from. These people are living in the most unsanitary conditions, *fifteen* to a room sometimes, and what's more... they're bringing the property values down. And when property values go down, City Hall responds by cutting back on the funding for local services. Law enforcement, schools, garbage collection... they're all being reduced, just when we need them the most. Everyone's complaining. The immigrants? They're screaming "racism!" (Bloody nerve.) Never mind *racism*, what about us? We were here first, and we've been perfectly happy here... until *they* came along. Now *we're* having to suffer for *their* sake!

But still... there *are* those in the local council who aren't prepared to abdicate their authority quite so easily. Now, I'm not talking about the majority of us, you understand. We don't have all that much to lose in the first place. But there is a core of those who are more... *enterprising,* shall we say... who see their future profitability being washed down the drain of 'progress.' I suppose I can't, in all conscience, blame them for feeling threatened by events, but it's possible that they might well have gracefully succumbed to those events, had they not been... *clandestinely*, if I may say, supported... nay, egged on, in fact, by the silent elite of Old Little Hurst, who have more to lose than even they.

Well, Old Little Hurst is an expensive and fabulous community of age old estates... which have been, quite rapidly, becoming surrounded by developments of a rather unappealing kind. Its inhabitants are, of course, the descendants of those old rulers of yore, whose power had *appeared* to have waned after the last great war. But everyone knows they still pull mighty strings, and control the comings and goings of our little town, secretly, and with a great and historical dexterity. Now, Taylor Bradley, possibly the richest and certainly the most powerful of these elite patrons, has been using his sway with a rather impressionable and, might I add, aggressive young council member named Nick Howe.

When I first met Nick he seemed a pleasant enough young fellow, always cracking jokes and such, but, after a while, I did find myself starting to feel nervous, let's say... uncomfortable, in his company. Oh, it's not that he's threatening in any manner. It's just that, well... he seems to possess a sort of nervous energy, which appears to adversely affect those around him. Perhaps I shouldn't talk for others. That's just me, I suppose, projecting my own feelings onto everything, but... let's just say that it makes *me* feel a bit uncomfortable to be in his presence. He seems too eager to please... everyone... all the time, if you know what I mean. If ever there were a dispute amongst the members of the council, he would be the one in there trying to calm things down. "What's wrong with that?" you ask. Not such a bad thing, I suppose, but... sometimes he would go to the extent of speaking untruths in order to achieve this purpose. Now, I do believe that there's no sense in us haggling endlessly over old issues, if there is, in fact, some way for us to resolve them. But I also believe that all outcomes are best served by a stubborn loyalty to the truth, even if it temporarily causes us a little trouble.

Then of course there's the other side of him. Where he could turn quite nasty, and snap at people in the most remarkable manner... smiling all the time, you see, and then... he would *always* apologize later – still smiling of course. A tense smile, it were, where the creases of his mouth were pulled into tight lines across his cheeks. I always thought it rather unusual for so young a man to have such deep creases embedded permanently onto his features.

It were my old dad who told me, on many occasions when I were a nipper... never to trust a man who smiles all the time. Anger— he would say, is a perfectly acceptable expression of a man's feelings, providing it were called for, and done with a sense of dignity and honor. I think by the word 'dignity,' he meant a sort of... orderliness, control... not ranting and raving and such. Of course he did not find it equally acceptable for the women folk to do the same. He felt it was an unseemly type of behavior for their fragile gender.

Ha ha! Many of the ladies today, I should imagine, would find him a bit of an old fashioned, er... 'sexist,' I believe is the term used nowadays. Well, I wouldn't know about that... I wouldn't dare argue with them about it, of course, but then I wouldn't dare argue with *him* about it either... *if* he were alive. On the other hand, I wouldn't imagine that he'd be too put out by being referred to as such... and might agree with it at that... proudly. What I do know, is that he were an honest man, and he would never abide a hypocrite. If he ever said that he would do something, well... you might as well have carved it in stone, 'cause you could be sure that *that* would be the very thing that he would do.

I don't believe that he'd have had more than a word or two to say to young Nick Howe, or about him, for that matter... *if* he'd have ever met him that is. Come to think of it, I don't believe Taylor Bradley had more than a word or two to say to him on that particular occasion I spotted them together in a car parked outside the supermarket. I remember it specifically because it seemed like rather an odd place for the two men to be having a conference of some kind, or so it appeared... and rather an odd time too. It was about one o'clock in the morning.

You see, the wife had woken up suddenly, she usually tucks herself in a couple of hours before I do... and she had a craving for a cup of Earl Grey. Now, having myself used up the last spoonful of that particular leaf on the previous day, I suggested that I go downstairs and brew her a nice pot of English Breakfast. But this idea did *not* seem to be in keeping with Mrs. Wright's wishes... she claimed that English Breakfast was, by definition, suited best for... breakfast. No— she insisted, it was *only* Earl Grey that would do, and she proceeded to dress herself for a trip down to the all-night supermarket. Nonsense— quoth I. If anyone must needs venture abroad this night, then shall it be me. (I believe a man has certain responsibilities in the household.)

Well... to cut a long story short, we decided to go together. On the way, I asked her if she might be pregnant or something – which was quite a liberty to take, as the wife doesn't normally appreciate rough language – but I thought I might get away with my little joke on this particular occasion, on account of the fact that we didn't *normally* get up after midnight and go for a little drive down to the supermarket. It was, sort of, well... a special adventure... and, er... she didn't clobber me, so I reckoned that she *must* have found it amusing, me being over sixty this past two years now, and she... well, I probably shouldn't blab, but... you know, being past the change, ahem... as it were.

I saw them in my rear view mirror just before we pulled out of the supermarket parking lot. I remember the wife getting a bit impatient 'cause it was taking me so long to get started for home... she looking forward to her cup of Earl Grey and all. But it was definitely Nick Howe in the passenger seat. And he seemed to be talking up a storm, waving his arms around... and smiling, of course, and... sweating. And Taylor Bradley was sitting in the driver seat. Big long silver car it was. Very flashy looking. But *he* didn't say much, just frowned most of the time. He's not a big one on idle chitchat, Mr. Bradley... or so I've heard tell. Anyway, just before I pulled away, they were joined by a tall... 'dark skinned' fellow who I hadn't seen before. My guess is that he weren't one of the local immigrant types. He was dressed in a style you tend to see more of up in the city. I hadn't imagined that Messrs. Bradley and Howe, with their particular backgrounds, would be too partial to *that* kind of company. Although... I *did* notice they didn't invite the young man into the fancy car with them. They just opened the window and he stood outside, leaning on it.

I haven't known too many of... *those* people, myself, so I suppose I shouldn't be the one to judge. But that which I have heard about them has not led me to think favorably of them. Of course, there are exceptions to every rule... singers... actors... and they *do* seem to be excellent sports people, but... well, my personal experience has only been that I've seen our neighborhood degenerate as their numbers increased within it. And, as such, it does seem that their appearance and our losses are directly connected. But still, my old dad... well, he were a man who never came to a hasty conclusion. He taught me that it were usually wiser to let a thing run its natural course, even if that course be not to your liking, rather than to interfere with things that you don't properly understand.

Now, Taylor Bradley... he came from a different class of people than my old dad... and, of course, me. It had been *his* ancestors belief, for many generations back, that they should maintain control of events whenever possible. They weren't happy when things weren't going according to *their* way of seeing it. On the other hand, they never seemed really happy when things *were* going their way, either. They were not a happy crowd. Took themselves a little too serious, my old da... well, anyway... George Burgess is from the same background. His father started the Popodell Publishing Company when George were just a nipper. I've heard it rumored that Popo was the family nickname that George went by as a youngster. And, apparently, the "dell" part came from his mother's middle name, Sophia Della Burgess. Although I've only ever actually heard of her referred to as Mrs. Burgess. Another rumor had it that it was, in fact, her *maiden* name that was Popodell. Well, anyway, those are the rumors. I don't know the family personally, you understand.

But George, er... as I say, is from that same ethic... you know, being in control. And, as a member of the town council, I suppose he feels it his duty to get things done, to make changes, to control the flow of things. In this way, his attitude is very similar to that of the other 'old' families of Little Hurst, and in particular... to Taylor Bradley who, although under a peculiar local trust ordinance is not allowed to stand for office in the council (on account of his excessive holdings in the community) nevertheless makes his presence felt through the nefarious proxy of his several lackeys, including, but not limited to the latest one... a certain young man named Mr. Nicholas Howe.

The difference is that George Burgess and Taylor Bradley have come down on opposite sides in the matter of the immigrant problem. And even though in this particular instance I tended to agree with Mr. Bradley, he was not a man that I would put my trust in. George Burgess, on the other hand, had always seemed an honorable man to me. He had proven himself, over the course of time, to be a defender of the workingman's interest above his own. Therefore, I have chosen to remain neutral in this issue, and to let the two warriors go at it on their own account. My feeling is that justice will be served no matter what the outcome, even if that justice were not immediately recognizable as such.

Well, the first conspicuous fray in this battle took place the very day after I had witnessed that midnight meeting, when bright and early, young Nick Howe got into a raised voice session with Mr. Burgess on the council floor, wherein he impugned Mr. Burgess's patriotism. Mr. Burgess retaliated by reminding young Nick, that it was in fact *he* who was standing up against the decisions of his own government. Young Nick wanted quotas set on the amount of immigration to be allowed in a given neighborhood, and that it should be relative to the amount in other neighborhoods, which didn't seem such a bad idea to me... although I felt he could have used a more respectful tone to a senior member. Mr. Burgess, on the other hand, was more interested in the funding of special services in order to feed the most poverty stricken of the immigrants. I also agreed with this action, as I believe it is not moral to let a hungry man starve, no matter what his background... providing, of course, you have the ability to feed him. Young Nick felt that the legal requirements for immigration should be more strictly enforced, in order— he said— to weed out those with no right to be here! And he pounded his fist repeatedly upon the rostrum as he said it. Mr. Burgess felt that it would behoove our community to offer special courses to educate the local citizenry about the culture of our new foreign compatriots, in order that we might promote understanding, and lessen discrimination. Young Nick indicated that he didn't give a fig for their culture, and that if they couldn't learn to speak our language properly they would get the kind of reception they deserved.

This went on for quite a while and tempers got rather heated. Others joined in too... on both sides of the argument, and people ended up resorting to personal slurs upon each other's characters. Young Nick made some rather nasty and uncalled for remarks, I must say, regarding Mr. Burgess' er... sexual preferences, which I'm sure are not true, er... and if they are... well, he certainly doesn't flaunt it, or behave in any way indecently in public. We heard a lot about such things when I were a young man in the military... as one does, you understand... but a true gentleman – as the officers were, in general – knew how to keep these matters discreet. There's nothing so tawdry as bringing this kind of vulgarity out into the public spotlight. Mr. Burgess responded, somewhat

harshly perhaps, by accusing Nick Howe of associating with gangsters...
although that may well be true (I wouldn't personally want to say). But
still, it's probably not good for old George Burgess' heart condition. He
was already out for two weeks at the beginning of this sitting,
undergoing all kinds of medical testing by Dr. Beecham, who told my
wife (in the strictest confidence of course) that the old fellow might
consider taking it a little easy from now on... if he wanted to see a few
more years.

Interestingly enough, although quite predictably I might add, as I
was walking out at the lunch break, I saw young Nick trying to apologize
to old George Burgess. But old George was having none of it. And,
whereas I personally might have tended to shake the young man's
hand... just for the sake of having the thing over with, I appreciated the
fact that Mr. Burgess didn't. I appreciated, I suppose, the fact that
someone was willing to hold to a principle, and take a stand... even
though I may not have the courage to do so myself.

Andrew Wright: Council member, Little Hurst.

Northcroft Avenue had once been a charming thoroughfare,
where pretty young ladies would promenade of a Sunday afternoon, in
bonnets and frills; where handsome young men in toppers driving pony
traps would offer them rides around the park... and come to rest their
hands eventually, and ever so lightly, upon the ladies laps. But that was
in Taylor Bradley's grandfather's day, and in George Burgess's
grandfather's day. Today the streets were littered with soiled wrappers
from Burger Mart and fast food emporia of every stripe and variety.
Ahmed's... and Harvey's Hungry Horse; Bunty's and Meaties; Veggies
and Slurpy's; Ka Ka's... and yes, Doodies; you name it, it was there.
Multiplex movie theaters with their horrendous black plastic awnings
and fluorescent flashing peep show fonts had defiled and defaced the
gorgeous Georgian crescent colonnade which had once arced
gracefully, with its yellow quarry-stone hue, along a quarter mile of

perfect elegance. Still, if you looked up above street level and blocked out all the traffic noise and the diesel fumes, you could see that graceful architecture sadly surviving its glory days. You might also see, in the second story window of number three hundred and seventeen, a smart, black and white, simple, old-fashioned, hand-painted sign for the Popodell Publishing Company.

From his position across the street, Dominic Devine's eyes scanned the window for signs of life. The roar of the road crew, drilling for the sake of nothing better to do, was hardly muffled by sealing shut the windows of the stuffy automobile in which he sat. Marvin suddenly appeared from the doorway of the building. Lighting a cigarette, he dodged traffic to reach the car and entered it, establishing himself in the driver's seat.

"Doesn't your air conditioning work?" Dominic grumbled, fanning himself vigorously with a copy of *Arms & Ammo* he'd found lying on the floor.

Marvin puffed on the cigarette. "Works beautifully," he answered. But before Dominic could proceed with his obvious request, Marvin (trying to muzzle a smirk) added, "only... they, er... never installed it." His sweaty cohort discontinued fanning for a moment, and leered at him with distrust. "Well..." he explained sardonically, "they wanted extra *money* for it!"

Dominic reached for the winder to crack the window down a smidge, and resumed his fanning, "In other words," he sighed, frustratedly shaking his head, " you don't *have* an air conditioner in this car."

"You know," said Marvin, " I read somewhere that the energy you have to expend to fan yourself actually *raises* your body temperature more than the amount you can reduce it by, er... fanning yourself."

The other man resignedly tossed the magazine into the back seat, picked up the black metal revolver which had been lying in his lap, and began nervously rolling the chambers.

"I hope you dumped those bullets like I told you," said Marvin.

"Yeah, yeah!" Dominic answered sullenly.

"Yeah? Well put that thing away now!" Marvin reached across

him to open the glove compartment. "If someone sees it we could be in big trouble!"

Suddenly, a sharp rap on the window startled Dominic, and he dumped the weapon, pronto, into the open receptacle before him, violently slamming shut its lid. The mid torso section of a police uniform hovered beyond the driver-side window.

"Shit!" said Dominic. "Do you think he saw it?"

Marvin calmly opened his window. "Yes officer, how can I help you today?"

"Move it!" said the cop.

"Excuse me?" asked Marvin feigning cordiality.

"C'mon Marv, let's go!" Dominic tugged lightly at his sleeve.

"I beg your pardon officer, but I was unaware that there was some kind of parking restriction on this block."

The cop clicked his tongue. He was looking down the street.

"Maarv..." insisted Dominic.

Marvin stuck his head out the window. He examined the sidewalk this way and that, as if he were looking for parking signs. But it was quite evident, despite his protests, that this single lane street was, nevertheless, a heavily trafficked thoroughfare. The infuriated trucks and busses rattling past him could faithfully attest to this, barely able to avoid scraping the paint off his passenger door, even though two of his wheels were well up on the curb.

The policeman, a descendant of generations of Little Hurst residents, started to produce his summons pad out of its black plastic rain proof wallet, and looked for the first time in the direction of this... *colored* driver. "Are you going to move this fucking thing?"

"Alright... alright," said Marvin, slipping the gear lever into first. "You don't have to be so fuckin' *rude* about it," he mumbled inaudibly as he pulled the car, one bump... and then another, off the curb slowly disappearing into the congested stream of busy workaday vehicles.

Officer Wallace looked up at the buildings of Northcroft Avenue. He thought they smiled slightly, relieved once again of the unnecessary tensions brought upon them by yet one more disobedient nigger; one more insensitive heathen, ignorant of the ways of society; ignorant of the great dance of manners and courtesy which all civilized people understand, which allows mankind to slide so easily from one state of advancement to another.

"So the gun will be filled with blanks," Marvin reminded Dominic.

They were sitting once again in Eric's – if there really *was* an Eric – enjoying a freshly cooked plate of something absolutely repulsive- looking... at least Marvin was. The ride down to Little Hurst had been almost three hours in each direction, and Dominic was deeply appreciative of the way in which Marvin was being so supportive. Who'd ever have expected as much from him? And perhaps that was because he'd never shown this side of himself on any previous occasion that Dominic could remember. Quite to the contrary, in fact, he'd always given the impression of being a sly and arrogant – if rather hospitable and entertaining – sonofabitch.

In fact, it was often whilst he was being a sonofabitch that he could be his most entertaining. It particularly amused Dominic that Marvin would provoke other motorists, whom *he* felt were driving badly, by cutting in front of them and then slowing to a crawl... repeatedly. Eventually he would allow them them to pull alongside and, amidst their curses and threats, he would feign deafness and complete ignorance of having done anything to them, which of course would frustrate them even more. Dominic often found it painful to suppress his amusement at these moments, and would burst into laughter the moment the other driver sped off, shaking his fist behind him. Admittedly, Marvin usually only inflicted this kind of treatment on *other* sons of bitches who had cut him (or someone else) off in a particularly aggressive manner, and so he could be thought of as some kind of an avenging angel. But, while Dominic's guilt regarding his pleasure at these pranks was assuaged somewhat by the feeling that nothing more than pure justice had been meted out, he could not help suspecting that one day the two of them might be gunned to death on the highway or, at the very least, be responsible for some kind of an accident. And yet, despite his own pleasure at it... despite the fact that Marvin probably only exhibited such behavior because of his overt approval, Dominic secretly disparaged him for it, and felt superior to him for his childishness and malice.

Marvin had other reprobate behaviors which delighted Dominic. One of them was his ability to be offensive at parties, to exactly the kind of people one would want to be offensive to... had one the pluck. Not only that, but he could do it in such a witty manner that it made *them* seem offensive or dim or, at least, in some way deserving of the offense. Sometimes, of course, it could be doubly amusing if that apparently prissy old thing – or wishy-washy young bookworm – responded in kind with an equally off-color comeback; or, for that matter, if they played dumb for a while only to reveal, at some crucial point, a sharper insight, just when Marvin wasn't expecting it. At such times, Dominic would cheer for them, inwardly at least, and rejoice in their victory over that bastard.

"The thing is..." said Marvin, "if you barge straight into this Burgess guy's office and shoot off a couple of rounds right away, you'll *definitely* get his attention."

"Well, I've heard," said Dominic, "that even blanks can kill you if you're close enough... the discharge. Of course I could shoot into the ceiling..."

"No, no, you don't have to worry about that," replied his advisor. "I caught a pretty good eyeful of his office when I was up there; the door was open. It's a pretty big room... at least twenty feet across. He sits *way* over yonder by the window. You could shoot straight at him, it wouldn't do him any harm – unless he dies of a heart attack, of course!"

Dominic giggled like a schoolgirl about to pull a prank, and then suddenly became serious. "Yeah, but won't he wonder why the bullet didn't hit him?"

Marvin mocked his tone of voice, "yeah, but if you shoot the ceiling won't he wonder why there's no plaster falling down on his fuckin' head?" Then he looked Dominic straight in the eye. "Look, if he thinks you're shooting at him, he'll be too fuckin' *scared* to think about things like that!"

Dominic cogitated for a while. "One thing I don't understand," he digressed, "is why that woman told me he was in the *other* office."

"What woman?"

"The woman who answered the phone. She told me that George Burgess was located in their other office, so she couldn't put me through."

"Maybe..." said Marvin, "That *was* their other office." But Dominic just looked confused, so he added, "I mean, maybe where *she* was, was a different place."

"Well that doesn't make any sense. The note paper had *that* address on it... and *that* phone number... where *she* was! Wouldn't you assume that..."

"Now you know what happens when you *ass*-ume things, don't you?" interrupted Marvin. And then he answered his own question before Dominic could get a word in: "That's right! You make an asshole out of Yoom."

"Who the fuck's Yoom?" There was something vaguely déja vu about this to Dominic.

"Haven't a fucking clue," said Marvin, "but... I have noticed these days, that many an upwardly mobile company has a phone center off the premises. Sometimes even in foreign lands – in order, you understand, to take advantage of the favorable exchange rates, and salaries, and so forth and so on..."

"Well... she didn't seem to have any kind of an accent," considered Dominic.

"That's as maybe, young man," said the younger man, "but sometimes they do it just to filter out the important calls from the riffraff. If you know what I mean." Dominic looked almost offended by this, and was just about to say something when Marvin cut him off again. "Anyway, what difference does it make? She was probably just lying in any case... trying to put you off, or something... it's... it's more than likely all part of their scam."

Dominic was pensive for a few moments. "Yeah... more than likely," he agreed. And yet, things nagged at his subconscious mind, the type of things which sometimes must be overlooked in order to get other things done. It had often occurred to him that there are two types of people in the world: people who spend a lot of time thinking about getting things done... and people who get things done. He knew which kind he was.

Chapter 23

All the way back to Prickly Bog Jocelyn had the sensation of being followed. But she never saw anything in her rearview mirror. She even pulled over once or twice, and waited, and watched... and there was absolutely nothing following her for sure. But there *was* something following her; only it wasn't behind her. And even if she could have figured out where it was – that... thing, which followed her – she still wouldn't have been able to see it. Okay, okay, so she would actually *have* been able to see it – because she had seen it before – but only once she'd stopped *trying* to see it. You know, sometimes, one needs to stop focussing on something, and just wait until one simply... falls into the hole. And right now, the hole did not want her to fall in. And so it floated mysteriously, invisibly, above her car.

Sixty-five... seventy... seventy-five, the V-eight throbbed; the old live rear axle was no match for its power. It juddered and crashed over pot holes, where once, in its youth, it may have merely wallowed. Although undisciplined then, it had possessed a tangible regard for bottoms and nerves. Whereas now, cranky, rust infested, metal leaves prayed to god – or possibly to the hole which floated up above – for some kind of mechanical redemption. And if not that, then at least... adhesion.

But a wingéd hole is ™Lexus-like in its disdain for mechanical imperfection, and cares not a fig nor a prune for a rattly fifties deathtrap hurtling down perennially untended highways in the rain. The former does, however, emit a powerful aura of prophylaxis around the *occupant* of the latter. So she was safe, Jocelyn, for the moment at least, while the whole hole, er... I mean the hole(y) angel – played by an invisible Marcello in the movie version, his voice the only clue to his presence –

floated dreamily above, shadowing her like a secret service man. (Eastwood, perhaps... with Marcello's voice, it's not important.)

But someone else was also following her. Another someone she could not see. No mystery here though, all you need these days is a simple electronic homing beacon, magnetically attached to the bottom of the car you want to follow, going beep, beep, beep on your dashboard monitor, so that you can stay well back out of sight, and still know which way to go. And those days were not *even* these days, but our future... an advancement, a progression, the fictitious perfection of our dreams and our desires. For what we seek is not some imaginary completion of what we are, but the constant incompletion of our memories pulling us onward, like a vacuum, to the future through the past. And the beep, beep, beep which she was unconsciously transmitting to that which was behind her, was saying, not this: fulfill my needs, but this: give me *more* needs. In other words, destroy quickly that which I, in my constant striving for perfection, rebuild, order and systemize, before I diminish my supply of imperfection, leaving me without meaning... leaving me content... leaving me numb.

And of he who received that message? He that peered inscrutably through mirrored lenses, even as the darkening sky reflected no longer upon them... what of him?

He went about his work with dignity and pleasure, wreaking havoc for the sheer joy of it... the pure spiritual ecstasy. He knew his mission – how many of us do? He was pure. Like so many ayatollahs and born again evangelists, he was simple and sincere in his singularity. It is *we* who are contaminated by complexity and doubt. We who strive to see so many differing sides of an issue that we can no longer know what is true. We... who are so conflicted in our motivations – and worse, so aware of our conflicted motivations – that we cannot strike, even when we need to. The man behind the mirrored lenses would not allow himself to be endangered in such a way. Should any man attack him, he would defend himself in the most brutal manner, and remain devoid of compunction. He could press a door key through a man's eyeball completely assured in his justification for the act, and never, ever feel a tinge of guilt.

Could you do that?

Even if your life depended on it?

Karl – perhaps that was his name – adjusted the lenses upon his nose, and then resumed a cheery but uncoordinated fingertip tattoo upon the steering wheel. He whistled tunelessly along with the unemotional muzak, flawlessly transmitted through opulent speakers, his listening pleasure undisturbed by the intermittent beeping of a flashing green arrow upon the screen of a little black box suctioned to the top of his dashboard. Karl was tone deaf. More than that, he was a man with no sense of rhythm. It seems consistent, of course, that the two should exist within the same body, when one considers the fact that harmony is no more than the rhythmic interlocking of two or more tonal frequencies. Dissonance, by that same reasoning, exists when two frequencies are *not* mathematically compatible.

For Karl everything was incompatible; therefore everything was compatible. His purity rested upon the basis of his inability to discriminate. It made no difference to him if things moved together harmoniously, or if they collided against one another. He was not a cruel man (he felt), and did not particularly enjoy brutality (he claimed); he had no feelings about it either way (at least none that he could discern). Should he be beaten, or even tortured, well... it was just a thing that people do; he didn't take it personally. But he would, however, extract his revenge when the time was right, in a righteous attempt to simply balance the books. He believed that pain was a necessary part of life which *must* occur from time to time. And when that time arrived, as it often did, if no other was available, he would inflict it upon himself –

although he preferred not to do so, as it can be *so* destructive and leave *such* ugly scars.

He admired those who approached their pain readily. In certain ways he admired those who fought adamantly against it. His admiration did not, however, reprieve the suffering of those upon whom he bestowed it. On the contrary, it made him relish the business all the more; it's good to work with good people. And, whereas he was not impartial to the punishment of those he admired, neither did he resent being the agent of the same upon those he hated and despised. His master was a man he hated and despised, and yet somehow he was also a man that Karl admired. But Frederick Greaves II would never, he knew, be the victim of his torture. Such is life, tops and bottoms. In every situation someone sits above whilst another crouches below. And Karl – if that really *was* his name – accepted the natural order of things with a philosophical resignation not found in ordinary men.

No, it was Margarita who tortured Frederick Greaves Junior; she was his wife. It was she, who lived alone in that great mansion these days. Alone, except for old Freddie (the first), of course… and his memories. Frederick II didn't go there very often, and today, only to welcome their special visitor. He lived in 62509 in a lavish duplex apartment – fitted with every possible amenity – surrounded by a roster of swimsuit models who usually cohabited the premises three at a time, and were replaced at frequent intervals by a management company hired specifically for the purpose. The engagement and removal of these young women was distasteful to Frederick (he had previously experienced unpleasant scenes with some of them when let go), and the "Friendship Management Company" were expert at the uneventful disposition of such matters. Needless to say they had programmed an extensive profile of Frederick's proclivities into their database, and sometimes he felt they understood his needs better than he did himself.

These 6-series towns were a little smaller than the 8-series, but they tended to be a little... cleaner – better kept, with a large number of small modern houses, interspersed with large luxury apartment buildings. The small houses were of a more... middle, or sometimes upper middle class status. But it pleased their richer neighbors, the inhabitants of those towering palaces which rose amongst them, to scan dramatic picture windows, from time to time, and be assured the populace they viewed below were *truly* their inferiors. On the other hand they still couldn't buy an egg, or freshly ground coffee, but no one seemed to care about that any more. Even the excessively wealthy had long since lost their taste buds to the march of chemical additives.

Frederick Junior got everything he wanted in 62509, and he always felt it an unnecessary annoyance to have to visit his wife. So he rarely did. There were no issue of their union to cause concern; Freddie III's mother had long since been disposed of, and Margarita had been Junior's replacement for her for almost ten years now – which was *more* than long enough for her appeal to have worn thin. Although, now that he'd been estranged from her for a couple of years, Frederick frequently speculated – when considering her still quite adequately sensual behind – upon the idea of popping down there and giving her a quick one... just for old time's sake. In fact, on one particular occasion he'd payed her a visit for *just* that reason. Although she didn't seem to respond very enthusiastically to his proposal. He'd had to *intimidate* her a little... you know, physically... in order to get her to cooperate. And even after all that, she didn't show much gratitude for his attentions; she hardly moved during the entire act. Since that time he'd taken to calling her Frozen Margarita... or just Frozen, for short. Karl didn't laugh. He didn't have much of a sense of humor. Maybe humor is somehow related to rhythm... or timing, anyway. Or maybe Karl had some other reason... you know, something personal. Whatever! Anyway, no... it didn't seem worth the trouble to visit her, and so Frederick kept those visits to an absolute minimum.

Karl, on the other hand, was over there all the time. His master sent him to the estate regularly, every fortnight, with a check for Margarita, and periodically on sundry and divers errands; it was after all Frederick's home. But Karl had developed the habit of additionally visiting the place at such times as his master knew naught of it and, over those visits, to spending their duration in the company of his master's estranged wife. She was a woman who seemed to derive great pleasure from the idea of a deception involving her husband's most trusted man, and she used Karl as an instrument of her vengeful game, trusting in his loyalty and discretion; believing it to be based upon his fear of discovery and his master's wrath. And Karl did fear Frederick... and feel immense hostility towards him, and consequently his motivation in this romance was not simply the lascivious embrace of a fine young body. In fact, his carnal pleasure often found itself in conflict with his disgust of the woman whose husband he cuckolded. As we already know, Karl did not register internal conflict, but instead, he sublimated those feelings which did not serve his purpose. Neither was his purpose served if his victim was not cognizant of the identity of his tormenter. In this case, not only was Frederick II ignorant whence came his cuckolding, but that such had indeed ever occurred. After some consideration, however, Karl realized that he had been afforded a splendid opportunity which, if he played his cards right, would allow him to torment both Frederick and Margarita simultaneously without either of them ever discovering his part in it. The disadvantage of this, of course, was that it would not be possible for him to gloat openly about his dominion, to their faces – at least not until the situation of his employment had taken a somewhat different turn – but then the benefit, which seemed worth that small sacrifice, was, that by remaining anonymous, he could continue his little game for as long as it gave him pleasure to do so.

It would be simple enough, he reasoned, to seed just enough clues to allow Frederick to discover his wife's deception, whilst obscuring his own participation in it. He would then be in the perfect position to collaborate in Frederick's cunning vengeance upon his wife, which Karl, of course, would help him to devise. Margarita would, in turn, complain to Karl about her husband's malignancy – as she often did anyway in their more intimate moments, when she coveted his sympathy and allegiance – never suspecting for an instant his own malignant complicity in her troubles.

It is ironic that those who employ underhanded methods in their attempts at gaining power over others are often surprised when others are underhanded towards them. They cry *foul* and curse the air that such a one could *stoop so low*, and they sermonize about the bad sportsmanship and evil nature of their adversary. Karl – if that really *was* his name – understood this dichotomy of hypocrisies, and took full advantage of it, performing his role to perfection. He was not motivated (he believed, at least) by his own inner demons. He was motivated instead by the atmosphere surrounding him; by the demons which inhabited the compass of his master, and his... ahem, mistress. He remained, always, aloof and uninvolved; the purity of his mission must never be contaminated by careless caring. He was merely the spirit of *their* deceit, and neither one of them could ever suspect just how easily his mischief might have been defused, by a simple act of trust... a simple act of honesty.

Beep, beep, beep. How refreshing— he thought— Jocelyn D'Orion was so honest... even without knowing it. She didn't require punishment. She deserved better, far better than life had dealt her up until this point. Yes, she deserved pain... but as a reward! The most blissful agony. It was the ultimate aphrodisiac, especially when applied by as great an exponent of the art as he – she deserved no lesser.

Sadly, however, these daydreams fell *not* within the purview of his present duties, and so he abandoned them for the time being. But he reassured himself that there was no harm in these tender fantasies. And he stored them away in the place where he kept such ideas, only to bring them out at a later date, and play with them – a little boy with his favorite toys, reclining on the rug upon his bedroom floor.

Beep, beep, beep. She was making a left turn onto the last leg of her journey. Prickly Bog was no more than an hour away now, and Frederick Greaves snored quietly in the back seat, as if the sounds he issued were responding to the chatter of the falling rain. No heavenly holes floated above *his* car. He didn't need protection; his life was a vacuum, and nothing could enter it.

He dreamed.

He dreamed of little white dogs which barked constantly, and peed upon one's leg. He dreamed of cracked and broken teapots which leaked their contents upon the kitchen floor like little white dogs. He dreamed that the rain fell for forty days and forty nights, and the roof leaked, and puddles formed around his feet... and tears flowed from his eyes, and fish swam in those tears as they fell through the air towards those puddles around his feet. And the fish cried bubbles of liquid air which rose up through those puddles around his feet, and through those tears falling all around him, and... popped!

And he dreamed that things became smaller as he looked backward into the distant past. People whom he had known floated back there, tiny versions of themselves, hung upon the spiraling concentric lines of oblivion. And sometimes, in their place, milestones hovered sentinel where this one had died, or that one had moved away. But all the way back behind these images, as they shifted their locations, he could see – buckled fast to the disappearing train tracks of perspective – a tiny giant locomotive pointed straight in his direction, its perfect round black nose, nothing more than a pinprick now, but growing... ever growing, a black whole, a dark star, threatening to consume his vision, his entire existence, with the complete and utter void. It was a long way off still, no present threat, but so ever present in its inevitability, as to be here now.

He was jolted from his dreams by the sound of lightning striking some place not too far away, and outside the protective buttery leather-sheathed womb wherein he reclined, the raindrops drummed an echoing counterpoint to his driver's fingertips upon the wheel. "Who am I?" he wondered for a few moments, until it all came flooding back. He was on the trail of disaster − that's who he was − which means that he could be no other thing. He had no choices, and that is a sad thing to be. He had not made himself, he had been made. He was nothing... could be nothing, by himself. He needed (always) others around him for reference, just so as to even understand who he was. He hated his aloneness... and yet he could not be with others. There was no connection. There was no honesty. There was no trust. He did not know what closeness meant; he could not. He was, in short, forever located in the one place he did not want to be. Alone.

Life sucks! Eh?

"Do you know something, Karl?" His baritone vibrations surmounted easily the distant roar of engine and of road.

Karl − it seems that *was* his name − flinched with surprise. Some irrational part of him feared that his thoughts may be overheard. They had been pouring from him unprotected within the sanctity of his imagined privacy. But he was not alone now, and could not guess how long it had been so. "What is it?" he challenged, and turned impatiently to glance over his shoulder. He had established, over the years, a technique of feigning concern with his passenger's thoughts, yet somehow − and indeed most professionally − maintaining his view of the road.

"I sometimes wish..." Frederick continued slowly, languorously, "that I owned absolutely nothing... that I lived on a beach somewhere... in a shack... built of driftwood... and palm leaves... where it would always be warm, and peaceful, and I would have no worries."

Karl nodded vaguely. His eyes shifted back and forth invisibly behind his lenses. This kind of talk made him uneasy.

"And there would be no people there, Karl. No wives, no fathers, no mothers, no children, no whores, no... not even you Karl. No one to pay. No money to pay anything with... I'd have a dog. A friendly dog. A nice big one, who would fetch sticks... if I threw them, but... who would go away and look after himself when I was tired of him." Frederick paused briefly but then, still staring off into the distance, he continued, "I'm tired, Karl. Ever so tired."

"Maybe you need a longer nap," Karl ventured in the direction of the rearview mirror, hopefully trying to avert the lengthy continuation of this philosophical colloquy.

"No, not tired in that way." (Karl sighed, but his passenger continued anyway.) "I'm tired of... of all *this*. This whole *business*. I'm tired of controlling this whole thing. Juggling a million details. Sometimes it feels like some automatic part of me is responsible for every thing I do... that I'm not really in control at all – I don't even really *like* much of what I do. But somehow I just... keep doing it. Can you tell me why that *is*, Karl? No... I suppose not. *You* wouldn't know. How *could* you?"

And I don't really care— thought Karl.

"Some part of me feels sorry for Jason Cyllabus Novedi, and even... yes, a sense of respect. In a way, I suppose that I'm rooting for him to survive... triumph, even, in his quest for... well, whatever he's on a quest for. I don't even *have* a quest for anything. So some part of me wishes him the best of luck, wishes for him to prevail... while I know at the same time that he cannot. That he must be killed.

"After all, I wonder, is *anyone* really so dangerous? I think not. There is, after all, a natural balance between purity and corruption." (Karl, strangely, found himself in agreement for a change.) "*We* shall survive, Karl, as we always do. How can we blame this poor stupid fellow for wanting to make everything perfect? How would he know that everything already is?

Jocelyn arrived in Prickly Bog at about seven in the evening. The rain had been falling relentlessly for several hours now, and even that great town's modern and ultra-efficient sewage system was finding the quantity burdensome. In fact, everything seemed to be going wrong here since the shooting at the cathedral. Although, to tell the truth, much of the shock which people felt was more attributable to Jason's sermon than to his apparent martyrdom. Whatever the reason, there was an air of tension about the place, as if *everything* were preparing itself for the ultimate collapse into ruination.

Now, we all know that once a historical outcome has been determined, any alternative conclusion seems not only less than remote, but it simply cannot be. Whereas, up until the actual materialization of that future reality, it often seems entirely possible that its development might yet be influenced, or changed, by a choice made now. This, of course can never be proven, as it is impossible to know whether that future we have influenced was in fact the same future which fate had determined in the first place... or, for that matter, whether our contribution was not simply the agent of fate's predetermination. It is a semantic argument at best... a thoroughly useless one at worst. Nonetheless, Jocelyn was at a loss for any decision. She didn't know what to do. She didn't know where to go. The hospital seemed out of the question for the time being – at least until things settled down a bit. She wondered if Jason had any trustworthy employee whom she might contact and ask for help. But she didn't have the first clue as to where to acquire such information. She wondered if Rebecca Burnside had in fact run off with Freddie III, and if they two were presently cohabiting some blissful love nest within a mile of her current location. But whom could she ask? The police? She didn't trust the police in *this* town; at least in 83047 she knew the sheriff. The town hall? It was possible that the town hall might have records of the entire community which were open to perusal by the general public. But it would be closed now. Tomorrow then, she would have to wait until tomorrow. Maybe something would happen, she fantasized, between now and then. Maybe she would accidentally run into someone she knew, preferably Rebecca or Freddie, or maybe some stranger would befriend her... answer all her questions... put her up for the night.

What the hell was she thinking? Was she out of her mind? She may be a country girl, but she knew better than to follow a stranger home. She checked in her wallet. There was a little money, but not enough to get a hotel room. Still, she could buy something to eat... and she could always sleep in the car for one night. She'd never done that before, it all seemed quite exciting for a second. No it doesn't— she thought— I'm homeless and friendless and cold, and parked in a dark, damp alleyway with the needle of my gas gauge kissing the letter E.

But it is usually at that very moment of despair – when things seem utterly, and completely hopeless, and one is resigned to sleeping in the car on a cold damp night – that actual things begin to happen. In real life, it can be the result of a refusal to accept one's situation which provokes some kind of action that forces things to happen. In stories, on the other hand, it is often something much more passive... something initiated by fate which appears out of the blue. And this particular situation was no exception to that fictional rule, for it was at that very moment that Jocelyn's attention was drawn to the wipers squeaking noisily across her windshield, and she noticed that the rain was almost over, and her prayers were answered in a flash of light. Up there, in the sky... well, okay, not in the sky but above her on the wall at the corner of the street... and, okay not so much in a flash of light, as a continuously flashing light... but there it was, unquestionably. An angel.

Well okay, it was the fluorescent outline of an angel at the top of a grocery store sign. And beneath it were spelled out these equally flashing fluorescent words:

ANGEL'S GROCERY • 24 HOURS
CARDS • BOOKS • MAGAZINES
EGG • MILK • JUICE
PAY PHONE • ARCADE GAMES • ATM

So why— you ask— was *that* the answer to her prayers?

Because:

It suddenly occurred to her that where there was a pay phone, there was information to be had. How silly of her, why hadn't she thought of it before. She could simply dial information, and ask for Rebecca's (or Freddy's) number. But more importantly, it made her suspect that if such obvious and simple solutions could pop out of nowhere, to puzzles which had previously seemed so overwhelming to her, then other solutions to other seemingly irreconcilable problems might lay hidden around some convenient corner, just waiting to be discovered. The thought cheered her considerably as she thunked the car door shut, and headed over to Angel's twenty-four hour grocery.

A large black limousine pulls away from the innocuous grey building. The misty air obscures its retreat, but sparks a halo of bouncing light around its shadowy form. Inside the small apartment a telephone rings... and rings. The hand no longer moves which had reached for it, but rests now, defeated by finality, just like these two lover's bodies which lie face down in pools of life's black syrup.

All hope is lost! All hope is lost!

Who did this thing?

All hope is lost.

Chapter 24

People are so cruel— thought Dominic Devine— I don't even *believe* in violence. Well... I know it exists, but... you know, if it's *necessary*. I suppose it *is* in some circumstances. Well... acceptable, anyway, even if it isn't *completely* necessary. Necessary, of course, being a matter of opinion... isn't it? I mean, is freedom necessary, for example? Mind you, I suppose the definition of freedom itself might be a-whole-nother subject for debate.

He leveled his gun at the mirror in the manner of some Jimmy Cliff baad maan look alike— They'll know, when they examine my gun, and find these blanks... that I wasn't *serious* in my threats; that this action was nothing more than a *parody* of a threat... a dance performance... an art piece, if you will. That's right, you see it's really just part of the book. It... and the book, well... they go together. They complete one another. The word... and the action. Without the other... either one is meaningless. If I don't fulfill this action, then I don't *deserve* to be published. And in fact, if this world doesn't have enough ingenuity to create someone who is capable of achieving this thing – this project... this combination of word and deed – well... then this world doesn't deserve to read it! I mean, I'm doing it for *them*! Aren't I? I need their support. If they don't support me, well... all is lost. And I think I can truly say that it wasn't *me* who did it. And it wasn't *me* who *didn't* do it. I am, after all, simply the vessel of *their* desires enacted... or denied. I am the manifestation of their inner purpose. If I appear to have no purpose of my own, it is because *they* have none. As I fail or succeed, so too do they. If I emerge crystalline, a beacon of accomplishment and power, it is *their* light which radiates out through my facets. But if I dwindle, sucked back into the sludge of anonymity, it is because of *their* fear of clarity and focus, *their* fear of character sharply defined. It is their own limp noncommittal which condemns them to forever wishing, forever wishing... to be born.

But wishes are wishes, and beggars walk.

He looked around the room. There upon the table, his half drunk cup of coffee lying cold. He placed the gun beside the cup, then raised the cup up to his lips. He sipped the coffee from the cup, then placed the cup beside the gun, which prior to, he'd placed beside the cup… when it was on the other side. He scrutinized the spot upon the table where the cup had been located and thought about the symmetry of change. The cup had been there just a second past, and now it was no longer there. Yet here it was quite clearly on the other side. It was, in short, somewhere else. And he remembered that old joke which proves with logic that you are not where you are:

> Abbot: Are you in Pittsburgh?
> Costello: No!
> Abbot: Are you in Arizona?
> Costello: No!
> Abbot: Then you must be somewhere else?
> Costello: That's right!
> Abbot: Well then if you're somewhere else, you can't be here!
> Costello: Aieeaieeaieee!!!

And Dominic Devine realized for the first time that this was no joke. It was true. If you're somewhere else, then you can't *possibly* be where you are. And he wondered where, exactly, he was. Somewhere else, or here? He felt an immense future resting heavily upon his shoulders, but he could not seem to summon up the strength to lift it. He reminded himself that it was *he* who was crucial to the flow of events which he was picturing. Without *him*, things would not happen. Without *him*, things would not have happened so far. And yet his body felt light and his presence, insignificant, and he was reminded of the man who thought he was disappearing because his family and his friends never seemed to notice him, or talk to him anymore. Dominic looked down at the back of his hand, watching the bloated veins run their wriggly courses like the blue branches of his family tree.

What value— he wondered— is a noble line, when cowardice is common like dirt, when fear inhibits all your most important decisions, and terror inhabits your every waking day. You can talk, and talk, and talk, all you want about how nothing is getting done, but all the while… nothing is getting done! And he knew, suddenly, and in a way that he had never known it before, that the time for action was at hand. It had finally arrived. There could be no more talk, no more excuses, no more promises or slogans. It was now or never! It was time to pay the piper! Seize the day! There could be no more hesitation! There is no time like the present! Just shut up, and get on with it! No more talking about it! No more stalling! Just do it! Okay? Here I go… any minute now!

He picked up the gun and examined it resting there in the palm of his hand. And all these thoughts were spinning at infinite speeds around his head which rested, apparently, upon his shoulders. But whilst within that head he conjured up those brave intentions, foretelling what he would or would not do, he noticed that another strange phenomenon was starting to occur: his hand was becoming translucent. The veins were showing clearly through the skin now… and now he could see all the way out to the other side. He could see, in fact, the table upon which his arm rested, right through the arm which rested on the table which he could see through his arm. And, somehow, he knew what it all meant. It meant that he, like the man in the story, had begun to disappear. And he knew, too, that whatever decisions he would choose to make in the future… that which was going to happen had already begun.

"I don't know *where* he is," said Marvin calmly.

The dapper, grey-suited young man he spoke to, seemed a pleasant enough fellow (although his face is not exposed to us, just now), but pleasantness can turn sour when expectations are frustrated, and one whose benign expression is a mask for his inadequacies, can breathe venom with a tone… a simple tone.

"I don't want this project cocked up!" he commanded. "We've put too much time and money into it." And then, with indignant and self righteous pessimism, he added, "I knew this wasn't going to work! This hair brained scheme!" He breathed heavily. "I tried to warn Mr. Bradley that your *type* couldn't get anything accomplished!"

"Look, Howe!" Marvin's tone could also be venomous. "I'm going to accomplish smacking you in the face in a minute, if you don't shut the fuck up!"

Young Nick recoiled, incapacitated by the threat of physicality. They were standing on the corner of Northcroft Avenue, about twenty feet from the entrance to the building in which Popodell publishers were situated.

"Don't worry," continued Marvin, easing up on him somewhat – if only so as not to attract attention, but perhaps also he felt a little guilty about intimidating so pathetic a specimen; it was just *too* easy. "Everything's under control," he added reassuringly.

"Well what time..." Nick sensed the threat receding and regained his bravado, "is he *supposed* to be here?"

"Three o'clock. Don't worry, he's only fifteen minutes late; it's a long drive down. Maybe he got caught in traffic." Marvin peered down the street, starting to worry a little himself now. "He'll be here in time to catch the six o'clock news... even if it takes him another hour to get here. Don't forget, he wants the T.V. news to sell his book for him. He's gonna be a big celebrity."

"Mr. Bradley doesn't care about any of that," said Nick. "He just wants George Burgess dead!"

"D'you think you could say that a little louder," spoke Marvin in an even tone. "I think that guy across the street didn't quite hear you!"

Nick pretended to ignore the comment but continued, nevertheless, in a hushed tone. "The point is, Mr. Bradley doesn't give a heck about Mr. Devine's literary career. In fact, we wouldn't even mind if Mr. Devine ended up deceased after all of this."

"Yeah, and me too, I bet!" said Marvin. Nick Howe just grunted and turned away. "Listen to me you little shit-head," Marvin continued, shoving an angry index finger deep into the other man's personal space. "Dominic happens to be a friend of mine."

Nick stepped abruptly backwards, moving his face away from any implied danger. "I'm glad *I'm* not one of your friends," he hissed.

Marvin shrugged off the comment, but only after having considered it for a moment. He dropped his hands to his side, and then inserted them into pockets before explaining. "I *promised* to help get him famous – it's the *least* I can do to help him out in this situation."

"This *situation*?" Nick almost laughed with disgust. "There *was* no situation until *you* created it for him. *You're* the one who sent him the letters. *You're* the one who hired the actor. *You're* the one who came up with this whole scam, having his book copied so that the actor

266

could quote his own words back to him and make him think that he was going out of his mind. Brilliant! If it'd been up to me, I would have just had Burgess terminated in a dark alley one night."

"No, no..." Marvin was shaking his head. "You have no imagination, no finesse. A murder would make people look for the murderer... who might be caught... and connected to Bradley... or me... nah! But a heart attack... because of *blanks* fired." He paused and examined Nick's face for a moment. "Nah... you're too stupid to understand the poetry of that, Howe!"

"I understand *results*," said Nick. "How do we know it will work? How can we be sure that he will even *die* of a heart attack? What if they get him to the hospital and revive him?"

"That's why I'm in charge of this..." said Marvin. "Cos I think of these things... which is why I have a man at the local hospital... to make sure."

"Well... well, what if he doesn't even *have* a heart attack at all?" Marvin chose not to answer, so Nick continued. "At least you could swap the blanks for real bullets... without Devine knowing."

"No! No... look, that would spoil the whole idea... anyway, Bradley *liked* my plan!" He waved dismissal, as if this trumped *any* objection.

"Yeah well Bra– I mean, *Mister* Bradley paid you a large amount of money to arrange this whole deal. It'd better not fail!"

"I've had a lot of expenses. I had to pay the telephone receptionist for three days each time, cos there was no way of knowing exactly when he'd call – not to mention the phone line, I had to keep that open for a while; it had to be the same number each time... don't you get the beauty of this plan? It was really all Dominic's idea in the first place. *He* was the one who chose the publisher. I tried to talk him out of it... at least, that's what he'll remember... anyway." Marvin checked his watch anxiously. "Where the fuck *is* that guy?" And then he added, "he'll be here, he'll be here!" Marvin wasn't sure if it was Nick Howe that he was reassuring, or himself. "...and then there was the actor. He spent a lot of time learning how to recite that chapter. He had to get it just right... and then he wanted extra money for going into the canal."

Nick was actually much more impressed with the plan than he

let on. It had surprised him that Dominic had bought into it at all. But he *could* imagine how it might seem a convincing reality to someone not privy to the background machinations which had made it all appear so real. The slight of hand of the confidence trickster. Like moviegoers at a western, who cannot see that the buildings of the quaint little town, are nothing more than flat surfaces supported by diagonal beams from behind. Yes, he might even have admired Marvin for his creativity but... well, his racism just wouldn't let him do it. How, after all, could one of *those* people be so clever. "Well, how did you know..." he tried to ask casually, "that Devine would take the old tramp home with him?"

"You see? You see?" Marvin was triumphant. "Just the same way that I know he's going to be here!" But then he acknowledged, "well I didn't know he'd take him home, but it didn't matter. It wasn't a necessary part of the plan. But I did know that Warren – you know, the actor – would interest him enough to get the con going. It was up to Warren to get him talking. And Warren is good... real good! You *see*? I know my people. And I know my Dominic Devine. He's just a guy who needs a little motivation. He's really pretty competent at some things, he just don't realize it cos he's so fucked up." Marvin looked at Nick Howe and added, "who isn't, eh?"

Despite himself, Nick Howe was touched by some emotion he didn't use very often. "I don't understand. You keep on talking like he's your friend... as if you really like him. Don't you see you're conning him, lying to him, getting him arrested?"

"He *knows* he's going to be arrested," said Marvin, "he's prepared for that. I'm doing him a favor; I'm going to make him famous. He's really pleased that all these mystical events are happening to him. I did that. I brought the magic into his life. I'm gonna make the predictions in his book come true... even if the truth isn't *exactly* the same as the one he imagined. His *belief* is what'll make it real. He wouldn't want to know the truth. It would spoil the illusion. I mean... if you went to a magic show, would *you* want someone to explain all the tricks to you? Of course not!"

"Yes I would, actually," said Nick.

"That's why you're an asshole," replied Marvin. "That's why you're trapped in a drab, grey suit existence. That's why you don't know what magic is. That's why Dominic Devine is my friend, and you're not!"

"You can't imagine," asserted Mr. Howe, "just how glad I am about that!"

"Yeah well, don't worry about it," Marvin reassured him, "it won't ever happen," and he turned his back on the man in the grey suit, as if awaiting the arrival of his good friend from the opposite direction. "And anyway," he continued over his shoulder, "you shouldn't really be here when he arrives. In fact, I wouldn't even be surprised if he saw you standing here talking to me – and left!"

"So you *don't* think he's coming," taunted Nick.

"Bullshit!" said Marvin. "He'll be here... just as soon as you fuck off." But in all truth, by this point, Marvin didn't really believe that Dominic would show. "Go on, fuck off out of here! I'll call you later when the job is done."

Nick Howe pooh pooh-ed him with a single wave of the hand as he turned to walk away.

"Hey!" Marvin called after him, smiling. "You'll see my boy on the evening news."

"Yeah... yeah," said Nick as he disappeared into the crowd.

Chapter 25

Jocelyn thumped the phone down on its hook— I can't believe they're not in— she thought. It had been so easy to get Rebecca's number... and Freddy's. Turned out to be the same number, after all. But the exhilaration of that small victory was dulled by the lack of response she was presently achieving. She exited the small phone booth, out into the noisy store, determined to wait there a while and try again later. She had, in any case, no other place to be, and – in comparison to any alternative she might possess – it seemed a warm and cheery place to shelter for the moment.

Every once in a while the loud mechanical hum in the store was interrupted by an even louder beep or rattle caused by a young fellow playing pinball in the corner. Sometimes he would slam the side of the machine, not so much out of frustration (as it had first appeared) but just because it was the style. A couple of times his friend had come into the store to obtain updates on his progress with the game. They had yelled things to each other in some unintelligible dialect of the English language, and the friend had returned to his post outside, chatting with the neighborhood bums, chatting with the whores, who had just emerged from their rain shelters, ready for work, ready for hanging out, ready for a smoke or a pinball game of their own.

The place smelled of stale fat, of burnt meat and bread, of the dust which hung in layers upon the cans of stale meat and fish and syrupy fruit cocktail which lined the shelves. Jocelyn sauntered over to the counter. Angel was a balding man; an unshaven, swarthy type, with heavy features folded comfortably over one another in a mask of utter honesty. He sat low behind his counter, behind racks of celebrity magazines and ™Chicklet and ™Marlboro displays... and lottery tickets, watching Greek soaps on a black and white, twelve-inch ™Ferguson, which illuminated him in blue-grey flashes from below. Amongst his exaggerated reactions to the show were interspersed rough words of advice, which he offered inattentively to a young man who sat on a little wooden stool on this side of the counter, holding his troubled head in his hands. They did not look at each other – they would not have been able to see each other over the counter anyway – but each aimed his head upwards when speaking, in order it would seem, to direct the sound over the top.

Jocelyn approached them. "What's an egg-milk-juice?"

Angel continued with his conversation for a few seconds, and then stopped abruptly. "What?" he said, standing up slowly and turning to examine his new customer.

The young man on the wooden stool looked up at her with a vacant and total lack of understanding broadcast quite plainly across his otherwise not unpleasant features. Jocelyn turned toward him and then back to Angel.

"On your sign outside," she answered, "it says *egg-milk-juice*. Is that some kind of a shake?"

Angel frowned at his young friend. His friend searched Angel's face for hidden clues. Angel looked down and wiped his hands on the soiled apron he was wearing. He cleared some newspapers off the top of the counter and lifted the flap open, pushing past Jocelyn as he stepped out from his sanctuary. He walked to the door, and then through it, turning only once he was outside, to face the flashing sign affixed above it on the side of the building. Jocelyn could see him framed there in the doorway, looking upward with his fists resting steadfastly on his hips; glowing intermittently in the misty air, illuminated from above by his own flashing name, and ignoring the persistent drip of water from some overhanging wire, which splashed his cheek at regular intervals.

After perusing the sign for a few moments, he suddenly

exploded into the most operatic sounding laughter Jocelyn had ever witnessed. The young man had by this point gotten off his wooden stool, and now craned his thin neck to observe his friend outside. Angel marched back into the store and, shaking the water off his muzzle like a wet dog, he halted directly in front of Jocelyn. He started to speak, but then stopped. He looked up at the ceiling and winced, as if he simply could not find the words with which to explain. He tried to pull the apron up to his face but it would not reach, so he extracted an equally filthy rag from his pocket and wiped the remaining moisture from his cheek.

Finally he raised one stubby thumb at Jocelyn and spoke: "I sell *egg*," he added a forefinger, "I sell *milk*," and now the middle finger as well, "I sell *juice!*" He looked at her quizzically. " What you want, lady?"

Jocelyn covered her face with her hands and laughed in embarrassment. "I am *such* an idiot!"

Angel was laughing too. "You very funny lady."

He grinned at his young friend who laughed, and then stopped, and then laughed again… and then stopped again, and said, "what?" But Angel just kept laughing.

"*What?*" the young man persisted. Angel just wiped his hands on the rag, and laughed some more as he pocketed the rag and then wiped his hands again on his apron.

"What?" the young man whined yet again, clearly starting to annoy Angel now.

"Later, Kostos! Later!" Angel reprimanded him, and resumed his original station, shutting the flap like a drawbridge behind him.

Jocelyn, still giggling a little, turned to face him now, "I'll just take a coffee," she said.

He moved over to the warming plate where a stained round glass container sat half filled with thick black gunk. "Regular?" he asked.

"Dark," she said, but then noticing what he was actually offering

272

her, she quickly added, "no... wait! Not coffee, tea! Give me some tea instead."

Angel stood there with the coffee pot in his hand and turned halfway to look at Jocelyn. "What kind of tea you want, lady? *Egg-milk-tea?*" They both burst into laughter at this, and Angel almost spilled the coffee he was holding.

On the other hand, Kostos, who had regained his seat by now, rocked back and forth a little on his wooden stool with a frustrated look, holding his arms extended and repeating, "what... what... *what?*"

Finally, Jocelyn gained control over her laughter. "Yes please, tea... with milk" she smiled. "Hold the egg."

"Wait," said Angel winking, "I hold egg." And he reached down behind the counter and came up with a real hard boiled egg in his hand. "You hungry, lady?"

"Thanks," she took the egg, wondering where he could have possibly obtained it. "How much do I owe you?"

He saw her rummaging through the loose change in her wallet; in this neighborhood, he'd seen *that* done many times before. "Eh!" he responded. "It's on *me* lady. Angel treats— *Kostos!*" He yelled at the young man, who jumped at the sound of his name. Angel gestured toward Jocelyn like Sir Walter Raleigh. "There is a lady present, Kostos."

"What?" said Kostos.

"How many seats are there in the house, Kostos?"

"Oh!" Kostos immediately got off the seat and offered it to Jocelyn, smiling at her meekly.

"Oh! No... no really, that's alright," she said.

"Go ahead," said Angel, "sit down."

"Go ahead," said Kostos, gesturing toward the chair like Sir Francis Drake. "Sit on it."

"Oh... okay," she capitulated, not wanting to offend, and she sat down and commenced to peel her egg.

"One tea-milk-hold-the-egg... coming up," said Angel, and he turned to make a ferocious face at Kostos.

"Coming up!" repeated Kostos happily, but then he noticed how strangely Angel was looking at him and he added, "*what?*"

"Later, Kostos," Jocelyn chimed in dryly, touching the young man lightly on his arm, "later."

Kostos smiled at her familiarity, and then they all three began to laugh again.

"Do you know where she is now?" asked Frederick Greaves. The limousine silently splashed through a puddle, soaking a woman who had been waiting at the corner to cross.

Karl smiled. "I have her right here in my little machine." He patted the dashboard monitor lovingly.

"I wonder what she's doing," whispered his master.

"She's having a cup of tea," answered Karl.

Frederick considered his answer for a moment. "How could you *possibly* know that?"

"Just a guess," said Karl, flashing a look at the rearview mirror and catching Frederick with a finger up his nose; it wasn't the first time.

But in truth, Karl didn't really know *what* she was doing. He couldn't even guess. He didn't really know *why* he'd said that she was having tea. He didn't even know why he'd said he guessed. In actual fact, Karl knew very little about himself... or his own actions; but he thought he did, and so he never questioned what was going on.

So what *was* going on?

Somebody was putting ideas into Karl's head. That's what!

Somebody was putting words into Karl's mouth. That's who!

But *who?*

Well, whoever it was, somebody was doing it in a consequential pattern. They were providing − not entire memories − but flashes of memory, which made it *seem* as if there was an entire memory hidden behind them. The history of a life which is rarely examined. It is stored in the attic somewhere, or the basement, under layers of dust. Is it denial, or repression which keeps them buried there? As long as there are flashes which promise the preservation of what was us, how often do we question them? Sometimes never. But flashes can be like the crack of light which gives the only solace, hour after hour, locked in the closet under the stairs. Flashes are the sting of cigarette burns on your thigh. Sometimes they are the pain of being raped from behind when you are just a little boy, playing peacefully on the rug upon your bedroom floor. Flashes bring us fear, and desperation... and anger. And even if there is no reality to the empty spaces between them, the flashes, like a dotted outline, can be connected to paint the most awesome picture of what a life has been.

For Karl, they did just that. And he believed in the past that the flashes had brought him. And we all know that what we believe to be true... is!

And yet, whoever it was who put those ideas into Karl's head, those words into his mouth, must have known what Jocelyn was doing at that very moment. Must have known that she was having a cup of tea. That she was eating a hard boiled egg... with ™Tabasco sauce. That she was the guest of two charming Cypriot storekeepers, who were listening intently − without even the *glimmer* of disbelief − to the crazy story which she, for some reason, just could not hold inside her anymore. But it was okay, they trusted her implicitly, every word she said. And like knights of old, Raleigh and Drake, they hurled themselves before her regal feet, and presented themselves at her disposal.

"An adventure," said Angel.

"An adventure," said Kostos.

And why— you ask— should these two men risk anything at all for a complete stranger? Why should they close up shop for the first time in eight years? Why should they wipe their hands on their aprons before removing them? Why should they throw out the young fellow playing the pinball machine, and turn off all the lights, including the big fluorescent sign flashing outside, and follow this strange woman off on some bloody fool's errand? Because it was an adventure, no?

No! It was because somebody had put the idea into their heads of course! Well… okay, that's not the only reason. After all, everybody's heard of the great Jason Cyllabus Novedi. Most everybody in Prickly Bog was a member of his church, but Angel always used to say that the Great God Bongo was just another manifestation of Dionysus— who was my ancestor… but way back— And he had never felt the need to become an active member of the local temple. He'd moved here eight years ago when his sister died, and left her only son, Kostos, in his care. Prickly Bog was rapidly becoming a boom town, but there were still some rougher areas one could buy into for a reasonable amount. So Angel and Kostos came to set up shop. They would make it big in the big city.

Somewhere along the way Kostos, as he matured, had met a sweet little thing named Kristina. Her father had a job at the J.C.N. building, where he sat at a computer terminal all day long. Nobody knew what he did. Jiggery-pokery, Angel called it. But nonetheless, that girl had persuaded her young suitor to accompany her to the temple once a week. K and K, they called themselves… or the KKs. Young lovers, together like two hearts carved into a tree. Same hearts, same love, same name. Ka Kas, is what Angel called them – pair of doody heads. But Kostos would not be taunted. He had read that book, you know… the one about the founder of the church of Bongovism – how he was born, how he would die. And he could quote chapter and verse from the Catechism of the Great God.

You know what Bongo says— he would tell his uncle— *the way you see things, depends a lot upon the way you look at things*— or sometimes he would quote— *if you don't like what's happening to you, try changing the way you behave*— if it was appropriate, and also sometimes... when it wasn't. Kostos really believed in all that stuff, from the history to the predictions. Everything in those books, he was sure, would come true eventually.

At first, Angel used to argue with him. "Bah!" He would say. "You talk like that book knows everything!"

"It *does!*" his nephew would reply.

"It doesn't have anything for me," was Angel's answer. "It's nothing to do with my life... or *your* life! That book is not for us, Kostos; we are not in there."

"We *will* be," replied the young man. "The preacher *says* we will... when our life is touched by the *one*, Jason Cyllabus Novedi."

"Ah, the preacher, the preacher... if the preacher told you to jump off a – never mind, you probably would!"

But even though he did protest so much, Angel had his own needs for belief and spirituality... and family, albeit of a subtler nature. And when he found that flyer shoved into his hand one day, it made him think that there might be another way in which he could comprehend the mysteries of the Great God Bongo, and in some way, perhaps reconnect himself with the sensibilities of his straying young nephew.

It espoused a different way of interpreting the words of the Great God Bongo, as written within the Catechism, and also within the book, "The High Priest of Prickly Bog." It was a more subtle interpretation, which appealed to Angel's somewhat mythical and metaphorical leanings. It led him to attend a *secret* meeting of the Bongovian order of the Intergalactic Temple of the Great God Bongo. *Secret*, one supposes because, technically at least, it was illegal to be a member of the Bongovian order. Admittedly, a few years ago there had been the

Bongovian suicide terrorists who had killed a lot of people and pissed-off a lot of people, not the least of whom were the many other pacifist Bongovians who had suffered a terrible repression in the wake of their actions. But, although a certain governmental department continuously did its best to stir up hatred against them, nowadays most people – including the police department – didn't see them as such a great threat to the establishment anymore, and, despite being officially frowned upon, they were left mostly alone to have their 'weird little cult meetings.' It would have been easy enough for the Patriotic Committee (the secret government organization which had been created to observe them) to infiltrate their brotherhood – and this most likely had already occurred – but the Bongovians naively believed that constant exposure to the inherent correctness of their doctrine would inevitably sway any potential spy from his mission, and turn his sympathies, inexorably, to *their* viewpoint. They were, therefore, prepared to take substantial risks when promoting their organization and philosophy. The only alternative to this risky behavior, they believed, was that their numbers would dwindle and they would eventually be forgotten, and consigned to the already jam-packed graveyard of defunct religions. The Patriotic Committee, on the other hand, desired their survival almost as much as they themselves did. It was in the interest of the authorities to keep available a scapegoat for whenever it was needed. The fact that they were non-violent just made them that much the easier to control.

Angel, not one to be unnerved by the potential of authoritarian disapproval (if anything, he was spurred on by it), underwent the initiation process – which was symbolic at best – and continued to attend meetings, whilst keeping Kostos uninformed regarding his recent conversion. He didn't believe his nephew would take easily to what many of his friends at temple considered a rather heretical group. But he did trust in the young man's basic common sense, and he believed, that were they to discuss matters from those holy books, that Kostos' deep devotion to the word and the truth would force him to see things from a more Bongovian perspective.

Kostos, for his part, was delighted that his curmudgeonly uncle had suddenly become so interested in his religion. Although during their discussions he sometimes felt that Angel, when he brushed up against Bongovian perspective, was sailing dangerously close to treacherous waters, and Kostos would try hard to shepherd the conversation back to more comfortable, and perhaps shallower, depths. In his wisdom, the older man did not push his nephew any further than he was ready to go, but it often frustrated Angel to take those two steps backward sometimes. He would never allow himself to fight with Kostos over the word of god, and therefore on occasion his frustration took inappropriate vent over other subjects... his work habits – Kostos was lazy, his dating habits – Kostos better be careful and not get up to any funny business with that girl, incase... well, you know what.

"What?"

"You know..." Angel would look away and shake his head, "babies... and such."

"The preacher told me and Kristina that it would be our duty to get married, and have babies for Bongo." He played a little dumb, but Kostos and Kristina had been practicing making babies for quite a while now, despite knowing that this was the one subject on which the preacher, and her father... and Angel, though he might not admit it, would be in complete agreement.

Angel just threw up his hands. "Aiee! The preacher!"

But even though they didn't realize it, uncle and nephew had strangely similar beliefs, and an unbreakable bond which resided deep within their natures. And somehow these recent weeks of connecting over Bongo had left both of them more open to the other's ideas. They had each, in their own way, reserved a space within themselves to be touched by the word of the great Jason Cyllabus Novedi. And here it was, grabbing them firmly, emanating from the lips of a virgin who had entered their lives simply to take shelter from the rain. Her purity irreproachable, telling them of the recent plight of the founder, the originator... *the* man responsible for their strangely shared belief. And they knew immediately – at least Angel did (Kostos tended to be a little more cautious when trying to make up his mind about any risky endeavor) – that they must rescue Mr. Novedi from his current predicament, as described to them by Ms. D'Orion. It was too late (as he informed Kostos) not to. They had already been touched. They were in the book now. They had become, through this simple meeting, part of the story. There was no turning back now. They must follow Jocelyn wherever she might lead them because, wherever she led them, it was towards their destiny.

And so they did. Out through the renewed rainfall, and into her nineteen-fifty-seven ™Chevrolet Bel Air, they all squeezed together in the front seat and, having dusted the water from their things, they drove off into the night. But not one of them noticed the silent black limousine which slipped into the stream of traffic a few cars behind them, and followed them as they went to get gas, and stayed with them all the way until they had reached the hospital, where the man whom they had come to help lay unconscious, dreaming of gardens, and fishponds, and statues of angels, and miniature clock towers, and fame and fortune, and unpublished manuscripts, and murder plots, and suicide, and treacherous friends... but never once did he dream of broken china, or little dogs who peed in the rain.

Chapter 26

The phone rang and rang, but as usual someone was dead on the floor, lying in a pool of blood.

The phone rang and rang, but this time no one had been murdered.

Because:

Someone had removed the blanks, him (or her) self, and had replaced them with the original bullets that Artie (or someone) had given (or sold) to him (or her) er... in the first place.

The phone rang and rang, and whoever's friend it was calling, was getting pissed off waiting for him (or her) down on Northcroft Avenue, in Little Hurst (or somewhere) and was now cursing out Dom... oops, I gave it away! Alright, alright, I admit it! It was Marvin calling. And it was Dominic Devine who was lying there, dead, on his own bloodstained carpet.

That stupid idiot had gone and topped himself!

And Marvin, in his own innocent way, was feeling totally betrayed, let down, cheated... whatever. He had a contract to fulfill. Money had been accepted... in exchange for services; there was his reputation to consider. That unreliable bastard— he thought— wait 'till I get my hands on him. But Marvin was, as yet, unable to fully appreciate the ironic futility of that statement.

So anyway:

Somebody's body, er... that is Dominic Devine's body... was lying there, dead, on his own bloodstained carpet. And it remained there all night long, with nothing but the flashing T.V. screen light to keep it company. The six o'clock news came and went, but there was no report about George Burgess, sixty-eight, the editor of the Popodell Publishing Company, having had a heart attack, whilst being held hostage in his own office in Little Hurst, a suburb of Lambden, by a crazed forty-something terrorist and aspiring author, Mr. Dominic Devine, who demanded that his novel be published. In fact, it had been a relatively slow news day, and viewers of the program found themselves regaled with the latest celebrity gossip that evening – weddings, babies, divorces, sex-scandals – rather than any such momentous and, quite frankly, even *more* titillating event... as such an abduction slash killing would have doubtlessly been regarded. No, it was not reported, simply, because it never happened. Now admittedly, later on that week, George Burgess *would* be found murdered in an alleyway close to where his office was; and the police *would* be searching for a tall, lean, dark-skinned man, who had been observed casually departing the scene of the crime, and may be a potential witness. But it wouldn't make the network news, although a brief blurb in the 'Town Crier,' a local tabloid owned by 'Lillerstian' elder statesman Taylor Bradley, would read (no photo attached) on page fifteen:

"We mourn the passing of Mr. Burgess. He was a great friend to all lovers of quality literature. He is survived by no family members."

Meanwhile, here was Dominic Devine, also gone forever, never to return... with nary so much as a page fifteen in the local chronicle – never mind channel seven, prime-time. Some people are just not destined for greatness. But then our fate, as they say, is nothing more than our temperament.

Why is that?

Because:

Some fools commit suicide and don't even leave a copy of your manuscript lying nearby... on your chest, possibly, with a little blood smeared on it for good effect. Well... maybe cut your thumb a little first; no way of knowing which way the blood will flow once you're dead. Or there might be too much blood, which could drench the manuscript rendering it totally illegible... or too disgusting, anyway, for someone to *want* to read. Look – if you're not talented enough to make your novel compelling, at least don't make it difficult to read. That's cutting your own, er... throat – so to speak.

So, what to do?

7 Step Recipe For Success

1. Cut thumb with razor blade.

2. Smear side of manuscript with blood from thumb (making sure not to obscure any script).

3. Cover thumb wound with ™Band-Aid.

4. Write note stating clearly the reason for suicide, i.e. inability to get novel published.

5. Secure note and manuscript in watertight plastic wrapper.

6. Lie on floor in public place with package on chest.

7. Shoot self in head.

But no...

Couldn't even do that. One last plug for immortality, wasted. Book hidden deep in closet, whence it would – no doubt – be disposed of with the rest of the trash; just before the apartment got a lick of white, and the young Jewish-Japanese yuppie couple moved in temporarily until they got enough cash saved for a down payment on a condo.

It would *never* get published. No one would *ever* read it. There would *never* be a time such as the future described between its nonexistent covers. No one would *ever* read his own life story in that book and be inspired to found a huge religeo-corporate social structure which eventually would take over a nation and control the lives of millions of people; despite the best laid plans of mice... or a certain murdering, conniving, tall, dark-skinned, arrogant, cocksucking motherfucker named Marvin Something-or-the-other. Whatever!

Not only that, but...

No such world would *ever* exist where angels named Mastroianni – or Gabriel, for that matter – grew taller, or shorter, or fatter, or thinner. Not in this reality, anyway.

Nope! It seemed that Dominic Devine's life had been a total loss, and he would be completely forgotten by all of those people who had never read his book (which was – let's face it – everyone), and also, sadly, by most of the people whom he had ever met. Of his family, he was survived only by his little sister, Damian, who, at fifteen years his junior, would have been about five years old at the time that he left the household, never to return. Any childhood memories she might have of him would be vague at best. Although, ironically, he *would* be remembered by a woman named Miranda Manley, who had always had a thing for clowns (ever since she was a child), and who nowadays masturbated regularly to the indelible memory of that sexy red-nosed bastard who had juggled four brightly colored balls at her kid's birthday party on the barge, those several years ago.

But wait, she's not the only one. There was this actor named Warren Something-or-the-other (unrelated – except by insidious guile – to the above named Marvin Something-or-the-other). He would remember Dominic Devine until the day he died. After all, his greatest and most memorable role was born in Dominic Devine's fevered mind. It was the part of a man named Henry Lewis. A man who was transported to the future by an angel. A man who changed his name to Jason Cyllabus Novedi, and who presently lies waiting in a hospital bed to be rescued by his virginal lover, and two Greek Cypriot shopkeepers. This role gave Warren Something-or-the-other (… er, let's just call him Warren from now on) some sort of connection to the fantasy of Dominic Devine. And maybe, for just that reason, he understood Dominic in a way that no one else ever had. As we all know, reality is nothing more than the conspiratorial fantasy of the many, and as soon as more than one person starts to believe in a thing… flying saucers… Jesus… AIDS… well, it all starts looking dangerously like reality to me.

And Warren… well, Warren was a trained and impassioned thespian. The fact that neither you nor I ever heard of him, speaks more to the superficial state of acting these days, than to his personal ability. If anything, it is indeed the proof – in this topsy turvy media entertainment atmosphere – of his quite estimable quality. When he took on a role, he would live the role. He would believe the role. He would become the role. When he first met Dominic Devine, that cold night on the deck of Miranda Manley's barge, he *had* just been transported there by an angel. He *had* just come from the future where, as Jason Cyllabus Novedi, he had been viciously murdered by… wait a minute, wait a minute! Not yet for that.

The point is this:

Something which was not real, which *is* not real, which would never *be* real… had, in the simple act of acting, become somewhat… real. Possibly not the exact *type* of reality desired by Dominic Devine;

nor the kind desired by Marvin, for that matter. It was, nonetheless, a *type* of reality. And *that* is a reality of some kind.

Of course the reality of the Taylor Bradleys and Nick Howes of this world would always be solid and fulfilled. They were the type who didn't sweat the small stuff... the details. Broken bones, a little blood splattered here or there... it all came out in the wash. As long as, in the end, there was power, and money, and the gratification of the ego.

But Marvin, and Dominic, and Warren, they were artists... of a sort. The *method* was important to them. The *journey* was the goal. If it couldn't be done a certain way, then it might as well not be done at all. They didn't want it any other way. Drama... yes, and romance, *these* were their addictions. So Warren had *become* part of that fantasy, and, in becoming so, he had become its creator. He had solidified it. To him, that day on the barge, there was no future moment that he would meet Dominic Devine at Chick 37 dressed as millionaire Henry Lewis. That was the past. It had happened *before* his many adventures in time. And when it actually happened, for all he knew, he could have been time hopping like some sort of latter day Billy Pilgrim, living all moments simultaneously, out of sequence, carriage before horse, arse over tit, but still in perfect synchronicity – like all things always are – this universe of no mistakes, every failure a lesson, every achievement a... well, there are no achievements.

And although – at some later date, in the instant before he died – Warren couldn't remember exactly *how* this tall, dark skinned man who shot him, fitted into this story, he simply took it for granted that while nothing had been achieved, no mistake had been made. And in this regard he was right. Because, as remote a chance as it might be that some policeman investigating George Burgess's slaying, might connect him to Dominic Devine's suicide (perhaps through a collection of rejection letters our intrepid hero had compulsively accumulated), and blunder somehow (in whatever flat-footed manner he was prone to) upon a failed actor who was trapped in his role, and had taken to wandering the streets, dressed as a homeless Henry Lewis, and through him, be lead eventually to the *instigator* of his remarkable performance... as remote a chance as that might be, it was, nonetheless, a chance that our Marvin was not willing to take. Therefore, suitable action would be called for; but this, of course, has not happened yet.

Meanwhile, Dominic Devine lies dead on his blood drenched rug. The six most important steps of the "Recipe for Success" have gone unheeded. No cut on thumb, no manuscript, no ™Band-Aid, no suicide note, no plastic wrapper, no public place. A simple bullet in the head, in the privacy of your own little home, may be aesthetically less repellent to some, but, from an entrepreneurial perspective, somewhat unartful. Nonetheless, when nothing is left and *all hope is lost, all hope is lost...* some whacky, flukish, unforeseen occurrence, brought on by somebody coming out of left field (whatever that means) can change the inevitability of (even) fiction. To whit: the complicity of a Mr. Actor Warren Something-or-the-other, in creating a possible reality out of a fantasy in his *own* mind – namely the fiction of a man named Jason Cyllabus Novedi, and a place called Prickly Bog – can somehow facilitate the transfer of reality from the obsolete mind of the recently deceased Mr. Devine, in the following manner:

Chapter 27

Once upon a time, a certain Jason Cyllabus Novedi lay dying upon a hospital bed. Now, the way in which he'd got there was by being plugged three times in the caboodle by a henchman of a Mr. Frederick Greaves... a fellow named Karl – that really *was* his name – who used to wear those awful sunglasses with reflective lenses, which made you feel as if you were talking to yourself when you looked at him. Karl was a legend in his own mind. A man of mystery. In fact, a mystery wrapped in an enigma wrapped in a puzzle wrapped in a – I don't know – a... banana leaf, perhaps. Okay, I'm not saying that he was a *total* fraud, but, not unlike many of us, his "act" might have deluded himself as much as it did others. Yes, we *do* become that which we *think* we are, but does that necessarily make us authentic? And Karl's act was, let's face it, severe, to say the least. But still, as deep and dark as Karl believed himself to be, and, as deep as he imagined was his knowledge of his master, there was something yet deeper and darker and more mysterious about Frederick Greaves Junior than even black hearted Karl could imagine. It was a secret... and a power, that had been handed down through time immemorial, from his father's father's father, to his father's father, and (need I say it) from his father's father, to his... father, that's right, that doddering old goose, Freddie Greaves Senior. Of course, *he'd* forgotten what it was by now. But to think that in his heyday, that sweet, pathetic old man had been quite the iron handed hierarch; hated and feared by all those who fell subject to his purview. (Jeez, why do you think his son turned out such a bastard?) So anyway – what the hell *is* this great secret? Alright, alright, I'm getting to it. The thing that even Karl did not know about the illustrious Mr. Frederick Greaves II, was that, at this very moment in time, he was the sitting chairperson of a shadowy, and ancient order of authoritarian power, known collectively (only to its members, of course) as the Dark Lords of the Guiding Star. There were only six men who belonged to this order, and this had been so since the beginning of time.

Now, I know what you're thinking. Six men... star... six pointed star... Jewish!

Right?

Wrong! Get that idea right out of your head. This story is nothing to do with a Zionist plot to control the world economy. It has nothing to do with racial, or ethnic groups of any kind. It is not a metaphor, an analogy, a simile, an ambiguity, an equivocation or, for that matter, a symbolism regarding any *specific* group or person. Although one *might* be able to make the case that it *is* in some way connected to religion... but more on that in a minute. For the time being, let's just say this story is about the six men who were... the Guiding Star.

These six men controlled the Universe.

Wait, let me finish.

They, sort of, controlled the Universe, inasmuch as they were themselves created by the conglomerated fantasies of all the individual sentient beings within that very universe, or to put it another way (and here comes the possible religious connection) the Great God Bongo. Well, these six men played an extremely important part in setting the balance of things *as they are*. And their very existence, not to mention the infinite longevity of their survival, gave proof to the notion that darkness is, indeed, the overpowering force of our dimension. In fact, as the sitting chairperson of the order, Frederick Greaves II considered his true name to actually be:

DARKNESS

The other five members were known to each other by the following names:

INERTIA

WEIGHT

LABOR

DEFEAT and

IMPRISONMENT

And when combined together, these six men presented the most powerful force which exists throughout the Universe; a power which makes even the Great God Bongo tremble in divine boots and lose focus. The name of that power is this:

DISTRACTION

For a man who is not completely DISTRACTED can never be successful in a universe where the Dark Lords of the Guiding Star prevail. The slightest glimmer of a connection with truth, or true feelings, can cause the intense focus of DISTRACTION to collapse. And when that happens, all kinds of absurd qualities such as... tolerance, self-evaluation, and nonjudgmentalism, which are of little or no useful value, start to appear and take hold and generally glom up the works.

Jason Cyllabus Novedi was a man who had lost his focus... I mean, his distraction; and he was starting to do stupid things. It was bad enough that he was questioning his *own* motivations, but he was also getting other people to do the same thing. That may be perfectly acceptable behavior for a man who has no power or influence in other peoples lives, but for a man in *his* position, it's a decidedly irresponsible way to conduct one's affairs. There is, in fact, a punishment for such behavior. It's called, '*death!*' And I, Dominic Devine, as his creator, felt that it was my duty to enforce such a punishment upon the creature which I had created. So I wrote it this way:

The guards in the hospital stepped aside as they passed. It made Jocelyn nervous. Surely it *couldn't* simply be that the sight of her two swarthy looking friends, as tough as they might be, was *so* intimidating to the guards that they would fade meekly before her approach. Perhaps it had not yet occurred to them that her mission here was to remove Mr. Novedi from their protection, and to take him home, to her father's farm, where actual chickens clucked whilst laying actual eggs, where she could nurse him safely and surely back to health, with real nutrition, and real care, and real... love. Her original plan had been to sneak in quietly, and get him out through a window, perhaps, without making too big of a fuss about it. But Angel and Kostos... well, Angel mostly – with Kostos in full agreement – had decided that it would be a more honorable course to march straight in through the front door, demand exactly what they wanted, and let the chips fall where they may.

Angel had never in his life been "distracted" enough to know exactly how one goes about implementing such a plan. He was neither a conniver nor a manipulator. He could fight a good fight, and he could bully with the best of them, but he'd never been one to cheat, or finesse matters in any way. He'd probably concede that being ripped off, once in a while, was a small price to pay for maintaining one's dignity. It wasn't in him to spend every second worrying about how he could get one over on the next guy. He was a man who, by all customary measures, was "destined to lose." And yet, someone not fully aware of the facts, might conversely argue that here was a man who'd had enough savvy to have procured a small business loan eight years ago, and from that humble beginning, to have generated enough trade so that now he could support himself and his young nephew in the fashion to which they were accustomed. Admittedly, not the highest standard of living, but at least they weren't working to make another man rich. But the truth was not so sunny a fable. Angel's store was in big trouble; he was mortgaged up to the hilt, he owed back taxes, and there was just not enough cash coming in to raise his head above the flood. Of course he hadn't broken the bad news to his nephew – possibly in an attempt to be protective of him, but more likely because he was just ashamed to admit it – and, whilst he had been pugnaciously holding on to the hope that something would indeed, er... turn up, he was finally beginning to accept the fact that the situation, as it stood, did not seem to portend any imminent reversal of his fortunes. It wasn't so much the location of his establishment. In fact the neighborhood was coming up slowly, but Angel wasn't keeping up with the demand of the newer residents. His traditional inventory was not up to the quality standards of the more affluent young people moving into the area, and Angel hadn't the slightest clue as to what they were looking for. He didn't have the knowledge to be able to change the situation. He didn't even have the knowledge to know that he didn't have the knowledge. What he did have was a great big stubborn streak that kept him believing it was nothing to do with his own actions, or his own need to learn new things, but that fate was simply conspiring against him, and nothing but an act of god could change the situation as he saw it.

Well, as much as the Great God Bongo encourages one to take the situation firmly in hand, and not be victim to the whims of fate, there are certain times when those whims can apply great pressure upon our abilities, and no matter how hard we work, we can't seem to get around even our own inner barricades. It is quite possible that this was just such a case. It is also quite possible that the way things were happening was nothing more than the way they should be happening. One thing is for sure, it certainly was the way that it *was* happening. And so, whether it was fate or temperament which had led Angel to this place... here he was, following this woman, and this boy – all three, in very different ways (Bongovist, Bongovian... lover) disciples all, somehow, of a fiction named Jason Cyllabus Novedi – as they hurled themselves down sanitized and empty white corridors, on a mission to rescue their savior. To save their rescuer. On a mission to save their savior.

And whether it was fate or temperament which had brought him here, it lent to Angel's expression the look of a man who had nothing left to lose. And, had one been present on that particular occasion, one may well have supposed that it was this very look which was responsible for the rapid withdrawal of those around him who might have presented some impediment to his progress. But that supposition would have been wrong.

What *was* in fact responsible was a simple wave of the hand, dealt by a suave grey-haired man in an elegant silk business suit, who followed them – just as rapidly, but silently and at a distance – remotely removing obstacles from the path of our intrepid threesome, just as he had done for all humanity since the beginning of time.

The name of this man was... Darkness.

In his universe no favor was without cost. More often than not, that cost was so high that it required sacrificing the thing for which the favor was needed in the first place. The gifts of Darkness were no gift at all, and in his universe he made sure that there was no such thing as a free lunch. Frederick Greaves swept silently through the hallways with a sad and confident expression upon his face. Behind him came Karl, his man, pulling tan buckskin gloves down tightly over his fingers. Behind him, the gathering throng of interns, nurses, orderlies, and security guards dared to emit neither statement nor breath in the presence of such immense power. When he and Karl arrived at the door to room 208, the two guards were lying scattered about the floor like ninepins. An angel had been here. Frederick stood aside and motioned Karl to open it.

Within, the three conspirators turned guiltily toward the silver-haired man who stood framed by the door. They looked like the fox with the chicken feathers coming out of its mouth. But Jocelyn immediately gathered her sense of righteous indignation around her once more, and returned to her attempt at resuscitating Jason. Behind her the voice of Darkness penetrated the atmosphere with an eerie, but almost pleasant command.

"Awaken Mr. Novedi, if you please, he has a visitor."

Immediately, a male nurse, a Filipino named Benjamin (his name and origin were of no concern to Darkness) scurried in and began to prepare a syringe. "It all right ma'am," he told Jocelyn.

At first she adopted a fighting posture— no one sticks nuttin' in my man. But there was something about Benjamin's voice which calmed her; which made her trust him.

"It all right," he repeated, gesturing at the implement in his hand, "I will awake him for you. No problem."

She backed away warily to allow him access. As she did so, Frederick Greaves and Karl slipped into the room shutting the door quietly behind them. The gawking throng of medicos were obliged to remain outside in the fluorescent white hallway, muttering inaudible speculations, wondering, not knowing what course of action would be appropriate. Uninstructed in the response to this particular eventuality, their degrees were of no help to them now. It is, of course, a gross generalization to claim that, despite their great education – or perhaps because of it – not one of them had the ability to think for themselves, to question the authority of someone like Frederick Greaves, whose portrait they had all seen hanging on the hospital benefactors wall. Not one had the courage to poke his face through that door, to ask what was going on, to satisfy himself that things were as they should be. No, not one.

Benjamin's syringe penetrated the vein, and carefully measured quantities of amphetamine-like substances began to flow rapidly into Jason Cyllabus Novedi's fingers... into his toes... into his brain... into his heart.

Visions of spinning gardens ground ever more rapidly to a halt, and the half-world, which Jason had inhabited since this crisis first started, began to fade away from him, and it twisted itself into an altogether different dream. It was the dream of a woman; a woman whose image he had fallen in love with; a woman who symbolized that which he was in love with. Her image filled his vision... like an obsession. It was a memory, far too powerful to even remember. It was a picture, far too close to even see. It was a distraction which had made him lose his focus. But now, before his very eyes, that blurred, distracted vision was starting slowly to take on a configuration. It was achieving a cast, a hue, a shade, a color. It was sharpening, pixel by pixel, until finally, it had achieved its blasphemous focus: Jocelyn.

"Good evening, Mr. Novedi," she said in a man's voice, like a ventriloquist, without moving her lips.

Frederick Greaves approached the bed, displacing Jocelyn from Jason's view. "We didn't want you to oversleep," he continued in the same voice. "You may be late for a very important appointment. An appointment with fate... or should I say... *temperament.*" He turned his head to examine the faces gathered around him – Karl first, then Jocelyn and Angel, and finally Kostos – as if he were making a public speech, as much for *their* benefit as for the object of his discourse, Mr. Novedi. "It matters not! They are the same," he concluded.

Jason looked around the room, his perspective blurring from one face, to another, to another. The harsh fluorescent lights above confusing his eyes with a trick of impedance. He felt unable to talk or to respond. Which reality was this— He wondered. Which focus? Which distraction? He could hardly understand what was going on. It showed in his face.

"Oh I *do* beg your pardon." Frederick Greaves seemed genuinely concerned. "How rude of me; it seems I have not yet introduced myself." And then he did. But to Jason, it seemed as if – whilst this man continued speaking normally – all the other people in the room had mutated into some kind of slow motion. Jocelyn was in the midst of turning to look at Greaves. Angel was moving to sit down upon the small, blue vinyl covered sofa in the corner of the room. Kostos stared dreamily out of the window into the darkness, where floating raindrops landed softly upon the glistening lamp-lit parking lot. Benjamin, the nurse, had his back turned, and was performing some function at a metal table. Karl was smiling poisonously, glaring at Jason, and stroking downward upon the leather fingers of his gloves.

"You do not know me," continued the speaker, "But I have followed your career with great interest. I must say, you were doing so very well, and for such a long time. But now this, this... *episode*, yes, seems to have turned things around somewhat... no?" Jason moved his lips to answer. "Shh... no, don't speak," the other man interrupted. "I shall tell you how things are, and how they must be. You will listen to what I say, for you have not long to live."

The lights seemed to flicker, but in actuality no change had taken place. It was as if the shadows were growing upon the walls, and soon the whole room felt as if it had been steeped in the rancid breath of Darkness.

"I will tell you of the balance of things, which you, in your selfishness, have chosen to disregard. Friend Jason..." the speaker eased himself down onto the edge of the bed, "... or would you prefer that I call you Henry? Do you really think that *you* are the most important person in the world, or just the *only* important person? Must you be reminded that this world was here long before you came into it... and that it will be here long after you leave? And, after you have gone, it will have changed very little – if at all. And if it does... change at all, then *your* contribution to that change will have been so *infinitely* small, as to be almost completely invisible.

"Do not even imagine... friend Henry, that you could possibly make any noticeable difference. *That*, is not the nature of our universe. Listen to me, and believe, for I am intimately acquainted with the prevailing characteristics of these times... and yes, of all others too. You may call them *powers*, or you may call them *fates*. They are my friends. I will tell you their names: Inertia, Weight, Labor, Defeat, Imprisonment..." and here he caught a glimpse of his own reflection on the side of a polished aluminum piece of hospital equipment, his face contorting artfully upon the imperfect metal surface as it moved, "... and Darkness.

"I tell you, *nothing* can ever be accomplished! No matter how much it seems that accomplishment has been obtained, it is a fallacy, and one must be, indeed, an arrogant man to believe in the reverse. And this is particularly true of you Henry Lewis, for you are one of the unlucky few who have seen the reality of things, and yet you have chosen to ignore the truth of your own unimportance. You have created a subterfuge in which you would glorify your own meaning. You have assembled a cast of characters who would support you in your megalomania, and convince you of the superiority of your existence.

"Others may also believe that there is hope for achievement, but their's is not an arrogant posture, as is your's. For they believe in the ability of the system to produce what is necessary. (Of course they are wrong, the system is debased and corrupt, so it will inevitably continue upon the course it has always taken.) But at least they do not think that they, personally, can change things. No, they believe in the system, and so they support it and, in doing so, they help it to survive... the way it is, the way it has always been.

"Don't you see, Jason Cyllabus Novedi..." his voice suddenly became tender and loving, as he furrowed his brows and raised one hand, slowly uncurling the fingers, and exposing his palm to the heavens. "Do you not see how subtle and delicate a balance it is, which holds all things together. It is only my brethren and I – the nominated keepers of the balance scale – who are responsible for the preservation of this system. Were it not for our considerable powers, and the constant distractions which we provide, the people of the world would ultimately come to recognize their failure. They would begin to taste the pungent and bitter flavor of their hidden misery. And they, like children, have no appetite for such an unsavory essence. Were this to happen, then all hell would surely break loose. Our system would collapse. Our fragile buttresses would come crashing down upon us, and that, truly, would be a failure for us all.

"We, the Dark Lords of the Guiding Star, have tended and preserved this exquisitely sensitive flower, for all eternity. We have fed it and nurtured it. We have defended it from all threats and assault. We have controlled the parasites, and we have achieved survival." Jason looked at him quizzically. But to Frederick Greaves, the contradictions inherent in what he was saying were insubstantial, or irrelevant. "Yes, yes," he seemed to respond to Jason's expression, "there is cruelty. Yes, there is pain... and suffering. Yes, there is unfairness and insensitivity. But... it is all for our survival. Firstly, you see, we *must* survive! We must not change, because when change occurs, that which existed before, can no longer survive.

"As for you, Henry Lewis, you have committed the greatest sin that exists. You have stared into the face of truth. You have seen the writhing snakes dancing upon your own head. You have tasted of the fruit of the tree of knowledge. You may no longer remain within this Eden. You shall be banished to the place where you belong... where you can thrive. But it's alright, you will be happy there. Have no fear."

The body of the Great Lord, Darkness, raised up above him and moved slowly away to make room for his minion. Karl stepped forward and approached the bed with his gloved hands raised up in front of him, fingers twitching joyously in anticipation of their impending duty.

297

"No!" Jocelyn screamed. Suddenly the motion clicked into fast-forward speed, and the lights began to flash like a stroboscope. Jocelyn jumped on top of Karl, kicking and biting and scratching his face with her fingernails. "I'm not going... to let you... kill him... you bastard!" Her words spat out between breaths. "I've never... loved... a man... before!" She turned to Angel and Kostos for support, but they were standing immobile, staring vacantly into the eyes of Darkness – yes, Frederick Greaves II – and a blue-green glow was emanating, like ectoplasm, from their bodies. She didn't know why, but she had the peculiar feeling that some kind of a deal was being cut. Karl, on the other hand, was quite mobile. He simply heaved one arm outward and slapped Jocelyn away like a bothersome fly. Splat! Just like that. Her body slammed into the wall behind her, and she slid slowly down its glossy surface, her arse squeaking against the paintwork, whilst she mumbled to herself through crooked lips, "but... we haven't... even had... sex... yet."

Karl sadly turned his attention away from her. "Soon," he replied over his shoulder (as if she'd been talking about him), and he began to ready himself for the nocuous duty he was about to perform upon the High Priest of Prickly Bog. But first, there was just one more little obstacle he'd have to overcome.

Benjamin, the Filipino nurse, had turned suddenly from what he'd been doing all this while. He was holding a freshly loaded syringe in his hand. "I'm not going to let you do this," he said. This was not, after all, just *any* victim of the powers that be, this was Jason Cyllabus Novedi, our most venerated leader, the founder of our culture. It's true, Benjamin *had* taken part in some of Frederick Greaves little *experiments* at this Hospital in the past. He had seen things which had disgusted him, but he had been convinced to participate, because Darkness has a way of inducing us to see things which are not necessarily there, and also a way of hiding things from us which are right in front of our eyes. But still, there comes a time in every man's life when he must choose to either stand up and be counted, or else fade from existence forever. Benjamin chose the former.

Karl smiled, and walked around the bed to where Benjamin was brandishing the syringe as if it were Excalibur. Karl made a grab for it, but Benjamin was quicker. He swiftly circled it around Karl's reaching hand, and stabbed it through the buttery buckskin leather glove, pushing in the plunger, in one move. Dark blood started seeping, firstly just around the thin metal point, and then staining the tan leather in increasingly larger circles of scarlet tincture. Karl had stopped moving, he was simply staring at his own hand. His blood dripped upon the gleaming white floor, and the drug tingled as it entered his system. He looked up at Benjamin, ecstatic bliss written painfully upon his features, unsure whether to resent the man or to thank him for this exquisite feeling. Benjamin released the syringe; his initial fear was subsumed into the rush of adrenaline his action had brought upon him. And seeing, within Karl's inaction, a further opportunity, he raised his foot and sent his heel ploughing, hard and deep, into Karl's solar plexus. Karl was sent flying and, with a huge gasp, landed on his back, straddling Jason's bed, the syringe still embedded in his glove. Jason's body jerked upwards in response. Benjamin moved in and applied his instep sharply to the area between Karl's outstretched legs.

"Aiee!" whined Karl, "that was great!" His head poked up above his chest. "Can you do that again?" he begged. So Benjamin did. "Whoa," sighed Karl. "That was *fabulous!*"

Benjamin was so amazed at this reaction, that he inadvertently remained just a little too close to Karl for his own good. As Karl's moans of pleasure turned softly into a chuckling sound, his legs wrapped silently around Benjamin's body, and pulled it tightly to his. His chuckles grew to a mad hyena's laugh, while Benjamin struggled for air, pounding on Karl's chest and face. This just made Karl laugh even more, even higher. But slowly the movement from this struggling brace of bodies – which had been lying, for what seemed to Jason an interminable period, on top of him – eventually subsided. Karl kissed Benjamin's forehead, with loving lips and a slimy wet tongue, just before he allowed his unconscious body to slip down to the floor.

Karl turned onto his side and looked at Jason straight in the face... and then at his own hand with the syringe sticking out of it... and then at Jason again. He smiled. With his other hand he reached over and lightly caressed Jason's chest through the bedclothes. Jason began shaking with fear. He looked helplessly over to where Jocelyn was sitting groggily upon the floor by the wall. He tried to speak but no word would come. "Shh," said Karl, holding an index finger to his lips. He pulled the syringe, slowly out of his hand, and stood up. It felt good to Jason to get the weight off him, and the proximity of Karl's face... his breath, his odor, had felt oppressive and constricting; but the fear did not subside, nor the shaking which it provoked.

Reaching down for a corner of the sheet, Karl wiped the blood off the syringe, and then kept on wiping – almost compulsively – until the implement was sparkling clean. He pumped it up and down a few times (the way Benjamin had been doing earlier) until it was dry inside. He pulled the plunger down and filled the syringe with fresh, undiluted air. He stood there for a while, again, looking at Jason, looking at the syringe, smiling. Eventually, he bent over Benjamin's supine form and lifted up one of the unconscious man's arms, revealing a thick blue vein on the inner forearm. After smiling once more at Jason, Karl glanced in the direction of his boss, as if seeking approval, but Frederick Greaves was locked in a visual embrace with Angel and (somehow) Kostos at the same time. So Karl returned to the business at hand; he administered the lethal dose. Ten cubic centimeters of deadly air. It took the bubble a few seconds to reach the heart. The body jerked once, and Benjamin's eyes opened wide with the wrenching pain of death. Having removed all obstacles from his path, Karl was once again in a position to resume his loving attentions toward the person of Mr. Jason Cyllabus Novedi.

Just before Mr. Novedi died, he made eye contact with a certain Greek Cypriot shopkeeper who had been waiting very patiently for just this moment. It's always nice to have a familiar face travel with you when you take that final journey down to the nether place. A familiar face? Of course, everybody knew that Angel was really Mastroianni all along, keeping an eye on Jocelyn, who would, despite Karl's tender promises, awaken safe and sound (after Frederick Greaves, and his man of course, had vacated the premises). And as for the angel? Well, he would end up right where he was supposed to be – with Jason Cyllabus Novedi, er... Henry Lewis.

You see, Mastroianni's final brilliant and multi faceted disguise as, not just one person, but two (yes he was Kostos as well), had kept the Great Lord Darkness busy, thinking that *he* was keeping Mastroianni busy, whilst Karl did his work. But Karl doing his work, was all part of the plan in the first place: Jason *had* to die, so that Henry could live again. But imagine, the immense power of the Great Lord Darkness, combined with the adolescent self centered mentality of Frederick Greaves II. Just think how much havoc he could wreak. Talk about arrogant, he had to be controlled, he could have ruined the whole thing, thinking that he was obeying the will of Bongo. What a moron!

"Henry..." Mastroianni spoke with a deep echo-y voice. "Henry, it's time to go home. Your mission is almost complete. There is but one thing left to do. You must seek out your creator, and you must tell him what you have seen."

"Everything?" asked Henry.

"Everything," said the angel

After a few seconds of cool looking psychedelic special effects stuff – you know, swirling colors and zooming in and out rapidly – accompanied by some freaky sounding music... Henry Lewis found himself, dressed like a bum, standing in the freezing cold, on some kind of pavement, next to a brightly painted barge, moored on a filthy and polluted canal. It was at that point that he encountered his creator, who was, er... well, me actually. Yours truly. Your author. Namely, Dominic Devine. At your service!

Later on, of course (after having gone back in time and playing himself in a younger, richer role) Henry Lewis finally reverted back to his homeless future self. He was found dead in an alleyway, murdered by a cheap con-man named Marvin Something-or-the-other, who had mistaken him for an actor he'd once hired.

Chapter 28

Well anyway, that's how *he* wrote it. But then that was just fiction, Dominic Devine's fiction. And so, that actor named Warren, who took on the role of Henry Lewis, lived it out the way he had read it. But in living it out so accurately – so exactly to the way in which it was written – what he did was, he (sort of) *created* it... in a way. He made it real. If not in this reality, then in some other reality... some other possibility. And the role which he created became a doorway to that other possibility. Not fiction this time, but in fact another reality... of a kind. Because in fiction, the future is inflexible. It's already been written. What's going to happen at the end of the book, is always what's going to happen at the end of that particular book. It is reality which is so uncertain, and as a result, so magical. Subject to the whims of random events.

In fiction victory is assured; as is disaster. A book can have a happy ending or a sad one. But a sad one cannot have a happy one. Not so in reality. In reality, disaster may well be assured, and yet in the last moment before it occurs... victory can be plucked from right in front of its nose.

So let us rewind a little to find out what *really* happened.

Firstly, a certain previously unemployed actor, a Mr. Warren Something-or-the-other, had created a possible reality out of a fantasy, by literally *becoming* a fellow named Henry Lewis (which, needless to say, included remembering all of his memories, and feeling all of his feelings). He actually achieved this persona on a dock, beside a barge belonging to a Ms. Miranda Manley. Now, as a result of this sudden change in the fabric of the Universe, a Mr. Jason Cyllabus Novedi, and a place called Prickly Bog sprang unexpectedly into being; complete with full biographies, employment resumés, family scandals, medical and dental histories attached. And then later on (or at the same time, depending on whom you ask) a certain Mr. Dominic Devine (being, himself, a co-creator of the above noted Mr. Lewis) was transported –

at the very moment of his death – into the supine body of the previously described Mr. Jason Cyllabus Novedi (which had, fortunately, just become vacated by the aforementioned Mr. Henry Lewis – as played, of course, by the unknown actor Warren Something-or-the-other) just as it was, in fact, in the process of being strangled to death by a man whose name really was, er... Karl.

Fortunately, Dominic Devine was transported over into the body of Jason Cyllabus Novedi still clutching the gun with which he was presently committing suicide. Well, two things occurred simultaneously in those two separate realities:

1) Dominic Devine succeeded in shooting himself dead. It was the major accomplishment of his life, and without which he would never have been able to transport over into the realm of Bongovia.

But:

b) Jason Cyllabus Novedi, who (let's face it) didn't want to die, was in the middle of being strangled, and, in fact, he *would* have been (it certainly was written that way) were it not for the mysterious appearance of a revolver in his right hand, which went off, accidentally killing his assailant, er... Karl.

Bang!

Suddenly the hands around his neck loosened their grip, and that body slumped back down on top of him once again. The adrenaline generated by this act of violence he had just perpetrated, caused him to speedily regain complete use of his consciousness. Suddenly he was no longer the undecided Dominic Devine. Suddenly he was no longer the impotent and inadequate Henry Lewis. He was a new man. In one spectacular move he threw aside the bed covers – and the body – which tumbled, no... *cascaded* to the floor; and he leapt up to his feet, standing there with his six-gun in his hand, looking like a regular 'Johnny Too Bad.' Yeah... but he wasn't 'Johnny Too Bad,' was he? No... he was a brand new Jason Cyllabus Novedi. The best Jason Cyllabus Novedi that he could be... well, that *anyone* could be, for that matter. He was alive. He was a winner. He was the conqueror. He was *fabulous*!

So anyway, there he was, in his hospital gown (with quite a draft blowing up the open back), pointing his six-shooter right into the face of a rather shocked looking Frederick Greaves, who could see all of his magnificent power draining away in front of his eyes. Standing next to him, Angel (who was now Angel again) smiled and tossed Jason a furtive wink. Kostos (who was the same old Kostos he had always been) noticed the wink but, as usual, couldn't understand what it meant.

"*What?*" he said.

Jocelyn was just starting to regain her bearings, sitting there on the floor. She shook the grogginess from her head a little, and quickly regained her focus. When she saw Jason up and about, she spoke urgently to him. "Jason! What's going on? You're hurt! You shouldn't be out of bed. You've got three bullet holes in your chest for krysakes!"

Jason glanced down at his chest briefly. He felt around down there with his left hand (still keeping the gun leveled firmly at Frederick Greaves' face with his right). "I don't think I do," he said, concluding that there *were* no wounds on his chest, "not anymore, anyway. Actually... I feel fine."

Frederick Greaves started fidgeting around a bit, looking nervous and uncomfortable. "What do you think you're doing?" he asked. "I wasn't just making all that stuff up. I've explained the nature of the Universe to you. You can't fight against that. You can't win here."

"Right..." said Jason, "... and wrong! You *have* been in control. But that was because *I* gave the power over to you. I allowed you to define *my* universe according to my own deeply held, negative subconscious beliefs. I just didn't realize that I was doing it, and you took advantage of my ignorance... my denial. You and your brethren – Inertia, Weight, Labor, Defeat, Imprisonment – are all the demons of my *own* making, and *I* shall be the one to decide when they are through, and *what* will replace them. It's not going to be *your* business any more, you pathetic lying bastard! Now..." he focussed an unflinching look straight into the eyes of darkness, straight into the heart of DARKNESS, and he spoke in a voice as clear as a bell, "do you have any last words for posterity?"

"Y-You can't do this," said Frederick Greaves, squirming this way and that, and looking desperately for a way out. "I always win in the end. You know full well that I will survive. You know how reality works. You know that you cannot prevail!"

"That's what I *used* to believe, because *you* had me convinced." Darkness began to smile a little when he said this, but Jason quickly amended himself. "No! I take it back. It was *me*. I had convinced *myself*. Because you, Mr. Darkness, are nothing but the part of myself who wanted me to fail, who wanted me to think that everything is too difficult... that there is no point in trying. But now I see clearly that you are nothing but the illusion of my own defeat."

"Nonsense," quoth Darkness. His smiled faded; it was getting too close in here. "I am real. Inertia, Weight, Labor, Defeat, Imprisonment, they are all real. You must obey us! *We* are the Universe." But his voice was not so potent now; his pronouncements less persuasive. "Think prudently," he implored, "before you act. Your actions could have momentous consequences... for you. Be careful."

Jocelyn, who had been paying close attention to this little interchange, spoke now, clearly, evenly. "Jason," she said, "are you sure that you know what you're doing? Are you sure?"

And Jason, Henry, Dominic... who had never been sure before, had prepared himself well for this moment, and when his woman asked him that magic question, "are you sure," the answer came straight to his lips, from his gut... from his mind... from his spirit... from his heart... from his soul. "Yes!" he said. "I'm sure!"

"What are you going to do?" she asked.

"I'm going to blow this motherfucker's brains straight to hell!" And he pulled the trigger and fired one single shot through Frederick Greaves head, ending the age old dominion of Darkness over that particular realm of reality known to the future world as the nation of Bongovia. Frederick Greaves II fell to the floor, dead, never to rise again. Jason took a deep breath and lowered the weapon.

Angel and Kostos smiled at one another and shook hands in some sort of ritualistic way.

Jocelyn stood up and ran to Jason. She grabbed one of his arms and spun him round to face her. "My hero!" she said, and then kissed him passionately upon the lips for the very first time.

Jason reciprocated for a few moments, then suddenly stopped for a second to ask her, "Meatball, or baloney?"

"Cheese," she replied. "With a pickle!"

"You're the pickle," he said, and turning her in the direction of the door, he affectionately smacked her behind. "Come on Pickle!" Then he glanced over at Angel again. "There's work to be done."

Angel smiled at him, and then turned and smacked Kostos on the back of the head. "Come on Pickle," he told his nephew. "There's work to be done!"

"*What?*" said Kostos, "what work?"

Jason stopped, "wait a minute!" He looked around for his pants. He slipped them on and threw a pale blue ™Terrycloth robe over his hospital gown. He strode over to the door in his hospital bedroom slippers and flung it wide open. The crowd outside jumped to attention.

"These two men," he pointed at the bodies of Frederick Greaves and Karl, "... tried to assassinate me. Have them removed." Then he added, "they killed the nurse, Benjamin, who fought to save my life. His family must be informed, and I will want to be in touch with them soon." He looked at one particularly reliable looking intern in the group.

"You'll notify me who they are?"

The woman nodded.

Then he took hold of Jocelyn's hand and strode away rapidly, leading her behind him. Angel and Kostos brought up the rear amidst a barrage of questions from the hospital staff who had suddenly come to life.

"Have the police investigators visit Mr. Novedi at his residence," Jocelyn was telling people. And, "please direct all your question to the hospital authorities and have them contact Mr. Novedi tomorrow." And, "please do not worry, all your jobs are safe; Mr Novedi will take personal charge of these affairs from now on."

Jason cut through this turmoil with a feeling of great confidence. He had begun to trust... the people around him, the woman he loved... that things were going to be okay. Phew, okay. What a great word. What a relaxing word. Whatever happened from now on, it was going to be okay. Suddenly he appreciated what the Great God Bongo had been telling him all along. You can *always* do what you need to do. There is no such thing as failure, only opportunities to learn. He did not fear his work anymore. He did not fear his success. He did not fear his obligations. He was not crippled by his duty. Whatever he could achieve would be his contribution. Whatever he couldn't... well, it would have to wait for someone else.

Kostos grabbed Angel's elbow, and asked him, "*What* work do we have to do?" Angel just smacked him in the back of the head. "No seriously," the younger man persisted.

"I hope you brought your pretty blue car with you," Jason yelled at Jocelyn, only slightly above the throng. "I don't think I'm dressed for the bus."

"Pretty?" She sounded resentful of the compliment. "I've got a Ram Jet 350 V8 and a ™Muncie 4 speed on the floor," she mumbled, but he didn't hear it – and he probably wouldn't have understood what she was talking about if he had.

They exited the building by the main entrance where the Bel Air still stood parked blocking the driveway, illegal almost certainly... belligerent perhaps, but pretty... beneath all that mud and grime and rain splatter? Well yes, actually.

"I feel awful," said Jocelyn. Jason turned towards her, concerned. "I mean, about Benjamin," she clarified, "the nurse."

Jason thumped the hood of the car with his fist. "Those bastards," he vented. "They've been playing me like a cheap violin. Well, this is my town! This is my dream! And I'm taking control of it as of now. I'm going to run it the way I see fit. And you know what? I'm going to do a great job. I know that I can, I know that I will... I trust myself. And anyway, it's *my* responsibility. The Darkness is over... Inertia better get moving outa my way... Weight had better lighten up... Labor is gonna get a good working over... I'm triumphing over Defeat... I'm locking up Imprisonment! I'm kicking them all out. They're finished. History! From now on there will be light in the dark places, there will be motivation, and freedom and balance... and accomplishment. It has been my fault, and no one else's, that these things have existed. In my weakness, in my stupidity, I have chosen them. Well I choose them no longer. I choose that things will be different from now on. As of this moment, it all changes!"

"Not so fast," said Angel.

"What're you talkin' about?" said Jason.

"What do you mean?" said Jocelyn.

"Yeah," said Kostos, "what *do* you mean?"

He'd certainly got their attention. But you know sometimes, when everyone's on a high, you have to calm things down a bit. It was Angel's function to be the moderating agent of the group. Not to flatten their energy, or to deter them from their purpose, but to channel them, to utilize their strength to its greatest benefit. We all go through moments of great change, which impassion us... make us believe that we are invincible, that we have attained the perfection of the ages, that we have nowhere left to go. But there is always somewhere else to go. There is always more to learn. And there is no place which is more perfect than any other. (Before enlightenment, chop wood, fetch water, build fire, cook food. After enlightenment, chop wood, fetch water, build fire, cook food.) "Well," he addressed Jason, "you yourself said that we have work to do." Now he looked at Kostos. "There were six of these men who controlled JCN. Killing one of them doesn't dispose of them all."

"That's right!" said Jocelyn, suddenly remembering something that she had forgotten. She had been lowering the top on the convertible whilst the others were talking. The rain had finally ended at some point during the nighttime of their arduous adventure, and the early morning sun was providing the golden lining to the disappearing clouds. She stopped what she was doing and, after rummaging around in her bag for a moment, produced the notebook she'd found behind Jason's garden bench. Holding it aloft she declared, "I have *all* their names in here." She tossed the book over to Jason like a ™Frisbee.

He caught it and flipped through the pages. "This is just what I was looking for."

"So what do we do now?" said Kostos.

Jason hopped into the front passenger seat of the pretty blue ™Chevy as Jocelyn completed folding down and latching the top. "One down," he said with gusto, inviting them all to join him within that splendid conveyance, "and five to go!"

The End?